MURDER

IN A SAN ANTONIO PSYCH

HOSPITAL, REVISITED

A Work of Fiction

By

John C. Payne

Other Books Written by John C. Payne

The Three and Out Trilogy

*The Saga of a San Francisco
Apartment Manager
*Murder in a San Antonio
Psych Hospital
*The Chicago Terminus

Stage Series

*Stage Three: Rod Richards Returns
*Stage Four
* Stage Five: The Reincarnation
*Stage Six: The Infidelity Murders

Annotations

I decided to springboard off the overwhelming popularity of the second book in my *Three and Out Trilogy,* that is . . . **Murder in a San Antonio Psych Hospital**. It is humbling that my readers enjoyed the fictional events that took place in an active mental health hospital. I trust you will also relish the storyline in this new book.

This story is a complete work of fiction. Names, characters, places, and incidents are products of this writer's imagination. The hospital's name, Mission Oaks Mental Health Hospital is fictional, as is its location within proximity and downstream of the famous San Antonio Riverwalk.

Enjoy!

Acknowledgments

First in line is my wife, Carol. She has the innate ability to tell me to "come to a landing" on long, drawn-out sequences. She also has a better "grip" on female emotions. Sometimes I tend to go overboard on feminine characterizations in my books.

Long-time friend and professional cohort Jack Selby offered his many observations and recommendations to make the "read" smoother and more authentic.

I have to admit the use of Wikipedia came in helpful at times.

Cover design and eBook formatting by Shelley Glasow, www.goodlifeguide.com

Prologue

The murder of the female CIA agent in the old Mission Oaks Mental Health Hospital had sent shock waves throughout the hospital community and the entire city of San Antonio, Texas. Finding the killer had been a challenging task for the multiple agencies involved in the investigation. The hospital was able to resume normal operations after the killer had been identified and captured. The Joint Commission on Accreditation of Hospitals had recertified the facility after an exhaustive inspection in the aftermath of the turmoil. A children's unit of 20 beds was constructed adjacent to the 50-bed hospital.

Hospital daily occupancy had hit an all-time high. The private, for-profit hospital was financially in the black. However, the roof caved in when the overachieving hospital administrator departed after three years of perplexing challenges. His young executive replacement became a drunken and sexually abusive tyrant. Deterioration of the facility across the board had become rampant. Routine maintenance ceased to exist.

The chief nurse was forced to resign. No cause for his abrupt departure was announced. Speculation pointed to his wife. She had been one of the government's principal agents in bringing the murder investigation to its successful conclusion. The marketing director was the last salaried person to be ushered out the front door.

The owners were forced to file for bankruptcy. The few remaining acute care patients were transferred to other local facilities. The children's unit was terminated.

The hospital was shuttered, pending disposition by the Bexar County Bankruptcy Court.

An eleven-month period witnessed a series of prospective suitors competing to obtain the desirable property. Nasty politics and legal gymnastics by the bidders were prevalent weekly. An investment group named Texas Coalition of Combat Veterans (TCCV) from Houston surfaced and became the top contender to purchase the property. Their collection of retired clinicians and health care administrators with a history of wartime military service outmaneuvered three national hotel chains to gain acceptance by the legal entities handling the bankruptcy.

The new organization charged ahead and began the onerous task of restructuring the former hospital after clearing the delinquent tax liabilities. TCCV gained renewed licensure from the state to operate a 50-bed acute care mental health hospital. A certificate of occupancy was obtained to activate a 20-bed extended care facility for special needs patients. Mission Oaks Mental Health Hospital was renamed Mission Oaks Treatment Center.

Chapter 1

January 2016

Boyd Bounder was slumped on a barstool, elbows anchoring his big body to the bar railing. His burnt orange jumpsuit no longer accentuated his muscular physique. It bulged slightly at the waist. Teddy's Tavern was conveniently located across from busy Alamo Plaza. It was mid-afternoon on a sweltering day in the tourist city. A tall, erect man with a trim GI haircut came up from behind him and tapped his shoulders. Bounder spun around and recognized the person.

"So, why'd you want to meet with me?" asked the six-foot-five former collegiate football player and dismissed former Mission Oaks Mental Health Hospital chief nurse. "You and your cohorts in management positions ignored my desperate pleas for help in the past. I always figured you knew the underlying reasons why I was canned. Must be something big coming down the pike that only 'yours truly' can resolve."

Howard I.M. Hill, a tall and slimmer version of Bounder plopped down on the barstool next to him. His worn, gray pin-striped suit and narrow red tie suggested his age. In the seating process, he jostled a young man maneuvering over to claim the last vacant stool at the long bar.

The chubby man lost his balance.

"Age before beauty," Howard bellowed at the man in his deep voice. The guy positioned his body to throw a punch but relented after Howard stood tall to face him. He backed up and snickered a comment to his cute date. "I don't want jail-time for assaulting a defenseless old fart."

Howard growled at him before the young lady led the couple's retreat to the other end of the saloon.

Boyd Bounder recalled their many conversations in the past. Some pleasant, others confrontational. Hill, the old Granada Invasion veteran took no prisoners. The 1983 threat to American nationals by the pro-Marxist regime in Granada was smashed by US troops within days. Hill's leadership in the assault was highly documented and resulted in the award of a prestigious combat medal.

"Still the tough old first sergeant not mellowed by these passing years," Bounder laughed. "Rumor has it that the I. M. positioned in your middle name stands for 'I'm Mean.' Is that true?"

Hill laughed, his heavily-frowned forehead an unwanted gift from years of heavy-duty stress. "I was sent to a foster home at age six when my parents were killed in a car crash. Nobody recollects what mom and pop had in mind with those initials when they applied for my birth certificate. The troops called me more descriptive foul names behind my back because I kicked butt. Didn't give a rat's ass—they survived."

Bounder chuckled at the wily veteran. "What're you drinking?"

"Iced tea, lime instead of lemon and no ice. Thank you," Hill smiled.

Bounder ordered the drink and another tall lager for himself. He forgot Hill was a non-drinker, having overcome alcohol addiction. The triumph over booze dependence inspired Howard to take advantage of the GI Bill. He earned an advanced degree in psychology and became a successful mental health counselor.

[8]

John C. Payne

Reputation had run rampant that Howard treated all his patients as recent inductees in infantry basic training. In the end, they all loved him.

"So, what've you been up to since they shut down Mission Oaks Mental Health Hospital?" Hill asked, not cognizant of Bounder's earlier cries for comfort and support in his previous position with the hospital.

"Nothing worth mentioning," Bounder deadpanned.

Hill put his hand on Bounder's shoulder and palmed him gently. "I heard through the infamous grapevine an alarming bit of news. You and Rod Richards had implemented all those superb upgrades and seemed to be doing an excellent job. Richards left. You were canned. New ownership came aboard naively allowing the place to stumble downhill."

Bounder pushed Hill's arm away.

Hill was quick to assess the man's moody disposition. "Okay, Boyd, I did have an inkling why they had let you go. Supposedly, your ex-wife took the liberty to tell false stories about some of your dealings at the hospital involving the opposite sex. Nobody in charge came forward to defend you, and the rest is history. A scorned woman can be a hellcat. Anyway, that's behind us. I have a proposal to discuss with you."

"I'm listening," Bounder said with a tight smile, not having a clue what was on the rugged man's mind.

Hill began. "I signed a contract to become the executive director of the 'resurrected' Mission Oaks Mental Health Hospital. I want you on my new team as the facility administrator working directly for me. You may have read a group from Houston purchased the facility. They are combat veterans aspiring to do something uniquely different helping fellow war veterans."

"I never served in the military," Bounder replied, not mentioning he took many measures to avoid the draft. "I'm not sure I'd be accepted."

"It matters not, Boyd. You have the background we need to move this outfit forward."

"Had you considered bringing back Rod Richards?" Boyd asked. "I respected him, as did the entire staff. He made the hospital the envy of the health care industry."

"Yes, I'm aware of that. I did contact Rod up in Illinois. He's a retired school teacher and has no desire to return to any sort of work. I guess he enjoys golf and travel like most older folks."

Bounder laughed, knowing Rod Richards did neither. "Did you try contacting Larry Richards? Rod's son did an outstanding job setting up the children's unit at the hospital. He might be available."

Hill nodded his head. "Larry had been recommended by some former hospital staff members. I tried to reach out to him but was unable to locate the man. Seems he has gone underground, or incognito since his wife was murdered. I'm sure you recall the newspaper articles and the gory details."

"Not really. I was in my private world after Marie left me. Things got nasty. I had no use for anything the despicable media desired to make known to the public."

"Sorry to hear that," Hill said. "I'm aware of the emotional impact of divorce, but one has to move on. I hope you will consider my offer."

Boyd hesitated for several long minutes before he responded. "Tell me more about this group of combat veterans who hired you. Sounds interesting."

Hill took a big slug of his iced tea. He loved to relate the story, careful not to embellish the narrative. "The Texas Coalition of Combat Veterans is a Houston-based 501(c) organization. This IRS grouping refers to a formal classification of 'Not for Profit' corporations, specifically those that are considered public charities, private foundations or private operating foundations. We refer to them as the TCCV group."

"What makes them so great?" Bounder asked. He wasn't familiar with the company, nor the different tax categorizations dreamed up by the IRS. He was a clinician, not a CPA.

Hill continued. "They are primarily composed of Vietnam and Iraqi war veterans. Most proudly wear Purple Hearts on their chests. Five are physicians and four are hospital administrators. Three of the investors were Dustoff pilots, the callsign specific to US Army Air Ambulance units. All twelve became successful practitioners and businessmen in the Houston area after their wartime service. They are mission-oriented."

"I'm impressed," Boyd said. "I admire former military types reaching out to other veterans in need of life-sustaining assistance at any level. So many of the troopers came out of combat with a myriad of health care issues. You saw them at the VA. I encountered several at Mission Oaks when I oversaw treatment protocols. They were a challenge."

"Well," Hill said. "Are you in?"

"Not yet. I need more specifics."

"Like what?" Hill seemed inpatient.

"I would like a written outline describing the organization in detail, the mission, proposed staffing and budget to name a few salient concerns. Do they intend to operate an acute care hospital, nursing home or assisted living facility? How about reimbursements for the diverse levels of care?"

Howard took a deep breath. At first, he was dismayed at Bounder's laundry list of questions. He was a "yes or no" man, not used to people dissecting his end game. Yet, he thought long and hard about Bounder's concerns.

The job will be demanding. Managers must be aware of the boundaries established by both the rules and regulations of the industry and the expectations of donors. I will be an added challenge, always known as a demanding person.

"That look on your face tells me that I poked a tender nerve here, Howard."

"No. I think it prudent you would express concerns. I'd be disappointed if you jumped at my offer without questioning the details," he lied. "Here's the deal. I will provide everything you ask for, plus additional resources and personnel I think essential. I'll include your job description and salary range with incentives in writing. You have five days to get back to me. We're anxious to move forward, Boyd. Is that acceptable?"

"Yes. Tell me where we'll meet again so I can pick up the documentation we've discussed."

"Simple enough," Howard replied. "Next Monday, noon at the Cantina Classica near the hospital. I'm sure you remember where it's located."

"Absolutely," Boyd laughed. "But I haven't been there in ages," he fibbed. "Is Clarisa Rios still giving the old hospital staff a tough time?"

"Find out for yourself," Hill suggested. "She always asks about you. I'm not sure why she poses the questions to me. I hardly know her. Was she the mysterious lady who put a wedge in your relationship with Marie?"

"I don't think we need to revisit any details regarding either woman," Bounder said with a slight tone of anger. "Clarisa is part-owner and manages the restaurant with an iron fist, yet she's warm and entertaining with her customers. It makes no sense to

[12]

me why you're so interested in why my marriage dissolved. Leave it at that." Boyd stood more erect.

"Settle down, Bounder. Fair enough, I agree with you. I've never been hitched. I have no right in rehashing old times when it comes to a man's relationship with a woman. Too many oddities I don't understand or care to know. See you next week."

Chapter 2

Howard Hill spent the remainder of the day in his apartment at the Pearl Brewery complex finalizing the paperwork for Boyd Bounder's employment contract. He faxed the five-page document to him. Hill was impressed with their session at Teddy's Tavern. Boyd hadn't changed much since his last contact with him. From all reports, he excelled in his duties as chief nurse at the old hospital. He seemed to have an interest in becoming the administrator of the new venture with TCCV. A telephone call interrupted Hill's thought processes.

"Good afternoon, Howard. It's Pritam Lozen here. Have you locked-in on our new administrator yet? I still intend to open Mission Oaks Treatment Center on schedule. The last hurdle is to get an administrator on board now, not tomorrow, nor next week. We need to get in gear to kick off the hiring process."

"Yes and no," Howard replied to Pritam Lozen's stern voice. Howard preferred the man's frontal attacks to wishy-washy, milk toast superiors. Pritam, or Tam as he preferred to be called, was an impatient man. He was one of the founding members of TCCV. Each board member of TCCV had been assigned to monitor one of the several major aspects of the non-profit organization. Tam drew the new hospital venture.

Howard Hill learned from an old army buddy that Tam had distinguished himself as a Dustoff pilot in Vietnam. He walked with a noticeable limp. His incapacity happened during the Tet Offensive of 1968. The air ambulance he was piloting was descending to a ground marker twenty-feet off the damp surface of a hot battle zone to pick up the wounded. The aircraft was hit by a VC rocket that shattered the tail rotor system. Tam was struck in the upper right thigh by an enemy bullet while scrambling out of the downed helicopter. A second-round shattered five vertebrae in his back. None of the other crew members had been injured. All were successfully airlifted out after a Cobra attack helicopter neutralized the entire area.

"Please be more specific, Howard. Clarify your 'yes and no' response about a new administrator," Tam loosened up with a slight snicker.

"Yes. I've identified and met with our leading candidate," Hill said. "I have finalized our proposal to Boyd Bounder as we speak. We meet again on Monday, and I expect him to accept our generous offer."

"Is he a combat veteran?" Tam was direct.

"No."

"Our board members prefer to hire outstanding military veterans, Howard. Is there a problem here?"

"No, I don't think so. Bounder is the most qualified candidate I've interviewed to lead our hospital staff. I've worked with him in the past in another capacity. You'll like him. He was an all-conference football player at UT. You were a collegiate athlete yourself. And a darn good one according to media reports that I was able to round up and dust off."

"Did you overlook the most obvious piece of information in those commentaries, Hill?"

"That you were a quarterback?" Howard was on thin ice, not knowing what direction Tam was coming from. He had heard Tam was a hard man to deal with. Sprinklings of humor were not evident in the man's resume.

"No, you blabbering fool," Tam shouted into the phone. "I was an Aggie. If Bounder doesn't walk on water, you and your Texas Longhorn buddy are histories. Get my drift, Mr. First Sergeant?"

"Loud and clear, colonel."

There was silence on the line, and then Tam broke out in a roaring laugh. "I trust your judgment, Howard, just having a little fun with you. You're being so strait-laced and serious whenever we meet tends to amuse me. Text me when you wrap it up on Monday. I repeat again—on Monday!"

The telephone went dead before Howard could respond. He decided the urgency expressed by Tam Lozen couldn't wait until Monday of next week. He called Bounder.

"Boyd, I've moved up our meeting. Where are you now?"

"I'm, ah, over at the Cantina Classica having a late dinner."

"Is Clarisa working tonight?" Hill hoped she wasn't because it was impossible to talk business with a nosey woman glancing in over your shoulder.

"No, Howard, why do you ask?" *At some point, I should tell him I'm dating her. He'll poke around long enough to confirm his suspicions.*

"We need some serious discussion about my earlier proposal, Boyd. I trust you've reviewed the documentation by now."

"No. It's still sitting on my desk at home. My thought progressions work better at three in the morning when I get up to pee. Hey, I just got my meal check. Why don't we meet at my place in an hour? You know where the Towers condominium is located?"

"Yes, right outside the gate at Fort Sam."

"Good. Go to the front entrance. Just give security my name and someone will let you up to my condo."

"Bring me a couple of her famous beef enchiladas," Howard said. "I haven't eaten yet."

"Will do. See you then."

The traffic on state highway 281was not its usual congested roadway at this early evening hour. Howard figured he'd take the freeway rather than scooting up Broadway. In the past, he'd cut through Ft. Sam to get over to that side of town. The base was now a closed post thanks to the terrorist disaster perpetrated on 9/11. He never took the time to update his military ID card to gain access to the base. He'd pick up a few grocery items at Central Market to kill time, hoping that Boyd would do a quick study of the paperwork before he showed up.

Boyd let him into his condo on the third doorbell announcement. "Your enchiladas are in the micro, Howard. Salsa has been warmed to room temperature. I'll dive into the documentation while you gorge yourself with the Tex-Mex."

Later, Hill rejoined Bounder in the study. He felt it was time to begin the negotiations. His hunger was now abated.

"Well, Boyd, any questions?"

"Everything looks great to me, Howard. Much more generous than I had expected."

Howard breathed a sigh of relief. He had prepared a counter-strategy in the event Bounder claimed he needed more time to decide.

"Yes, I agree with your observation, Boyd. Tam Lozen had already interviewed three candidates recommended by a search committee hired by TCCV. I reviewed the three resumes and wasn't comfortable with two of the contenders. The third person was a female who served as the chief nurse of a busy evacuation hospital in Vietnam. She later became executive director of a children's hospital in Denver. The woman is originally from Corpus Christi and wants to get closer to home. If it had been a psych hospital where she had earned her spurs, I probably would've opted for her. Tam wasn't happy with me holding out until we had a chance to run this by you."

"Tell me more about this Pritam Lozen guy, Howard. He seems out of place. Has he ever been a hospital administrator?"

"Not to my knowledge. When a medic earns as many medals for his heroics in war, few will argue his credentials. I may have told you earlier he was one of the founding fathers of TCCV. He led the organization to growth and financial stability through his many initiatives. They're not a Fortune 500 company, but they are well-known and admired throughout the region."

"Lozen has an unusual name—part Hispanic, part something else," Boyd commented.

"Yes, to both observations, Boyd. He is a proud descendant of the Coahuilteque nation, a collection of hunting and gathering Lipan Apache and Comanche bands going far back in history. He told me some of his close ancestors had lived in the several missions around San Antonio. Tam was one of the major participants that lobbied heavily for the San Antonio Missions to gain the UNESCO Worldwide Heritage site designation. The five missions built by the Franciscan missionaries during the 18th century integrated the Spanish and Coahuiltecan cultures."

Boyd had more input. "I've visited all the missions. Some of them have Mariachi bands playing during Mass. You need to take in some of the great mission sights."

"Been to the Alamo," Hill said. "That's all I needed to see. I can't figure out why any commander prepares for a battle he's destined to lose. The lack of discernable intelligence on the enemy was not an issue. Guess I'm not a true Texan."

"Seems like Mr. Lozen has a burning grasp of Indian history," Boyd said.

"One last comment about Tam before you sign off on the paperwork. He is a student of military history. He is proud of the Indian warriors that fought in WW II, primarily the code talkers."

"What?" Boyd asked with interest. "Who the hell are those characters?"

"A code talker is the name given to the American Indians who used their tribal language to send secret communications on the battlefield. Most people have heard of the famous Navajo code talkers who used their traditional language to transmit secret Allied messages in the Pacific theater of combat during World War II. Other tribes also participated. Japanese soldiers had no idea what was going on. Their actions saved a lot of US Marine lives in the hotly contested islands."

"Guess I need to take a few steps backward on my assessment of this Mr. Tam Lozen," Boyd said. "My not having a military background is no excuse. Thanks for filling me in. I'm ready to sign the paperwork."

They shook hands and bear-hugged each other. Both laughed at the impromptu gesture of male bonding.

"I'm pleased you finally agreed to head up the operation at Mission Oaks for us, Boyd. I know the huge challenge of a 50-bed psych hospital is nothing new for a person with your background. As you may have noted in the summary document I provided you, the 20-bed extended care unit is a horse of a different color."

"How's that, Howard?"

"It has to do with licensing in the State of Texas. Let me explain. We have been granted an exception by the state because of the uniqueness of our operation. Keep in mind that the TCCV is a powerful organization in the eyes of our political friends in Texas."

"Go on, Howard, this wasn't completely spelled out in your documentation. Do I need to reconsider signing?"

Howard thought for a moment and said, "Perhaps I failed to attach that agenda—unwittingly of course. We are combining the state-enforced criteria for 'Long Term Care Facilities' with that of 'Extended Care Facilities.'"

Boyd agreed. "I'm familiar with long-term care ventures, Howard. They furnish food and shelter and personalized care to four or more persons unrelated to the ownership."

"Go on my good friend. You're on a roll."

Boyd nodded. "This arrangement includes the administration of medications by authorized personnel. The length of stay varies. Reimbursement by third-party payers likewise differs."

"Good, but the second mission of Mission Oaks is a 'bastardized' version of how Texas defines long-term care facilities."

Howard pulled in closer to discuss the distinction. "Traditionally, long-care facilities offer residents health and personal care assistance in a homelike environment. Mission Oaks will operate more like a retirement home, still stressing personal dignity and promoting a greater degree of individual independence. Our residents will be allowed flexibility to come and go for short periods after being vetted. They have to prove reliability to our satisfaction."

"I understand why TCCV decided to offer this big benefit," Boyd stated. "I'm comfortable that Mission Oaks will be reimbursed for the psychiatric services delivered by our staff. At the same time, I don't see any reimbursement streams coming from days occupied in the retirement center."

[20]

"There might be an occasional third-party payor they can link to," Howard laughed. "However, the founders of TCCV have deep pockets. A list of free services is outlined in its mission statement."

"That's hunky-dory, Howard Hill, but I see a major control issue staring us in the face."

Howard shrugged. "We took that under control consideration advisement. Tam Lozen has authorized the hire of an executive director to oversee the 'retirement' unit. You'll have total responsibility for the mental health hospital. The next person I bring aboard will run the 20-bed component of Mission Oaks Treatment Center. Both of you folks will report directly to me."

"I can live with that," Boyd said. "Do you have anybody in mind to run the retirement home?"

"Yes, Molly Pritcher. You'll love working with her. Rumor has it she's a doll."

Boyd stood up. "Wait for a jiffy here, that's a red herring if I ever envisioned one. I suspect most of the residents will be of the male variety—worldly, horny and difficult to deal with. Don't you see potential problems surfacing in the face of management?"

Howard chuckled. "Of course, I do."

"What am I missing here?" Boyd asked.

"Molly is Tam Lozen's adopted daughter."

"You're kidding me, Howard."

"No, sir. That's a fact."

"Care to share some of the backgrounds on Tam's family? Then I might be able to put my arms around some of these disjointed pieces of information." Bounder was more than curious.

Howard remarked, "I think that's fair. This is all I know. Pritam Lozen never married, but he loved kids. I'm not sure where he was living at the time. He decided to adopt a 13-year-old girl.

A 10-year-old boy came later. Not sure of Molly's nationality, but for some mysterious reason, she doesn't carry the Lozen name. I elected not to inquire further. Perhaps I'll have the opportunity to chat with her after she becomes more comfortable with my engrossing personality."

"Good luck on that assumption, Howard. But 'engrossing' is a fuzzy-wuzzy word and doesn't describe a warrior like you. Let it be argued that your persona is not one giant magnet to those who get to know you. Anyway, I must admit the family makeup is interesting. I know all I need to be familiar with her at this time. Her ethnicity doesn't concern me. Tell me about the boy."

"The son was adopted off an Indian reservation in South Dakota. The records indicate he is from the Lakota Tribe. He was given the name of Jase Lozen. Tam Lozen is not proud of this kid."

Boyd perked up. "What's the buzz on him?"

"His son was always in trouble, according to Tam. Disrespect for authority and the lack of acceptance of personal responsibility were major issues. Some have suggested there might have been a cultural clash because of the differences between the Lakota and the Coahuiltecan customs and traditions."

Boyd was aware of San Antonio's early heritage and marveled at the city diversity.

Hill continued. "Without his father's consent, Jase applied for conscientious objector status with his local Selective Service System board even though the military draft ended in 1973. The Gulf War was on the horizon. He didn't want to chance the draft being reestablished by Congress. Peace lovers can be assigned several alternatives by the Selective Service System. The board approved his convincing application. Somehow in the absence of a military draft, Jase finagled a 24-month stint with a state-sponsored environmental program in Mississippi."

"I thought these moral or religious opposers were all put in the medics," Boyd commented. "I've met a few military nurse veterans who fit in that category. They were exceptional caregivers."

"Some did migrate to the medics, even earning the prestigious Medal of Honor," Howard responded proudly. "Other folks are given the opportunity for alternative service. Jase Lozen studied archaeology after his work with the state, even earned an advanced degree from an Ivy League university. That made his daddy proud."

"How interesting," Boyd said. "The kid has brains if nothing else."

Howard nodded and continued. "Armed with extensive knowledge of humankind, he left to 'dig' in various parts of the world. Some excursions were funded by his home university. Others were 'gifted' by unknown geezers interested in measuring cranial skulls or some shit like that. Jase narrowed his searches to the Yucatan Peninsula as he became more sophisticated in his field. The son even bedded and then wedded a young maiden from Campeche. The interesting bit of scuttlebutt is that young Jase Lozen hasn't been heard from in over five years."

Chapter 3
June 2016

Mission Oaks Treatment Center opened with a well-coordinated and expensive media blitz. Every TCCV director was involved with the detailed planning, to include rehearsing the opening ceremonies. Unfortunately, the weatherman didn't cooperate, and a slight drizzle, followed by spurts of high winds delayed the opening ceremony. A portable bandstand had been set up in front of the hospital. The tight semicircular arrangement wasn't designed to accommodate an uplifting ballet performance but to seat selected participants. Temporary bleachers were erected facing the bandstand.

The state governor and the San Antonio mayor sat in the first row of stand seats, each accompanied by a Purple Heart recipient in full military uniform. Spouses and friends of the dignitaries sat in the row behind them. TCCV's notables and their families occupied the third row. The remaining seating was open to media personnel and other attendees. Additional chairs were brought in to accommodate the overflow crowd, not dissuaded by the unpleasant weather.

A military band from nearby Ft. Sam Houston marched in and presented the colors. Pritam Lozen trooped in from the rear of the edifice followed by Howard Hill, Boyd Bounder and Molly Prichard. The TCCV chairman of the board of directors introduced Tam as the master of ceremonies.

The hour-long formalities included a brief history of TCCV and its motivation for embarking on the challenging enterprise. The military hierarchy in attendance sat proudly when Tam acknowledged their presence.

Local media couldn't absorb enough of the story as evidenced by their week-long cannonade of facts, figures and community involvement. Pictures and lifetime accomplishments of Howard I.M. Hill, Boyd Bounder and Molly Pritchard were featured weekly. The press went to great lengths to pay tribute to the TCCV founding fathers and the impact that the organization would have on the local community.

The 50-bed hospital was operating at thirty-percent capacity within three weeks. A major hurricane occurring in the Gulf of Mexico battered southern Texas and closed several mental health hospitals along the stretch of coastal cities. Inpatients were transferred to inland hospitals away from the destructive forces of nature. Mission Oaks was the recipient of ten patients.

The adjacent 20-bed long-term care unit had just opened for business, waiting eagerly for its first long-term resident.

"Stop fretting, Molly," Howard said with a concerned voice. "TCCV is almost done screening the applications for residency in your unit. They've decided to select only five aspirants from the initial group to set the standards for all future candidates. Tam told me they hadn't completed the prerequisites by the time we opened the hospital. In other words, first things first. It is my humble opinion they didn't want to put any undue pressure on you."

"Screw you, Howard I. M. Hill. I'm a big girl, fully capable of making solid decisions on my own. Why the hell do you think they hired me? For my good looks?" She laughed. She'd been advised of Howard's patronizing personality but felt comfortable in being herself.

"Not really," he answered the six-foot-two, auburn-haired beauty. "I had the opportunity to review your resume, not that you needed one."

"What the hell do you mean by that statement, Hill? Are you assuming my father led the charge for his only daughter to run our challenging unit?"

"Whoa, Molly, of course not. Piloting an Apache AH-64 attack helicopter during Operation Desert Storm tells me the entire story—all I needed to know. I couldn't have achieved success in that specialized training. Hey, I got sick jumping out of perfectly good airplanes during my stint in the army. I hated anything that had to do with altitude. I don't know how you did it."

She sprang off her chair and faced him. "Apples and oranges here, Mr. Hill. I served with distinction in the Army and was proud of it. I elected not to make a career of it. One wartime experience was enough for this body." She rolled up her left sleeve and exposed a foot-long, jagged, discolored scar racing down from the elbow.

Howard stared at the disfigurement. "Ugh, nasty I might say. Care to tell me how it happened."

"No, not relevant. Bottom line—I would've lost the entire arm if it weren't for a skilled surgeon in the combat support hospital. My father never encouraged me to stay in the military. However, I knew he harbored thoughts of me being a general officer one day. Did you happen to read my post-military achievements?"

"I scanned them. Noted you had an advanced degree in management, followed by several years of work with Goodwill

Industries. I trust you were in positions of leadership with them."

Molly smiled. "In my last five years, I served as a regional manager in their busiest geographic area in the northwest. I also became the public relations delegate for the entire organization. Putting out brush fires blown up by media scoundrels was challenging.

"Sounds like fun. I'll bet the Army never trained you for that juicy delicacy."

"Yes and no," she said. "But let's face realism. You've been there, done that in your capacity as a first sergeant. I was told early on in my short career that no problem was too great for the 'top dog' in the outfit."

"We kicked ass, took names and never looked back," he said with a grin. He liked her already and knew they could work well together.

"In your scanning process did you note I played volleyball at a Division I university before military service? Even earned the coveted All-American classification."

"Yes, don't shed us underlings, here and run off to coach jumping-Jesus female wannabees. I notice you've been able to maintain a conditioned athlete's body."

"I take that as a compliment, Howard." She softened with a weak smile and sat down. "I try to jog five miles, three times a week. You might want to join me to tighten up that puffy midriff some."

"Too old, two bad knees, no motivation," he smirked.

"Then I have the ideal practice for you to engage in. It's a form of Tai Chi that might be known to others as a moving meditation. Energy sources in your body are activated, circulated and balanced. The 'mindfulness' gurus in the world pontificate on the documented positive results from this ritual. Hey, you don't have to do the 'daily dozen' anymore at your age. You don't need to run, do pushups, get on the ground to achieve a relaxed state of mind. Yes, I put into practice what I teach."

She saw Howard mulling her comments over in his mind. Then he commented. "A shot and a beer, multiplied by the number of times I've been stressed out during the day tend to achieve this, ah, state of mindfulness." He didn't drink. She didn't have to know that.

"Suit yourself, old man. Don't let the good times pass you up."

"I'll take it under advisement," he said. "Would you care to share the ambiguous circumstances why TCCV brought you here?"

"No. Are you concerned because I'm a woman?"

"I've never experienced the characteristics of sound leadership in the few women that I've supervised," Howard shot back. "Highly-strung emotionalism tends to interfere with objectivity. Furthermore, having little crying babies while wearing a uniform is not my definition of combat readiness. Perhaps I tended in the past to hold females to a higher standard than their male counterparts who I've trained to kill people with their bare hands. But, having said all that, don't be alarmed. My peers have told me I've mellowed some in recent years."

She said nothing, expecting a dialogue of outdated thinking.

Yes, Molly, I did voice my concern before I had this opportunity to talk to you face-to-face. Now that we've had this nice chit-chat, I'm no longer apprehensive."

"Thanks, I appreciate your frankness. I guess General Douglas McArthur's parting assurance to the West Point military graduates that 'Old soldiers never die, they just fade away' certainly doesn't pertain to you, First Sergeant Hill."

Howard doubled up laughing. "Touché, my dear woman. Oh, I have one last question, Molly. Where are you living in the Alamo City?"

"I've rented an apartment out at the Quarry, off state highway 281. It overlooks a beautiful golf course, not that I have the time or inclination to take up an old fart's sport."

"Is that right?" he said with a hint of sarcasm. "I try to play at least once a week—usually whip the other three hamsters your age in my cutthroat foursome. Look out your apartment window some Saturday morning and you might be lucky enough to see us in action. Anyhow, welcome aboard. Glad to have you."

She nodded and started to leave.

"Hold up. Just a few words of advice before you get off and running."

"And what might they encompass?" Molly was confused.

"Be careful of Boyd Bounder."

"Huh?" She had no clue what he was referring to. "What's that all about?"

"He's single, handsome and likes women," Hill said. He knew Bounder was dating a woman who owned a popular restaurant frequented by hospital staff. Bounder had mentioned it in passing one day when they'd met at Starbucks for a quick cup of coffee after work. Howard got the impression from Boyd this lady was a good catch but a little unpredictable at times. He remembered Boyd's comment when they were leaving. *"She's a real challenge, Howard, but well worth the effort."* Keep that in mind if you have the occasion to deal with him on a personal basis."

"Thanks for the warning. I think I can handle it."

Chapter 4
February 2017

Boyd Bounder was happy with the state of affairs at the hospital. Operations were functioning effectively and efficiently. The assembled staff was performing as though the group had been in place for several years. He was fond of the new art pieces that had been installed in the larger offices, hallways, and the main entrance.

The interior decorators had removed all the stuffed animal heads from the busiest areas of the hospital. Boyd cared less they were oversized trophies from the previous owner's Safari expeditions. The TCCV group provided framed prints of the most famous US military engagements dating back to the Indian Wars.

The hospital dayroom was enlarged by removing the wall from the large adjoining room which had been used as storage. The interior decorator redesigned the enlarged room into two components, separated by a sliding wall partition.

One space contained the dayroom used for recreation and leisure time. A large green-felted pool table was located in the center of the room. Several leather loungers were located against the outer wall between a huge bay window. A mahogany V-shaped bookcase with the most recent hardback best-sellers stood in one corner stood. Framed pictures of POTUS and the Pentagon's chiefs of staff of each service branch adorned another wall. The American flag stood tall and erect next to the main entrance door.

The other space partitioned-off the renovated huge room housed the location for physical and occupational therapies. At first glance, an outsider would think it was a miniature version of LA Fitness. The latest and most expensive equipment was stationed along the inner walls. Soft, colorful photographs of the Grand Canyon, Niagara Falls, Mount Rainier, and the Golden Gate Bridge were interspersed between written procedural rehab guidelines pinned on the walls.

The rooftop pool and volleyball court underwent a minor renovation that had been in process for some time and now enjoyed by many patients. Water volleyball teams were formed. Competition between the patients of the different military branches was awesome. Former Navy SEALs were ineligible to select their teams. Interspersed among the "inferior" troopers had been a major adjustment to their more vocal teammates.

Howard Hill didn't office in the hospital complex. He elected to use an upstairs conference room when he was on-site for meetings, inspections, and complaint sessions. The staff was aware his temporary office space was minimally equipped with only a laptop computer and a wall-mounted telephone. The chain of command was compulsory, with no exceptions. He limited his incoming calls to two important individuals—his hospital administrator and the long-term care executive director. If the patients wanted to voice a complaint, they had to resolve the issue with a member of their treatment team.

One rainy day Molly was busy behind her desk preparing a purchase order when interrupted by Marco Simone, her administrative assistant. The stocky, blond-headed Italian wore a huge grin. "How do you like your new office, Molly Pritchard? Jazzy enough for you?"

"Not too bad compared to previous workplace settings I've labored in. Perhaps the word 'labored' is misleading. But, you know what I mean. You were with me at my four previous jobs."

"If pushed, I'd have to agree with you," Marco said. "But, my first encounter riding shotgun with the super-duper female pilot in an Apache attack helicopter in Iraq would be in that, ah, 'labored' classification."

She chuckled. "Yes, there's no comparison to flying that killing machine to working in the bona fide civilian world. I don't ever remember a plush office like this when riding a big desk job in the military. Let's face and enjoy the here and now—leather chairs and a private bathroom."

"I'm fine in my little cubbyhole," Marco laughed. "A coffee pot and spittoon is all I'll ever need."

"I thought you got rid of that stupid chewing habit when you left Iraq."

"Don't push it, boss, I'm working on it."

She nodded. "Other then that filthy distraction, I have to admit you do pretty damn good with that foot prosthesis. The VA did you well. Maybe it' s my fault you still don't have two real feet to put shoes on."

Marco shrugged and said nothing. He plunked down in one of the leather chairs facing her. "Why were we so stupid to volunteer for that disastrous combat patrol in Fallujah while the Apaches were down for maintenance? I stepped on that fucking mine and woke up ten yards from the other guys. You were luckier," he lamented, then pointed to her arm.

"What do you mean by that comment, Marco?"

"Just thinking. That high-velocity round that almost severed your arm was probably aimed at your pretty head. They had one hell a time hauling us to that combat support hospital. Look at you now—tall, beautiful and highly desirable."

"Shut the fuck up, you flake," she snickered. "You're revolting, clumsy and married with kids. If you weren't so proficient in your job, I'd have your wide butt tossed out on the street."

They both doubled-up laughing. Marco knew he was a chiseled, Hollywood-handsome hunk. That fact never escaped her. He was also true to his spouse.

She then reverted to the original subject about office decor. "My associate Boyd Bounder over there in the hospital lucked out. His furnishings must've cost a mint. The leather lounging guest chairs are to die for. And a wet bar in a hospital office, yak!"

"Do I detect a hint of jealousy?" he sneered.

"Huh, no, just pouting. Bounder has a more important job, so should be 'dressed out' accordingly."

"I don't agree," Marco jumped in. "He only has to deal with the crazies for a few days, or weeks at a time. You've got these hardened combat veterans for maybe the rest of their lives. Granted, we only have a couple in-house at this time. They think and act like this is a country club. Perhaps we need to tighten things up."

"Mr. I. M. Hill doesn't think so. He suggested we give them as much freedom as possible. He'd be the first one to 'right the ship' if he felt necessary."

"What does the I. M. stand for?" he asked with a smirk.

"Everybody is hesitant to ask him for some reason or another. Scuttlebutt has it that the 'I' stands for Immortal and the 'M' stands for Majestic."

"You got to be outright pulling my leg," he quipped.

"Who cares," she said. "Just bow or genuflect whenever he comes over here."

"For sure," Marco snickered. "When I see him walk across the water in that swanky rooftop swimming pool next door. Otherwise, it's business as usual."

"One last comment on I.M. Hill," Molly said. "I had a nice chat with that grizzled, bearded veteran we recently admitted. He told me not to use his given name in the facility. I don't know why. Grizzly is the handle he preferred. Anyhow, Grizzly served with Howard during the US invasion of Granada in 1983. The man shared with me the grim story about I. M. taking a bullet for him."

"Good Lord," Marco said.

Molly nodded in agreement. "Grizzly was walking point during a patrol Howard vehemently disagreed with. As always, rank had the final say. Unfortunately, the squad ran into a well-concealed ambush."

"Sounds familiar," Marco said. "Please go on."

"Grizzly raised his hand in the air to alert the squad of a potential problem ahead. Trailing behind, Hill caught glimpse of a slight movement far ahead in the thick bushes. He raced up and knocked Grizzly to the ground. A sniper rifle cracked, and a round struck Hill while lying on top of Grizzly. Fortunately for I. M., it was a through-and-through deep flesh wound of his right shoulder. One of his many medals was awarded because of bravery in combat."

"I'm more than impressed with him now," Marco added. He walked to the window behind Molly's desk. He stared out at the Tower of the Americas several blocks away. "Your friend Mr. Bounder doesn't have this spectacular view from his office window," he pointed out the casement. "What's the history of the tower?"

"It's the second thing I learned after arriving here," she said. "That 750-foot tall structure was built for the 1968 HemisFair hosted by San Antonio. You need to take your kids up there in the revolving observation deck. It offers a fantastic view of the entire area. But, the primary history lesson in San Antonio for newcomers is the story of the Alamo. You'll know a lot more about the mission when you have more time to explore the city."

"I'll do that—even have the wife tag along."

"That's mighty considerate of you, family man. Don't you have some catching up to do? I've got my notes here and haven't crossed out a few of the assignments I gave you three days ago. We have some new 'lifers' coming in next week."

"No sweat, boss, I got it covered. But, do we need microwaves and small dormitory refrigerators in each room? These lads aren't students. Are they too lazy to haul ass to the dining room?"

"We'll encourage it. Lest you not forget, we were funded to provide these conveniences to our special guests."

"Yes, Molly," he smirked. "Thy will be done."

"You may excuse yourself now, Marco. Let me be alone for a stretch. I'm overdue on the report Mr. Hill requested last week. To the drillmaster, it's already past due one day before the suspense date. Get the drift?"

"Loud and clear. I'm outta here."

Chapter 5
April 2017

He was sprawled face down on the tiled hospital dayroom floor. No signs of movement. No outward signs of trauma. Nobody was around. No alarms were sounded. The mental health aide assigned duties in the dayroom had skipped outside for a quick smoke and extended break.

The prone patient had been the first admission to the newly-opened hospital. Little ballyhoo was made for his celebrity status. He'd only been an inpatient for a short period but made a few friends. The TCCV organization will be furious when they learn of the incident.

Eduardo Munoz was motoring down the hallway toward his room when the dayroom aide rounded the corner. Eduardo sped past him. "Better slow that high-speed chariot down, mister. You almost ran me over."

Munoz carried a bulky, 200-plus pounds with narrow brown eyes and a mohawk crewcut. He was short in stature, a few inches above five-feet tall. Eduardo usually wore camouflaged fatigues when he was journeying around the facility. He had a shrill, annoying voice, almost feminine.

"Sorry, sir," Eduardo apologized as he gave him a sharp salute. He braked the motorized wheelchair. "I was passing the dayroom when I heard a commotion. Obscenities and other unspeakable words were flying out of there. I burned rubber, not that I'm a coward or anything like that. Avoiding trouble and confrontation seems to be a daily challenge for me. Sir, I suggest you run in there and find out what's going on. Meanwhile,

[36]

I'll head back and police up my untidy room less the colonel beats me there. I failed his last inspection."

The aide laughed. "My friend, that Bronze Star for Valor you earned during the Korean War tells me you don't run away from conflict. Get lost. Go take a nap. The colonel is on R&R in Hawaii." *The crazy son-of-a-bitch with delusions of grandeur should've stayed at the VA. I was told he had been a patient in the old hospital but transferred back to the VA when Mission Oaks Mental Health Hospital shut down. Now TCCV petitioned for him to be the second patient in the new hospital. He's scheduled to be transferred to the long-term facility next week. Good riddance!*

The aide waited until Munoz headed back to his room, then stopped in the bathroom down the hall heeding nature's call. He finished up and went outside for a smoke—thought he'd earned it. Then he ambled back to the dayroom. The aide was in a heightened state of anxiety when he saw the patient lying next to the pool table. A broken pool cue stick was perched on top of the green-felted pool table. A ball-peen hammer was on the floor in the corner. Two metal chairs were turned upside down, five-feet from the corpse.

The shocked aide raced over to the prostrate man and rolled him over on his back. He was cold to the touch. There was no heartbeat, no breath, bulging eyes were opened wide. A huge black and blue indentation was visible in the middle of his forehead. Percy Radcliff was dead. The aide yanked out his cell phone and called Boyd Bounder, imploring him to rush upstairs to the dayroom.

"Jesus H. Christ," Boyd shouted when he entered the dayroom and saw the dead man. He pushed the aide aside. He noticed the broken cue stick and overturned chairs. "Call 9-1-1 and tell them we found a patient dead in the dayroom, a possible homicide for all I know."

The aide grabbed his cell phone and placed the call. Bounder began CPR procedures. He placed his hands, one over the other in the middle of the man's chest and using his full body weight, pushed hard in rhythmic sequences.

"They're on the way," the aide shouted as he hustled out the entry door, fearful of the impending consequences about to descend on all parties. He wanted no part of it.

Bounder began to tremble. He knew he had to call Howard Hill before the cops arrived. *Hill will be mortified when he learns of this disaster. We should've anticipated this possibility based on the series of threatening telephone calls we received last week. But in our line of work, intimidating calls happen all the time. Where the hell was that dayroom aide when this went down?*

The dead man was the son of a popular Texas State representative from Houston. Percy Radcliff had the distinction of being "the first man in" when he was admitted to the new hospital. Percy had served with distinction as a marine sniper in Afghanistan. He'd left the service after his enlistment expired, returning home to a wife and two children. His adjustment to civilian life was wrought with behavioral disorders, several DUIs and a brief incarceration behind bars. His brutal battery of a defenseless homeless victim did not go down well. He had rejected all authority figures, including his strong-willed father. His wife and children suffered through his troubled times.

Percy tried to re-enter military service but was rejected. He was diagnosed and treated for a post-traumatic stress condition, manifested by outbursts of violent acts resulting in bodily harm.

[38]

Lance Radcliff was Percy's father, and he felt best to have his son undergo further treatment in a facility away from his Houston suburban home. The wife was emotionally drained and disagreed with the treatment plan, pressing hard for local intervention. She finally caved under the intense pressure of his demanding father.

Enter TCCV and Pritam Lozen, a former US Army Dustoff pilot serving as co-pilot for Lance Radcliff in Vietnam. Thirty-five missions to the jungle and rice-padded countryside bound the two together for life. Appropriate arrangements were made to have the emotionally encumbered Percy admitted to the new mental health hospital in San Antonio.

"Stand down the hospital and secure all exits," the burly police lieutenant with a starched blue shirt and razor-sharp creased pants ordered the other officers. They had arrived minutes before Howard Hill.

"The perp might still be hiding out in the hospital. Examine all patient rooms, closets and storage areas. Be careful, the bastard might be armed. Bag that hammer over there and the broken cue stick with your gloved hands," he ordered one of the officers near the dead body.

"Check his hospital robe pockets and underlying garments for any items of interest. Bag and identify everything you find. I don't care if it's snotty tissue or grimy false teeth. Don't leave anything behind."

"Look what I found in his pocket, lieutenant," another officer exclaimed with an excited voice. He held up an index card with four scribbled words.

"Good job," the lieutenant said with a huge grin. He took the card from the officer and tried to read the note, looking puzzled. "Not familiar with the jargon. Bag it and give it to the coroner when she gets here. Damn, she should've arrived by now. Probably dilly-dallying at her favorite Starbucks. Anyway, it might give us a clue to this tragedy once the words are interpreted."

Hill walked in and saluted the tall and muscular lieutenant. "Hello, Baldy, glad you were able to come to our unplanned party. I hadn't seen your smiley face since the grand opening ceremonies. On top of that, you haven't responded to my calls challenging your many skills on the golf course. Playing the game of cops and robbers appears to be more than a full-time job. Anyway, hope you can help us here."

The big lieutenant with a boxer's cauliflower ears had been a patient of Howard's when he ran the VA addiction center several years ago. At first, they butted heads, each with his stubborn agenda. Hill won out. They had maintained a close relationship after the police officer regained control of his life. Howard had hired one of the chief's cousins as an administrative assistant at the VA.

"Sorry to spoil your day, I. M., but duty calls. I assure you we will get to the bottom of this." He shook Howard's hand, wrapped his thick arms around him and then rejoined his investigative crew.

Hill cornered Bounder and led him to the back part of the dayroom away from the frenzied activity. He demanded a quick assessment of the situation. "Weren't you told to keep eyes on this patient at all times? You knew his history. You were aware of the threatening phone calls that you shared with me. This rotten state of affairs could've been avoided. Who was with him in the dayroom?"

"One of our senior mental health aides was assigned the duties," Boyd said. "I haven't had a chance to talk to him yet. The
police lieutenant has already rounded him up. Two uniforms are
in the outer office next to the dayroom questioning him as we
speak. I can't believe something like this could happen here.
We've followed protocol at every step."

Hill stared him down. "Yes, obviously every stage of his activity . . . minus the events leading up to the killing field." Hill
wanted to focus on the sequence of activities where patient control and supervision broke down. The death of a high-profile patient had the potential of widespread negative press. Damage
control measures had to be implemented. He'd assign the task to
Molly Pritchard. He needed to capitalize on the quick-thinking
and high-speed action capabilities that stood out in her resume
and job recommendations.

The county coroner arrived, followed by the forensic team.
They reported to the lieutenant as he exited the outer office. The
lieutenant gave her a quick look. She wore loose-fitting clothing
to hide her stretched-out old tattoos and excessive bulk. Her ap-
parel appeared as though it came from the local thrift store. The
doctor was old and disheveled but firm in her gait. Soon after her
arrival, the lieutenant walked in and gave her a quick summary
of the situation. They knew each other from many previous homicides and were cordial. She began her evaluation. He stood to
the side and watched her detailed assessment. Hill and Bounder
were still parked in their chairs further off to the rear. They listened intensely to the conversations.

"What do you think, doctor?" the lieutenant asked. "Did you
read the scrawled wording on the index card my associate gave
you?"

"Well, lieutenant, I looked at it and didn't recognize the dialect. I'm English, Spanish and Cajon schooled. We have a linguistics expert back at the shop. He'll figure out the hodge-podge in no time. Look, I'm just starting here, but I don't think it was self-inflicted," she said slowly.

The lieutenant's eyes displayed a quizzical appearance.

"I haven't experienced anything quite like this before," she said. "I've been involved in numerous odd-ball killings in the past. You of all people know that. This scenario is nowhere to be found in the textbooks. You've got the hammer and damaged pool cue stick to fingerprint. I got the dead body to explore. We'll do an autopsy, DNA and toxicology tests and see what shows up."

"Got it," he said.

"My first inclination leads to a homicide," she continued. "The only thing I can't understand is the circumstances involving the deep indentation in the forehead. A killing blow with any type of hammer would've broken the skin and discharged a bloody mess on both the corpse and the floor. There was none apparent in this case. The absence of blood leads us to other potential causes."

The lieutenant was patient but edgy. He scratched his bald head. "And what would those be?"

"First, so much depends on whose fingerprints are found on the hammer. The smashed cue stick is another story. That is to say, who broke the wooden rod and under what circumstances? I might find some bruise marks on the body during my examination. I don't believe you'll find the victim's prints on the hammer. Secondly, the squiggled words on the index card will give us another important clue. And lastly, my autopsy will determine if he had a congenital malformation of his frontal skull, or maybe some other precarious medical condition not recorded in his medical files. The bottom line, however, I think he was the victim of an assault. It could be another patient, a visitor, a hospital staff member, janitor, or housekeeper. The whodunnit falls in your lap."

"We'll get to the far end of this," he said assuredly. "It's not my first dance on the big stage."

The coroner nodded her head. "You always do, my favorite police lieutenant. I'll determine the cause of death. You find the perpetrator. We'll split the generous monetary achievement award."

Meanwhile, the forensic team came into the dayroom without saying a word. They set up their equipment on a sheet strewn over the pool table and began to assess their duties.

The lieutenant laughed at her assertion about the prospects of success. "Yea, the city and county officials are generous to us peons."

"There's always a first time," she said with a straight face. "Oh, by the way, you can have your fingerprint guys go to work now. Make sure they get prints off the hammer and the cue stick. There might be other surfaces you want to be printed. That's your call. Thanks for holding them off and not allowing them to get ahead of my physical examination. Have a nice day."

"Wait," the lieutenant ordered. "Can you give us a time of death?"

"Too early." She waddled past him, glanced at Hill, gave Bounder a wink, and then disappeared through the doorway.

The dead man was fingerprinted and placed in a body bag. The coroner's crew that had followed her into the dayroom removed the dead body. The remainder of the police unit that searched the premises reported back to the lieutenant.

"All secured, boss," the team leader said. "However, we did run into a crazy character in a motorized wheelchair roaming the hallway. He stopped us, wanting to know why the uniforms were after him. He claimed to know all about the incident that took place in the dayroom. I told him to return immediately to his room and don't leave under any circumstances."

"Good. I want to talk to him but only in the presence of Mr. Bounder and Mr. Hill. Go back and get him, ASAP! Have another officer retrieve the mental health aide who discovered the body. Mr. Bounder here will give you his name and whereabouts.

The lieutenant walked over to the other officers. "Did you run into anything bizarre that waived a red flag?"

"No, sir," one of the senior officers said. "Just a bunch of inquisitive patients wondering what was going on. I told them we were here at the request of the administration to conduct a security drill. Three patients volunteered to be a part of it. One told us he had appeared in a sci-fi movie in Hollywood. I wrote his name on my business card and told him he might be contacted for the next drill. He said he would donate his fee to the local food bank, of all places."

"What about the other two patients?" the lieutenant asked.

"Oh, they said they liked to play hide and seek."

The lieutenant laughed. "First-rate job, officer. Round up the building and grounds search party and get the hell out of here. I'll stay behind and quiz the wheel-chaired jockey and the aide. Our forensics are getting the fingerprints and will remain with me until I finish up here. If it was a murder, the perp is long gone."

Hill and Bounder joined up with the lieutenant.

"What's next, Baldy?" Howard asked.

"We'll turn this case over to our detective staff to handle the continuing analysis. An expert will review the security camera tapes generated at each entrance of the hospital. They'll put out an APB if anyone noted suspicious vehicle activity around the hospital complex. They'll even run an inquiry on the hospital's incoming and outgoing telephone calls since Mr. Radcliff was admitted. Also, cellphone tower scrutiny has provided valuable information to us in the past. I hate to say it, but there are too many loose screws running around here for me to feel the least bit comfortable. This could develop into a long and drawn-out exercise in futility."

"Let's sit in on the conversations when they bring Munoz here, Boyd," Hill suggested. "I'm sure Baldy won't mind. We might be able to explain some of the uncanny fairytales only that clown Munoz can generate."

The lieutenant nodded in agreement.

Eduardo motored in at top speed, followed by a police office frantically chasing after him, screaming for the patient to slow down. Munoz clipped the corner of the door housing on his way in. Colorful sparks flew from the metal portico. The quivering mental health aide arrived several minutes later with the other officer.

"Put that aide in another room and stay with him while I question this speed demon." The lieutenant ordered. "I'll get to him later. Wait, better yet, take him down to the station and let him sit on ice and think about what happened here during his duty shift."

The officer did as instructed and led the freaked-out aide from the dayroom. He didn't resist the forced trip to the police station.

Bounder looked over at Hill with a smug face.

"Pretty bad, huh Boyd?"

"Yeah. We'll get bottom of this."

The lieutenant thanked the other policeman for his help in the speedy recoveries and told him to return to the station. He then motioned to Hill and Bounder to come closer and join him.

Chapter 6
One hour earlier

Molly Prichard jumped from her office chair and raced to the window. She had witnessed the commotion taking place over at the hospital. She wondered what caused the police squad cars to circle the facility and race to a screeching stop at the front entrance.

She walked over to check the back window of her office to see if anything out of the ordinary was going on there. She took in a deep breath when she surveyed the area, noticing an old, beat-up military ambulance variant of the Humvee sitting near the staff parking lot.

Molly stepped over to the tall book cabinet and snatched a small set of binoculars from the top shelf. She trained the device on the truck. It displayed a visible, but weather-worn symbol of the Red Cross. The lorry was a replica of the one that transported her and Marco's wounded bodies to a combat support hospital in Iraq years ago.

There was no visible sign of activity in, or around the vehicle. Molly grabbed her cellphone and took a picture, then thought for a few moments.

No, I must be seeing things. It couldn't be. I got to show Marco when he gets back from picking up the new patient. I wish I'd sent another person to the San Antonio International Airport other than Marco. I'd feel better if he were here to help assess the situation. He always had the skill to explore alternatives at the last second and opt for the best course of action.

Molly rushed to her desk to call Boyd—no answer. She called Howard—same non-response. Upset and also confused, Molly left her office and decided to hustle over to the hospital and find out what was happening. *Why would an old field ambulance be parked on the property?*

Fifty-feet out from her side-office door to the outside plaza, she heard the grinding of a truck engine. Within seconds, the Humvee was racing toward her. Molly spun around at the last second to avoid a head-on collision. She fell hard to the concrete surface and rolled away from the oncoming truck.

It sped past her, turning sharply away from the front of the hospital. The steel monster started to lean on its side, two wheels off the ground, but the skilled driver was able to avert a rollover.

Molly sat up, took several deep breaths and shook off the near disaster. Nothing she could do about the fleeing Humvee as it dashed out of view. She ran across the plaza and reached the hospital front door. It was locked. She peered inside and began banging on the glass door with her bruised knuckles. Nobody was inside. There was no activity. She raced around to the side door. It was locked. The same scenario existed at the rear hospital door near the garbage bin.

She retraced her steps to the front entrance. A uniform was now standing inside the locked door. She rapped again. He saw her and waved her off with a hand and arm gesture. She kicked hard at the steel plating at the bottom of the door.

The police officer unlocked the door. She barged in.

"Whoa, lady, cool down, you almost knocked me over. I have orders that nobody enters or leaves the building." He hadn't noticed the blood dripping from her elbows, nor the ripped blouse.

[48]

Molly showed him her ID badge depicting her position on the facility management team. "What the hell is going on in there?" she shouted at him.

"Don't know for sure, but my job is to guard this entrance until I'm relieved."

Molly moved in closer. "Can you please tell me why you were called to the hospital in the first place?"

"All I know is we got a 9-1-1 that somebody was hurt. It could've been an accident, assault or even murder. I don't know any of the details, but you're not coming in here, ma'am."

Molly was almost out of control but put her raging emotions at rest while trotting back to her office. She treated her bruised elbows with medicated wipes stored in a desk drawer. The seeping blood had abated. She tried calling both men again. Nothing happened. She plopped down on her office chair in deep thought, formalizing her next course of action.

A few minutes later her cell rang. It was Boyd Bounder. He had no clue about the frustrations she'd experienced in the last hour.

"Hey, Molly, glad you made it back to your office so soon. I thought you were going to run some errands today. I want to give you a quick 'heads up' about the calamity taking place next door. I trust you've noticed the police cars parked out front."

"Yes, hell yes, for Christ's sake, Bounder. I was almost killed going over there to find out what was happening."

"Almost killed? What do you mean by that?" His voice had become more serious.

"I'll fill you in after you get your ass over here. You can tell me why the police are guarding your place with the tenacity of the Pope's Swiss Guards."

"Sit tight. I'll be right over."

Within minutes, Bounder was standing beside her. He shuddered at Molly's disheveled attire. She motioned for him to sit down. She returned to her desk chair. Boyd noticed the torn shirt, but not the condition of her elbows. He insisted on hearing her story first before he would address the jumbled mess across the plaza. She became more relaxed but adamant that he get on with his narrative. He conceded to her argument.

Boyd then briefed her on the sequence of events leading up to their questioning of Eduardo Munoz. "It was lengthy and tenuous," he said. "Munoz wouldn't shut up. He bragged incessantly about his military heroics in the gassed trenches of Verdun during WW I. More evidence of a tattered brain. We decided to take a short break from the onerous grilling process. So here I am."

"You mean that crazy son-of-a-bitch killed one of your patients?" she asked, scratching her head.

"Hold on, you're drawing a conclusion that hasn't been proven. Munoz is not the killer-type according to the delusional archetypes we've examined. He'd rather be killed for outrageous acts of heroism than take another human's life. You may have forgotten that we intend to transfer him to your 20-bed unit next week. That will take place unless the cops decide another course of action after cross-examining him."

"I told you before, Bounder, that I don't want him here."

"The TCCV loves the guy for some odd reason," he said. "The VA dumped him here as soon as we opened. Let's not draw any conclusions at this point. As I told you, the old geezer is harmless."

"Yeah, so why do the cops have him in the center of the bull ring?" she asked.

"He seems to be the only witness to the patient's demise."

[50]

"By the way, who's the stiff?"

"Percy Radcliff," Boyd sighed loudly.

"Oh my God, not him." She stared up at the ceiling.

"Why the reaction? You must have had some kind of association with the guy in the past. Do you want to talk about it?"

"No."

"Suit yourself. Molly. Now, please tell me about your 'near-death' experience."

She gave him every detail of the event, including a quick peek of her bruised elbows after her long tale.

He shuddered when he saw the jagged scrape and swollen elbow joint knowing that it could have been much worse. "I'm so happy you're safe now, Molly. Thank goodness. Why don't you go home and rest up? I have to get back to the hospital day-room. Howard Hill is beside himself. In his words—ready to court-martial the entire hospital staff. We're about to reconvene the questioning with the police lieutenant. I'll relate your story to the lieutenant about the ambulance situation. He'll know what action to take. Are we still on for tonight?"

"Maybe. I'll let you know later."

They'd had a few dates after Bounder's relationship with the restaurant owner had cooled. Howard Hill had made a comment to her in their initial meeting about Bounder and the woman. Regardless, she had grown to like Bounder. He was another established athlete and a reliable gentleman.

"Is there a problem, Molly?"

"Ahh, no, not really. I guess I haven't had time to reconnect with reality after that truck almost killed me today. I'll be alright."

"I have no doubt about that, Molly."

"Thanks, Boyd. Okay, we're on for tonight."

[51]

Chapter 7

Boyd returned to the hospital and took a seat close to Munoz. The questioning was still going on in great detail. He waited to discuss Molly's breath-taking account with the police lieutenant, but first things first. They needed to finish the long harangue with Eduardo. But, the patient had other thoughts on his quizzical mind and shifted the thrust of the conversation.

"Mr. Bounder, I'm sure you remember all about me from the past," Munoz said sharply. "I spent time in your hospital. You know, when that CIA lady was murdered. I took home the grand prize in the capture of the badass who killed her. Now you people are squeezing me to confess to this unfortunate state of affairs."

Bounder reminisced about what had happened back then. *Yes, he's correct. Give the man credit. Great job.*

Baldy was getting impatient with Munoz. "Look here, Mr. Wheelchair, you were the only person identified as being in, or near the dayroom when all this happened. Stop leading us into the land of fuzziness and give us some facts. Were you with Mr. Radcliff in the dayroom before he died?"

"Yes. The colonel told me to keep an eye on him before he went on leave."

"What colonel?" Baldy asked.

"You know, the former commander of the 55th Brigade who is on temporary duty here at the fort."

Hill was at wit's end. "Eduardo Munoz . . . did you and Mr. Radcliff have a heated argument that led to blows?"

"Of course not. How dare you! I learned all about the man the day after he came to us. Percy almost lost his life in the last war. He is a renowned hero. We played a game of checkers and he whopped my butt. I was getting angry at him always humiliating me, so I grabbed one of those pool table wooden spears off the wall rack and snapped it in two."

"Did you strike Mr. Radcliff with the stick?" the lieutenant asked, pushing Hill and Bounder back behind the pool table.

"Certainly not. I respected him too much. I tossed the pieces on to that pool table over there."

"Then what did you do?" the lieutenant asked.

"I heard the mess hall chow bell ringing in my ears. I suffer from a rare form of tinnitus, but I can still hear things. I left Mr. Radcliff sitting in the comfy lounger by the window. He began reading the *Army Times*."

All of a sudden the dayroom overhead lights went off. The hospital emergency generator failed to kick in. All electrical outlets in the hospital became inoperable. It was still daytime, so darkness was not a factor.

"Maintenance automatically checks the generator when this happens," Bounder announced. "Nothing to worry about, folks. They'll reboot it."

A low humming sound was heard as the battery-driven wheelchair began to chug toward the door. With cat-like quickness, the police lieutenant seized Eduardo's arm as the motorized unit tried to ease past him.

"Hold on there, cowboy," the lieutenant shouted. "You're not going anywhere." With a powerful tug, he spun the heavy wheelchair around to him and prevented it from moving forward.

Munoz did as directed and bellowed out a string of profanities in the officer's direction. The lieutenant poked him in the stomach with his nightstick, then slapped his face. "Shut the fuck up and listen to me," Baldy yelled out, frustrated and at wit's end.

Hill jumped into the fray, told Baldy to get a grip and ordered Bounder to give Munoz something to calm him down. Bounder went to a treatment room and secured sleep serum and a syringe from a locked cabinet. He returned and administered the sedative. Shortly thereafter, Munoz was led away, escorted by mental health aides and returned to his room.

There had been a lapse in the conversation. It was time for Bounder to discuss Molly's scrape with the ambulance. Baldy and Hill were astonished as the story unfolded. They looked at each other and couldn't believe this new twist in the saga.

"Did she get hurt?" The lieutenant finally asked.

"Nothing serious, a few scrapes and bruises, and a pissed-off attitude."

"I would've expected that of her," Hill grinned. "She's the warrior type."

"That throws an interesting variable into the equation," the lieutenant said and then jotted down several more pieces of information in his notebook. "We'll put out an APB as soon as possible. We'll find that damn truck."

With nothing more to accomplish, Bounder decided to return to his office. He had to get caught up and then wrap things up for the day. A pile of pressing paperwork was strewn across his desk. He hoped Molly was eager and awaiting a relaxing late evening meal with him.

Hill waited until Bounder and Munoz departed, then called Molly. "Sorry so late getting back to you," Hill apologized. "Sit tight. Bounder discussed your 'near-death' experience with the mysterious ambulance. You sound relaxed now, thank goodness. I'm on my way over to your office. The rain has subsided. I know Bounder gave you a short briefing about the action that took place over here. We need to put out a press release."

"Yes, he did, Howard. Do we have a murder scene on our hands? Bounder was hyped-up. Is that the way he always acts when confronted with a violent problem?"

"Bounder never served in combat, Molly. We're different. Believe me when I say this. I'll fill you in completely when I get there. Did you survive the electrical outage?"

"We heard a loud bang over here. I hit the deck as quickly as my butt allowed. No one shouted 'incoming,' so I was at a loss what caused the noise. It was Fallujah all over again. Then one of my guest room associates came in and gave me a little history about the outdated transformers in the neighborhood. There's also one near our office not far from the hospital Dumpster. She said it happens several times a year. The utility company vowed it wouldn't go down again. I wouldn't bet on it. I'll put a pot of coffee on."

On his way across the plaza, Hill was in deep thought. He was aware that Molly and Boyd had enjoyed lunch together several times in the past week. *I wonder if there is an attraction developing between them. I think Boyd let loose of Clarisa for some unknown reason that he hasn't shared with me.*

They sat around a coffee table in Molly's office sipping the hot brew. "I need to buy one of those Keurig dynamos like yours, Molly. Takes all the labor out of making that first cup of mud in the morning. Let's talk."

Howard closed the gaps in the events that took place next door. Molly made copious notes and underlined several key phrases. She jotted down questions on the other side of her ledger.

When he finished his detailed report, she asked questions and wrote down his responses—brief and concise. She then waved him away, got off the visitor chair and then sat down at her desk. She pulled out an old folder that contained all the press releases covering the CIA murder in the old hospital. Howard stayed seated, crossed his arms and said nothing.

"What's your take on this state of affairs, Molly," he asked after a ten-minute hiatus. "We have to get moving before the buzzards start circling overhead."

"I am doing nothing, Howard."

"What the hell are you talking about? We're going to get crucified!"

"You are going to inform Tam Lozen on his hotline immediately. Tell my father what happened and get his input. He's an old pro on these delicate matters. He'll tell you that Percy was a close friend of my brother. In earlier years, he often stayed at our house for periods when his father traveled. It's weird because they were not compatible. Jase was weak and contentious, always arguing about some far-out crusade on human rights. He supported any plight involving the American Indian, historically and at the present. On the other hand, Percy was humble and hated politics, more into the sporting scene to include chasing after cute cheerleaders."

"Were there ever fisticuffs?" Howard needed more details.

"Oh, no, Percy was a physical specimen not to be messed with. Jase was a weakling, his venomous mouth more damaging than any right cross he could throw at you. Anyway, my father will know what information to release about Percy Radcliff's unfortunate demise. He'll brief the TCCV board members and then coalesce with Percy's father and the wife. And then he'll tell you to let me determine what action we'll take on this end. Lastly, he'll probably threaten to fire you."

"You got to be outright pulling my leg," Hill snapped back.

"Nope, but I'll tell you how these things work."

"I'm all ears, Molly. This better be damn good."

"We are not going to put out a press release. That's inviting a bucket of worms we don't need in our lap at this stage of the investigation."

"I disagree," Hill yelled. "The enemy is at our doorstep."

"Howard, you don't seem to get it. We're ahead of the curve. We don't know a fucking thing that went down over there. Were you in charge of operations when that CIA agent was murdered in the old hospital?"

"No. How is that relevant?"

"She had gigantic scissors buried in her chest," Molly said. "What do we have here?"

"A dead man with a caved-in skull," he shot back.

"Apples and oranges, Howard. You presume some fool pounded-in Percy Radcliff's forehead with a hammer. We don't know that. Maybe he tripped on a banana peel and clunked his skull on the floor. We are going to wait until we get the prelims from the coroner. Meanwhile, have Bounder assemble every breathing hospital employee and brief them on the situation. He needs to tell them not to form any conclusions until we're advised by investigating authorities. They are to avoid all contact with elements of the media. There is only one person in this entire complex who will meet with the media when the time comes. You're looking at her."

"Well, if your old man fires me over this mess, I'll take you down with me."

[57]

"I don't respond to threats, Howard. In the end, I may save your white ass."

"Don't bet on it, sweetie."

Howard left her office with mixed feelings. *Molly's a bitch to the nth degree but tough as nails. I kinda have a soft spot in my hardened heart for her. She's tall, attractive, unhitched and has her shit together. Few people have the guts to stand up to me. I like that. I can't believe she may have the hots for Bounder. He's a good man, works hard, but not her fancy. Perhaps I'll toss my hat in the ring.*

Molly brewed another cup of coffee and peered out the window. She watched the erect and proud Howard I. M. Hill marching across the wide plaza. He was going to call Boyd Bounder and give him a heads-up about Molly's scheme.

Marco Simone returned from the airport with the new admission to long-term care. He parked in the rear of the facility and saw a police car in front of the hospital. *Nothing new in our line of business. Must've been a patient under extreme stress to be hauled in by the cops. I'll check in with Molly once I get this new guy settled.* He had a guest room attendant escort the man to the admissions office. The night-shift clerk processed the nervous without a problem.

The extensive file on the patient had been delivered by UPS the previous afternoon. Marco observed the new admission being escorted to his room to settle in. He peered down the long hallway and saw Molly's office light still aglow. He knocked on her door and walked in.

"Hi Marco, I regret having you make the airport run," Molly said with a glum look.

"Huh? Why, did I miss something?"

[58]

"You sure as hell did. Didn't you see the cop cars? One of our patients was found dead next door in the hospital dayroom. To make matters worse, I almost got run over by a speeding Humvee."

"Jesus H. Christ," he muttered. "Report please."

Molly thrashed out every detail of the past several hours. When she described the Humvee ambulance catastrophe, he shuddered. She pointed to her bruised elbows and ripped blouse.

"What the hell—a Humvee ambulance? I wonder why it was still on hospital property while the police were doing their thing."

"It does seem weird," Molly countered. "Maybe they get their jollies off by filming episodes of frantic disorder and mass confusion."

Marco got excited. "Maybe they were stupid enough to try and take on the entire police force. They may have had a concealed .50 caliber machine gun mounted in the back. Hey, enough of this ranting. Thank goodness you're still alive. Tell me the rest of the story, and I'll fill you in on my experience at the airport."

Molly elaborated. He listened intensely to every detail, then shot up from the chair.

"You won't believe this, Molly, but I saw a beat-up old Humvee at the airport when I picked up our new admission. The piece of junk was parked several spaces away from me in the parking garage. I did a doubletake—Fallujah all over again. I had the urge to stroll over and check it out. Nobody was in the area, so I snapped some pictures for old-time's sake. I couldn't hang around because my flight was arriving at the gate. You know, that had to be the same Humvee you talked about. Let's go back to the airport and find those fuckers."

"No, hold on, Marco—not a good idea. I'll contact the police lieutenant who supervised the investigation. You give him the specifics of what you saw and what action you took. Send him the pictures of the Humvee . . . stat! Let them run with it."

"Dial him up now," Marco urged. "I'd like to ride with them and show the exact location of the getaway truck."

"Not your call Marco. You'd only get in the way and complicate things."

"Me? Get in the way? I'm a born and trained super warrior with one steel foot ready to kick some radical asses."

"Marco?"

"I guess you're right, Molly, as usual."

Chapter 8

Molly headed back to her apartment to get cleaned up for her late dinner with Bounder. She felt the need to take a hot shower to flush away the seriousness of the day's events. The scare with the old converted Humvee ambulance and Marco's airport sighting came to mind as she soaped up.

Where'd those bastards get that relic? I know the government has periodic sales for unserviceable military hardware. The police lieutenant assured me an all-hands alert went out and a squad car had been dispatched to the airport before we even concluded the conversation.

The skinned elbows were no longer an issue. The swelling had almost disappeared. She relived her tour of duty in Iraq and shuddered thinking about being shot by that sniper. Marco told her the radicals' expert marksmen prided themselves with the success of their long-range headshots. The road to her recovery had been a formidable challenge. *I got to stop reliving Iraq.*

She looked forward to her dinner session with Bounder. She sat in her recliner and enjoyed a glass of red wine before Bounder picked her up. Again, the thought processes took front and center.

I keep contrasting Bounder and Hill as though I'm grocery shopping for my evening meal. Bounder is sweet, unassuming and steeled with a gentleman's respect for the opposite sex. He proved his mettle on the tough Texas gridiron. He's good company and I enjoy being with him.

Hill is old enough to be my father. Stern, battle-tested, yet sensitive. We're both combat veterans living with the ravages of our wartime experiences. Somehow he appeals to crazy me.

Maybe I need one of our psychologists next door to analyze my state of affairs and point me in the right direction.
Dinner at the premier steakhouse in downtown San Antonio on Houston Street was a delight for both of them. Boyd had frequented the restaurant on two occasions. He was sure she'd love the special touch given to all customers. They were famished.

Boyd Bounder and Molly Pritchard drove back to his new two-story home in the King Wilhelm neighborhood for after-dinner drinks. They had opted to forego libations before dinner. Wrapping up the dead body disaster at the hospital took several hours. It was late. He was despondent about the day's calamities at the hospital. Blame will rain down on him from all directions. Failure by the hospital administrators to provide a safe environment for patients and staff is paramount—no exceptions, no excuses. Sharing his concerns with Molly at dinner had helped relieve the stress. She was comforting, supportive and caring.

"What made you buy a home in this neck of the woods and give up a neat condo at the Towers, Boyd? This home is antiquated."

He perked up. "Hey, that's why I like it here south of downtown. Most of these colonials have witnessed the rise and fall of the German influence in the Alamo City. Prominent family figures walked these old streets, many pushing baby buggies on the cobblestone surfaces. You haven't been in town long enough to witness the gentrification of this area. I treasure this category of progress, makes me feel young again. Mothers chasing active toddlers, husbands walking dogs, and young kids kicking soccer balls in the streets invigorate me, Molly."

"Whatever," she said and shrugged her shoulders. "I'm dying of thirst. Are you going to whip up those margaritas you promised, or did you delegate that mission to me?"

"No ma'am, sorry about the delay. I'll get right on it."

Molly strolled around the large living room, tiny dining room, and peeked into his private office. A large framed picture of Boyd hung behind his desk. He was in a Texas Longhorn football uniform reaching skyward to snag a forward pass. She walked in and read the citation below the photograph. She took a deep breath noticing that he had won All-American honors as a tight end.

Molly then scrutinized the contents of the mudroom next to the kitchen. She had no clue why he elected this oblong room to display his exclusive collection of rifles on one wall and antique swords on the opposite wall. Most collectors would house these weapons in locked cabinets somewhere in the depths of the home, not adjacent to the rear exit door. She made a note to ask him later.

"I'm glad you like our popular local drink, Molly," he said as he beckoned her to the sitting room next to the living room. Four overstuffed loungers circled a mahogany coffee table. A caricature of the State of Texas was carved into the top surface of the table. The heavy unit sat on a black bearskin carpet. The head was almost the size of a basketball.

Molly was impressed. "Did you kill this bear with one of those rifles mounted in the back room?"

"Yes, Molly."

"Was it the shotgun? Tell me about the hunt."

"No, the Remington rifle. I hate to brag. Leave it at that." *I should've told her the truth. My hunting guide actually shot the bear with that rifle.*

[63]

"Fine, Daniel Boone. I need to comment on a person's choice of liquors. I profess to be a Jack Daniels fan if you want to know. To me, margaritas seem to go better with spicy Mexican food. Not thick juicy steaks. And by the way, thanks for not taking me to the Cantina Classica tonight. The busy steakhouse just down the street was more impressive and the food of higher quality."

"Sorry, Mr. Daniels is not sitting in my liquor cabinet. I thought you'd opt for red wine. I'll pick up a couple of bottles of Jack tomorrow for, um, insurance purposes."

"Sounds fine to me," she laughed.

Boyd hesitated before responding to her reference to the Cantina Classica. "I think you know that I no longer feel affection for Clarisa, the owner."

"How would I know that?" Molly roared back.

"I thought Howard Hill might have passed that on to you."

"Good gracious no. Why would he even think of doing that, Boyd?" *He doesn't need to know about Howard's earlier advice to me on the subject.*

"Howard has a jealous streak in his moral fiber. Don't quote me on this, but I think he is interested in pursuing a relationship with you. He sees me as the opposition now that Clarisa is history."

"Why Boyd Bounder, I am so impressed that two senior warriors have an amorous interest in me. How do I rate such affection?"

Bounder skirted the answer with another question. "Why don't you have a boyfriend?"

"What makes you think I don't?" She gave him a hard look.

[64]

"You seem so settled and happy here. Howard told me you had a love interest, but you broke it off when this opportunity in San Antonio took precedence over existing relationships back on the home front."

"Aha, you've been checking up on me. Having said that, I need to flip the magical coin and see whose face shows up—you or Mr. Hill."

Boyd chuckled. He didn't remember Howard grilling him on his love life. "Don't believe everything the old first sergeant tells you. Howard's a great mentor, but his history with women is another story."

"I'm not interested in digging up old personal events here, Mr. Bounder. I live in the 'now' world. So many people are bogged down by dragging around unpleasant memories."

Boyd relented. "Allow me to join your domain."

The second and third rounds of margaritas came quickly. They were both getting light-headed. He became more touchy-feely. She became more somber and changed the infatuation landscape, still recalling Howard Hill's earlier chat with her about Boyd and Clarisa.

"Tell me about your early meeting tomorrow morning with the entire hospital staff," Molly asked. "You plan on discussing our collective marching orders as it pertains to Percy Radcliff's death. I'll be present. What do you intend to tell them?"

Boyd thought for a moment. "Howard and I got together for a quick strategy session before I picked you up. He filled me in on his earlier discussion with you."

"And how did that go?" She was anxious to hear Howard's play on the staff briefing.

"He referred to his 'skirmish' with you," Boyd added.

"Yes, we did have a little chat," Molly said. "But, it was more of a verbal boxing match. He agreed with my approach to the hungry media and other intrusive hangers-on. He also cleared the air and told me I'd be representing the hospital for the media briefing when scheduled."

Really? The old boy backed down." Boyd then asked her if she was ready to listen to his pitch for tomorrow.

"I'm all ears," she said. "Let's hear it."

"I'll inform the staff of the unfortunate incident concerning our patient Percy Radcliff. First, a little history that led to his death. He had gotten into a heated argument with another patient in the hospital dayroom. It almost came to blows. He wanted none of that and ran toward the door to get out of the room, tripping on the corner of the pool table leg. The poor man lost his balance and fell hard to the concrete floor. He smashed his head and dislodged the metal plate that had been implanted in his frontal skull as a result of a combat injury in Iraq. Unfortunately, the fall dislodged the plate and it penetrated the brain. Resuscitative measures were unsuccessful. The medical examiner is evaluating this detailed scenario."

"Bravo, Boyd Bounder. That's exactly what I had planned to release to the press. Now, let's hope it's true and factual. We should be hearing from the county coroner in a few days. The detectives investigating the case have to resolve the fingerprint issue. Perhaps that will necessitate another course of action. We'll address the developments at that time."

"It's late, Molly. Would you like to stay here tonight? You haven't had the chance to explore the rest of my new real estate. I have a comfortable guest room upstairs. Not sure I can drive you home safe and sound."

Bounder's tongue was thick. He had snuck in an extra margarita during the long discussion. To add to the alcoholic binge, he decided to double-pump the tequila bottle top pourer. He was tipsy, a rare occurrence for the light drinker.

"Thank you, Boyd Bounder. I'll take you up on the fine offer. We don't have a designated driver on board. Is there a deadbolt on the bedroom door?" she kidded him.

"Yes, but I have the only key," he laughed. "The guest bedroom is upstairs on the right. Nobody leaves or enters but yours truly."

"I don't intend to lock the door," she beamed. "I'll keep it wide open, then we'll see what happens. Goodnight, Boyd."

Molly excused herself and headed upstairs. The guest bedroom had a king-sized canopy bed that occupied half the room. A small desk with a laptop computer and printer on top was in one corner. The only chair in the room was a small La-Z-Boy recliner in the other corner. Two large windows on either side of the bed allowed ambient streetlight to filter in. Oil paintings pictures adorned the walls. The huge one over the desk depicted a remote highway scene with bluebonnets displayed on each side of a two-lane road. She had read somewhere that the colorful wildflower was the Texas state flower.

On the wall next to the door was another oil of the wildly popular Texas roadrunner, a long-legged bird—the subject of much folklore. She was surprised not to find a print of the famous Texas longhorn grazing in an expansive green meadow. Boyd elected not to have a TV in the guest room—too distracting for whatever might be going on in there.

The alcoholic haze in her brain dissipated to a lesser degree and allowed her to revisit the recent past. Molly had mixed feelings about the short-term relationship she'd developed with Boyd.

The grown men around here think I have a boyfriend stashed back home. If they only knew! I was branded as the "one and done" girl in high school. None of the young men came back for a second chance with me. My father ran them off with threatening actions if they attempted to touch me. Even with his slight limp, dad was known throughout the community as a no-nonsense tough guy.

In college, I was pegged as a loner. My intense involvement with sports didn't allow me to socialize on a steady basis. Now I'm ready for a new escapade, but Boyd might be too inebriated to take advantage of a golden opportunity. I'll do my best to stay awake and see what happens.

Chapter 9

Bright sun with great intensity raced through the bedroom windows. Molly had to pull the cover sheet back over her eyes. Then she popped up and checked herself out. She was wearing an old pair of his pajamas she'd found in the closet. Loud snoring and a fully clothed Boyd Bounder was lying next to her. She glanced at the alarm clock. The time was already eight. An unopened package of Trojan's was neatly positioned on the bedside table next to the clock.

She leaned over and punched Bounder's arm that wasn't coiled beneath him. Nothing happened. She jumped out of bed and rolled him over, hard, nearly plunging him to the wooden floor.

"Huh? What the hell. Hey, stop that, Molly. I'm awake. Holy shit, what time is it now?"

"One hour after your scheduled meeting to brief the hospital staff," she said in a sarcastic voice.

"Oh, no! Give me a minute to shake off the muddled mess in my brain."

She chided him. "I'm shocked. I thought you were dead, judging that you still hadn't undressed from last night. Should I be disappointed?"

Boyd took several minutes to assess the damage. He tugged at his waist and tucked his shirt back in. *She looks hot. Did I seduce her last night, and then get dressed again?* "Molly, you best get serious about today. Call my secretary and inform her I got delayed, and I'll be at the hospital in fifteen minutes."

"Nope. Call her yourself," she said. "I have to get dressed and hustle out of here as fast as I can. I'm meeting Howard at nine, and I best not be late. He's not known to accept failure for any underling not to report on time. We're to finalize our communications to both the media and TCCV." She walked briskly out of the bedroom and into the hallway bathroom.

Boyd wasn't sure how to wrap his arms around her temperament. *I screwed up in more ways than one. I know I can salvage the situation at the hospital. But not so sure about my rapport with her. She seems pissed.*

He went back to the master bedroom and cleaned up. He heard the hallway toilet door shut and her heels clicking the uncarpeted wood flooring on her way out and down the stairwell. Twenty minutes later he pulled into Mission Oaks. The staff parking lot was full.

"Oh, there you are, Mr. Bounder," his secretary said as she rushed into his office. "The staff meeting went well in your absence. You failed to tell me that you had asked Mr. Munoz to address the staff about the dayroom fiasco. I was there. You need to hire the old maestro as your public relations representative."

Boyd hesitated and shook his head in disbelief. *What the hell? She assumed I authorized him.*

"I'm happy to hear that. I'm on my way to his room to check out if he modified my script for the briefing. I'm sure he followed it to the letter."

"Oh, I'm not sure about that," she said with a serious look. "It seemed to me he talked off the cuff, not referring to any written notes. He is a good public speaker."

Boyd did his best to hide the embarrassment. "Hold the fort down until I get back. I'm sure the media caravan is on the way over."

"I doubt that, Mr. Bounder. I heard the story already made the local area news report."

"Oh, what did they say?" Boyd sat down.

"Not much. I can't quote the exact wording for you. They said something about the police department planned exercise involving a terrorist taking over the hospital. And hospital authorities were pleased with the exercise. Nothing was said about the dead body found upstairs."

"Good. I'll go up and thank him for the brilliant job he did on my behalf." Boyd shook his head. He wasn't sure he'd heard correctly everything she told him.

On his way up to the second floor, a patient came up from behind him and poked his shoulder. "Sorry to waylay you, sir. Did you receive that FedEx package my mother sent me? She said it should be put under lock and key when it arrives."

"Huh, no. Hans Schmidt, I'm sorry. What are you expecting from her?"

"You know, I put a note on your desk two days ago."

Boyd didn't remember any note having been left on his desk. "I think you're confused, sir. May I ask again, what is she sending you?"

The patient saluted Boyd. "Sir, it contains some personal items I had stored in my footlocker while in Afghanistan. I need to make sure everything is still intact."

Boyd was concerned. "What did you do in Afghanistan?"

Hans was eager to tell him. "I was with an EOD specialized unit."

"Sorry, I wasn't military. What do those initials stand for?"

[71]

"Explosive Ordnance Disposal, sir. My job was to disarm those personnel mines the Taliban planted along the roadside. Too many of our soldiers lost their limbs because of the booby traps. I was damn good at it."

"I'm sure you were, soldier. May I ask what you intend to do with the, ah, things you receive in that box from your mom?"

"Oh, sure., I worked with both the Houston fire and police departments before the TCCV sent me here. For one year on the job, I was called out to examine suspicious packages and boxes. I had to neutralize a handful of explosive devices. Didn't you see the award for heroism tacked to the wall above my bed?"

"No, Hans, I must've missed that the last time I checked in on you. By the way, I asked you before . . . what do you plan to do with the FedEx box you're expecting?"

"I intend to start a business that will help protect this community and its citizens. Maybe you can help me prepare a resume to send to all the local agencies involved in law enforcement."

Boyd put his right hand to his lips in thought, then said, "That's interesting, Hans. Your ability to blueprint your ideas is remarkable. Let me think about it. I'll have my staff standing tall to await the arrival of your goods, and then I'll get them to you."

"Thank you, sir." The patient saluted, did an about-face and returned to his room.

Boyd watched him leave and shook his head. He questioned how any soldier could have the guts to crawl around on the dirty ground trying to locate and disarm highly explosive materials. He also dwelled on Schmidt's comments.

Good Lord, what have we gotten ourselves into with this patient? I'd like to know what's in that big box on its way to my hospital. Hopefully, it contains simple bits and pieces of souve-

[72]

nirs he'd grown attached to while in the service. All I need is a weapons expert making bombs in the dayroom. Hold on, stop it, Bounder! Maybe I'm going overboard with my thought processes. I didn't get much sleep last night. In any event, Howard can't hear of this. I'll talk to Marco Simone, Molly's guy. He's more experienced in these matters than I am. He'll be sworn to secrecy.

As he neared Eduardo's room, he heard the last words of a telephone conversation emanating from inside. "And when am I going to receive the new vehicle? That's fine, thanks, goodbye."

Boyd walked in without rapping on the door. "What the hell was all that about, Munoz?" he asked with a stern voice.

"Well good morning, Mr. Hospital Administrator. You don't seem to be wearing a good mood. My guess is you haven't received any feedback on my marvelous talk this morning to your staff."

"No," he lied. "What's this I overheard about buying a new car?"

"Oh, that? Relax, sir, not a car. I just ordered a new Tesla, self-driven motorized wheelchair with oversized tires and big headlights. I'll be able to drive on the streets of San Antonio. And don't you go worrying about who is going to pay for it. The VA presented the invoice to me as a going-away gift when I came over here. They told me I was a valuable source of comfort and support to the other patients on my floor."

"But, why get a new unit like that one? You're not leaving the hospital grounds under any circumstances."

"Mr. Bounder, sir, you appear to have forgotten who I am."

"Impossible, Mr. Munoz. I know you like the back of my hands."

Eduardo sneered. "I received an order from Sam Houston to be his intermediary to deliver orders to Colonel Travis at the Alamo. He told me he's tied up with recruiting new soldiers to defend Texas. What greater honor could a man receive?"

"Did you take your medications this morning, Eduardo?"

"No way."

"Why not?" Boyd demanded.

"I needed a clear and open mind to deliver the talk you asked me to convey to hospital personnel. And I needed to be careful about how I related the story last night to my girlfriend. She works at the radio station."

"Girlfriend? Radio station? Last night? What's this all about?" Several new grey hairs began to mature on Bounder's head.

"You haven't had the pleasure to meet her, sir. She had worked at the VA and did me favors—big time favors. Know what I mean, Mr. Bounder? Anyhow, she's now living out her dream. I didn't want her studio bosses to learn secondhand about the murder in the dayroom. Otherwise, the whole community would be up in arms. I assured her the police department conducted an annual exercise required by the American Hospital Association.

"What kind of exercise is that?" Boyd knew where this was heading.

"A simulated terrorist attack to blow up our building."

"And was that the subject of your talk to my staff?"

"Yes, I'll give you a summary. But before recap, be advised I visited that senior mental health aide who was the first person to encounter the dead body. The police department had released him back to the hospital after they'd thoroughly questioned him. Even gave him a lie-detector test. He was still shaking like an epileptic creature about to pass out. I had my pearl-handled pistol given to me by General George S. Patton strapped to my side. I threatened to have the stupid aide hung naked at high noon if he ever told anybody about the actual situation in the dayroom."

"Don't you think that's a bit extreme?" Boyd asked.

"No, of course not. The aide assured me he never witnessed the killing, only telling Percy Radcliff he was going out for a smoke. He told me he'd probably be fired for leaving the patient alone for so long. I believed him—his not being there when Radcliff was killed. The future of his job and possible termination is up to you, sir."

"Alright, Eduardo. Thanks for the great job filling in for me. And yes, the aide will be seeking employment elsewhere. Now get back in bed and lay down. I'm going to give you two pills that will make you sleepy. You're over-hyped about the situation here. Stop reliving the important talk. We're all gratified."

"Sure thing. You're a medical genius Doctor Bounder. You know what's best for me," Eduardo sighed.

"I'm not a damn doctor. I have a nursing background, but I now run this hospital. You best never forget that, Munoz."

Bounder finished with the patient and walked past the dayroom on his way back to the office. Everything appeared to have returned to normal. Two patients were playing pool, and a third was working a Sudoku puzzle on the other side of the room. He remembered Howard Hill telling Baldy not to put the recreation area off-limits with yellow barrier tapes. No need to prolong memories of the unfortunate nightmare.

"I left a message from Mr. Hill," his secretary said as he came in and sat behind his desk. "I'm not sure what it meant. There's a fresh pot of coffee over there on the credenza."

"Thanks for the heads-up. I don't have to read the note. Howard must be on his way over, right?"

"Yes, and Molly Pritchard will be accompanying him."

Boyd changed his mind and opened the memo. He needed to confirm there wasn't a hidden agenda so he could better deal with the old, cantankerous first sergeant. He was pleased with the precise verbiage only Hill could spawn. The exact wording was . . . **Thanks for the smokescreen you created by coaching the crazy old geezer to articulate your release to the fawning media.**

Chapter 10

An hour later, Howard Hill and a beaming Molly Pritchard came marching through Boyd's office door. Molly perched on a chair. Hill remained standing in front of the administrator's desk—like a schoolteacher ready to reprimand a sassy student.

Boyd was uptight. Molly more relaxed. She was attired in a pink jogging outfit—Hill in tight jeans and cowboy boots. He seldom wore his grey, pin-striped suit while conducting business in the hospital.

Howard was the first to talk. "Tam Lozen called. He's flying in from Houston tomorrow morning. I'm happy to report he wasn't ranting and raving about our situation here. I had contacted him earlier about the dead patient. He'd already heard the radio news release about the police training exercise at Mission Oaks. The Houston media outlets keep posted on any news related to the TCCV activities across the state."

"That's fine and dandy," Molly said. "I guess they put my recommended news release in the proverbial shit can."

Howard ignored her. *Typical female reaction. She'll get over it.* "The four of us will be attending the county coroner's release of her preliminary findings on Percy Radcliff's death," Hill said.

"Will the police lieutenant also be there?" Boyd asked, now more relieved.

"Yes. He will brief us on the status of the investigation when the coroner concludes her assessment. She called me late last night congratulating our release to the media folks. She said it makes her job a lot easier not having to fend off the circling buzzards, though she is shielded by several layers of administrative types. She hasn't conferred with the lieutenant yet. He wanted to wait until everybody was present. It's a good idea. Everyone will be reading off the same sheet of music to eliminate confusion or misconceptions as we all prepare to take the next steps."

Molly retrieved the pot of coffee from the credenza, poured three cups, and then served the steaming brew. As if choreographed, the smiling secretary brought in a plate of glazed donuts and skirted back to her office. Everyone sat down, munched and sipped. Nobody talked. Boyd was ingesting Howard's remarks. Molly had already been briefed. She ignored Howard and grinned at Boyd as though nothing of any consequence happened the previous night at his residence.

"What are the next steps you referred to, Howard?" Boyd asked.

"Several courses of action as I see it," Howard responded. First, you will develop an in-service series of classes on overall hospital security practices, patient safety procedures and interactions with external individuals and agencies."

"Good idea," Molly added. "I'll include my group next door in the training."

Howard nodded in agreement. "The next undertaking will be predicated on what we learn tomorrow from both the coroner and the police lieutenant. Lastly, never let a hospital patient broadcast anything to outside living, breathing bodies. I repeat—any event that happens under our roof . . . stays under our roof. Is that clear Bounder? You dodged a gigantic bullet by employing that media-magnet goony, wheelchair-bound idiot to do your job."

Bounder remained silent, not wanting to take credit for the successful airing or the "no-no" of a hospital patient doing his dirty work.

Molly laughed. "Hey, that ingenious patient saved the day. We should award him a medal of some type."

"No thanks," Boyd said. "I already took him behind the woodshed and laid down the law. Howard, you need to contact the purchasing agent over at your old VA facility for me. He approved and requisitioned a new kind of motorized wheeled-vehicle for Eduardo Munoz. Request it be canceled as soon as possible."

"Whoa there, Boyd. What the hell are you talking about?"

Bounder shared his earlier discussion with Munoz.

"Consider it done," Howard said. "And now, folks, it's goodbye. I have to grace myself at another meeting in an hour."

"Anything we need to know about, Howard?" Molly asked with a concerned look. "I know the man you are meeting. You best be prepared for demanding questions that might arise."

"No, I got it covered . . . duty calls." He left the hospital, not about to tell them he was meeting Clarisa Rios in a lavish downtown hotel room—not at the busy Cantina Classica.

The secretary popped in and picked up the empty donut tray and coffee pot. "Mr. Bounder, the FedEx delivery person buzzed me at the side entrance. He has a big box for Hans Schmidt. Want me to sign for it and have someone bring the container up to him?"

"No. Call Drake in maintenance and have him secure the box. Tell him to lock it up in the storage room in the basement. Nobody is to inspect the contents or remove it unless I approve. Tell him to report to me when he completes the task."

"Will do." She gave him a quizzical look and left the office.

"What the hell was all that about, Boyd?" Molly asked. "Does that have anything to do with the hospital dayroom misfortune? Is there something I should know about?"

"No, it's a private matter involving another one of our TCCV patients. It's on my plate. Relax."

Boyd walked to his office window and looked out for several minutes. Hill was chatting with the FedEx driver. One of them apparently told a joke because both were laughing. Howard patted the young man on the shoulder, strolled to his automobile and sped off.

I guess their brief encounter didn't involve the delivery of Schmidt's mysterious box. Otherwise, he'd be standing in front of me cussing and issuing directives. I hate his damnable habit of micro-management. Still wearing the blasted uniform!

Molly used Boyd's office phone to call Marco Simone. She wanted him to confirm with admissions about the pending transfer of Eduardo Munoz to her doorstep. She didn't hear Boyd coming up behind her but felt a hot breath enveloping the back of her neck. She swung around and slapped him hard on his cheek. He retreated back toward the window but maintained his balance from her blow.

"Hey, that was nasty, Molly. Are you pissed about last night? Are you wounded that I didn't share anything with you about the FedEx delivery? Please tell me." He stopped massaging his cheek.

"I don't want to discuss last night, other than to say there won't be another night like it soon. It's obvious to me that I didn't appeal to you. Let's act like professional adults and concentrate on our efforts to make Mission Oaks the envy of the community."

Boyd stiffened—not sure she was serious. He'd like another go at her but using a different approach—one that worked in college with the adoring cheerleaders.

They were interrupted by the barking telephone. Boyd answered. It was from Marco.

"Hi, Boyd, is Molly still there?"

"Yes, of course. I'll put her on."

He gave the phone to Molly. She shook her head expressing displeasure with the conversation. Her face turned crimson.

"What's up?" he asked.

"Eduardo Munoz," she answered.

"Go on," Boyd said and sat down. She took a seat next to him before she spoke.

"I've seen and heard enough about that devious screwball. I'm going to talk to my father when he gets here tomorrow. Munoz is going to become history if I have any say in the matter. The goofball should be sent back to the VA where he belongs. Better yet, transfer him to a long-term care unit in faraway Houston."

"Humm, not a bad idea," Boyd smiled.

Molly continued. "Marco also advised me we have another admission on the way over from the Greyhound bus station. I'd like to be here when she arrives."

Boyd looked surprised. "A she-person?"

"Yes. I'm going to be the first one to greet her. I'm out of here. Goodbye."

Molly passed Drake on her way out. He knocked and came into Boyd's office. "I got it done, boss. Everything locked down and secured. Anyway, what's in Hans Schmidt's big box?"

Boyd shrugged his shoulders. "You never know about Schmidt. The man's upstairs for a reason, Drake. He's got some priceless personal effects according to his mother. She wants them near him, otherwise, he goes ballistics when anyone mentions Afghanistan."

"Yeah, probably some of those genetically altered poppy seed plants to harvest cocaine. Maybe he plans to go into business here."

"Get serious, Drake. We're running a hospital on these grounds, not some experimental organic nursery."

"I am boss—spent a tour of duty in that godforsaken place nobody wants but us and the Taliban pricks. I never got hooked on the stuff, but I witnessed too many buddies go off the deep end and ruin their lives."

"Schmidt is here for another reason. I don't have the liberty to share his medical diagnosis with you."

"No problem," Drake said. "Nice chatting with you—got to run off. The supervisor scheduled a month-ending inventory of consumable items in our department. They seem to disappear as fast as they're requisitioned. See you later."

Boyd liked the clean-shaven, soft-spoken man. The energetic maintenance man was a dependable and hard worker. His proficiency in electrical and mechanical matters was worth the above-standard salary for workers in those technical classifications. The man had overcome many obstacles in his personal life after military service and a subsequent divorce.

I'm curious why Drake always wore different colored leather moccasins instead of sturdy work shoes—maybe an OSHA violation. I'll let it ride. Different strokes for different folks. Probably watched a slew of cowboy and Indian flicks growing up.

His telephone rang interrupting his thoughts on Drake. It was Howard.

"Tam Lozen moved up his schedule at the last minute. He's arriving on United Flight 809 in two hours. I'm tied up at that downtown meeting I told you about. One of the 'do-gooders' in attendance is talking about making a big donation to Mission Oaks. I can't rightly leave that possibility sitting untouched on the table. Will you break loose and retrieve him?"

"Sure, I'll do that for you, Howard. Tam and I had some interesting discussions during the opening ceremonies held for the new Mission Oaks Treatment Center. He was gracious enough not to belittle me for my lack of military service. Hey, I know the importance of downtown meetings with our community supporters. We ask—they give . . . at least on most occasions."

Howard said nothing.

Boyd was confused. "We're not meeting with Baldy and the coroner until tomorrow morning? Why the big change of plans?"

"Tam wouldn't tell me why the meeting was moved up," Howard said. "Maybe he's going to shit-can all of us."

"Where is Tam staying?" Boyd asked.

"At the Haxton Hotel downtown. I reserved a big suite for our main man. I hope he appreciates it. Tell him hello for me, Boyd."

Chapter 11

The next morning, Clarisa Rios was cold and naked as she tip-toed into the bathroom. Her hair was tousled and unkempt. Howard was asleep on the ruffled king-sized bed. She looked forward to a hot shower before she woke him up. *He didn't tell me earlier why he had to run over to Mission Oaks when he gets dressed. There was a heap of fallout from a patient trying to commit suicide. At least I think that's what Howard had told me on the phone. Maybe I'm confused.*

Howard joined her in the steamy shower. "Thought you could sneak away from me, young lady? I was playing dead soldier, begging unconsciously for mercy." Globs of soap were dripping from her arms and legs. He nestled up to her, intense body heat pervading his entire body. The green iguana tattoo on her belly looked anxious and alert. There was no resistance from Clarisa. She wrapped her arms around his neck, kissed him and then nibbled on his lower lip.

"Stop, stop, Clarisa, you're going to draw blood. I'm getting big down there again. I told you about my important meeting coming up. This old soldier doesn't intend to wear a Purple Heart clip-out on my shirt pocket."

"You big baby. Your close friend and business associate never complained. You're growing mellow, Mr. Hill."

Hill moved backward. "I'd like to ask you a personal question. You don't have to answer. If Boyd Bounder was so magnificent, why'd you throw him under the bus?"

She gave him a wicked smirk. "Boydie dear had all the tools of the trade for the task at hand. Know what I mean?"

Howard glared at her.

She continued to answer his pointed question. "I didn't do such an awful thing to the sweet man. You got it all wrong, Howard. He tossed me in the trash can like yesterday's leftovers. Bounder was a good lover. Must've found a better lay. Do I sense a bit of resentfulness?"

"That's not the story he shared with me, Clarisa."

Clarisa was startled. "You mean he shared details about our most intimate moments?"

Howard grinned, saying nothing and watching her squirm.

She pushed him away. "Well for Christ's sake, it doesn't matter now, does it?"

He laughed, then got serious. "Sorry about that. What's done is done."

"I tend to agree with you there, Howard."

"Your spicy demeanor turns me on," he said coyly. "Let's hop back in the sack for an encore and forget about the past."

"Where's Howard?" Tam Lozen asked when Boyd greeted him at the airport baggage ramp. The small man was limping more than usual according to Molly's earlier description of his impairment. Boyd speculated he'd been drinking on the flight, though not picking up an alcohol whiff when they talked.

"He's attending an important meeting downtown," Boyd replied. "Thought you were coming in tomorrow."

Boyd was worried he might be walking on thin ice. If the sledgehammer was coming down, he thought it would be best for him to face the music, here and now, rather than letting the notion of being fired boil away in his bloodstream.

Tam picked up a small suitcase from the conveyor belt and stood next to him. "Molly called me yesterday and asked me to come here as soon as possible. I asked her why. She was sobbing—said she'd discuss matters when I arrived. Bounder, you've spent enough time with her to know what's going on. Don't hide anything from me."

"I wish I knew," Boyd said with a smirk. He was certain it had nothing to do with their unsuccessful foray last night in the bedroom. It had to be related to the dayroom misfortune.

"I'm sure Howard has the answer," Boyd reported. "I suggest you wait and talk to him. They have been working late hours together. She may have confided in him."

"It can wait. I heard from several sources of your tactical approach to the media situation surrounding young Percy Radcliff's death. It was handled well. The fellows at TCCV were delighted indeed. Are we going to walk into a buzz saw tomorrow when we meet with the police lieutenant and the coroner?"

Bounder looked quizzical. "Neither Howard nor I have received any feedback from them. Whatever they've found, be assured they're holding their findings close to their collective vests."

Tam nodded. "The other board directors heard through their intelligence network that the county coroner working the case is old and incompetent. I don't know why they were overly concerned. You have any insight on that matter?"

"Not really. I've worked in the behavioral health field for years. Mental health hospitals are seldom faced with patient deaths on site, let alone homicides. She is retiring in six months. On the plus side, Howard knows the police lieutenant in charge and has great confidence in his abilities. They've worked together in the past. I was impressed with the cop's approach to the awful situation in our dayroom."

[86]

"Got it, we'll find out soon enough. Take me directly to Mission Oaks. I'll check into the hotel later. I need to see Molly right away."

The traffic on state highway 281 was building up due to a stalled vehicle on the right shoulder near Hildebrand. "Fucking rubberneckers," Tam shouted. "You'd think we had a head-on collision with strewn bloody bodies littering the highway. What's wrong with your people?"

"We're almost there," Boyd said, ignoring Tam's reference to San Antonians. "Should I call Molly on my cell to let her know we're ten minutes out?"

"No need, just get there." He seemed impatient which bothered Bounder.

Marco Simone saw them pull up from his office window and chugged out to meet them. Boyd maneuvered to park, but Tam hopped out before the car came to a complete halt.

"Hey, Marco, my main man, it's great to see you again," Tam shouted. "How's the bum foot?" He was responsible for hiring the veteran and putting him with his daughter in San Antonio. Marco was a true hero in Tam's eyes. He'd stepped on an enemy mine while serving to protect his country.

"Which one? The one I was born with or the toy one?" Marco said with a straight face.

"Well both, of course. Do you have this place shaped-up yet?"

"Sir, I work for your daughter. She runs a tight ship, won't accept anything less."

"Glad to hear that. Where is she now?"

"In the lounge upstairs. Shall I get her for you?"

"No, I'm sure you have more important things to do than escort me around. I know the location. Talk with you later."

Tam surprised her in the lounge, seated by the window flipping pages in a journal. "It must be nice to relax reading a magazine on company time, young lady."

She tossed the publication on the floor and ran to greet him. There were signs she had been crying earlier.

"Thanks for coming sooner than scheduled, father. I know you are a busy man."

"What's on your mind, Molly?" He cut right to the chase. She led him to the sofa by the bookcase.

"Jase called me this morning."

"Jase—Jase Lozen?" He cut her off.

"Yes, your son . . . my brother. Let me talk, dad. It's important."

"Sorry about that, Molly. You stunned me. Jase has been out of touch with everybody for so long I can't recount. Please go on."

"Jase heard about Percy Radcliff's death—thinks he was murdered. I don't know how he came to this conclusion. Jase told me he had talked to Percy a few days ago. He warned me to be careful and watch my back. I asked him why. He didn't elaborate."

"Huh?" Tam expressed disbelief.

"Jase said anyone close to him would die an unnatural death."

"You mean close to Jase or Percy?" Tam demanded clarification.

"Both," Molly answered. "And his warning was directed to each of us."

"Jase must be smoking some exotic weed wherever he's digging these days."

"He's moved on from that," Molly argued. "He said he's taking up more important issues impacting the greater good of mankind—whatever that means." She threw up her arms in disgust.

"Maybe he's found a way to eliminate hell on earth," Tam pitched in. "Perhaps newborn babies from this date forward are hereby declared free of future disease and injury. I have no clue about what's going on in that boy's disturbed mind."

"Whatever it is, I think it involved Percy Radcliff in some way," she said. "He asked me if poor Percy was wearing a blue and red feather in his long hair. I'm not sure why these colors have any significance. They may have started a new political faction dealing with global diversity issues. Maybe Jase discovered some hullabaloo about his or your Indian ancestry in several of his archaeological sites. Perhaps he found some adversity in his excavations about my ethnicity, whatever it is."

Tam looked distressed. "I'm not sure what the colored feathers represent. I have a vague idea but must research our family historical collections that go back several centuries."

For some reason, Molly wasn't sure she believed him. He appeared distant and unsure of himself.

"On the other matter," Tam continued. "I'm sorry that I never shared with you the facts and circumstances regarding your cultural and biological origins. Some day when you're back in Houston we'll visit my safety deposit box. I'll unlock the past and lay it out in the open for you."

"That complicated?" She had no idea what strange items he had stashed away in a locked box.

Tam nodded a yes.

"One last comment regarding Jase's phone call, dad. He wouldn't continue the conversation or answer my more pressing questions. He told me to be careful and asked me to alert you. Then he hung up on me."

"Where was he calling from?"

"I don't know, dad. We had a bad connection."

"Thank you, Molly, for insisting I come to San Antonio right away. The news about Jase is unsettling. Several complicated scenarios are bouncing around in my thick skull." He pondered whether Jase was getting ahead of himself. Their strategy was far from coming to fruition. *No need to bring her into our scheme at this time. It's best for her to be confused.*

"My thoughts also," she said with a deep groan. "I hope we can get to the bottom of this mess."

"First things first," Tam said. "We'll put family matters on the back burner for the time being. The big meeting tomorrow should give us some pointers where we're headed. Different strategies need to be addressed based on Percy's death, be it a murder or accident."

"If you think that's best, dad. Guess I overreacted. Would you like to go to the Cantina Classica for something to eat? It's my favorite Tex-Mex go-to when I'm hungry."

"Yes, but I was hoping to catch up with Howard first. When do you think he'll be back from his crucial meeting?"

"Talk to Boyd. He knows Howard's schedule."

"Speaking of Bounder . . . how are you two getting along?"

"In what way?"

"You know what I mean," he laughed.

"No, I don't." *How would he know what's going on around here? Maybe Boyd talked about it on the drive over.*

Marco poked his head through the doorway, interrupting the banter between father and daughter. "You guys hungry yet?"

"I am," Tam said. "Let's go down the street to the famous cantina. If I recall, Molly never likes to eat a full meal. She can nibble on chips and spicy salsa dip if she doesn't bail out on us. I enjoyed bantering with that woman owner when I was here during opening ceremonies. What's her name? Oh, I remember now. It's Clarisa something or other. Call Bounder and see if he wants to join us. See if Hill is back from that pressing confab in the city. I'd like to know what the hell that was about. Marco, you must join us."

"Yes, sir." Marco saluted and carried out his order. He stepped in the hallway and made the calls. Neither man answered their cells. He strolled back in to see Molly at the office window staring outside in horror.

She was shocked to see Hill and Bounder arguing in the parking lot. It appeared to her Hill threw a round-house punch at Bounder and just missed his jaw. "Good Lord, she yelled out. "These two jokers are either working on their dancing footwork or fighting with each other near the garbage bin. What in the world is going on down there?"

Tam and Marco slid over to the window and joined her. They both began to howl when they witnessed the skirmish of two old, seriously out-of-shape grown men.

Hill bent at the knee and hooked his left leg around Bounder's right ankle and flipped him on his back, huffing and puffing like a steam engine. Bounder was unable to right himself quick enough because of arthritic knees. He crawled over to the hospital wall and shimmied upward with his back against the concrete.

Hill began to laugh, then waved Bounder back for more punishment.

Bounder wasn't done yet. As Hill approached for the kill, Bounder squatted, moaned, and then shot up with the crown of his head smashing Hill's protruding jaw. The surprised Hill backed off, vigorously massaging his painful chin. He spits a few times as if disgorging a broken tooth. Nothing flew out, other than some globules of red mucus.

They disengaged and stepped back at least five feet from each other. The combatants glared at their adversary while summoning up volumes of air from exhausted lungs. Neither man spoke—just scowled.

"I wish those comedic buffoons put as much effort into the operation of this new enterprise," Tam said, tongue in cheek. "TCCV board members would be appalled if I filmed the foray and shared with them the inglorious highlight of my visit to San Antonio."

"Boys will be boys," Marco laughed. "It'll end soon."

Chapter 12

The tussle between the two big men did not end. The mano-a-mano contest across the plaza was now viewed by several patients hanging on the fence up on the hospital swimming pool deck. Cheers rang out . . . for no one in particular. Some patients peering out their room windows thought it was a scheduled recreational program for their entertainment. They enjoyed the program.

The outside ruckus continued after a brief pause. Bounder tackled Hill and fell on him to the ground. Hill reached down and put a bear hug on his opponent. Bounder kicked free, got to his feet. Hill stood up in time to anticipate another Bounder punch and then laughed.

Bounder pulled his fist back, stopped and then chuckled. They were winded, staring at each other and physically unable to continue their scuffle. Forty years ago, it would have been a blood bath—probably to a draw.

"I hope you're satisfied Bounder," Howard said. "Now that you've exhausted your inventory of football gridiron bad boy techniques. Sit back down and let's talk. We're too fucking old to be carrying on like two jealous schoolboys sniffing after the same skirt."

Bounder shook Hill's hand in agreement and said, "I don't know why Clarisa felt like she had to call me and discuss your romantic misadventure at the hotel. She—"

Hill interrupted. "Wait one damn second, please. I have a question. Did she call you—report back to big daddy? I just dropped the lady off at her restaurant."

Bounder didn't answer but laughed. "Now I get it. You haven't had a hot, finagling female in the sack for a long time, old man. Can't get it up anymore? You forget about the downbeat ramifications that a good fuck entails. She wants something . . . something desperately—and you pulled your zipper down for it."

"Clarisa is a sweet, loving person," Hill objected. "She's kept the local food bank supplied with Mexican food items for ages. She volunteers at the homeless shelter, sponsors a food truck and donates all the proceeds. What are you getting at, Bounder?"

"Pure and simple, and you fell for it, soldier. She is maneuvering for that juicy contract to operate our food service program at Mission Oaks. The request for proposal is going out next week. You signed off on it—must've alerted her to watch for the announcement. Need I say more?"

Hill was stunned. "I can't believe it. I don't remember ever discussing classified information with her, or anyone else. You'd better cough up something much more specific. What made you come up with this ludicrous conclusion?"

"Why do you think I dumped the woman, Howard I. M. Hill?"

Howard shook his head, bruised face turning a bright red—couldn't figure it out.

"Allow me to offer a few words of advice," Boyd said with a stern face. "Drop her like a hot potato. She's a walking troublemaker. We don't want this female Godiva to get in the way of our relationship. Objectivity outweighs emotion when it comes to contracting. More importantly, the future success of our Mission Oaks enterprise is at stake."

[94]

Howard gave him a bear hug, spun him around and said, "Partner, I've got to hand it to you. You saved my fat behind. Let's head over to Teddy's Tavern and I'll buy."

The patients above cheered, then resumed their rehab in the pool. Molly watched them walk over to Bounder's car and take off. She turned to Tam. "Still want to go eat. Those two clowns are off to no good. Let's not get in the way of their reconciliation."

Marco couldn't stop laughing. "I had my money on Hill. We army guys stay united. Just happy nobody got hurt."

Tam agreed. "True enough. We'll likely hear more tomorrow from these two pranksters about male bonding. I'll closet them in a tight corner before we go to the hearing. I'll get a piece of both their fat asses, believe me. We can't have senior hospital executives waging physical conflict in this environment. By no means is it conducive to the healing profession. I hope nobody around here filmed the damn thing."

Clarisa greeted them at the front door of the restaurant, then disappeared. Molly changed her mind and decided to join them. She wanted to spend more time with her father. "I wonder why she took off so soon," Molly commented. "She normally yaks on about the specials of the day and then finds a quiet and comfortable table for us to do our thing."

"Not a problem with me," Marco said. "Time to eat, talk comes later."

The Cantina Classica was packed and loud. A hostess appeared and told them they had a fifteen-minute wait for a booth. They declined and then were offered three vacant stools facing the open kitchen as an alternative. They accepted.

Molly always liked to watch the activity taking place behind the main counter. Plates of all varieties were hustled back and forth by the uniformed service staff. Beef enchilada choices took the lead two-to-one over soft and crispy tacos. It was here that Molly experienced the many different Mexican food selections that looked yummy enough to eat. But her father was correct. She'd never finish any of the plates she'd ordered in the past. But, today she wasn't hungry . . . still cogitating on the bruhaha back in the hospital parking lot between two men she highly respected.

Tam surveyed the busy operation looking for Clarisa. Tex-Mex food was at the bottom of his food chain. He then turned to Molly and said, "Has that crackpot Eduardo Munoz been transferred over to you yet? I'm anxious to hear how he's adjusting to the 'more relaxed' atmosphere of extended care living. The man has a record of disrupting every place he's been offered to live and receive needed care. He's flown too high over the cuckoo's nest as far as I'm concerned."

Molly looked over to Marco for the answer. She wanted that man gone. She thought Marco could engineer an acceptable solution.

Marco had dealt with her father on a different plateau than her. Guy to guy, more factual, less emotional. "Sir, he's getting settled in as we talk. I saw him through the rear car window when we drove off. He was motoring his contraption over to our building. We're putting him next to our new female occupant."

Tam thought for a moment and said, "Refresh my memory. Who's the woman?"

"Sallie Sake," Molly said. "She'd been in a long-term physical rehab unit in Houston. You should remember her, father.

I'm told your vote was the deciding factor in approving her application submitted to the TCCV board of directors."

"Ah, yes. How could I forget? She appeared in person—the most beautiful Japanese-American woman I've ever seen. The working group wanted her transferred to Bounder's psychiatric hospital. They insisted she wasn't completely over the recovery hump of her depression."

"If I might be so bold," Marco jumped in. "What are you talking about?"

Tam seemed confused. "Bear with me, I'll go into more detail in a few minutes."

"Consider it done," Marco said but restated his question anyway. "I'd like you to explain your thinking on approving her application."

Tam wondered why he was so persistent. *Maybe he doesn't want female residents. I'm not so sure I would either.* "Sallie had served honorably on a US Coast Guard cutter several years ago. Her ship was patrolling a sizable quadrant of the Bering Strait for possible interdiction with a pirate Russian ship posing as a friendly fishing vessel."

"Wait, hold on a second, sir. Excuse my ignorance, but where is the Bering Strait?"

Molly jumped in. "It's a body of water in the Pacific that separates Russia and Alaska. I believe it's a little south of the Arctic Circle."

"That is correct," Tam said as he looked up at the waitress balancing a large tray of food. He had asked for a bowl of chicken tortilla soup. Molly ordered one beef taco. Marco asked for three cheese enchiladas. She served them quickly and then maneuvered to a table behind them.

They paused their discussion of the new patient and nibbled at their meal selections, seemingly not as hungry as when they were first seated.

"What happened to her on this mission," Marco asked, as he forked a large portion of his spicy enchilada and shoved it into his mouth. A long string of cheese dangled from his lower lip, struggling to reach his chin.

"Let me tell you what transpired," Tam said coldly and newly enraged. "She damn near lost her life. That's what happened." His eyes began to water. "The cutter fired several .50 caliber warning shots over the fishing vessel's bow to stop the escaping trawler. The shots were ignored."

"Stupidity on the high seas," Marco said. He was already half-finished with his plate. The other two hadn't touched their food.

Tam went on. "The cutter caught up with them. Sallie led a team of five Coasties to board the armed fishing boat. Nobody was visible on deck. As they sidled unhindered to mid-ship, three of her men were cut down by automatic weapons."

"Was she hit?" Molly asked, alarmed by the sequence of an impending ambush she had once experienced in combat.

"No, and that's part of the problem, "Tam continued. "Sallie and the remaining Coastie exchanged fire. They killed two pirates emerging from concealment and wounded two more who were scrambling for cover. Her partner was bleeding from his arm—she was unscathed."

"So, Tam, what's the problem you're alluding to?" Marco asked. He wiped the strip of cheese from his chin and then scarfed down the last couple of tortilla chips from a bowl on the counter.

"The hidden pirates surrendered and tossed out their weapons. They begged for mercy. Her partner approached them and handcuffed the first man. As he tried to cuff the second one, he failed to see the hidden stiletto soar to his neck, slashing his throat. Sallie shot the pirate between his eyes. Her Coastie partner slid to the ground and bled out."

"Oh, shit," Marco cried. "I know what happened next."

"Yes," Tam said. "Sallie shot the other pleading and handcuffed asshole five times in his face. She searched the rest of the vessel and found two young naked girls hiding in the galley. Sallie presumed they were whores to service the pirate crew. She blasted both girls multiple times in the middle of their bare chests—then sauntered over to the fallen bodies to empty her rifle in their guts. She didn't feel the large arms from behind clasping her shoulders in a tight grip. It was the captain of the cutter."

"Wow, a hell of a story," Marco said. "I have a question. How did the Coast Guard cutter know the fishing boat was Russian?"

"Prior intelligence reports," Tam said as he finished the last three spoonfuls of soup. "The Coastie brainpower had been alerted by other friendly fishing vessels operating in proximity of the buccaneer ship for several days. They became suspect. It turned out they were transferring illegal contraband to smaller, motorized crafts not displaying flags of their origin countries."

Molly had heard enough about the woman's heroics. She hadn't touched her taco—never intended to. She wanted to know more about Sallie's medical condition and how she had hooked up with TCCV. Molly was forced to wait. Clarisa sauntered up to the table with complimentary margaritas.

"Sorry to have neglected my friends from the sanatorium down the street. We had a major issue come up in the kitchen which I had to defuse. I'm getting tired of all the ridiculous shenanigans that take place around here. You'd think we were a culinary school cranking out white-tasseled glorified chefs, for Christ's sake." She threw her arms up in disgust.

"That bad?" Marco commented. He stared at the green iguana dancing on her exposed midriff, the big eye winking at him.

"Yes, I need a stud like you to supervise this place." Clarisa touched his shoulder, then squeezed his right biceps. She had eyed him earlier and liked what she saw. "Discipline and ingrained responsibility are long-lost personal traits. Maybe I need to retire, go off to a sandy Caribbean beach. I'll find me a rich man to coexist with." She stared Marco down. "Perchance, are you available?"

Marco sat up taller on his stool. "Too late, ma'am, but I'll keep you in mind if my situation goes south. Uh, or, wait until my kids get out of college. I'll have some free time on my hands."

"Sorry about that, young man," Clarisa said. The hostess came over and beckoned her away from the counter. "I hope to see you all again before you leave my palace of fine foods. Ta Tah."

"What an interesting character," Tam said. "I'm glad our luncheon neighbors behind us finished eating and left the cantina shortly after they seated us."

Marco snickered, then said, "I agree, now close the Sallie Sake loop for us, Mr. Tam. Molly asked a pertinent question about the woman before we were interrupted by that tall screwball proprietor."

Tam hesitated, then nodded. "Yes, Molly asked about her medical condition and why she was referred to TCCV. I'll be brief. She tried to commit suicide twice in one month. She couldn't overcome her remorse about leading her boarding crew into an ambush that wiped out all the male members. Killing two innocent young females increased the severity of her guilt. You might not be aware but suicide in Japanese culture had been considered an acceptable way of restoring one's self-esteem."

"Like falling on the proverbial sword?" Marco cut in.

"I wouldn't go that far, Marco. This regrettable behavior had its onset at their home station after docking from the episode in the Bering Straits. The provisional diagnosis was suicidal ideation. This judgment caused Sallie to be medically discharged from the Coast Guard."

"Fine, dad, that answers Marco's first question." Molly was getting fidgety. "Under what circumstances prompted the referral to TCCV?"

"Her father was a Medal of Honor recipient from an earlier wartime conflict," Tam said proudly. "He and his family settled in the Houston area where Sallie grew up, went to college and then joined the US Coast Guard. Mr. Sake became a millionaire by developing a small software company into an international powerhouse. When bought out by an internet conglomerate in Silicon Valley, he donated half of the proceeds to TCCV. Need I say more?"

"No, I think Marco and I can fill in the rest of the blanks. It's time we head back to Mission Oaks. I want to meet this young lady before Eduardo Munoz develops a relationship with her."

[101]

"Oh, no, Clarisa is heading back over here," Marco sighed as he was getting his credit card out to pay the bill. "We didn't organize our retreat soon enough."

Clarisa caught up with them and said, "Thanks much for coming here for lunch. Sorry, you folks didn't touch the margaritas. I understand no drinking on duty. I know there are many restaurant options in this fine city. Let me comp your meal. No, don't jump up and down and argue with me. She looked at Marco and blinked her eyes. Have a great rest of the day, people."

Tam nodded and Molly shook her hand. Marco seemed to express approval. He retrieved his credit card from the checkout counter and shoved it back into his wallet. He moved away from them and checked out a tray of food a male waiter was serving a table near the front of the restaurant. He was impressed with what he'd observed. Marco made a mental note to ask for the teeming green enchiladas, white rice, and refried beans next time he frequented Cantina Classica.

Clarisa had one last thing to communicate, wondering if it was appropriate under the present circumstances. She sensed an atmosphere of uneasiness with her guests. Clarisa took Molly aside, pulled her closer and looked squarely in her face and asked, "By the way, have they found that slimy bastard who killed your patient the other day?"

Chapter 13

Later that afternoon, Bounder and Hill had retreated to Teddy's Tavern after their bravado in the hospital parking lot. They had talked out all their issues on the drive over. They had no intention of revisiting the "blow by blow" salvos thrown at each other. As far as they were concerned, the short-lived match ended in a tie.

Alamo Plaza was extra busy hosting the Daughters of the Texas Republic. A Mariachi band was playing music in the rotunda pavilion in the plaza. Even the popular horse-driven carriages were forced to take alternate routes. It was busy and loud inside the popular drinking hole. Willy Nelson was blasting out a tune in his pronounced nasal delivery. Wayland Jennings was in the on-deck circle.

"What are you drinking today, Howard?"

"My usual iced tea," he said. "And you?"

"Same old, same old," Boyd chuckled. "What are your thoughts about tomorrow's meeting with the coroner? I hope they have the toxicology results in by now. I have this eerie feeling Percy Radcliff suffered a painful death."

"How did you come to that conclusion?" Hill looked confused.

"I was with him soon after he was found on the dayroom floor. I did everything possible to revive him. His skin color had a strange hue—one I wasn't the slight bit familiar with . . . and I've been witness to many deaths."

"My money is on that ball-peen hammer crushing his skull," Howard said with conviction. "I've been a bystander in a host of military bar brawls over the years. I've seen claw hammers buried in the top of some men's skulls. Not a pretty sight."

"I get it," Boyd laughed. "The guessing game should be resolved tomorrow. Do you think Tam Lozen was pissed that you didn't pick him up at the airport?"

"Probably, but the little man never demonstrated flexibility in the past, at least from the skinny I've heard bantered around. I'm not concerned—getting too old to be bothered by what one would consider 'established protocol' in business circles."

"Suit yourself, big guy. You're cut from a different cloth than these martini-drinking hotshots around these parts."

Happy hour was beginning at Teddy's. Tourists and locals alike streamed in for the cheaper libations. The proprietor was generous, providing enough snacks to constitute one's evening main meal. Tortilla chips, salsa and pretzel sticks took center stage. Neither man took advantage, allowing the other tipsters to indulge until the bowls were empty. Willie and Wayland got tired out, and the local favorite George Strait took over.

They overheard an argument getting louder in the back of the saloon. A thin man dressed in surgical greens was shaking his head and denying everything a fat lady was verbally throwing at him.

"No way was the guy murdered," he said. "I don't know where you got your information, lady, but you need to be made aware of the facts."

"Bullshit," she shouted at him. "My husband was there. He witnessed the terrible act. One of the crazy patients pulled a pistol from his bathrobe and shot the poor man in the head. Of course my dumb husband tried playing hero but was brutally shoved aside by the killer on his way out. Thank God he's still alive."

[104]

"Let's get out of here," Hill said. "The real news will be plastered on the street soon enough. That is, if these nitwits were talking about our situation at Mission Oaks."

"Did you recognize the guy in greens?" Hill asked as they stepped outside. "Was he one of yours?"

"No, Howard. Let it be known that none of our employees wear greens."

"Ah, if you say so. But one of the days I officed in your conference room, I saw that patient next to Eduardo Munoz's room decked out in greens."

"You're probably talking about Hans Schmidt. He wasn't a medic in the military. Probably caught sight of his camouflaged green pajamas. He's an odd case. I'm keeping my eyes on him."

"Why is that?" Howard rubbed his sore chin and surveyed the inside of his mouth with his tongue, checking for a missing tooth. There was none.

Boyd didn't want to alarm Hill about Schmidt's footlocker contents stored in the basement. Drake had met Bounder in the hallway several days after the footlocker had been stored. He re-assured the administrator there was nothing to fret about. Bounder had always been leery about anything stored in military-issued boxes or containers.

"Howard, I just have a gut feeling that Schmidt and Eduardo could pair-up and become big-time buddies. Eduardo is plain out crazy, not telling how he's going to influence the younger Schmidt."

"Why? What's Schmidt's problem?"

"Paranoia, distrust, suspicion or whatever else you want to label it. TCCV thought our structured system of patient care would provide the means for recovery."

"Hey, fine with me," Howard said. "I thought Eduardo was moving over to Molly's unit?"

"Yes, the transfer was made today."

"Glad to hear that." Howard didn't have a dog in the race—made no difference to him.

"However," Boyd said. "Keep in mind Eduardo never met a stranger in his entire life. Schmidt possesses the kind of personality that Eduardo will take advantage of. Probably make him a corporal in Napoleon's army. Munoz already holds the rank of brigadier."

"I know Munoz is not your management problem anymore," Howard said. "For your information, we were able to deny him his new motorized, super-duper wheelchair. The VA backed off."

"Molly will appreciate that," Boyd said with a sigh of relief. "The man does good enough with the electric unit he has been running with in the past. I can't even come to grips what might happen if Munoz hit the busy streets of San Antonio."

They left Teddy's without finishing their drinks.

Howard grinned as they stopped walking at the corner of Houston Street waiting to cross. A hop-on, hop-off bus of cheering tourists passed in front of them. Someone on the top tier was singing "The eyes of Texas are upon you" in a deep baritone voice.

"Oh, if we could be so enthused," Boyd commented. "Where are you going for dinner?"

"Home. Take a shit, shower, eat, and then watch Tom Selleck in *Blue Bloods*, then hit the sack. I want to be super alert for tomorrow. I have this feeling we're going to be blind-sided by both the coroner and my friend, Baldy. We best be as sharp as a tack. Tam Lozen will be measuring us with one of those wicked liability measurement gauges he carries with him at all times. Remember, his ass is hanging in a sling next to us. We'd better hope for the best. See you tomorrow, bright and early."

"Make sure you put some ice on that thick chin of yours, Howard Hill. We don't need to field any inquiries tomorrow if perchance someone spotted our over-charged testosterone cells on display."

Chapter 14

Early in the morning of the following day, Tam Lozen called Howard from the Haxton Hotel. "Get Boyd Bounder and bring him here right away. I need to talk with both of you gentlemen."

"Good God, Tam, it's six o'clock. What's going on?"

"Just get here, Hill," he said briskly and terminated the call.

An hour later, all three men were sitting in a conference room off the main lobby. There was limited activity in the area.

"I am utterly dismayed about your little quarrel in the hospital courtyard yesterday," Tam said. "What in Satan's name was that all about? Stop, don't even answer me. I am putting you two ruffians on notice. One more display of childish behavior on either of your parts will result in immediate termination of your duties. Is that clear?"

Neither man spoke, just looked at each other.

"Well?" Tam said. "I'm waiting for an answer."

Hill went first. "I want you to know Boyd and I have put that little scuffle behind us. We understand it wasn't a professional thing to do. Shit happens. That's all I can say."

"Yes, Tam, I agree with Howard's comments," Boyd said with conviction. "Believe it or not, we're good friends and work well together getting the hospital complex squared away for TCCV."

"Alright, you're excused. I'll see you at the inquest."

Later in the morning, all parties were upset that the preliminary meeting with the coroner and police lieutenant was canceled. The authorities admitted they weren't prepared with enough conclusive evidence to hold a meaningful conference. The toxicology findings weren't in yet. The detective investigating the murder was recovering from an emergency appendectomy.

Tam Lozen took advantage of the five-day delay to shoot down to Harlingen to discuss the possibility of opening a TCCV outpatient clinic. The community leaders in the Rio Grande Valley had petitioned TCCV with what they felt was enough justification to put it on their agenda. Tam was concerned about the number of illegals crossing the border and seeking medical care wherever and whenever they could find a willing source to take them in. He thought about the consequences of such a glaring potential injustice. *I feel strongly that both political parties aren't doing enough to protect our own indigenous population living down there.*

It would be difficult for him to justify TCCV providing health care services to foreigners sneaking across the Rio Grande. In his mind, everybody knows they would carry a whole host of communicable diseases with them into our country. Former military members for which TCCV was organized to help would be squeezed back in favor of "aspiring new US citizens." *We need to build a big wall and keep those law-breaking indigents out of our country."*

Molly and Marco were preparing for three more admissions to their unit. Occupancy goals were taking shape. Her full staff complement was already trained and in place. Marco was lauded for developing the orientation package for new employees. TCCV officials were using his training protocol as the boilerplate for all their business activities.

Boyd Bounder had agreed to admit several mental health patients from three separate health maintenance organizations in

South Texas. His staff convinced him that they needed more "patient diversity" on the wards. Military patients tended to form cliques. Army hung with Army—Marines hung with Marines, sometimes allowing Navy to join in—Air Force to Air Force, and of course . . . the SEALs were a breed apart. Reimbursement rates for the new patients and their different levels of care became an issue.

Less than twenty-percent of the Mission Oaks staff had experienced the mandates of military service. They were concerned that the hospital was beginning to experience some of the nuances often associated with the VA inpatient system.

Howard agreed in principle but was hesitant at first to open up the ranks to the unknown. Tam Lozen was consulted. He dropped the final say-so in Howard Hill's lap. Hill sought opinions from Molly and Marco. Marco was not happy with the reimbursement rates when comparing them to like facilities. Molly felt they shouldn't stonewall the proposal as rates were not buried in concrete. They could always be manipulated by the diligent bean counters.

Medical inflation runs rampant and hospital controllers have to constantly readjust fixed and operating budgets. They finally supported the idea for Bounder's psych hospital bringing in non-military but not for their long-term care unit. Hill finally gave the "green light" after the input from his trusted associates.

Chapter 15
Meanwhile in South Texas

They were lined up in rows of five, seated cross-legged on the damp ground listening intently to their leader. The younger attendees were arranged in a separate group off to the side of the main assemblage. All participants, young and old were adorned in blue and red colors—feathers for the adults, face paint for the male adolescents. The young female members wore long, blue buffalo-hide jeans.

The abandoned ranch twenty-two miles north of the Mexican border served as an ideal headquarters location for the new-age warriors. The two-lane road leading into the ranch was nothing more than a dead-ended pathway with overgrown weeds providing heightened security to the property.

A makeshift wooden control tower hovered above and next to a retractable gate barrier. The passageway was manned around the clock by two gun-toting braves. An armed dune buggy continuously circled the camp perimeter. They encountered all types of darting wildlife but no human intruders—too barren, too dangerous for most folks.

Their move from neighboring Louisiana was tedious but successful. The 125-acre spread allowed ample grazing fields for their milk cows. The airplane-sized old hanger was ideal to store the two school buses and six older camouflaged-painted Humvees.

Their guide was often referred to as Chieftain. No first or last name. He was astute in selecting the site implementing the age-old Indian tradition of "Squatter's Rights." The entire area was considered "spooked" by area indigents who avoided the property entirely. It was believed that one of the two bodies of water on the property devoured several young children floating on a truck innertube.

The site was far from the air corridor of commercial air traffic. The main homesite had been reduced to rubles by looters and illegals crossing the border into the United States. A water well near the remaining foundation was found operable after undergoing some minor repairs. The new occupants were temporarily housed in tents and assorted, makeshift wooden huts. No permanent dormitories were planned. The nearest farm or ranch site was thirty-five miles west. The distant, paved road was fifteen miles north with a hook-up to IH-35. From there it was a long four-hour drive north to the outskirts of San Antonio.

Some of the members complained about sleeping in tents and being fed K-rations, most dating back to WW II. The hot food truck scheduled in advance of the day's meal plan was often delayed. They hadn't been conditioned to the more spartan existence. It didn't matter. They were on the threshold of living out their dreams.

Strict security measures had to be enforced, including the use of alternate routes of egress to avoid surveillance. Strait-laced conservative Texas ranchers live by a creed not easily swayed toward neo-colonialism movements. The Humvee ambulance used in the recent hospital death mission had been ditched fifty miles east of their location. The Chieftain believed no person would ever find it submerged in a spring-fed pond that had served their ancestors for many hundreds of years. The stolen license plates had been removed and buried several miles distant from the pond.

The assemblage Chieftain stood up and hushed the crowd. They were excited, yet apprehensive. "Our exalted leader bids all you warriors a warm greeting. He apologizes for not being here with you today. He was asked by the Bureau of Indian Affairs to undertake a secret mission in Mexico. The request was made by the Mexican government and authorized by our own US State Department. We're proud of his international connections and reputation. His professional status serves us beyond all means in our continued war of remembrance."

Cheers erupted from the gathered crowd. "We will overcome, we will overcome. No human population will deny us our rights, borne and sanctified in the blood of our ancestors. It is ours . . . it is ours alone."

One of the younger, more vocal and exuberant Indian in front questioned why the blue and red colors represented their laborious undertaking. Chieftain frowned. "Your father was negligent, young man. He should've schooled you warriors properly before he ran off to San Antonio. At least that's the latest report I have on the deserter's whereabouts. I'll admit though, he was a fine mechanic—kept our vehicles running and our electronics humming. I'll answer your important question because he's no longer with us. All you other youngsters take heed in what I'm about to tell you."

The entire congregation stood, then became energized and shouted out, "We will overcome. It is ours. It is ours alone." Chieftain used his hands and arms to silence the crowd and signal them to resume their squatting positions. He paused for a few moments to collect his thoughts and gain their full attention. Then he began in a loud voice to ensure all parties heard him.

"Our colors support one of the most important goals in our history. The blue color signifies sadness—sadness for the many inequities forced upon us by the white people. The red color embodies our present ambitions, war—war to take back what is legally ours. We shall never forget the famous words from out great Lakota warrior Chief Crazy Horse . . . "The Red Nation shall rise again, and it shall be a blessing for a sick world—a world filled with broken promises, selfishness and separations—a dark world longing for light again."

A rumbling noise was heard off in the north. Two vans appeared as tiny black specks far off in the open and flat horizon. They were heading toward the assemblage. Small swirls of mist churning behind the slow-moving vehicles weren't visible to the crowd. A prolonged early morning rain barged in to help lessen the long drought experienced in the south of Texas.

The food trucks finally arrived. Cheers erupted from the group. The youngsters scrambled to their feet and ran toward the vehicles. A loud referee's whistle halted them in their tracks. They walked back to their designated locations.

Chieftain then proclaimed the session was over. He still had to announce more updated information, but he gave way to the hungry and tired members. Another group of vehicles coming from Mexico was scheduled to arrive together with the food trucks. It was hauling more temporary building materials.

It didn't happen. Chieftain presumed the cluster was held up at the border crossing. Nothing new. Though he hoped to see the small convoy arrive soon, preferably before dark. In a matter of days, their entire community would be celebrating the unification of their clan. The long wait would pay big dividends for the dedicated group. Chieftain still didn't know when the clan's lionized leader would return from his mission in Mexico.

Tonight, he would inform the members of their movement's first major accomplishment. The murder in a San Antonio mental health hospital on their hallowed grounds would impact positively on their wilting morale—a cause for celebration.

Chapter 16
June 2017

Six days after the law enforcement inquiry in San Antonio was delayed, Tam Lozen returned from his visit to the Rio Grande Valley. He had mixed feelings. Local officials had provisionally pledged the funds to build a new TCCV clinic in McAllen. His organization vouched to provide additional monies for the complete finish-out including furniture and equipment. Howard Hill was programmed to provide technical guidance. Marco Simone was slated to conduct the training for the new staff using his newly designed teaching module.

Tam was assured illegal immigrants would be banned from receiving any level of health care services. He still had his doubts some would slip through but relented to the urgent pleas of valley leadership. The projected goal for the clinic to be built and operational was eighteen months after all funds were released for construction.

Hill was busy reviewing his notes for the ten o'clock meeting with the authorities working the Percy Radcliff murder. He was prepared for a question-answer format and had covered every potential detail of the investigation that might surface in the dialogue. It was time to reach out to Boyd Bounder again.

"Good morning, Boyd. I'll pick you up in an hour for the conference with the coroner. You're at the hospital, right?"

"Yes, I'll be ready. I'm up in the dayroom shooting the breeze with Lefty."

"Who in the world is Lefty?" Hill had a difficult time keeping up with new admissions. He was out of the loop, too busy with other more demanding challenges.

"He's one of our new patients, and interestingly—he's a second cousin to your former combat comrade Grizzly. I'm sure you haven't forgotten old Grizzly."

"How could I ever forget. I'm still carrying around some shrapnel from saving his no-good ass. Tell me more about the left-handed patient."

"Lefty presents one of our more interesting medical challenges. He walks around here dazed and confused. Shadow-boxes in the mornings and sleeps in the afternoon. On one occasion he punched a framed picture off the wall in the hallway. Guess he saw the face on the picture throwing a right cross at him. If you talked to him, he'd tell you he's the second coming of Jack Dempsey—God forbid."

"Who referred him?" Howard wondered why the man needed this level of care.

"He came up from a hospital in Corpus Christi. They thought we might be able to help him. He gets too aggressive at times but then becomes apologetic and remorseful. I trust the other more mature patients will rally around him, settle him down."

"Maybe, maybe not," Howard said. "From my experience, patients like Lefty need some time in our rage room. You told me earlier it's now operational."

"Yes. I tried out some of the instruments with Donna Mae Phelps, our new recreational therapist. She auditioned me on one of the gadgets to control rage. Believe it or not, I was successful with that oversized hammer pounding down the narrow nail heads into the thick oak, redwood stumps. You need to make a go at this challenge, but we have to clock you. You're limited to a time-based quotient adjusted by the severity of your rage."

"Screw you, Boyd Bounder. Pound your own fucking nails. By the way, is this Lefty character a veteran?"

"Yes, he spent his entire three-year enlistment in Germany, then left the service under honorable conditions. Lefty was the All-Army boxing champ in Europe during his tour in the nineties. He has one of the most comprehensive health insurance plans I've seen recently. His rich daddy wanted to ensure his son would never be without the requisite care he needs. We'll work with him and see how we can minimize his outbreaks."

"Good luck, brother," Howard chuckled. "Put your gloves back on and start training to improve what I witnessed the other day. You telegraphed every wild-ass swing you threw at me."

"No, not going to happen. Maybe I'll put him in the ring with you, Mr. Hill. Incidentally, did you ever find that tooth?"

"Go to hell Bounder, never lost it."

Boyd laughed at Howard's refusal to acknowledge who came out ahead on their little free-for-all the other day. "Hey, are Molly and Marco planning to attend the session with the coroner and police lieutenant?"

"Molly—no, Marco—yes," Howard replied. "Tam Lozen nixed her attendance. He didn't feel she could offer anything more informative than the comments in her written statement to Baldy. What more can you say when a speeding truck is trying to flatten you? I think he's wrong not allowing Molly to be there, but what recourse do I have? Baldy has some questions for Marco regarding the pictures he took of the Humvee ambulance at the airport. By the way, did Clarisa call you?"

"Huh? Why?" Boyd asked.

Howard said nothing.

"The answer is no on that ridiculous question, Mr. Hill. The Mexican jumping bean and I are not communicating with each other."

Howard snickered. "You know her, wants to keep all options open, a typical frustrated, middle-aged woman indeed."

"You said that. There are no options open on this boy's mind, Howard. I told you before . . . we're history. What the hell did she want from you? Another romp in the hay? Not a one-and-done physical exercise in the love-making department?"

"Boyd, Boyd, I thought we got over that. Anyhow, she called me, told me something strange happened at the cantina last night before the closing hour. One of her new customers got in a heated argument with the wait staff, almost came to fisti-cuffs. The young man was inebriated and had to be helped out of the restaurant by friends. The drunk made several comments about killing crazy people, getting the nuts off the street, or comments like that. Clarissa thought his utterings might relate to what happened at Mission Oaks."

"Why didn't she call the cops?" Boyd asked. "I think the la-dy has been watching too many NCIS conspiracy theory TV pro-grams. She likes to stick her big nose into everything, even our business at the hospital. Keep away from the woman."

Howard didn't respond to his mandate. "I'll see you in six-ty minutes. Be ready!"

The county conference room was brightly lit but unembel-lished—no pictures, no rugs, no piped-in music, no humor, just the sensation regarding the dissolution of life. Boyd thought it could pass for the inner office of the morgue, less the cold steel vaults. The coroner and Baldy were seated next to each other at the long oak conference table. A pitcher of cold water and sev-eral glasses were situated in the middle of the tabletop. A dozen chocolate chip cookies were sitting unattended on a cracked plate.

"Please have a seat and grab one of these tasty cookies, folks," the coroner said. "Mr. Coffee died last week, and we haven't found any caffeinated alternatives. The water is healthier for all concerned, trust me. Oh, and ice cubes are a no-no in my healthful living book."

Boyd, Howard, and Tam pulled up chairs opposite the other two. Marco sat at one end of the table and a sinister-looking stenographer came in and sat at the other end. She eyed Marco, adjusted her thick-rimmed glasses, and then proceeded to further check him out.

"Where's Molly Pritchard?" Baldy asked after surveying the other three visitors.

"She's not available," Tam said smartly. "I have her plugged-in on another more important mission. I don't believe she has any additional input that would add to our discussions here."

Baldy seemed annoyed, but he kept his composure. He didn't agree with Tam Lozen and felt it best if he tabled his thoughts for later in the presentation. It had to come up sooner or later.

"Agreed, let's get started," the coroner said. "Baldy will lead off because his findings are more complex than mine. Baldy, you're up."

The police lieutenant wasn't as sharply dressed as in the past. His shirt was wrinkled as though he had slept in it. But his big shoes stood at attention with a glossy military spit-shine. "I want to thank every one of you for the super cooperation we've received from you and your staff. We've left no stone unturned.

You might ask, have we identified any persons of interest? The answer, unfortunately, is no."

Tam sat up straight in his chair. "That's not a brilliant start in a murder investigation, lieutenant. I could envision a half-dozen candidates who might have murdered the patient. Well, maybe three or four."

"Let me continue, Mr. Lozen, the obvious never takes front and center in situations like these, otherwise we wouldn't need the investigative resources on our competent police staff. Wouldn't you agree?"

Tam said nothing, just cleared his throat a few times to indicate it was time to move on. He expected facts, no equivocations. His good mood had dropped a few degrees after the elation he'd experienced from his visit to the Rio Grande Valley.

The lieutenant continued. "Fingerprints taken at the crime the crime scene revealed some interesting findings. Eduardo Munoz was true to his statement. He handled the broken pool cue stick. His fingerprints were all over the pool table, on several chairs and the doorframe leading into the room."

"What about the ball-peen hammer?" Howard asked.

"We traced the prints to one of your employees in maintenance," the chief said, pointing at Bounder.

"Oh no," Boyd cried, then slouched back in his chair.

The lieutenant went on in a concerned voice. "A man who goes by the name of Drake. He's in every national fingerprint database we've examined. He hasn't been convicted of any offenses warranting prison time. A few DWI's, possession of a controlled substance and disorderly conduct in several public demonstrations showed up. He had also served three years of active duty service in the marines—spent a year in Afghanistan but received a less than honorable discharge from the Corps—not honorable as most do."

"What were the public demonstrations all about that resulted in his arrest?" Howard asked.

Baldy cracked a smile. "We broke through some red tape and scored a hit. Two were related to diversity disputes involving Indian suffrage. An unknown tribe was denied voting rights in a small Louisiana town and took to the streets. We weren't able to pinpoint the exact nature of the other demonstrations but were led to believe they were related to some political malcontents."

"Did you bring Drake in for questioning?" Howard asked.

"Yes, and I was satisfied with his answers."

"Well, what were they?" Tam asked impatiently.

"I'll elaborate more to include Molly's testimony when the coroner discusses her findings. I hope you'll be relieved."

Tam shook his head and then stood tall looking over to Boyd Bounder. "You didn't vet this scumbag inside out—outside in. How could you put him in an important hospital position with that abysmal record?"

Bounder took offense. "His misdemeanors happened at a young age and after he'd left military service with some dark clouds behind him. The man had two tours of duty on the front lines facing hostile forces and earned a Bronze Star for Valor. Sources indicated he left the army with a burning question . . . 'Why was our government attempting to impose a model of democracy on a tribal culture whose only goal was survival among warring factions?' Makes good sense to me I might add."

Marco sat patiently, a slow burn in his gut for all the nonsensical bantering.

"Hold on here," Howard butted in. "Boyd Bounder, you never served a day in this man's army. What gives you the right to agree with a non-conformist?"

"You'd better hang tight there, Mr. Hill," Bounder laughed sarcastically. "I had brutish enemies when I served on the gridiron for good old UT. I didn't get any awards for valor when I got coldcocked by an oversized gorilla linebacker from the hated Aggies—spent three days in the hospital."

Tam's face reddened at the mention of the Aggies. He jumped in to cut them off. "Gentlemen, please, let's have the lieutenant and the coroner present their findings without arguing about the merits of one's personal beliefs. We've got a murderer running around, maybe still on our campus or in the area. We need to find him, or her."

"Thank you, sir," Baldy said with conviction. "The coroner will discuss the cause of death in a few minutes, at which time you can draw your conclusions. Now, let me talk about the Humvee ambulance that almost ran over Miss Pritchard. By the way, I thought for sure she'd be present today." He was still stifled.

"I made the decision she'd not attend," Tam shot back in defiance without a clarifying reason.

"Whatever," Baldy said. "We dispatched a patrol to the airport based on Marco Simone's insistence. The vehicle was nowhere in sight at the location specified by Marco when we arrived. We concluded it dumped one of the perps off for a flight and then took off. We did put out an APB in hopes of nabbing them. Thank goodness for the detailed photos Marco snapped in the airport parking lot. The license plate was stolen. We figured that much."

"Hooah, Marco," Howard shouted.

[122]

Baldy raised his hand. "But, let me add . . . the close-up photo of the base of the windshield depicting the vehicle ID gave us something tangible to work with. The Humvee was purchased through an auction process by a government contractor in Louisiana. A company by the name of Indian Extraction, L.L.C., dba as 'Our Inherited Land' is the owner of several inoperable Humvees. They were deployed during the war in Iraq and written off as combat-damaged trucks."

"Did you contact the agency that sold the Humvees to the Indian outfit?" Tam asked. "I'm sure they have names and addresses."

"Yes, of course, Mr. Lozen. We sent a detective to two locations—warehouses in Baton Rouge and a truck garage in Lake Charles. Both sites were unoccupied. The detective talked to several neighboring businesses and got the same answer. In a nutshell, whoever had leased the two buildings vacated the properties several weeks ago."

Marco had a comment. "Nothing new here," he said. "They're professionals and these scoundrels only left one barely recognizable trace behind. They must've removed the big Red Cross symbols in a hurry because they left behind a vague outline of the symbol on the top front overhang of the cabin. My photos weren't detailed enough to pick this up. I'm sure your man followed-up with the leasing offices for descriptions of the renters and any forwarding addresses."

"Yes, and you are correct, Marco. They are pros, not a trace to be found."

"No sir, not pros in my book," Howard interjected. "They failed to desecrate the vehicle ID numbers after their purchase. Numerous former government-owned vehicles are running around America with and without traceable vehicle IDs. Hells-bells, I even bought a broken-down jeep from a GI that didn't have the numbers stamped on the frame. Of course, I was young and naïve at the time."

"I'm bringing Molly Pritchard to my office after our session," Baldy scowled as he looked over at Tam. "I'm convinced she might be able to add something of importance from her initial statement . . . did she see their faces, how were they dressed and how many were in the vehicle."

"Good luck on that end," Tam said. "Molly is perceptive. Maybe she can fill in some of the blanks. Are you done yet with your briefing, lieutenant? It's getting late, and we need to move on."

"Yes, for the time being. I'll amplify some of my comments during the coroner's presentation. Madam Coroner, are you ready to begin your remarks?"

"No," she replied. "It's time for a thirty-minute break. One's brain can only absorb as much as the 'behinder' allows. Sorry about that Tam. The restrooms are down the hall to the right. Take your choice . . . they're unisex."

Chapter 17

Molly Pritchard was making her rounds of the facility while the other managers were attending the hearing. She stopped to talk to Eduardo Munoz. She was dressed in a trim, aqua blue jumpsuit—the same outfit Marco had warned her last week not to wear around the unit for fear of "feminine overexposure."

Eduardo was parked in his mini-wagon outside his room talking to Sallie Sake. Both were laughing at each other. Molly had reflected earlier to Marco that the male creatures in her facility would be in awe at this woman's physique. She was tall for an Asian but curvy in the right places. Her boobs and butt would stop a grown man cold in his tracks. As far as she knew, Sallie never took the liberty to flaunt either asset around the complex.

"Good afternoon, folks," Molly chimed. "Care to share the funnies with me? I need a boost of any bit of humor to make me relax. Rough day. The stress level in my part of the world is elevated today." She looked drained to both of them.

"Why is that?" Sallie asked. "Your appearance suggests you had jogged 5k to decompress. Never mind, I don't care to know. Mondo here is a riot. Give him five minutes, and you'll be in stitches."

"Munoz, not Mondo," quipped Eduardo. "I don't understand why you beautiful females can't correctly pronounce our exquisite Spanish names. My buddy El Conquistador Cortés would disembowel everyone of you sweethearts if he'd heard you talk in this sullied accent."

"Your buddy, Eduardo? Is he reincarnated?" Sallie put her hands on her hips.

"Of course not. I was with him when he overthrew the Aztec empire and won Mexico for the Spanish crown."

Sallie frowned. "That's wonderful, Mr. Munoz. And how does your German male friend next door address you? *Mit an umlaut* accent mark above one of the precious letters in your name?"

"Not so. After Hans Schmidt got transferred over here from the hospital, I found him to be a polite and educated person. Schmidt's military service acquainted him with many of the brave Hispanic soldiers who fought for our country. You might want to listen to him whenever he comes out of his room. He tends to be solitary and indifferent, but he's not."

"How old are you now?" Sallie asked, changing the subject. She didn't like the skinny German the day she'd met him on her orientation tour of the facility. Perhaps that would change over time. Judging a person on the first contact was never one of her stronger character traits.

"I lost count at the turn of the last century," Eduardo chatted on. "Let me think. Oh, yes indeed, I'm a one-hundred-seventy-three-year old man as of three weeks ago."

Molly couldn't hold out any longer. She broke out laughing. "How did you come up with that number, E-d-u-a-r-d-o?"

"By a well-known algorithm that was passed down by my Spanish family through the ages."

"Care to explain?" Molly asked. *I might regret it.*

"I have no objections. In fact, I'm proud to educate you uninformed folks on matters of life expectancy and religion. First, I will list the quantifiable variables that affect the aging process. We identify five major categories, but I won't elaborate on the mathematical calculations—too complicated. I have them written down somewhere. An oath of secrecy was sworn and witnessed when I celebrated my one-hundredth birthday bash in Mexico City. Oh, yes, the first category involves vital statistics compiled at birth. Components include the city of birth, the exact physical location of birth such as home, hospital or elsewhere. We add in gender, weight, height, birth order, and number of siblings by sex. And lastly, the age of mother and father at the time of birth."

"Done yet, Eduardo?" Sallie asked. "This is starting to bore me."

"No, just getting started. I trust you read the Bible. If not, allow me to inform you. The Old Testament scriptures have passages on a fellow by the name of Job. He lived to be over one-hundred-forty years of age. I'm sure they didn't have algorithms back then, only the word of God."

Molly smiled and asked, "What's the second category you want to discuss and please be brief?" She was now beyond curious with the mindset of this zany creature.

"Sure, boss. This grouping pertains to environmental factors. The first element being the amount of time, in days, spent living above fractured fault-lines in the subterranean. The second element relates to the linear distance from the center of the equator where you've spent the first thirty years of life. Another applies to the cumulative effects of smoking, drinking, and carcinogenic exposures since age fifteen. We also look at —"

"Enough!" Molly said, shaking her arms high in the air. "We've heard ample illustrations and hope you continue to lead a good life regardless of the algorithmic calculations on your behalf."

"Not so fast, Miss Molly. You asked me for a detailed question and I'm giving you an itemized account. Be patient, I'm coming in for a landing. A marital history and occupational stability are also major factors. We rate them on a scale from one

[127]

to ten, based on exposure to dangerous ventures . . . to that of sedentary deskbound jobs. I'm finished, done. Any questions or comments?"

Molly looked at Sallie and began to laugh. "Aren't you a rare specialty among the millions of folks wandering the earth conjecturing when they will be called to meet their creator. Speaking on that subject, Eduardo, weren't you going to give us your thoughts on religion? If so, please give us the summarized version." She became more relaxed, having fun.

"Aren't you out of gas yet, old man?" Sallie snickered.

He ignored her. "Oh, thanks for asking, Molly. Ah, dear old religion—how could I not address this delicate topic? I'm a smorgasbord-type of person. I trust you all know what I mean here."

"No," Sallie responded in disgust. "Try elaborating or hold your tongue. I don't care for Western food served in drive-ins or cafeterias. You're long-winded, drawn-out soapbox dissertation is infringing on my nap time. Please be brief, or I'm out of here."

"I wouldn't think of holding you up, my dear. We all value the need for more rest time here. What I believe and practice on any given day depends on my mood. Some days I elect to follow Christ and all his doctrinal underpinnings dictated by the Pope in Rome or other world-known prelates. I'm courteous, respectful and helpful to those I encounter. Other days, I'm sitting at the right hand of Satan, cogitating on how to send people to hell. Who can I abuse, hurt or made to suffer? In other words, Sallie, I choose daily what fits my temperament."

"Thank you, Eduardo. I'm impressed and delighted to have you as my friend," she lied with a straight face. "I know we'll have these thought-provoking discussions as time goes by. Hopefully, on those days that the 'prince of darkness' hasn't descended upon you. Good day, my friends." Sallie skipped to her room down the hall, shaking her head in dismay.

Eduardo asked Molly if she had any time left to sit down and talk with him. He had something heavy on his mind to share with her. She suggested they sit down in the card room at the end of the hallway.

"What's on your mind, Eduardo?" she asked. "Make it brief. I hear my desk beckoning for my return."

"I want to know why you're not at the courthouse attending the inquest about Percy Radcliff's death?"

"I wasn't invited there," Sally countered. "Rest assured, we're well-represented." *What's on his mind? How did he know about the inquest?*

Eduardo scooted his motorized wheelchair next to her. "I woke up this morning after a sleepless night with a befuddled sense of awareness. Then something poked hard on my brain. There's one situation surrounding the man's death that I didn't tell the cops."

"Oh, what was that critical piece of information?" Suddenly, Molly became more attentive to his ramblings.

"Drake, the hospital maintenance man was in the dayroom sometime before the medical aide discovered the dead body."

"What? How do you know?"

"Because Drake told me one day at lunch. He said he had a quick job to complete. I failed to ask him what the task entailed."

Molly was alarmed. "I'm going to call Howard right this moment and tell him we are on our way to the courthouse. He called me before I stopped by to visit you and Sallie. He informed me they were on a long break. Hopefully, they'll delay their inquest until we get there, and you can tell your story. I be-

[129]

lieve it has a direct bearing on this case. I'm glad you felt the need to bring this up, Eduardo. I'll call Howard on the way over. Let's go."

The coroner had not reconvened the hearing after the planned twenty-minute break. She had been called to the county supervisor's office on another important matter not related to the present inquiry. She returned thirty-minutes later with a humble apology.

"What's up?" Howard asked. "They're not going to let you retire as planned? Your tour of duty has been extended until this case is resolved, and the killer has been tried and convicted?"

"Something like that," she moaned. "I can't go into details. Local politics has always been a thorn in my thick side. Retirement can't come soon enough. Are you folks prepared to begin again?"

"No, ma'am," Howard said. "While you were gone, one of our patients informed us he had withheld some important information on the case that he hadn't told Baldy's investigators. Molly Pritchard is bringing him here as we speak. Maybe you can have an assistant bring us more coffee while we wait—and forget the stale cookies."

"I don't have an assistant, sir. The position got cut from my meager budget. Why do you think I'm leaving? I have a morgue attendant, but he doesn't do coffee. I'll go fetch it myself." She then hustled out the conference room to carry out the request.

"Can we believe anything this Eduardo Munoz is going to tell us?" the police lieutenant asked. "The guys a flake of the highest degree. I had a difficult time assessing his credibility when we conducted the initial investigation."

Tam looked morose. "Is the patient going to tell us he killed Percy Radcliff?"

Boyd Bounder stood up. "Let's hear the man out. I feel I can gauge his reliability better than most. I've known him for a long time. Oh, here they come."

Eduardo wheeled into the conference room with heightened exuberance, as though he was going to collect the Texas lottery payoff in one-hundred-dollar bills. "Molly's right behind me," he said. "She's jabbering with the deputy who frisked her after we entered the building. I didn't know she was carrying—maybe not. Chances are the uniform was working on asking for her telephone number. Cops have a big advantage wooing the girls. Knowing Molly for the short time I've been around her, she's simply being polite and respectful."

"Cut the crap, Munoz," Tam spoke sharply. "If we need your opinion on matters of amorality, we'll ask for it. In the meanwhile, shut the fuck up and speak only when you're spoken to. Do I make myself clear?"

"Yes sir, Admiral, carry on." Munoz wheeled to the back corner of the conference room, turned toward the dirty window, killed the small wheelchair motor and began sulking.

Molly walked into the room as the coroner was setting the pot of coffee on the conference table. The coroner said, "Aha, I see we're all present and accounted for, plus one newcomer in the corner."

"When do I get to talk?" Munoz turned his little vehicle around asking in a soft voice. "Nobody seems to care that I have overwhelming evidence who killed the patient. This investigation should be over in two days."

"Who is this person?" the coroner asked nobody in particular as she looked around at the other faces in the room.

The lieutenant spoke up. "He's here to add additional testimony to the happenings in the hospital dayroom at the time the deceased was found."

"Oh, goodness," the coroner said. "That might add credence to what I'm about to report. In that case, escort him out of here. I don't want an outsider butting in on my presentations. You need to interrogate him somewhere else . . . and on your own time, lieutenant."

"Yes ma'am, I'll do that." He walked over to Munoz and signaled him to follow. Munoz hesitated, not wanting to leave. He loved the audience and had more *spiel* to lay on them. The lieutenant was infuriated by the theatrics of the chatty patient. He grabbed the clown's shirt collar and give it a strong tug—enough for Munoz to get the hint. They left the conference room and found a vacant chamber down the hall where he parked Munoz.

"Stay here until Molly comes back to retrieve you, understand?"

"Yes, sir, hope it's real soon. I tend to get impatient"

The lieutenant considered slapping handcuffs on the imbecile to ensure he wouldn't become a disruptive spectator. He gave up on that idea and returned to the coroner's ongoing inquest.

Chapter 18

The coroner was brief and explicit. Nobody in attendance could believe what they had just heard.

"Percy Radcliff was poisoned to death," she said. "The notion the ball-peen hammer that everybody suspected killed him is null and void. His skull wasn't crushed. He had lived from birth with a congenital bone defect that resulted in a 'sunken' appearance in his forehead."

"Excuse me for interrupting," the lieutenant apologized. "I need to take one minute to talk about the hammer and put everybody at ease. Drake's fingerprints were on the ball-peen hammer. He'd been in the dayroom repairing a damaged windowsill. The man forgot to retrieve all his tools after the repair job was completed and inadvertently left the hammer behind in the corner. The chief of maintenance submitted the completed patched-up work order to me as evidence of the labor performed. Drake was then cleared by the police investigators of any malfeasance in the case."

Hill and Bounder were relieved and more relaxed after hearing the lieutenant's comments. Tam seemed indifferent, almost non-caring. Marco gazed at the door expecting Eduardo to crash in any moment.

"Thank you, sir," the coroner said. "Good job. Now I'll continue with my report. According to the released death certificate, I listed the cause of death as a respiratory failure—the consequence of cardiac arrest from a lethal injection. The poisoning agent was determined to be Micotil. The product contains Tilmicosin phosphate used to control respiratory disease in cattle. It has no known antidote if overdosed. Micotil is sold only to licensed veterinarians. Do I have any questions?"

Nobody responded. They were too stunned about the use of Micotil to reply to her remarks. Micotil "poisoning" was a new twist from the norm in related homicides. They were having trouble putting their arms around the unusual "cause and effects" summation by the coroner.

Tam finally became alert and then asked Howard and Bounder pointedly, "Do we have any person on our staff or even one of our patients who is a licensed veterinarian?"

Howard looked at Boyd and said, "Not that I'm aware of. Boyd, what is your response?"

"We don't have such a person. Molly, do you have any thoughts?"

"I'm as stunned as you are. We don't have anybody I'm aware who has worked with the product. Marco, do you have any input?"

"Yes, I do, but it's for the coroner. I'm new around here and only have limited working knowledge of our staff and patients."

"Go ahead, young man, don't hesitate to probe," she said. "Sometimes I inadvertently omit items that others deem important to hear."

Marco stood up. "Where did you locate the needle marks on the body where the syringe injected the poison?"

"Jugular vein on the upper right side of the neck." She looked sharply at Marco, wondering what this was leading to.

"Thank you, doctor," he said. "If I were sitting in a chair and someone came up behind me and tried to shove a needle in my neck, I would fight like all hell to prevent it. Was there evidence the dead man tried to fight off the attacker—like contusions or bruises of the upper body?"

[134]

"Yes, though minor," she reported. "We believe the deceased knew the attacker and may not have been cognizant of the impending assault."

"How potent was the poison?" Marco wouldn't let up. "In other words, was death immediate?"

"I would probably say yes to your question." She tried to recall what she'd told the lieutenant earlier at the crime scene. He had asked for the exact time of death.

The doctor continued her report. "Veterinarians inject the vaccine subcutaneously, that is, beneath the skin for a slower absorption rate into the animal. They've found that it would prove fatal if injected into a major vein going directly to the heart. We concluded that the dosage of Micotil administered was potent enough to vaccinate a full-grown milk cow."

Shaking his head, Boyd asked for more specifics.

"Sure, let me amplify. Our research found the dosage used by most veterinarians adds up to 1.5 milliliters for every one-hundred-pounds of animal weight. I think you get the idea of why death was almost instantaneous."

"Thank you, doctor," Marco said. "I can see why no shouts of distress were heard in the area or at least reported to authorities. Bottom line—Percy Radcliff knew his killer."

"Is there anything else on your mind, Marco?" Tam asked, as though he was waiting for the long-winded inquiry to conclude. He'd heard enough—was ready to return to Houston to deliver the news to TCCV staff and Percy Radcliff's family.

"Thank you, sir, but I'm not finished yet. Sorry to be such a pest and thorn in our coroner friend's side. There are too many loose ends here in my mind that weren't addressed."

Molly agreed and motioned for Marco to continue.

"Have you checked with all the local and state veterinarian professional societies to determine if any veterinarians were blacklisted? If identified, what reasons were listed? Have you checked all the distributors in the area that sell Micotil? It would determine if they maintained an inventory of veterinarians who routinely order the prescription for milk cows. I'm convinced there is a farm or ranch in Texas that owns milk cows to sell its products to the big dairies. Or maybe even to provide milk for their large family and friends. I could go on and on, doctor. How about telling us what detailed actions you and your staff have taken to identify a 'person of interest' in this murder case?"

The coroner was intimidated by Marco's verbal barrage. "Look, young man, you need to ask the police lieutenant. Your questions fall in his bailiwick. I cut and dice. Know what I mean?"

"Yes, I'm fully aware of what you do on that stainless-steel slab," Marco said. "I'll ask the lieutenant my questions later. What about the four words written on the paper the police folks found tucked into the dead man's pocket? Are we going to hear about that?"

The coroner smirked as though she scored a humongous one-handed leaping dunk from the foul line. "I was about to tell you an interesting fact. The police lieutenant had asked me to follow-up on this vital piece of the investigation, knowing I had better access to a forensic expert. Our linguistic scholar did his research. You won't believe his findings."

"Trust me," Marco said sternly. "I've got a plane to catch."

Molly stared at him and got his attention. She put her index finger to her lips wanting her associate to hush up and allow the coroner to finish.

The coroner picked up again. "The learned man found the words come from the Classical Nahuatl language of the early Aztec empire. The more modern dialects closest to this interesting language is spoken in the Valley of Mexico."

"That's wonderful, doctor," Marco said, ignoring Molly's suggestion. "Please tell us what they mean in the neo-modern English language."

"I'd be happy to do that," she smiled, now seemingly back in control. "*It-Is-Ours-Alone*. That's the exact interpretation. Do we know what's involved here? No. We have asked the police experts to run with this message and see if it makes any sense to them. Perhaps you folks at the hospital can put your heads together and solve the interpretation."

A humming noise was heard at the door. Munoz and another county staff member came back to the conference room. Munoz was clapping his hands. "I bribed this young man standing next to me to bring me back to your hearing."

The coroner addressed both the staff member and the lieutenant. "Anything you two want to add based on your several interchanges with Mr. Munoz?"

"No, thank God we're done here," the lieutenant responded. "I'll boil done our two-minute discussion in one sentence. Eduardo Munoz accepts the fact Drake did not kill Percy Radcliff."

"I'm relieved," she said. "My formal portion of the hearing is completed. I'll hang around if anything comes up that I can add any relevant comments. Molly Pritchard is standing by if you want to quiz her on the malicious people in the ambulance that tried to ramrod her as they were leaving the scene of the murder."

"Thank you," Baldy said and then turned to Molly. "Do you have a description of the driver of the big Humvee and any passengers?"

"Lieutenant, I almost got run over by a two-ton truck. The HMMVV is a lightweight, diesel-powered, four-wheel-drive tactical vehicle weighing 7,700 pounds. It can accelerate at least sixty-five miles an hour."

"I guess you know your cookies, Molly. Are you also a trained, heavy-wheeled vehicle mechanic?" He wasn't sure why he asked her the question.

"No, but in Iraq, I ran an army motor pool in an emergency for two months while the person in charge was recovering from a gunshot wound. So, these are facts, sir."

"Thanks for the clarification. Please go on with your story, Molly."

"My point here is a gigantic, heavyweight steel monster was racing toward me at top speed trying to pancake me. Did I recall anything? Yes, my brain ordered 'get the hell out of the way or die an unpleasant death.'"

Tam jumped in. "Molly, stop the dramatics. The lieutenant wants to know what the driver and passengers looked like. Can we get your impressions?"

"I'm sorry for the theatrics, folks," she said. "I happened to spend time in the back of that boxy vehicle on the battlegrounds in Iraq—bleeding and in shock. All I can recall in this aggravation was the driver had a funny-looking face."

"Explain," the lieutenant said with renewed interest.

"It appeared to me the driver was wearing a mask."

"Huh, what type of mask?" Tam took the lead.

"I couldn't distinguish specific facial features at all, but the colorations stuck with me."

[138]

"What were the colors?" the lieutenant asked, anxious to hear where the story was heading.

"Blue and red pigmentations were smeared all over the driver's face." *I do recollect Jase telling me something about those colors when we had last talked. Perhaps I'm dreaming.*

The room became silent. Every mind in the room was processing data, facts, and suppositions as rapidly as a NASA computer. The attendees began looking at each other, hoping the next person could translate something meaningful from Molly's comments. The silence was interrupted by a squealing, machine-operated, four-wheeled mini-vehicle repositioning itself in the spacious conference room. All turned to look over at Munoz.

"Everything you're talking about here describes the radical Indian faction we're beginning to hear and read about. These savages are trying to take over the USA!" Eduardo Munoz shouted out at the top of his shrill voice as he headed toward the conference room door for a speedy exit.

"Anybody know what that's all about?" Howard asked. "Tam, you have Indian blood racing through your veins. Are you aware of any such activity?"

Tam hesitated and turned red in his face. "That man is crazy, and I've said that before. He needs a craniotomy, not an extended paid vacation in our facility. The American Indian has been marginalized in our society since the West was won by the Great White Father. Sure, I hear rumblings from time to time, but it's no different than the plights of other disinherited populations treated as undocumented immigrants. I'm not in the law enforcement business. Let's ask the police officer here for his expert opinion."

Baldy smiled. "Yes, we see reports of periodic Indian unrest. But I've witnessed nothing as dramatic as that Indian tribe who took over Alcatraz and created such a stink in the San Francisco area many years ago. The Bureau of Indian Affairs is quick to react to any adverse activity that would bring discredit on any Indian nation."

The coroner had absorbed all the mumbo-jumbo iterations she could take. "Lady and gentlemen, this formal inquiry is over. As with any other homicide in my jurisdiction, our efficient law enforcement troops will prevail. I'm out of here. Good day."

She left without fanfare, racing off to the eminent glory of her pending retirement.

Tam stared her out the door in absolute disgust. "I hope the county gets a young, friendlier coroner than the woman who just deserted us. The bitch has taken on the personality of every poor soul whose body she opened up and sliced apart."

"She did enlighten us on the unusual and mysterious cause of death," Baldy said. "I sure hope—"

He was rudely interrupted by the neatly dressed detective who rushed into the conference room out of breath.

"I'm so sorry sir, but I have some important information for your action that can't wait any longer. It had a "Read Immediately" dictate when it crossed my desk. I know you're in the middle of an important segment of the inquiry, but this takes precedence. My lead detective in the investigation has identified a 'person of interest' in the murder case. We have to take immediate action if we hope to nab the bastard."

Tam Lozen yelled out . . . Who the hell is it!"

Chapter 19
Elsewhere

Jase Lozen had always been proud of his father and adorable sister. Tam Lozen's strong passion for his cultural upbringing and the barriers he had to overcome to achieve success were never forgotten by Jase or Molly. Jase loved them but feared for their lives. The inescapable web being woven by his uncompromising followers could result in their untimely deaths.

His mission in Mexico was completed. The Bureau of Indian Affairs was delighted with the success of his brief expedition. Working day and night, Jase's team unearthed tons of mucky, grime-impacted soil until they discovered remnants of an ancient Aztecan village. The primordial civilization was confirmed by university scholars in Mexico City. Mexico subsequently sought to apply for the UNESCO World Heritage site designation for the historical revelation.

The monetary award he earned contained an unexpected huge bonus. The funds assured him that his growing community in Texas would sustain itself for another year. By then, they would certainly have achieved their ultimate objective.

Jase decided to spend a week in the Yucatan peninsula before returning home. He needed to regain his body strength from continued and onerous physical exertion. At the same time, rest and moderate recreation would relieve the mounting stress he'd been under. There were times he thought seriously about aborting the campaign. Too often fleeting doubts of achieving triumph and the odds of lasting success gnawed away at his optimistic frame of mind. Uncompromising efforts like theirs seldom sway the thinking of the citizenry. The crusaders are discarded, discredited and thrown to the dogs and left to suffer their humiliations.

He often deliberated whether his wife would've stayed with him if he hadn't joined ranks with the group of young radicals hell-bent to change the world. She was passionate, supportive and faithful during the early years of their marriage. She worked long and hard hours supporting his educational endeavors. Perhaps the negative outcomes would've been different if they had sired children. She was game—he couldn't produce.

Drake had been Jase's first choice as Chieftain. The man could persuade and instill confidence in the younger, thrill-seeking members. His organizational talent was superb. As the population of the encampment increased, Drake created a team of mid-management supervisors for five major functions—training, security, education, food- service, and property management. He called them "Mids," deciding not to use their given names.

Drake fell in love with the whiskey bottle, and that choice proved to be his downfall. His wife had left him and returned to her home in Georgia. There was no question he had to be removed from authority. His expertise as a mechanic and skilled technician was beneficial, but he had to be eased out of leadership for the good of the struggling faction.

Jase was informed by his new leader that Drake was "defrocked" and forced to leave the tribe. His two children remained with the clan but under the parental guidance of the tribe's medicine woman. She was barren and childless. Drake sought employment in San Antonio. Chieftain had no reason to keep track of the ousted trailblazer.

Jase was thankful that he had appointed the current, hard-charging guide to lead his flock during his temporary absence in Mexico. The man, only known as Chieftain, was a true warrior.

[142]

As a teenager, he had the guts to fight his way out of an uncompromising gang of street criminals in Newark, New Jersey.

Chieftain had dispatched a courier to Mexico to deliver a coded message to Jase while he was organizing his team for the historic dig. The traitor Percy Radcliff was no longer in their midst. He had become an extremist, oppositional and argumentative to the point of total disruption whenever he visited the camp. Percy tried to introduce a new religious movement from his comfortable Houston home to all who'd listen to his passionate sermons.

The impact on a small contingent of young warriors was pronounced and not appreciated by the more-seasoned elders. Dissension arose and drastic action had to be taken against the cancerous Percy Radcliff to quell the muddy waters.

Initially, Jase Lozen's earlier ploy to deceive the TCCV was successful. He had convinced his father to help Radcliff's family by arranging admission to a Houston area hospital for observation and treatment. Percy became more dysfunctional alienating other patients to boycott their treatment teams. Two psychotic patients later went AWOL on Radcliff's prompting.

The former family friend became a walking time-bomb ready to explode and derail the supreme design. Tam Lozen felt something had to be done to alleviate the rebellion. Tam stepped in and arranged Radcliff's transfer to their new hospital in San Antonio. Everybody was happy with that decision—that is, until his abortive stay at the busy hospital created shock waves in Houston.

Chapter 20

Seven days of physical healing and regenerating his psyche proved indispensable. Jase Lozen was fully committed to the repeated calls from his ancestors. No human force existed that would impede all-out victory. He was anxious to resume control over his tribe.

The first item on his itinerary was to pick up Chemist at the San Antonio International Airport. Jase wouldn't drive one of the community Humvees for this task. He was enraged that the Humvee used in the recent hospital exploit involving Percy Radcliff was left unattended in the airport parking garage. The young scout assigned the mission of returning Chemist for his flight back to New Mexico wouldn't commit the same blunder again. He was mutilated. His headless body was propped up in the driver's seat of the Humvee ambulance when it was laid to rest in the ancestor's pond in South Texas.

The American-Indian bred Chemist had been a paratrooper in the French Foreign Legion in his late teens. Other troopers steered clear of the big, mean Indian because of his foul temperament and physicality. In his early twenties, he joined the US Army and was deployed to Afghanistan as a field service veterinary tech. Chemist completed an additional three-year hitch as a food service inspector. He became disgruntled with following "nonsensical" orders and got out of the army.

His academic resume was superb, demonstrating a highly motivated and energetic pursuit of higher education. He enrolled in a veterinary tech program in Wisconsin after his military commitment. Chemist became obsessed with the study of chemistry after completing his associate degree. He went abroad for an accelerated regimen of advanced courses, finishing with a Ph.D. in chemistry in Switzerland. He elected to pursue a research position with an international fertilizer corporation in the US. It was in this capacity he befriended a young archaeologist in Egypt.

Jase Lozen had been aware of the man. During a drug-induced stupor with one of his former archaeology confidants, he learned that Chemist performed "dirty work" for a negotiated fee. The job had nothing to do with the discipline of removing mounds of earthen soil for cultural research in the fertilizer business. The spouse of the friend's older brother was unfaithful with two different lovers, one a teenager. The adulterous woman had disappeared—quickly and permanently.

Chemist migrated to a new and more exciting line of work. The overriding exhilaration of killing human beings consumed him. He had no first, middle or last name. Identity monikers weren't requirements in his occupation. Those who needed his services used the website, triangulating through several levels of "darknet" encrypted networks until contact was made with World Funds, LTD. The bogus investment house located in Quebec, Canada was a clearinghouse for hired assassins with huge financial charges for their hired guns. Chemist made millions in his growing career of dissolving human life.

Jase Lozen performed extensive and costly research on Chemist before he had hired him. He learned through several trustworthy resources that the Indian and the traitor Percy Radcliff had known each other. Chemist and Radcliff met in Afghanistan. On one occasion in a war-torn village, they drank and gambled all night. Radcliff lost over a thousand dollars, half of which never got repaid. Chemist never forgave him that debt. Now Radcliff was no longer a threat to their glorious campaign.

[145]

It was a less difficult task obtaining public records on Drake's relationship with Chemist. They had been active at Standing Rock Indian Reservation in 2016 protesting the Dakota Access Pipeline. Their mob of disgruntled kinfolk considered the planned crossing of the Missouri River would be a threat to the region's freshwater and destruction of ancient burial grounds.

It was reported that Drake blamed the big Indian's physical tussle with the authorities as the reason for their arrest. Chemist was defiant and uncooperative with the authorities. They spent two days together in a dark cell, arguing and cursing at each other waiting to be bailed out. According to one of the deputies, they didn't leave jail as friends but as hated rivals.

Jase wasn't concerned about the man's abusive history with white women. The associate who had hired Chemist didn't beat around the bush. He wanted a proven assassin.

The flight from New Mexico arrived early. It gave Jase and Chemist time to become better acquainted while enjoying a snack at the airport. Both enjoyed the Tex-Mex offerings in one of the corridor restaurants. Jase got hooked on enchiladas de Santa Cruz while on assignment in Mexico. Chemist preferred the margaritas and opted for a plate of puffy tacos.

Initially, Chemist was hesitant to go into great detail about his history. He assumed the man he was meeting with had vetted him thoroughly. An hour later, they departed San Antonio for Houston. They would finalize Jase's strategy for the next phase of the grand plan.

Chapter 21
Meanwhile, the hearing continues

The police lieutenant had been upset with his lead detective investigator in the Percy Radcliff murder case—but not for barging unannounced on him in the conference room. The lack of progress in aggressively pursuing every lead in the murder case became a thorn in his side. He was ready to fire the detective for his incompetence.

"Sir, if I may explain my rudeness, you and those present will be pleased with my account. As I reported, we've identified a 'person of interest' in the murder case."

Baldy had cooled off and hoped they could corral the killer without delay. "You have center stage but be brief. We've been sitting here on our collective asses most of the day chewing on the forensic details that resulted in Radcliff's death."

"Yes, sir. First, I want to complement hospital management for putting a security camera in a strategic location to film all transactions at the visitor sign-in desk. We were able to identify all the guests within a twenty-four-hour window on the day the patient was murdered. We obtained facial recognitions, addresses, and telephone numbers."

Howard acknowledged, "I don't usually brag, but it was my idea from the get-go. We used this system at the VA, and it saved our butts on more than one occasion. So, what'd you find detective?"

"Seven visitors signed up during that period. We ran our high-tech, visual detection software program to determine if any of them had a record of arrest warrants or other misdemeanors."

Baldy smiled. He felt they finally garnered some good news. He motioned for the detective to continue.

"Six individuals cleared the screenings without any histories necessitating follow-up actions by law enforcement. The seventh person's screening profile lit up like a Christmas tree. His name is Damian Coahuila, age 33 and residing at 1375 Strathmore, San Antonio, Texas. He spent three years in Huntsville for assault with a deadly weapon. Coahuila was arrested for four DWIs over the past five years. His occupation was listed as 'General Contractor' with specialization as a pipe-fitter. The facial screen reflected severe skin disfigurations on both cheeks and a three-inch scar in the center of his forehead."

"Did you pick him up?" Tam asked before anyone else could comment.

"Negative," The detective said. "Nobody was home. We initiated 24-hour surveillance of the residence—nothing. We obtained a search warrant and found the house empty and severely trashed. Going house-to-house, we learned from neighbors Coahuila was a loner, didn't own a vehicle and was rarely seen on the property. We will continue surveillance for five more days. Our initial conclusion at this point is he skipped town without leaving any footprints. We won't pursue him any further."

"What? That's all you got?" Tam acted distraughtly. Howard crossed his arms in apparent disgust. Molly, Marco, and Boyd looked at each other and shrugged.

Baldy took over. "Gentleman, there's no tangible evidence Coahuila killed Mr. Radcliff. The police department doesn't have the resources to justify continued, round-the-clock surveillance of the house or other city locations. We will alert law enforcement agencies nationally to engage their technology to watch for him and take appropriate action. We'll shift into phase two and allocate our limited manpower accordingly. The man will resurface somewhere. Be assured, we'll get to the bottom of this."

Marco stood tall, bypassed Baldy and walked over to the lead investigator with an intimidating stare. "I did a tour as a military policeman early in my army career. I don't doubt the efficacy of your established protocol, but I do question the lack of effectiveness in your investigation."

"Marco, settle down," Molly ordered her associate. "Let's show some respect and courtesy here. I'm sure law enforcement is as frustrated as we are. We have some of our own in-house cleaning up to do to prevent the recurrence of such a tragedy. Let them do their part without us looking over their shoulders."

Tam came to Marco's defense. "I have to agree with Marco to some degree. Allow him to continue his thoughts on the matter." He then sat down. Molly stared boldly at both men.

"Thank you, sir," Marco frowned. "I'll be brief with only three questions. The first is a matter of curiosity, the second a possible lead that needs to be checked out further, and the third is a major point of contention."

"Move out on your thoughts, Marco," the lieutenant said. "Time is another enemy we're having to deal with."

Marco sighed. "Sure enough. The man's last name is unusual. What's his ethnicity and would that racial background have a direct bearing on his desire to kill Radcliff? My second point pertains to the other six names on your listing. Do any of these individuals identify as family, friends, staff or anybody local we might have an interest in? Please read their names from the manila folder you're holding."

"Of course," the detective said. "Mr.—"

"Simone."

"Thank you." The detective opened the folder and read the seven names on the list. "We have a John Smith, Jamie Jones, Pamela Cruise, Vincent Italiano, Clarisa Rios, Donald Hone . . . and of course Damian Coahuila."

Marco pointed to everyone in the room and asked, "Do you folks recognize any of the names just read to us?"

Howard went first. "Clarisa Rios."

"Ditto," Boyd Bounder said.

Molly and Marco shot their hands in the air to signal they also knew the woman.

"Now we're getting somewhere," Marco beamed. "Boyd, do we have a column on the sign-in sheet listing the patient or patients these seven people visited?"

"Yes, but not everybody fills out the patient's name. I see where we need to revisit our procedures to ensure we know who is going where in our hospital."

Marco turned to the lead detective. "Can you tell us that information from your interviews with these folks?"

The man beamed. "Yes, all but two visitors listed the patient he or she was visiting over a 24-hour period. We were able to get confirmation from those patients that were visited by John Smith, Jamie Jones, Pamela Cruise, and Vincent Italiano. All but Smith stayed at least until eight o'clock. He had to leave for a late afternoon appointment with a bank in Seguin. We're confident these folks were not involved whatsoever with patient Radcliff."

"That's fine with me," Marco said. "Please continue."

"I will do that. Only Clarisa Rios and Damian Coahuila left that 'patient visited section' blank on the sign-in roster. It was an oversight on our part that we didn't ask Clarisa Rios who she was visiting. I told you enough about Coahuila."

"Thus, we have two persons of interest—right detective?" Marco implied.

"No, we've cleared Miss Rios. She satisfied our investigator's screen. She told us she frequently visits a few military patients because her brother was also a veteran but had died on active duty. She brings them goodies from her restaurant. We verified the fact with several of the unit aides who work on the wards."

"Thank you," Marco said, satisfied that the scatter-brained purveyor of food substances performed welcomed charity work with her morale-building visits. "Now, it's time for my third and final question. I have a burning desire to know whether you've contacted local, state and national veterinarian organizations to determine if this Coahuila character is a veterinarian?"

"No, we simply haven't gotten that far yet," the detective frowned.

"Thank you," Marco said. "I'm almost done here but have one last question to you, lieutenant. Earlier you said, and I quote . . . 'We'll shift into phase two and allocate our limited manpower accordingly.' Please discuss what you mean by the term 'accordingly' so we're all reading off the same sheet of music."

Molly walked over to Marco and grabbed his right arm. "Marco, you're done with further disruptive and inexcusable behavior. You've embarrassed us with your prosecuting attorney's argumentative approach to a highly-skilled and dedicated police department!"

Marco said nothing.

"One last thing, Marco Simone," she commanded. "Go retrieve Eduardo Munoz from that room down the hall and bring him back to Mission Oaks.

"Yes ma'am. I hope the person assigned to babysit Munoz hadn't fallen asleep on him. You know that wheeled contraction of his has concealed wings." Marco spun around and took off.

Chapter 22
July 2017
Three weeks later

The bad blood spilled in Marco Simone's disdain for the police lieutenant and his investigative staff had finally abated. Cooler heads prevailed. Several days after the inquest, Marco Simone had sent a sincere and highly emotional letter of apology to Baldy after his belittling verbal assault against the police department's progress in the Percy Radcliff murder case.

The lieutenant had acknowledged Marco's expression of regret and called him. Baldy encouraged him to continue to express his opinions on any matter that would help everybody involved to bring this case to a final resolution.

Marco went to see him. In a slightly comedic gesture of friendship, he asked Baldy what his real name was. Marco didn't care for nicknames. He was Tubby until he entered the army.

"Edgar J. Wactenshutt," Baldy said with a chuckle. "If you tell anybody at the hospital . . . I'll pack you up and ship you to Mongolia. Oh, by the way, Howard knows my given name but was sworn to secrecy long ago."

Meanwhile, Molly's 20-bed, long-term unit was at capacity. TCCV had dispatched a small van with veterans from Houston-area nursing homes. Before their arrival, Lefty had been transferred from the acute care hospital to Molly's unit. Clinicians felt he could thrive in a less restrictive environment if monitored appropriately. He opted to take over the room of his second cousin

Grizzly who had been discharged to a VA nursing home closer to his Alabama home.

Before long, Lefty and Eduardo Munoz became best buddies. They played water polo together in the pool on the rooftop of the hospital. Two former Navy SEALs being treated for chronic anger management issues took exception to the spirited play of Lefty and Munoz in the pool. Recreational therapist Donna Mae Phelps intervened before the heated discussions resulted in a physical altercation. Munoz, in all his bravado, had the last word—"don't mess with army folks, dudes." He might live to regret it. SEALs are like elephants. They never forget—or in most cases, forgive.

Molly had mulled over the possibility of designating one of the residents as a coordinator of patient activities. She had been spending more time with Baldy's detectives. She was the only professional staff member at Mission Oaks Treatment Center that Baldy's staff felt confident could explain the nuances of mentally sick people on a common person's level of comprehension. It didn't hurt she was attractive, physically active and fun to work with.

The idea of a resident coordinator was fully supported by all residents and put to a vote. The final tally was unanimous. Sallie Sake accepted the non-paying position of Unit Coordinator. She would report directly to Marco Simone. Eduardo was distressed that his brief campaign for the appointment fell on deaf ears. There remained a trace of friction between the two residents.

Drake spent considerable time in his off-duty hours with Hans Schmidt, though Schmidt was tagged a loner by most other residents—except Munoz. They were both cribbage addicts. Hans also was a fanatic playing electronic war games that drew Drake's attention and participation.

[154]

Between the fun and games, Drake learned the contents of the mysterious footlocker secured in the storage room. Schmidt also shared with Drake his plans with the unusual contents. Schmidt was ready to develop a business plan but needed help, not knowing the ins-and-outs of making that happen. He didn't want to seek assistance from leadership fearing that Miss Molly or Boyd Bounder would deter his ambitions.

Drake possessed the solutions involving the technicalities, but the crafty maintenance man had the "end—game" target deeply embedded in his fiber. He never lost his fervor to level the playing field and bring honor and parity to his former family in South Texas. It was thought that Hans Schmidt would play a vital role in the next few weeks. Eduardo Munoz had all the answers for the design of such a business plan. His girlfriend at the radio station boasted to them she had all the contacts necessary to secure a big contract for the German.

The time had come for the next step to evolve. One night in the basement storage room, Drake and Schmidt opened the footlocker. Schmidt intended to construct a newfangled device to demonstrate to law enforcement agencies what he did in combat. He hoped such an effort would result in some form of consultancy to either the fire department or law enforcement.

Conversely, Drake had planned to develop a prototype explosive device but was disappointed with the contents scattered around loosely in the big box. Even though he was unceremoniously discarded from his clan and other tribal members, he never abandoned his pledge for redemption at all costs, being willing to suffer a hero's death if necessary.

Drake found the footlocker contents were mere keepsakes of bits and pieces Schmidt collected during his tour in Afghanistan. There were no switches, fuses, containers, explosive devices or batteries to construct and detonate an IED. A dozen pieces of varied sizes of shrapnel were tagged with dates and locations where Schmidt had collected them in Afghanistan. Some of the fragments still had evidence of dark coagulated blood.

Drake should've known better. The kid was a paranoid dysfunctional type not to be taken seriously. The footlocker was a complete dead end as far as he was concerned.

Before I was cut loose from the tribe, it was my responsibility to obtain the explosives needed for the final phase. I still maintain my role is sacred. I'm still deeply committed to the cause.

Eduardo Munoz wasn't told of the various keepsakes in Schmidt's footlocker. He wasn't aware of an arrangement that would result in the ultimate instrument to achieve both Drake's and the tribes' final solution. His propensity to envision future events would come into play before the final act.

Chapter 23
September 2017

Progress in the Percy Radcliff murder investigation had decelerated. The police lieutenant and the new county coroner Evelyn Augustin summoned the TCCV representative and hospital leadership to the long-overdue promised update on the inquest proceedings. The coroner was a young, ambitious forensic pathologist recruited from Toronto by the County Commissioners. The police department was thrilled with the depth of experience she had displayed with complicated homicides. She was young but experienced.

Evelyn's dogged efforts to revisit questionable assumptions and discarded leads proved vital to the closure of outdated cases. Four older, unresolved murder cases had been pending from the previous coroner's docket before the woman retired. In each case, the perpetrators were prosecuted and sent to prison. Evelyn dove into Percy Radcliff's pending case file with enthusiasm rarely displayed by the previous pathologist.

There were rumblings of discontent by the TCCV executives about the stagnant proceedings. Tam Lozen drove over from Houston with the disgruntled TCCV legal counsel who insisted he be present for the updates. Boyd Bounder and Howard Hill were the only Mission Oaks attendees. The police lieutenant didn't invite Molly or Marco. They had become nuisances to his staff, believed to be encouraged by Tam Lozen's insistence to stay involved for some unknown reason.

The lieutenant introduced the new coroner and began the report. "Thank you again for being here today," Baldy said. "I know you folks are just as anxious as my investigative team to get this case resolved. We finally found Damian Coahuila."

"Thank the Good Lord," Bounder exclaimed. "Is he at long-last sitting in your jail?"

"Ah, no, Mr. Bounder. Several days ago, we received a detailed narrative from the police department up in Waco that Damian Coahuila was killed in a motorcycle accident on IH-35 north of the city. His body was positively identified by the church authorities he worked for in the little town of Abbott. The pastor reported that Coahuila had been hired as a janitor eight days ago. He pleaded the fact he had no family, no friends and no home, but was an ardent follower of Jesus Christ. The vagrant was hired and lived in the basement of the church."

"So, you've closed the books on him?" Tam asked.

"Yes, he's history. There's no evidence he killed Percy Radcliff as far as I'm concerned."

Howard Hill sat tall and cleared his throat in a loud belch as though he had a piece of beefsteak caught in his sagging craw. "Baldy, what about word from the various veterinary organizations you made contact with—anything show up?"

"Nothing under the name of Damian Coahuila. There were two Damián's listed in their membership rosters but no Coahuila. The bottom line at this time is we have no other suspects. I feel—"

"Hold on, Lieutenant," Evelyn stopped him. The police lieutenant had involved her earlier than normal in her orientation to the new position because of her innate ability to perceive things external to her occupation of dissecting dead bodies. "Tell these folks what we found when we went over the video surveillance tapes again and again. You know, the colorful films depicting persons signing in to visit patients at Mission Oaks on the day of the murder."

"Oh, yes, thank you, Miss Augustin. I was just getting around to it. We focused-in closer to Damian Coahuila's signing in and noticed a person standing by in a white doctor's smock, probably male. The person circled Coahuila, moved to pass the desk and quickly entered the lobby. We weren't able to get a face or even a sharp image of the back of his head. What we did observe was a huge, well-built person, bigger than Boyd Bounder or Howard Hill. Believe me, that's big. He wore a blue and red scarf around his thick neck."

"So, where does that lead us?" Tam asked, getting angry and impatient. He directed his next question to Boyd Bounder. "Do your physicians and other mental health workers wear white smocks?" He made no reference to the scarf.

"Never," Bounder said. "No, too stark—boosts everybody's blood pressure. It's obvious now we had an imposter walk into our hospital who could have killed Percy Radcliff."

Tam nodded his head in agreement. The stiff legal counsel looked like a fat bulldog ready to jump into the lengthy discussion but again, restrained himself. Evelyn glanced over at him adjusting the headband anchoring his long, flowing greyish-black hair.

The lieutenant continued. "Before Evelyn Augustin went to medical school, she served in the Canadian army veterinary corps as a procurement agent. She learned during the Vietnam conflict DOD procured beef from Australia for feeding the troops. As a part of the contract, the US funded research in Australia on how to protect the bovine population from diseases that would imperil or limit their growth and development. The drug Micotil was used in the study. It was found to be the best protective agent to vaccine the cows against respiratory diseases prevalent in their species."

"So, what?" the legal counsel boomed out in a deep voice. "Get to the dog-gone point." Evelyn thought his voice resembled that of Perry Mason. She loved watching old American movies.

"Hmm, sure," the lieutenant said with alarm at the tenacity of the new player in the game. "I was about to address that. Our new coroner, excuse me, the medical examiner went to DOD and obtained a listing of all personnel involved in the Australia research protocol. She was able to pull up a list of three US government personnel overseeing the research. Two people are now deceased. The third person named Chetan Hawk in military records was an American Indian who in later years became a Ph.D. chemist. He was last traced to a fertilizer company in the US, then all of a sudden fell off everybody's screen. We are looking for him as we speak."

"Again, what's his name?" Tam asked, trying to recall if he'd ever heard of him. Jase had been delinquent in not making contact with him on a recurring basis.

"Chetan Hawk, but we're not sure what name he goes by at this time. He has changed his given name on official documents three different times over the years. At last report, he goes by the name of Blue Red. We have every law enforcement agency looking for the man."

"Why would the killer use Micotil?" Howard asked the coroner. "Aren't there other more readily available lethal poisons he could have injected into the man's neck that would do the same thing?"

"Yes, there are dozens," she said. "But we believe the killer probably had an existing supply of Micotil stored somewhere in a convenient location. He had worked with the product before and learned of its lethal potentials. Why would he expose himself to an incriminating audit trail of a professional purchasing a controlled substance?"

"I'm not sure it's a controlled substance," Bounder reported.

Tam got up and marched to the front of the room. "Correct me if I'm wrong," he said, changing the subject. "But, didn't Molly tell us during the earlier inquest the man driving the Humvee ambulance had blue and red pigmentation smeared on his face—or something to that effect?" *I need to continue to express my concerns to them.*

"Of course," Bounder said in an excited tone. "I remember we were all perplexed with her comment—even deliberating how she could be so descriptive facing near-death. It could be this Hawk guy, or Blue Red or whatever his name is who tried to run her over."

The attorney nodded his head, seemingly happy with the flow of facts and circumstances. He was content to sit and wait this out.

The lieutenant sat taller and agreed with Bounder. "Let me get back to the Micotil discussion for a second, and then I'll shut up. Even though our coroner, er, medical examiner here felt we'd have a difficult or impossible task of linking Mr. Blue Red directly to the Micotil, she took one step further. Evelyn checked with every distributor of Micotil in the country. She ran all the possible combinations of the names we were working with. Even throwing in some bogus ones."

"Bravo," Hill commented "I might add . . . meticulously. I guess she came up negative. Right?"

Evelyn smiled. "I was able to get two leads that are being checked out as we speak. I'm not encouraged though. It's a longshot. I'll keep you posted."

The lieutenant was elated, relieved that some pressure had been lifted off his big chest. "Please give Doctor Evelyn Augustin a big hand for bringing us closer to a resolution that has bedeviled us since the beginning of this complicated hunt for justice."

All but the legal counselor clapped their hands in appreciation for what the police lieutenant had reported. They felt law enforcement was getting closer to uncovering the person and the motive for killing Percy Radcliff.

Mr. Lawyer held his fat hand in the air to halt the celebration and walked to the front of the delighted group. He tugged several times on his pencil-thin mustache and exhaled loudly for all to hear. "Tam Lozen is a respected director at TCCV and represents the membership's position as best he can. Let it be known that I care less about being respected and adored by an old group of combat-hardened idealists."

Hill and Bounder were ready for another physical skirmish but this time with a different opponent. If Molly and Marco were in attendance, all hell would've broken loose at the reference to "combat-hardened idealists." The lieutenant and Evelyn were waiting to hear what knockback was about to descend on them.

"I'm aghast at the entire proceedings I witnessed here today," the counselor barked out. "I trust that nobody in attendance can comprehend the magnitude of financial liability we're dealing with here. The hospital is on the verge of potential bankruptcy if this ship isn't righted soon, and I stress . . . very soon. TCCV is vulnerable, as is every person in this room. Good morning," he said curtly as he walked briskly past them and out the door.

[162]

Tam Lozen quickly excused himself and followed him out, not saying a word.

"Good fucking goodbye." Marco muttered.

Chapter 24
Meanwhile, back at Mission Oaks

Hans Schmidt had returned from breakfast at the long-term facility pumped-up with enthusiasm about finalizing his business plan. Eduardo had told him that his ingenious girlfriend at the radio station was printing out the final plan and assured everyone it would work. He had no interest in checking out the footlocker—not relevant in his opinion.

Hans was convinced he was on the threshold of a new and rewarding career. Drake had built in some realistic scenarios. His bedside telephone barked, jolting him from his thoughts. He answered quickly and was told by the caller to shut the door to his room and speak softly. It was Tam Lozen ringing him from Houston.

The old man was terse and to the point. Hans was surprised because his relationship with Tam Lozen had always been cordial and uplifting. Not this time. Three minutes later Hans hung up, confused but acknowledging agreement to their change in plans.

His thoughts were then interrupted by a text message from Sallie Sake. She asked him to join her downtown at Alamo Plaza. Drake was across the street at Teddy's Tavern reminiscing with an old army acquaintance who came to town a few days ago. He wanted Sallie and Hans to join them.

Schmidt enjoyed homecoming celebrations. He texted her back and agreed to meet them. He didn't vacate his room until he was sure that Munoz and the other residents were not lingering about in the hallways. He locked the door behind him and decided he wouldn't sign out. Nobody would miss him. Bed-check was no longer in play at this stage of his supportive treatment. He figured the busybody Marco Simone must've been dressed down by Molly Pritchard for some unknown reason. The man was no longer as temperamental and self-assured as in the past.

Hans jumped out of a taxi and caught up with Sallie near the bandstand in the Alamo plaza.

Sallie gave him a long hug. She liked Hans . . . had so much in common with him. She took his hand and they crossed the busy street.

Teddy's wasn't busy when Sallie and Hans sauntered in. They saw Drake immediately, but not his friend. Drake came over and put his arms around her while firmly shaking Hans' hand. Sallie and Hans sat down at a table across from Drake. The chair next to Drake was empty.

"Where's your long-lost friend?" Sallie asked him, wondering if they were still friends after what happened at the Cantina Classica two nights ago. *I can't believe these two are colleagues when they almost came to blows and disrupted the friendly atmosphere of the popular restaurant.*

"In the latrine making a phone call." Drake's words were slightly slurred. "He'll be out in a few moments."

Sallie was disappointed. She assumed the two men had been drinking all afternoon. His more frequent love with the bottle worried her. *Was he on the verge of becoming an alcoholic and losing his grasp of reality? I like him a lot, but my concern cautions me to tread slowly.*

Hans perked up. "Your friend is in the toilet to make a telephone call in private? That's a little unusual—must be sworn to secrecy or something weird is coming down."

[165]

"Not sure," Drake said. "Don't draw any conclusions at this point. He did seem a bit nervous when I met him downtown near the Messinger Hotel. The guy has changed since we were last kicking ass and taking names. For some reason, I can't fully recall all the situations in the past when we were side-to-side—like dates and places. This old brain doesn't summon-up like in the past. But, you have to keep in mind, copious events for both of us have washed over life's dam since then. Hey, doesn't matter, he's more serious now but still friendly. Don't let that bother you. I'm sure you'll like him, Hans."

Sallie didn't care for the guy when she'd met him with Drake earlier at Clarisa's restaurant.

"So, why'd the man travel to San Antonio and hook up with you again?" Hans asked. "Did he look you up on Goggle and feel a need to reconnect? Did you invite him? What gives with you two?"

Sallie remained silent. She knew bits and pieces about their relationship from dinner the other night with them. She reached under the table and playfully rubbed Schmidt's inner thigh. He looked over at her and smiled. She liked to tease the German. He was always uptight, had a difficult time relaxing.

There was no response from Drake to Schmidt's question about the reason for the friend's visit. Drake wasn't sure how to answer the pointed questions. He didn't remember who had made the initial contact. *Me? Him? Times have been tough on me. Too much going on in my life to keep things neatly compartmentalized.*

"Oh, here he comes now," Hans said, no longer caring about the details of the mysterious reunion. "My God, he's a giant. Must be five fingers short of seven feet." He turned to Drake.

[166]

"You never mentioned anything about this creature from outer space when we last chatted."

"Slight oversight," Drake laughed. "He's even bigger than he looks."

Hans extended a hand to greet the stranger, and then pulled back. He noticed the scarred disfigurements on the man's hands and fingers.

"Hello, my name is Hans. Sallie and I are Drake's comrades. What's your name, my friend?"

"My name doesn't matter to you or anybody else in that regard," he said curtly. "Drake told me more than I needed to know about you—mostly good and some not too comforting. Glad you were able to come downtown from your little infirmary to meet up with me and party with us. Drinks are on me."

"Fine with the drinks," Hans said. "Sorry, but I have to call you something other than Mister. It bothers the hell out of me. I'm a detail man."

The tall man stiffened and then relaxed. "Call me Chemist, little man and we'll be alright with that. I see you've noticed my hands. That's how I got my nickname. Well, sort of. I loved science classes in high school."

"Great," Hans said. I did to."

Chemist indicated agreement. "I studied my butt off while other guys played sports and screwed with the little cutie pies. I couldn't get enough chemistry lab to satisfy my thirst for the subject. So, my father bought me one of these fancy chemistry sets. One weekend I concocted a new experiment, though cautioned about the multiple dangers of working with chemicals and other compounds. The fucking scorching glass beaker containing the chemicals blew up in my hands. Enough said about that silly stunt. Let's get going on the drinks."

Hans nodded a smile. He didn't sense the big man had consumed as much alcohol as Drake.

Sallie ordered a glass of house white wine. Hans asked for a German beer. Drake and his friend shared a bottle of Scotch whiskey. The bartender put two new shot glasses in front of them and walked away without saying a word.

"I love San Antonio," Chemist said. "Look across the street and you'll see why. Who can deny the ferocious battle that took place over there in that broken-down church? The Texans took it on the chin, bigtime. Now your city is full of Mexicans. Am I right?"

Sallie and Hans glanced at each other. She said defiantly, "Who gives a shit. We're not from here. Nobody in this group cares what happened many years ago. I don't." She lied with a straight face. Chemist glared at her, not liking her pugnaciousness.

Drake snickered but felt it was time to get serious. He was thankful the place had emptied. The several happy tourists were probably taking their party to another watering hole. There wasn't going to be a celebration in the saloon as Hans had envisaged.

"Folks, we have to talk about where we're at and what lies ahead for us," Drake said with a serious look on his face. His words were now precise and to the point.

Sallie thought Drake's demeanor was recovering somewhat from the after-effects of too many libations. His friend sat uninterested with the chatter but kept his eyes glued to her lithe body. Sallie noticed and wished she'd dressed more conservatively.

"Hans, my dear colleague," Drake began. "According to Eduardo Munoz, you have finally developed the explosive package that will level the damnable puzzle palace. The detonation

[168]

will bring down everything within 100 yards of its foundation. Our collective act of revenge will proclaim to the world about the righteousness and justice that will deliver us to our end goal."

Sallie nodded. Hans looked confused. *Drake has lost his mind. He damn well knows what I have in the footlocker. Why is he going off about a bomb? Did he forget about my business plan? I had no intention to build any bombs or mines to blow up the hospital. Tam Lozen was referring to a bomb when he called me this afternoon. That's why he arranged my transfer to Mission Oaks. I must get back to him and straighten things out. I'm no fucking terrorist.*

"Well?" Drake said, staring at Hans Schmidt.

"Don't ever listen to Eduardo Munoz," Hans shot back. "He's a quack of the first degree. Tam Lozen told me a third party was contracted to handle the blitzkrieg," he fibbed, hoping Drake would back off on the subject.

Drake hesitated and then shrugged his shoulders. He looked over at Sallie, hoping she'd join in the dialog. Drake wanted her to help clarify the situation about the bomb. Hans may have shared the contents of Tam's phone call with her.

Sallie had no idea what Hans was talking about. He was tossing in German words again. She finally interacted but changed the subject and turned to Drake. "What does your bored-to-death friend sitting next to you have to do with our big plans?"

Chemist glared at her and said nothing. He then stood up and appraised her body, scheming on devious ways to enjoy her physical assets. He didn't care what the others might be thinking.

Sallie tried to read his mind, thinking he might throw a punch at her if she rejected his advances. *I saw the deviousness in his glaring eyes calculating the how and when.*

Drake broke the ice and laughed. "Please sit down, Chemist. My friend came to San Antonio to assist me in our endeavor to end the disparaging existence we've all been subjected to, my dear Sallie. Why else do you think he's in San Antonio?"

Sallie didn't care to respond.

"Hey," Hans jumped in. "I probably should hustle back to the facility before too long. I have a one-day pass to be out with you folks," he lied again. "I don't want to violate patient privileges. I believe Sallie understands. Don't you?"

"Of course, I do," she smiled, almost laughing, then continued. "That bastard Marco Simone will send out an armed patrol if you're one minute late. You'd think he was a member of the reorganized German Gestapo the way he pushes himself around the facility." Now she was taking the liberty to use a word in Hans Schmidt's native tongue.

Drake cut in. "I wouldn't have guessed. He seems meek and mellow to me."

Hans Schmidt agreed, referring to his earlier assessment of Simone.

"No, what I just said is a fact," Sallie said. "I'm not sure why the sweetheart Molly Pritchard puts up with him. Maybe they have something going on between them that we don't know about. Who cares? I don't."

Sallie and Hans continued to probe both Drake and his friend about their past histories and what had brought them together. The big man was brief and elusive in his responses. He didn't like being grilled by two loonies from a nuthouse. He'd be gone within two days and out of everybody's sight and minds forever.

Drake was now a bit more lucid. He'd enjoyed his days in military service but was concerned when Chemist contacted him about meeting up for "old times sake." They'd had their differences, but he concluded the overused adage that "time healed old wounds" was valid.

He laughed when Chemist told his young friends the story about his unsightly hands. It didn't happen that way. One evening in Afghanistan, Chemist was high on some heavy-duty cannabis he swiped from a local. He suffered severe burns of both hands trying to pull out a searing spit of charred goat shank from a flaming wood-fired pit.

Sallie and Hans had ordered one more drink and watched Drake drift back into an alcoholic miasma.

The owner of Teddy's Tavern stopped by to check on customers in the vicinity of heightened activity. He introduced himself as Big Teddy Bear to the group who had just taken over two tables in the far corner of the tavern, then moved on to Drake's group. He didn't want an all-nighter to develop on his watch.

Teddy kindly suggested that Drake consider wrapping up their three-hour reunion and take it elsewhere. Rather than objecting, all four discussed other possible places to hang out. They couldn't agree where to go next and decided to call it a day.

Before heading their separate ways, Drake suggested meeting later to dine again with Clarisa Rios at the Cantina Classica. Chemist hated the Mexican food he had the other night but didn't want to create a fuss. A protest might encumber his end plot to kill Drake.

Hans Schmidt figured he'd return to Mission Oaks. Nobody at the long-term care facility would be around to question him.

Chapter 25

Sallie and Drake were the first to leave Teddy's Tavern together. She'd been with Drake for the last four nights. They had become lovers. She had faith in him and seemed willing to join his aggressive crusade of correcting the inequities borne by his adopted Indian nation. She couldn't wrap her arms around the malicious act of Drake being expelled from the tribe's encampment. He'd lost parental control of his two young sons in the process. Yet, he maintained his pledge to continue the battle, even though exiled from the only safe-haven he'd ever known.

Hans Schmidt and Chemist found another table and stayed behind to talk more. In an oddball sort of way, Hans liked Drake's friend and sensed the Indian was comfortable with him. Chemist had always wanted to visit Germany, but Switzerland was the closest he'd come.

They had several more drinks before deciding it was time to leave. Chemist asked his new friend for a favor. He needed a ride to the closest sporting goods store. He didn't have a car because Drake drove him to Teddy's Tavern.

Hans didn't own a vehicle but called Uber for a lift. He decided to go with Chemist to the store. Maybe he could find a letter sweater. He always enjoyed football but was never big or strong enough to work his way off the end of the team's bench. It was late afternoon. Traffic was heavy on IH-410.

They shopped for a time and met up at the cash register. "Why'd you buy a skinning knife, of all things?" Hans asked him. "Do you plan to go hunting somewhere?"

"Hmm, yes. Another old military acquaintance here in town offered to take me deer hunting over the weekend. He goes to a place called Camp Bullis north of town. He guaranteed we'd kill one, maybe two. The least I could do is skin the deer for him."

Hans thought this was unusual, not knowing or caring when deer season commenced and ended. He figured the man knew what he was talking about. His disfigured hands were large and strong enough to rip the skin off the dead animal without using the carving knife. He didn't pursue the thought any further.

"Why'd you buy that sweater, Hans? It's hotter than hell in this city."

"Always wanted one—like the green and gold colors. Our team logo was a shamrock. I went to an Irish school."

Chemist shrugged and slapped him gently on the shoulder. "Good boy."

Hans contacted another Uber and headed toward Chemist's motel on the south side of the city.

They were speeding down IH-37 when Chemist pointed at the tall tower across the freeway from the Alamodome. "It's gigantic. What the hell is it?"

Schmidt wasn't sure but said, "The control tower for our international airport."

The Uber driver snickered but said nothing. He enjoyed the banter of bizarre characters riding in his hyper-polished Camry. He thought both passengers had been smoking some super-grade pot.

"I'll drop you off at your motel before heading back to the hospital," Hans uttered. "I'm starting to get confused about things, lightheaded—maybe too much booze, not used to drinking that much. Besides, I haven't taken my medication today."

"No hospital, friend—my place," Chemist said. "I can help." He needed Hans assistance in the final stages of completing his contract to kill Drake. He asked his new acquaintance to come inside his motel room for a few minutes to relax and chat some more. He needed a clearer picture of what was making Schmidt act a little out of character from their earlier session at Teddy's.

Hans didn't resist, thinking it might be wise to slow down and relax for a while.

"What ailment are they treating you for at the nuthouse, Hans?"

Hans looked dazed but responded. "They call it a paranoia complex."

"What medication did you forget to take today?" Chemist became more inquisitive.

"My Xanax pills, but I hate them—makes me think about awful things. Sometimes I want to reach out and strangle the therapists who think they're improving my strolls through the stumbling blocks of life."

Chemist moved closer to him. "I have something much better for your condition—trust me, I'm a clinical whiz. I'm sure you're not aware of my doctorate in pharmacology." *This kid will believe anything I tell him Maybe this is normal for his condition.*

"Really? This is exactly what I need, not some clinical type in pressed blue jeans whispering pleasing words to me." Hans had begun to perspire profusely. His brow was wet, his blond hair matted.

Chemist unzipped a leather pouch, reached inside and pulled out some large tan-colored tablets. As a trained chemist, he knew Hans' psychoactive drug would cause confusion, dizzi-

[174]

ness, slurred speech, memory problems, or even a sense of dere-alization. He felt a supplement of his favorite remedy would help the thin boy misinterpret reality.

Years ago, Chemist and a female scientist associate had made a foray to South Texas while on a summer break from college. He and the woman harvested the button-shaped seed from the peyote cactus. Then they ground it into powder and capsulated it for easy usage.

Chemist claimed the recreational use of mescaline got him through the academic rigors of college. Not only that—the violent lovemaking with the woman under a fantasized cloud of eroticism was unworldly. One other benefit was derived for the value of mankind. The psychedelic alkaloid from the peyote cactus had been used in religious ceremonies for his ancestors. Weren't they on the threshold of such an event?

Hans Schmidt didn't object, figuring anything reasonable would settle him down. He willingly swallowed the pills handed to him. Chemist convinced him not to return to his hospital home but to rent the room next to his. It was vacant. Chemist figured it might be useful for his strategy tonight. His room had a door that opened into the adjacent room designed to accommodate larger families.

Hans believed it was a great idea. *Sallie might be able to join me if Drake is too drunk and incapable of romancing her tonight. She's always flirting with me. The beauty could lasso any cowboy she'd set out to seduce. Back at Teddy's Tavern, I thought she squeezed my family jewels when we were seated across from the two boozed-up old pals. Hey, stranger things have happened to me when I put my Romeo playact in motion.*

Hans decided to rent the adjacent room. He lurched up and sped out the door toward the front office, almost losing his balance—his motor skills befuddled. Upon arrival, he was greet-ed by a grubby old man with a handlebar mustache who had been snoozing on a beat-up loveseat behind the office counter. Few words were exchanged between them. Hans tossed a twen-ty-dollar bill on the counter. The old man swiped it quickly and shoved it into the front pocket of his dirty bib overalls.

Five minutes later, Hans stumbled out the door with a room key—no questions asked—no registration form completed. Chemist suggested he stay with him until they were scheduled to meet Drake and Sallie for the planned dinner later that evening at Cantina Classica.

Schmidt agreed with the friendly giant who'd entered his life and was eager to help him out. He had compassion for Drake's friend and his hard-to-believe history. For some reason, he believed the strange man harbored a streak of uncontrollable violence. Hans knew he shouldn't return to the hospital in the condition he was exhibiting at the time. Chemist assured him he'd be feeling better and to look forward to a tasty Mexican dinner at the popular restaurant.

Hans had eaten lunch on one other occasion at Clarisa's place. He preferred an outdated German restaurant down-town—homey food not seasoned like a jalapeno bazooka.

Chapter 26

Sallie and Drake entered the Cantina Classica that evening in a happy party mood. She set aside her disturbing thoughts about the unpleasant episode she'd experienced the other night at the restaurant. Hans Schmidt wasn't with them that first evening she'd met Chemist. She recalled Drake's Indian friend was a first-class asshole. *He stared me down as though I was interfering with whatever he was trying to accomplish with Drake.*

Hans was wandering around the back of the restaurant out of sight and in a state of total confusion. He didn't remember how he got there and slipped out the back door. He perked up when he noticed Drake's red Lincoln SUV parked in a handicap slot. He climbed in the front driver's seat and dozed off.

Drake led Sallie to a table in the back of the restaurant near the restrooms. A Mariachi band was playing Mexican music in the far corner of the busy restaurant. Each band member was dressed in a white shirt and vest, colorful tie, and long black pants.

Ten minutes later Drake and Sallie were joined by Chemist, the hulking man with a mean face and traumatized hands. He was wearing a blue and red bandana tied around his thick neck.

Chemist nodded to Sallie and hugged Drake. All three had enough alcohol still running amok through their systems. They didn't question Hans Schmidt's absence from the gathering.

The two men pulled their chairs together and ignored Sallie. She was no longer a participant in their game, sitting aside with her arms crossed and staring around at the other customers.

Chemist and Drake's moderate temperaments changed in ten minutes. The two men began screaming profanities at each other. Sallie swirled about and tried to calm them down—no luck. Drake and Chemist continued to shout and curse at each other. A passing waitress cautioned them to be quiet. Several customers seated near the arguing men left their half-eaten meals, repulsed by the madness happening around them.

Clarisa was on duty at the time and came over to investigate. Chemist shoved her aside and told her to get lost and mind her own business. Sallie got up, brushed past an astonished Clarisa and raced out the front door, screaming obscenities as she left.

Outside the restaurant, Hans snapped out of his catnap and glanced through the side window of Drake's car. He was vaguely aware it was his friend Sallie getting into a taxicab in front of the restaurant. The cab then spun away quickly.

Where the hell was Sallie going? She knows the motel where I'm staying because I had texted her earlier after I had rented the room. Maybe she's heading there. I'm beyond hope that she will have sex with me if I can get my downstairs' equipment aroused enough to engage her fantasies. I think she knows Chemist also has a room in the dump. But where is Drake staying? At his apartment?

His head began to throb again. He squeezed hard on both sides of his forehead in despair. Hans begged for the pain to rush out the top of his head. He popped in two more pills Chemist had stuffed in his pocket to use in case he needed immediate relief. He dozed off again.

An hour later, the scene inside the Cantina Classica had drastically changed. The Mariachis had returned from their break and assumed their musical sets. Drake and Chemist left the restaurant, laughing and slapping each other on the butt.

Through an advanced fuzziness clinging to his brain, Hans Schmidt sensed the exact moment when Drake and Chemist hopped clumsily into the back seat of Drake's car. They began a ritual he couldn't comprehend.

Chemist put on a pair of surgical gloves from a small bag that was left in the car. He still had a small supply of cocaine in his small sack. Next, he pulled out a hypodermic syringe and injected Drake with the drug that caused the man to shriek, then began to shake and start giggling. A ceramic pipe with a bulb on the end was also in his sack of illegal "goodies" but wouldn't be used tonight. Instead, he lit up a marijuana-laced black cigar.

Chemist became fully cognizant of Hans squirming upfront in the driver's seat. "Hey there, you creep, stop reaching back here at Drake. Let him be. He's at a new, all-time level of excitement. Don't interrupt his glorified mood in any way. Aren't those happy pills still working for you? Chemist reached in his back pocket and got out two more tan pills. Here, Hans, toss these down your fucking throat right now."

Hans did as he was directed. He gagged as each pill went down, anxiously waiting for the expected surge to ignite him.

"Now control your abominable anxiety you squirming shithead," he shouted at Schmidt. "You're getting on my nerves. If you want to live another day, disregard us. We're rehashing old times entertaining ourselves. You aren't allowed in this family picture. Think about that slut Sallie Sake. The street broad's got the whole tied-up gift package. Jackoff if you have to, but don't screw with us."

Hans looked askance and slid down deeper in the driver's seat, the steering wheel caressing his engorged crotch. He

Murder in a San Antonio Psych Hospital, Revisited

stared up at the blinking, bright neon sign on the restaurant roof. It was humming a soft lullaby to him. *Was it the words of "My Sweet Lorelei" or another tune so dear to my German heart?* He grinned and left the two alone in the back seat to enjoy their mutual ecstasies.

Twenty minutes later Chemist told him to wake up and switch places with Drake who was going to take the wheel. Hans had a difficult time processing the request. The words directed at him intermingled with the soft humming he was enjoying. Then the appeal became a stern verbal directive.

Hans continued to exist in a daze. Chemist leaped out of the car, opened the front car door and punched him in the face, yanked him to the ground. Then he stomped on his chest several times. Blood began a slow creep down Hans' face. He didn't know what was happening. Maybe the car door hit him. He didn't care. He'd live another day.

Hans switched places and slid into the back seat already vacated by Drake. The befuddled Drake tip-toed to the driver's side, pulled hard on the steering wheel and then slipped in. Chemist positioned himself directly behind Drake.

"Buckle up, sports fans," Drake shouted. "We're going for the mega spin of our young lives—one you'll never forget. If you think motoring a race car in the Indy 500 gets it on, you'll chill out on a few happy laps around the Alamo." He backed out and eased the car to the street.

Chemist looked closely at Hans, then pulled him to his chest. "Wipe that blood off your repulsive-looking face, Schmidt. You look like Bozo the clown. Take that skinning knife out of the pouch in your back pocket and hand it over here," Chemist commanded. "Now, dopehead, not five seconds later."

[180]

Drake was higher than a forked-tail bird of prey singing, "♫ Off we go . . . into the wild blue yonder flying high . . . into the sky ♫." The car was racing down Roosevelt Street, bouncing off the fenders of two parked cars and began to slow down before jumping the curb coming to rest.

With his left hand, Chemist reached over the front seat headrest and grabbed Drake's forehead. He pulled the man's head upward. Griping the skinning knife in his right hand, he slashed Drake's throat wide open. Blood sprayed all over the windshield and most of the dashboard. In the process, Chemist nicked his left hand with the sharp knife. "Son-of-a-bitch," he yelled in pain, his blood dripping down the front of Drake's shirt.

Hans Schmidt ignored the vicious assault on Drake's life but couldn't stop laughing. "Wow, that was some wild-ass shit," he exclaimed. Getting got out of the stalled car, he waltzed around to the driver's side and opened the door. Drake was slumped over the steering wheel, his body quivering in jerky motions as he bled out and muttered, "Ya nooo . . . gooood, ahhh . . . prick I ... I —"

Drake was dead.

"Push the dead fucker over to the side, get in and restart the engine," Chemist screamed at Hans. "We gotta get this wreck outta here. You know the city. Wipe some of that stinking blood off the windshield so you can see out. Find someplace where we can dump the dead body."

Hans thought for a minute and then shouted out with joy. "I got it. I got it. We're heading just a few blocks away from my favorite stomping grounds. We're taking Drake back home."

"What the hell are you talking about, Schmidt? You better straighten up. No more medicine shit for you."

"We are going to joyride over to Mission Oaks," Hans giggled. "The big Dumpster near the staff parking lot is beckoning for Drake's inglorious remains."

Hans started the engine and sped off. He was delusional on the resupply of magic pills Chemist pushed on him when he and Drake came out of the restaurant and got in the car. The additional pills sustained the brain freeze, then released.

Mid-morning darkness greeted them in the parking lot behind the hospital. A slight drizzle scattered droplets across the windshield. It was quiet. There was no evidence of activity in the entire area.

"There it is, sir," Hans pointed and whispered. "The new tomb of the unknown zealot."

"Pull up by the Dumpster and let's get this marvelous christening over with, you fool." Chemist was anxious to get rid of the dead man and leave the area as fast as possible. He'd noticed some vehicle activity several blocks over.

Hans parked alongside Drake's burial chamber, then got out of the car. Chemist joined him. Hans jumped up on the dented hood and waited for the entombment to begin. It reminded him of sneaking into a theater to watch a horror show on the big screen. He sat down on the hood, then slid to the ground.

The assassin opened the front car door and pulled the dead man's head over to him. He then forced the mouth open and nipped off the end of Drake's tongue with the skinning knife. He inserted damaged organ down the wide slit in the dead man's damaged neck.

"Hey, man, why'd you have to do that?" Hans cried, then stood up next to the front-dented bumper. "He has to talk to his creator and beg forgiveness. No, that's not how it goes. He

[182]

needs to plead long and hard with Satan not to burn him into the smoldering ashes of hell."

"Stop blabbering," Chemist shook the knife at him. "I'm in no mood to listen to your stupid dissertation, little dopey man. We're in a hurry here."

Then Chemist tugged the dead body out of the front seat, slung it over his shoulders and heaved it inside the Dumpster. One leg was left hanging outside the opening. Chemist reached into his pocket and pulled out the index card Jase Lozen had sent with him from Houston.

"Come over here, Hans, buddy. Take this card and tie it to Drake's tennis shoe with one of the shoelaces."

"Huh, what's that, his last will and fucking testament?" Hans laughed out, then began to quiver and lose his balance. Confusion, loss of anything rationale all of a sudden riveted him.

"Something like that," Chemist said. "Pull yourself together and do it now, you idiot. We got to scramble out of this sick graveyard as soon as possible." He scanned the area again. No traffic was heading their way.

Hans tried to read the note, but the prevailing darkness wouldn't let him. He unlaced one shoe, poked a hole in the corner of the index card with his motel key and affixed the note to the shoe.

Chemist had climbed back in the driver's seat, cranked the ignition and then spun the vehicle around, ready for a quick retreat. At the last second, Hans vaulted at the opened passenger door, grabbed it with both hands and swung in. His feet were still dragging along the parking lot tarmac as the car sped away to the neighboring street.

[183]

"Where are we headed?" Hans asked as a series of wheezing and coughing overcame his irrational thoughts and speech. He lost control of all bodily mechanisms, then puked chunks of vomitus all over himself.

Chemist reached over and punched the sick man hard on the side of his jaw. "You vile bastard, go to sleep. I'll wake you when we get to the motel."

Schmidt was still conked out when Chemist pulled into the motel parking slot. He tossed the dead-weighted Hans over his shoulders and struggled to open Schmidt's motel door. It was locked. He dug into the drugged man's pocket and pulled out the door key. He went inside the darkened room, felt his way around, then tossed Schmidt onto the nearest twin bed.

Chemist went outside to the blood-spattered car and looked around to see if anyone was lounging around in the area. All clear, he quietly drove the car to the back of the motel. He was able to hunt around and find a water hose. It took a long time in the darkness to flush out the messy interior of Drake's Lincoln SUV. He washed the blood and other residual human waste down the nearby drain.

Chemist's contract to kill Drake was now fulfilled.

Chapter 27
Meanwhile at Mission Oaks

Hospital officials had been pleased with the feedback they were getting from Evelyn Augustin, the new medical examiner. However, their optimism for a quick resolution of Percy Radcliff's murder never materialized. The TCCV's legal counsel shattered their resolve with his threatening assessment. The leadership of TCCV was in a quandary, wondering if this entire undertaking was a huge mistake. Law enforcement was not close to solving the terrible murder in the hospital dayroom.

Week after week they were no nearer to rounding up the killer and solving the mystery than when the group had last met. Every clue, every mistaken identity and every reported location of the suspect moved on without success. The Houston officials of the TCCV finally recommended the FBI be brought into play. When queried, the federal agency determined it wasn't a crime that fell within their realm of exploration.

Despite the adversity, Howard Hill was satisfied with the clinical progress of his appointed staff at Mission Oaks. Bounder developed new and exciting methodologies to enhance the clinical treatment of hospital patients. Donna Mae Phelps, the relatively new recreational therapist transformed the rooftop swimming pool into a major hub of activity for the elated patients. Eduardo Munoz and Lefty were ecstatic for a comical reason. They were voted "best warriors most likely to succeed at sea" by the grizzled military veterans.

Molly Pritchard and Marco Simone weren't as successful.

The residents at the adjacent long-term care facility were a constant thorn in their collective sides to maintain a physical and mental stimulating agenda.

Before Hans Schmidt had disappeared, the staff had commented about his continued weight loss. One staff member had observed Hans was not eating properly and often skipped meals. Others viewed him as nothing more than a skinny scarecrow with his sunken eyes and straw-like course blond hair.

Sallie Sake was another challenging patient. She had a habit of wandering from the campus too often and without signing out. Then one day she'd vanished entirely.

Few residents could tolerate Eduardo's eccentric behavior. Lefty was fine, but several other long-termers had refused rehabilitation and signed out against medical advice.

Molly was not as assertive as her position demanded. To the contrary, Marco became more rigid and demanding.

At Howard Hill's request, Tam Lozen sent a consultant to work with both Molly and Marco. They had agreed that an external review of their performances might prove helpful. Neither were intimidated by the more mature and nationally recognized expert in hospital operations.

The change was inevitable, and a major improvement became evident soon after the consultant's visit. The staff at the acute care hospital began to work more closely with the staff at the long-term care facility, a much-needed cooperative effort. Treatment plans and subsequent execution were reviewed daily, not semi-weekly. A degree of patient satisfaction was noticed as the result of a revised management approach conducted by Molly and Marco. Even Howard Hill noticed on his unannounced visits the patients seemed less combative and more open to constructive suggestions by the clinical staff.

[186]

It didn't take long before another far-reaching setback raised its ugly head at Mission Oaks Treatment Center. The cataclysmal aftermath was fierce enough to cripple and become the final blow to management and ownership—not to exclude the patient population

The affair happened on a murky dark and wet early morning when the hospital housekeeper approached the large Dumpster behind the building. She switched on her iPhone flashlight as she neared the huge container, having tripped over an empty cardboard box the previous morning.

As she stuffed a huge bag of garbage under the slightly opened big lid, she screamed out in revulsion. A stubby leg with a bloody tennis shoe wrapped around the ankle was suspended over the side of the trash receptacle. Her iPhone light picked up an index card with four squiggly words tied to one tennis shoe. The Dumpster contained a dead body covered with some food scraps, medical refuse and soiled paper plates.

The woman was horrified, racing back to the rear entrance of the hospital not daring to fully open the lid and inspect the body. To her dismay, the door was locked. She began screaming unintelligible gibberish at the top of her lungs.

The housekeeping supervisor was coming to work and turned to park his auto in the lot behind the complex. His headlights honed-in on the shocked employee pounding on the rear door of the hospital. He jumped from his car and raced to her aid. He was unable to decipher her babbling comments. She was crying and pointing and jumping up-and-down and made no sense.

The supervisor unlocked the hospital door and ushered her in. She finally regained her senses after settling down in his office. Sobbing, she told him about the body in the Dumpster.

[187]

Within twenty minutes, a team from the Metro Police Department arrived announcing their presence with whirling red rooftop lights and blaring sirens. At the same time, other hospital personnel began arriving for work. The neighborhood was now awakened as the armed officers disseminated to begin their investigation. The dead man was a respected and popular hospital employee.

He'd only been known as Drake.

Chapter 28
Back in Houston

Tam Lozen was in a quandary after he had last chatted with Hans Schmidt. Something major was amiss. He couldn't put his arms around the disconnect. Schmidt was supposed to be manufacturing their bomb.

I should've been more cognizant of the unprogrammed ramifications of his paranoia when I visited and finally recruited him in that lousy Houston psych hospital.

I championed him to the TCCV admissions manager. His heroic actions in Afghanistan warranted his selection to our new program in San Antonio. Nobody on the board disagreed with my sentiments.

Schmidt appeared willing to accept the societal prejudices against our culture and how we planned to avenge that bias. Perhaps I misread him when he told me his mother was shipping the footlocker with the explosive supply parts to Mission Oaks Treatment Center. It was scheduled to arrive after he was transferred there.

Tam's thought process was interrupted by the unexpected call from his son. Jase was phoning from the tribe encampment.

"Jase," Tam mumbled. "I'm shocked to hear from you. However, you should know better than calling me on an open line. Hang up and go through the security protocol we've developed. You should've remembered that I had that requirement stamped in you thick head long ago."

A few moments later, Jase was on the line again. "Father, I know we've grown apart over the past several years. It's time we work together on the embryonic final plan you embedded in my brain, then nourished repeatedly while growing up. I've matured many times over in bringing those ideas to reality."

"Yes, son, becoming a glorified grave-digger was a brilliant scheme to get where we needed to be."

Jase was annoyed at this undignified reference to a highly complex career choice. "I resent your frame of reference to my graduate training and successful explorations. I knew you wanted me to become a career soldier in the army—anybody of average skill can make that choice for his or her country. You seem to have forgotten I became one of the leading bioarcheologists in the field."

"Yes, I'm aware of that," Tam said without emotion.

"The Bureau of Indian Affairs even awarded me their 'Lifetime Achievement' gold-framed certificate of distinction. If it weren't for my skillful discovery in San Antonio, we'd never have found the overwhelming rationale for our grand plans. Look where it's bringing us."

"Refresh my memory, son. Two major events have lingered in my deteriorating mind over the years that need rehashing," Tam laughed.

"You got to be kidding me," Jase fired back, unhappy with the direction the conversation was heading. He was not read-in on his father's recent hospitalization for a series of mini-strokes and now reportedly in the early stages of recovery. At Tam's insistence, medical authorities were directed not to notify his family. They needn't be concerned about his failing health. It would be an unnecessary detriment that would bog them down and complicate the success they're striving for.

[190]

"Allow me to remind you, father, our courageous people are now laboring side-by-side to fulfill the all-encompassing pledge catechized by your leadership. Do you want me to spell out the specifics for you? No. Hold your tongue. I had the opportunity to recertify physical evidence of the scattered remains of the Coahuiltecan Indian tribe in various locations throughout San Antonio. Without my persistence, we'd still be floating around like a buoy at sea with lack of direction."

"Of course, Jase. During your time of 'blowing your own horn' with that wonderful declaration, I was sitting on the TCCV strategic planning committee that recommended the purchase of the bankrupted, aged psychiatric facility near the San Antonio River. I boned-up on the history of my heritage and petitioned the city library to make certain historical documents available to me. They had been retired in the library annex across town. Initially, I was denied but persisted and succeeded in having them released to me. I frantically leafed through the numerous chapters I was interested in."

"Yes," Jase said. "I remember that."

"How in the world could you ever forget the specifics?" Tam stated as his voice started to quiver. "Never mind. I learned that the land I had zeroed in on was first cleared for a hotel to be constructed on the site of our present hospital complex. The hotel ultimately failed, and a group of psychiatrists bought the property and repurposed it as a mental health hospital. Their efforts were noteworthy, but the hospital also failed."

"I seem to recall that," Jase said.

Tam wouldn't slow down. "We jumped in with an offer that was accepted and purchased the property. I alone knew that the buildings were constructed on the sacred burial grounds of our forefathers. Not to alert TCCV officials, I secretly had you travel to San Antonio and covertly corroborate my findings. Your education and documented success in your field could not and would not be challenged."

"Thank you for the chronicles." He noted his father's rapid breathing and voice fluctuations. "Now, what was the second major event you wanted to go over?"

"Um, let me think. Oh, yes, it has to do with relocating the tribe from their safe-haven in Louisiana. You had no authority to do that. I've been the leader of our oppressed clan since the inception of the grand vision—the goal to restore our dignity and rightful place in the world."

"Yes, father. How did you know we moved to Texas?"

"Skyhawk, the man you call Chieftain."

"Huh, what the hell," Jase expressed with skepticism. "Skyhawk?"

"Yes, sir. I grew up with his father in New Jersey. Both of our parents picked blueberries and strawberries as seasonal migrant workers. Every summer we headed north to Maryland and New Jersey. When I was eighteen, I declared my independence and decided to remain in the area. No more shuttling between South Texas and the East Coast. Skyhawk's father and I followed different paths to adulthood. He moved to Newark to labor in the local industry. I joined the military to fight wars against our adopted country."

"I'm proud of you," Jase said. "I'd would've done the same thing under those trying circumstances."

Tam ignored the comment and continued. "I learned through various reliable sources his son Skyhawk was a problem—running in gangs, getting in trouble with the police. I contacted my old friend and offered to send the young troublemaker to one of our progressive reservations in New Mexico. The rest is history."

"Father, I hate to tell you this. Please bear with me. Skyhawk is no longer the leader. Our group in South Texas was falling apart when I got back from my Bureau of Indian Affairs consultancy. Morale was at an all-time low. Some of the underlings told me he was absent for long periods. They said he found a pretty young maiden and stashed her in a quiet village near the border town of McAllen. Skyhawk lost sight of our crusade for justice. Drastic measures had to be taken. I relieved him of all his responsibilities and resumed my rightful place as head and master of the tribe."

"Why didn't you—"

The encrypted communication device went dead. Tam forgot there was a restrictive time limit on the equipment. Sometimes the short-wave signal drifted. He figured his son would call him back. He didn't.

Tam was exasperated. He needed to get on the same page as his son. They seemed to be working in opposite directions. It was naptime. He was getting too old and much too fatigued to re-establish the call with his son. Tomorrow would bring another set of frustrating news.

Jase slammed the transmitter device down on his lap and stared at it. *Was this my father I was talking to? He seemed distant and spoke with a fragile voice. If we are going to succeed in our quest, I must get him refocused. He's been in the driver's seat too long—I have to take the wheel. It's time to run up to Houston and surprise him. Maybe, I'll find time to visit San Antonio and see Molly. Chances are it might be the last time we are in this world together as one unique family.*

He walked outside his hut and surveyed the sprawling grounds of the complex. The young braves were undergoing a complex rifle drill led by one of the senior associates he recruited from Laredo. They were inspired, well-conditioned soldiers readying themselves for the ultimate battle. The two sons of the deposed Drake were leading the competitive scoring chart. *Those are good kids. At the appropriate time, I will sit with them and tell them the rest of the story about their father, but not before the successful execution of our end plan.*

Jase relaxed watching two female participants keeping up with the more gung-ho males. There had been a drastic change since he relieved Chieftain and took charge. The whole camp welcomed him back as though a rebirth befell them. He decided not to participate in the Chieftain's family preparation for ceremonial burial in the adjoining county. The interment took place on a small, Indian-owned farm. Only the immediate family was in attendance. After the entombment, no family members returned to take up arms in the hallowed campaign.

Everything appeared to be in order except for the explosives. The delivery means were already housed in the big shed. Two repurposed Humvees would lead the attack. His famous father and leader of the movement let the ball drop. Tam Lozen's favorite psychotic and emotionally challenged patient of German heritage had not followed through. Hans Schmidt was recruited and coached for the sole purpose of procuring the delicate high-explosive ordnance needed to pull off the planned onslaught of the complex in San Antonio.

He'd discuss the next move with his father when he visited him in either San Antonio or Houston. It was imperative to sort out and address other potential stumbling blocks that might arise and bring an end to their pursuit of justice.

Chapter 29

Tam Lozen was awakened early by a telephone call from San Antonio. It was from the police detective heading the investigation in the newest murder case. He'd been advised by his boss to contact Tam and advise him about Molly. She'd been asked to assist the department with the murder case. Tam objected. He felt her stability was needed on the job, not running around in circles with local law enforcement.

The detective was persistent. He knew Drake had visited Hans Schmidt often in Molly's long-term care unit. The murder was creating havoc among hospital employees. Most patients were living in fear they might be next on the killer's hit list. Without being asked, the Navy SEAL contingent grouped and developed a course of action. There would be no surprise attack on their combat-hardened lives.

"Go ahead, detective," Tam said. "Do what you feel best for all concerned."

Sallie Sake had been missing from the long-term care facility for several days before Marco Simone informed Molly of the disappearance. He wanted to round up Hans Schmidt to help him with his off-site search to find Sallie. Hans had a habit of popping in and out of the unit periodically as leadership relaxed some of the standing attendance policies. Boyd Bounder had briefed him about Schmidt's footlocker shortly after it had arrived at Mission Oaks. Marco blew off Bounder's concern as a gross exaggeration. He knew how combat troopers collected harmless war trophies to brag about with the boys and girls back home. Several of Marco's prized possessions adorned the walls of his office.

Marco was aware Hans and Sallie had become close friends before both had disappeared. He followed their social and treatment programs carefully. He perceived both felt their ethnicities of Japanese-American and German-American were cultural deterrents in this close-knit environment. Marco was sure if he could round up Hans now, the patient could provide valuable insight regarding Sallie Sake's mysterious departure.

When Marco last spent some meaningful time with Hans, he had the gut feeling Schmidt was in a declining mode mentally. Clinicians disagreed, explaining the many ramifications of his mental health disorder. Hans had excused himself from further "pep talks" with Marco, feigning a spell of forgetfulness and fearful the fiery demons were on his doorstep.

Marco was disappointed. He'd never experienced an obsession with terror, suspicion, or distrust with mental health patients. He believed he'd earned Schmidt's profound loyalty as a fellow soldier who had faced the perils of combat operations. Schmidt was nowhere to be found. It was time to bring Molly aboard and advise her of both of their unexcused absences.

Molly had also sensed that something was amiss with Sallie. In the recent past, the woman had avoided her whenever possible. When confronted, Sallie had alleged spells of intense pain from migraine headaches. She had claimed the intermittent episodes put her out of action, not able to communicate with anyone or understand their concerns about her. She suspected that Sallie might've been involved in some mysterious way with Drake's slaying—simply intuition and not based on her work with the police. Now she was gone. Marco disagreed with Molly's view point. He thought she might be overreacting to her new role working with homicide investigators.

"Have you reported Sake's AWOL to the police department?" Molly asked Marco. "I had been disturbed about her change in behavior. She'd stopped going next door for her therapy sessions. To make matters worse, she hasn't been around to perform her bed-checking duties. Eduardo Munoz told me in confidence he thought she had a lover downtown. Before her final unexcused absence, he said he was aware she'd been skipping out periodically at night, probably to meet with that person."

"No, Molly, I haven't been in touch with the police. I'm still hoping Schmidt might show up in hopes he can provide more answers. You are the main point of contact now that you're working so diligently with them. The situation is an internal matter as far as I'm concerned—no hurry to involve them. Now I'm seeking your guidance on how to proceed in-house. I think our residents are showing signs of anxiety. They need clarification about some of our new and relaxed policy guidelines."

"Really? I'm astounded to hear that," she commented. "Maybe I need to quit my work with the police department and get back to my duties here. I feel certain demands on my position of leadership are not being addressed."

Marco tugged on his lower leg, readjusting the old prosthesis which was starting to irritate his lower stump more each day. He looked long and hard at Molly. "Well, what I just reported is true," Marco said defiantly. "Mission Oaks has a major calamity to deal with. Our patients sense it. They were militarily trained to act aggressively when confronted with possible injury, or even death. First the Radcliff murder and now the Drake killing dumped in our collective laps. Radcliff was an obnoxious loner here with just a handful of friends. Drake was immensely popular among the professional staff and the patient population. He

[197]

did everybody favors during his off-duty hours. We may be forced to close our doors."

"Don't jump to conclusions, Marco. The police don't think Drake was murdered on hospital grounds. I've been hip-to-hip with the cops for the past several days. They base their assumption on what they found on his body when it was retrieved from our Dumpster."

"Care to share that with me?" he asked, placing his hands on his hips.

"Sorry, Marco, I've been sworn to secrecy regarding the ongoing investigation. You know I've been officially detailed to work with the law enforcement folks."

"Yes, of course, I know that 'officially' means closed mouth. Everybody around here knows that. But can you at least tell me what the autopsy revealed? Then I'll get off your back."

Molly led Marco over to the soft chairs in her office and told him to sit down. She closed her office doors and brewed a Keurig for both of them. She sat next to him and patted his folded hands.

"Drake's throat was slashed, and his tongue cut off," she said sadly. "It was stuffed deep down his throat. Both legs were broken at the knees. Each hand was gashed by a razor-sharp instrument. The coroner surmised there had been a struggle with his killer. Blood samples on Drake's torn shirt and pants were analyzed. Genetically, they didn't match his DNA profile. He must've staged one hell of a fight before succumbing to a stronger and more lethal opponent. The killer also tied a weird note to the victim's shoe. It's being analyzed as we speak."

"Oh, my glorious God," Marco said with a hurt look. "That's horrific and miles beyond vicious. The killer must be found before he strikes again. But why Drake?" Marco shook his head with a confused look. "It had to have been someone he knew in the past who held a major grudge against him."

"We think it goes deeper than that, Marco. That's what I'm unable to share with you at this point."

"I get it, Detective Pritchard. Have you pinned Eduardo Munoz down about the 'mysterious' lover Sallie may have been seeing?"

"No, Marco, I want you to do that for me. I can't deal with the crazy goon anymore. He fabricates scenarios better than a bestselling fantasy author. You have a knack for extracting details from a person's brain cells that I lack. Let me know what you find out. I've got to run."

As she left her office, she bumped into an excited Clarisa Rios. Marco was still seated, massaging his neck and chin trying to make sense of their newest catastrophe.

"Whoops, sorry, I should've knocked," Clarisa apologized, looking concerned and several shades haggard.

"No problem. What's up?" Molly had no idea what brought Clarisa to her office.

"From the date I was awarded the food service contract for Mission Oaks, I've made it my business to get to know all the folks who work here and frequent my Cantina Classica. My first contact was with maintenance and your Drake character. He helped me so much in rewiring electrical outlets in the hospital kitchen after I took over the dining operations. I am in a state of shock learning about his death. One of the beat cops who frequents my restaurant told me you're working with them to find Drake's killer. Is that correct?"

Marco overheard the conversation, got up and walked over to Clarisa. He then turned red-faced in anger to Molly. "Don't answer that question, Molly. She has no right to be questioning you and poking her big nose in our business."

"Huh?" Clarisa mumbled, wondering why Marco was so agitated and upset.

He got in Clarisa's face. "You don't seem to miss a trick when it comes to our part of this world—do you? Have you seen Sallie Sake lately?"

"Oh, sure." She backed away. "Miss Sallie had been visiting my restaurant every night to eat. Usually, she was alone. It's strange though—she normally came in about fifteen minutes before closing time. I found that behavior extremely rude and discourteous to my staff."

"Why is that?" Molly asked, more subdued than Marco's intensity. She hoped to learn more about Sallie's prolonged absence from the unit.

"Well, my hard workers are more than anxious to get home with their families after a long and busy workday," Clarisa clarified. "Wouldn't you also feel that way?"

Marco looked at Molly, then said nothing. He wasn't going to engage himself any longer with this snooping woman.

Clarisa continued. "I spoke with Sallie once about her total disregard for politeness, and then let it drop until I had a chance to discuss her actions with you, Molly. During one of her first visits to my restaurant, she became hysterical, crying, swinging wildly and cursing me out like a salty sailor drunk on shore leave. She had to be restrained. I know she belongs here with you folks, and I can't figure out why she is free to come and go as she pleases. Can't you control your patients?"

Marco threw his arms in the air, did an about-face and stormed out the door.

[200]

"We're glad you called on us, Clarisa," Molly said gently, not offended by the piercing question or upset with Marco's bolt from the room. "We have a set of rules and living requirements for all our long-term guests. On a rare occasion, one of our patients will take advantage of us, and we have to reinforce our policies. Worse case, they are discharged. Sallie is a special person. She's been missing for some time now. We're worried about her not being here for treatment. Would you please call Marco the next time she comes to your restaurant."

"No ma'am, I refuse to lower myself. He's a maniac. But, I agree with you. She needs to be taken off the streets. It might be too late to do anything. I'm afraid she's in a heap of trouble, maybe way over her head."

"What are you trying to tell me, Clarisa?" Molly stiffened.

"Several nights ago, Sallie came in with Drake. I saw them take a table in the back of the restaurant by the restrooms. Ten minutes later they were joined by a hulking man with a mean face. He may have been an Indian. My cousin married one and they don't look anything like us Latinos. The man had a blue and red bandana tied around his thick neck. I didn't think anything more about the situation and went back into the kitchen to help the cooks."

Molly could hardly believe what she was hearing. This connection between Drake and the Indian startled her. She remained silent for a few moments mulling over the woman's comments.

"Please go on, Clarisa. You said Sallie came to your restaurant often. But, Drake and this other man—interesting to say the least. Do you think there might be a reason to believe this Indian could be the killer?"

"I don't know. It gets confusing. You know how hard I work at the two locations." Clarisa whimpered. "I think we finally upgraded the food service operations here."

Molly shook Clarisa by the shoulders. "Why didn't you call the police?"

"Hey, hold on sister, they didn't cause any material damage in my restaurant. They didn't commit a crime as far as I was concerned. What stood out was the big man's contempt for Sallie being with Drake."

Molly called the police lieutenant and advised him of this new state of affairs. He told her to bring Clarisa to the station right away.

After shedding tears and refusing to go to the police station, Clarisa finally relented. "I love Sallie and her friend Drake. The poor man had no reason to be slaughtered like that. I'll do what I can to find the terrible person who took Drake's life!"

"Thank you, Clarisa, I knew you'd cooperate. This whole state of morbid affairs is gaining a cruel momentum. It's going to hurt us all if it continues in this direction."

"I agree with you, Molly."

"Please wait for me outside in the plaza, Clarisa. I'll be there in a few minutes."

Clarisa left, and Molly summoned Marco back to her office. He marched back in with an apologetic expression on his unshaven face.

"First at the police hearing and now in my office," Molly unloaded on him. "If you ever act out again in that contemptible and temperamental manner, I'll fire your fat behind faster than a rattlesnake strike and send you back to the ghettos of New York! Do you understand me?"

"Yes, Molly, loud and clear. Sorry, I guess I'm the hot-headed Italian difficult to keep his mouth shut. This whole murder scenario at our place of business troubles me more than I can express in neatly packaged dialogue.

She continued to lock in her glare at him

"I'll reel it in. You have my word on this. And at the same time . . . you have my back."

Chapter 30

Mission Oaks Treatment Hospital did not witness the public relations onslaught they were expecting. Molly took the initiative to meet with the press, explaining the unfortunate murder took place elsewhere. She convinced them that an external radical group was targeting the hospital for some unknown reason. She assured them the local police department was on top of the investigation. Eduardo Munoz's lady friend in the media had coached Molly through the intricate sequence of events to placate the news-starved media types.

The affable Lieutenant Baldy called Boyd Bounder and Howard Hill to a conference at the coroner's office. They had been unduly patient waiting for information needed to reassess their strategy of gaining stability amidst another crisis. Baldy felt it was time to share more specifics regarding the ongoing investigation. Molly was already in attendance. Evelyn Augustin was expected momentarily.

"Thank you for coming over on such short notice," the lieutenant said apologetically. "I want to update you on our progress to find the killer. Let me also say that Molly here has been a helpful resource to our team of investigators. I know you're trying to determine who in God's world wants to destroy you. Tam Lozen sent me a detailed text several days ago because the FBI request by TCCV was denied. Their brain trust has also been working tirelessly to unearth something—anything that would help resolve the crisis. I noticed some changes in Lozen's speaking out recently. Not good is my assessment of the man's personality."

"What did Lozen have to say, Baldy?" Howard asked, not concerned about personality disorders. Nothing new with Howard—everybody had hang-ups to be reckoned with.

The lieutenant hesitated, then said, "I'll get to your contact with Lozen in a few minutes. The work you're doing for our brave soldier and sailor veterans is truly remarkable. City Hall has been impressed. Your hospital complex is one-of-a-kind, so to speak. You've improved the lives of those military warriors sent to you for care and rehabilitation. Everybody realizes the untenable situation you're in."

Molly smiled, wishing Marco was present to hear the compliment.

"The young men and women enter active military duty as healthy, impressive specimens," Baldy exclaimed. "When they leave their military commitment, we must return them in good health. Otherwise, we compensate them for the loss of any of their physical or mental fitness. Two murders on your watch in such a short period is unacceptable by any stretch of one's imagination."

Molly took the floor, impatiently moving past the lieutenant. "Tell them why you're convinced the murder took place elsewhere. Also, lieutenant, tell them what the killer's note said."

"Thank you, Molly. I'll defer those questions to the coroner . . . er, ME . . . as she likes to be referred to. Oh, she's coming in now."

"Good afternoon, folks," Evelyn said warmly as she took her seat at the head of the conference table. "I have some good news and some bad news to report. I'll go with the good news first."

There were quizzical looks on the faces of all assembled. Any sprinkling of news was welcomed—preferably good.

"As you already know, the corpse's throat was slashed, and the victim bled to death. The outer portion of his tongue was excised and wedged down the gap in his sliced neck. Why such an inhumane act? We don't have a clue. Maybe the dead man ratted out somebody of importance. Having said that, there was enough residual blood remaining intravenously to perform minimal analysis. You might've suspected the toxin Micotil would show up somewhere—yes, based on the other murder you folks dealt with. But it didn't. There were no toxins or other lethal poisons in his system, unless you lump cocaine abuse in that category."

Hill looked disappointed. Bounder appeared pleased.

"In summary," she continued, "The official cause of death was heart failure due to excessive blood loss from the devasting physical attack on the victim's throat. Death probably occurred within a two-hour timeframe. One other interesting finding showed Drake was also intoxicated. The alcohol content was elevated high enough in itself to cause his death. We also think he was of Indian heritage but can't state that unequivocally."

"Why did you try to determine his ethnicity?" Boyd Bounder asked. "Is there something we're not aware of here?"

"Tam Lozen requested the testing," she said loud and clear.

"Does that tie in somewhere with the TCCV investigation?" Boyd went on. "Do they think the radicals behind the murders are a group of Indian dissidents?"

"I'm not sure, but I'll table that thought for now," she said. "We also tested the bloodstains found on Drake's clothes. They weren't his—presumably the killer's, according to two of my young associates. I cannot make that assumption because the

[206]

stains were indistinct, probably old and clinically difficult to analyze. They could've been from another third party not involved with the assassination."

Howard jumped up and took the floor. His furrowed forehead making small waves at them. "What in the hell do we have
here? An Indian slaughtering another Indian?"

"Let's not go there at this time, Mr. Hill," Evelyn cautioned. "I don't have the time or inclination to describe the
complicated process of proving one's chromosomal origins beyond a reasonable doubt. Genetic variations sometimes referred
to as 'markers' vary considerably among different cultures.
Please allow me to continue."

"Sure, ma'am, I get it," he sighed loudly, then sat down.
"I'm as anxious as the rest of the people sitting here to find out
more about the attack."

"Okay, Howard, then allow me to proceed. First the good
news I alluded to earlier. We're confident the food and medical
refuse found on the victim's body did not originate from your
hospital or long-term care unit."

"Wow, that's a big sign of relief," Bounder uttered, his eyes
opening wide.

She continued. "How do we know this? At our request
your foodservice operator Clarisa Rios analyzed the food scraps
for us. They were Asian foodstuff leftovers, probably Thai or
Vietnamese according to the seasonings. She hadn't introduced
those delicacies to the patient population yet, waiting to gauge
their interests in a variety of foods."

"True," Bounder said. "Military types like the more traditional American offerings. You know, like pizza and burgers
with French fries. They are numbers one and two on the request
list."

"I would've expected that," the ME grinned. Howard didn't. He was always fed a wide variety of food offerings in the army, not greasy, high calorie fried food, but declined to contradict Evelyn Augustin.

She smiled, then continued. "Clarisa opened up with us after she'd agreed to the visit. Of special interest was the comment she'd shared with the lieutenant about the old next-door neighbor to your facility. She thought he might be the culprit. She's spotted him out her hospital kitchen dining room window walking his dog in the early evenings. Sometimes he's toting a small bag, presumably garbage. On more than one occasion he veers over to your Dumpster and tosses the goods into it."

"Hold on," Howard interrupted. "Shouldn't he have noticed the dead man's leg hanging out the Dumpster?"

"I asked Clarisa about that. She told me he always approached his garbage run from the opposite side of where the body was found—plus it was never in bright daylight. Anyway, the old gentleman probably has poor vision."

Howard nodded in agreement. He just had his optometrist renew his prescription to a higher reading level enhancement. The news about cataract formations was another matter.

The ME paused briefly, then continued her report. "Clarisa told me it's hilarious how the old geezer looks both ways, up and down the street. Then he crouches down and springs up, tossing the bag mimicking a LeBron James's three-point shot. She says the old coot makes her day and elects not to go after him to demand he cease and desist."

Laughter erupted at the coroner's story, a welcomed break from the serious discussion on the important findings of Drake's death.

"What about medical refuse?" Bounder asked. "How do you know it wasn't ours? Where did it come from?"

"Correct me if I'm wrong, Boyd, but you folks don't perform any surgical procedures in your psychiatric facility. Am I right?"

"Yes, a good point, ma'am," Boyd said. "Performing craniotomies is no longer a preferred choice to release the pent-up demons . . . so to speak. I trust you found standardized surgical instruments, bloody gauzes and empty medical containers used in surgical procedures."

"No surgical instruments, but some of the other items you suggested, Boyd. I spent two years in a surgical residency and never forgot the medical supplies and equipment we used in surgical techniques."

"Fine and dandy," Howard spoke up again. He was getting impatient. Too many facts and not enough conclusions. "Let's have the bad news."

Evelyn Augustin looked over at the lieutenant. "Do you want to take it from here?"

"Yes," Baldy said. "It's police work. I want to address the note attached to Drake's foot. Again, like the note left with Percy Radcliff, we needed to have the message interpreted. I don't know why the killer was so adamant about using a dead language to relay his message. The four words read *'Next, you all die.'* We believe the killer is the same culprit who killed Percy Radcliff."

Molly got up and stood next to the lieutenant and faced the others. "As you know, I've been spending time working with the police department in this case. I believe a radical group, possibly a militant Indian faction intends to take over our facility.

Please don't quote me on this, but my gut feeling is usually right on serious matters such as this."

"Isn't that a little hypothetical when we don't have more reliable facts to make that claim?" Howard commented angrily. "That would mean war!"

"Don't anybody in here start making conclusions —please people," Baldy exhorted. "That's what we're getting paid for. We've researched Indian radical activities over the past fifty years. This scenario could reasonably fit, although the two assassinations in our case are extreme. Protesting is the one common denominator of dissent—murdering people elevates it to another level. This is a serious business. We may have to call in the Texas Rangers to help us."

"Agreed," Howard said. "They're a damn good outfit dealing with these complicated cases. They know how to rope 'em and hang 'em."

"I have one last comment," the lieutenant said, ignoring Howard's picture of justice. "What I'm about to say further causes difficulties in completing the investigation. We're looking at possible inside collaboration."

"What in Christ's name are you implying here, Baldy?" Howard was smug and impatient challenging his old friend. Boyd Bounder had been a quiet participant but popped up when he heard the troubling allegation. Molly said nothing.

"I'll get to that in a moment, Howard. Please sit down and cool off, otherwise, I might have to ask you to leave."

Howard was red-faced but declined to get into a verbal confrontation. He wasn't about to leave, thinking the confab was finally concluding.

"Listen up, everybody," the chief said. "My final comments relate to the findings of our fingerprint analysis taken from the murder scene. I know you're aware we have a detailed fingerprint file on your entire staff. Employees agreed to it as a condition of their work contract. Not sure it was legit, but we turned our heads. The department had Drake's prints on file, loud and clear. Fortunately, you also asked us to print every patient and long-term resident you admit for care and treatment in your facilities—probably legal from a medical-forensic point of view."

"You bet," Howard concurred. "Right Boyd?"

Bounder nodded, pleased that something positive was said about his hospital.

The police lieutenant continued, "However, brace yourselves. We also conducted fingerprint analyses on all the significant debris found inside the Dumpster. Our investigators were thorough, hoping these actions would give us a clue who we're looking for, and this is what concerns me. It should trouble everybody else in this room."

Molly stiffened. She had already been advised of the results, but with a high degree of skepticism. "Go ahead and tell them, lieutenant," she said dourly.

"Sure, Molly, and again, thanks for your help with my team. We did find Drake's prints lifted off two instruments we retrieved from the Dumpster. We're not sure why he would've handled these items. The hypodermic syringe and ceramic pipe with a bulb on the end are used by crack cocaine addicts. Evelyn found some traces of cocaine in the cadaver but not in the drug apparatus."

Boyd Bounder was in awe and finally spoke up. "We have no evidence that Drake used or dealt with any form of narcotics. We knew he had experienced some run-ins with the law years ago, but those arrests didn't involve drugs. Maybe they belonged to the killer."

"We'll never know," Baldy said. "Our team also checked out the smudgy prints on the exterior face of the Dumpster thinking they might be the killer's but found nothing conclusive. The assassin had to be wearing some type of protective covering when Drake was encountered and disposed of. Surgical gloves perhaps."

"So, we're still stifled and without a clue who murdered Drake," Howard asserted, as he got up to leave, disgusted with the entire report.

"Er, yes and no, Howard . . . don't leave me yet," the lieutenant insisted. "Earlier, I told you to brace yourselves and here's the reason. There was another set of prints we lifted off the index card attached to the victim's shoe. We are somewhat confused here and—"

"Please get to the point, lieutenant," Molly urged in a loud voice. "Tell them!"

Baldy forced a fake smile. "The experts reading the prints reported they were perfect specimens. They belong to one of the patients under your care and control."

Bounder got up, confused, and at the same time sickened. He slumped back down in the chair. Molly closed her eyes. Howard grabbed a seat.

The lieutenant ended his report. "We believe one of the sick people involved in the hideous act of killing Drake was your own Hans Schmidt."

Chapter 31
Two weeks ago, the day after the murder

Hans Schmidt had awakened with a severe headache. The room was pitch dark. His head was about to explode like many of the roadside bombs he'd defused. His paranoia kicked in. *What did they give me last night? Do they also plan to kill me? I'm going to die a terrible death. I just feel it. The devil visited me and gave me no options.*

He stretched over to turn on the bedside table light to see if Sallie was still lying in the other bed. She wasn't. He noticed his dirty clothes were still tangled in a mess on the floor. He then checked the doorknob where she'd hung her backpack. It was gone.

Hans scanned the dirty and disheveled room, wondering what had brought them to a cheap motel south of town. *Is the weird stranger still renting the next room? He scrambled my mind, then tied it into a tight knot . . . the bastard.*

He struggled to get out of bed, grabbing the headboard and began to limp over to the beat-up wooden chair next to the bathroom door. The table light began to dim, got dimmer and then the bulb went dead. He was afraid to ambulate to the motel door and peer outside, fearing he'd fall flat on his face and not be able to get up.

The renewed darkness was challenging to negotiate most of his body movements. Nothing resembling his fluid action to locate a buried bomb in Afghanistan without being blown away.

Every bone in his body screamed in defiance. He collapsed in the chair and worked to clear his mind, then he scrambled over to turn on the lamp nearest him. It was flickering, not long before it would join its twin's demise on the other bedside table.

Hans leaned against the adjoining room wall to listen for any activity or unusual sounds. There were none. He looked back at the bedside table. The skinning knife was still sitting there next to the blue and red headband she wore last night. The pouch for the knife was missing. He didn't notice the tiny blood residuals adhered to the blade.

Why is that sharp knife on her table? Sallie Sake is as brave a person as I've ever known. It appears my suicidal friend decided not to go through with the final act. She'd shared that with me several times in the recent past she'd threatened to slice her wrist wide open in hopes of bleeding out to a glorious death. The demented wheel-chair jockey Eduardo Munoz claimed he'd saved her life on at least two occasions back at the hospital. Who would've believed the fool? I surely didn't.

Schmidt tried to recall the sequence of events last night that brought them to this flea-infested roadhouse. The pain in his head began to dissipate. The state of confusion was slowly being replaced by traces of rationality. Slowly, he attempted to slide the pieces of the puzzle back in place. His brain had returned to near-normal functioning. Miraculously, he was able to recall portions of the conversations and activities that took place over the past several days.

He shuddered severely at what might have happened to Sallie. He wrestled with the events surrounding Drake's disposal and the whereabouts of his imposing gorilla friend. And before all that—what about Tam Lozen's puzzling call about explosives?

Cringing, he reached over and grabbed the skinning knife from the other table. He moved it under his chin, the sharp blade against his shivering throat. *I might as well end it all here and now. What the hell, Sallie is not here to talk me out of it.*

The following morning Hans Schmidt was in bed, still alive. He was naked, reaching for two more Xanax pills when the motel room door came crashing down. His head was as heavy as a bowling ball. The intense sun raced through the flattened door and blinded him. Two uniformed cops with pistols drawn pulled him from the bed and slammed him to the floor.

"You're under arrest, pervert," the cop named Pudge screamed while waving his weapon at the petrified occupant. "Wrap that bedspread around your skinny waist. People like you should be hung in the village square in broad daylight."

Hans did as ordered and tried to chase away the fuzzballs obliterating his sight. Blinking like a berserk pinball machine, he saw the old man in ragged bib overalls pointing at him saying, "Yes, officers, he's the one. He checked in yesterday and I caught him pushing drugs. Two teenagers across the street ran in and told me he propositioned them, offering drugs to entice them to commit an immoral act. I'd shoot the fucker if I still had my old .410 shotgun handy."

"Take it easy, old man, I'll take it from here," Pudge ordered. "Go back to the front office and don't let anybody enter the motel grounds or leave this place until we are finished with this vagrant."

"Ain't no problem, officer. He's the only customer still in my motel. The big fellow in the next suite checked out earlier—didn't pay his fucking bill—said he never slept in the bed."

"Okay, pops, now please get out of here," Pudge said.

"Oops, sorry ma'am for the nasty word," the innkeeper apologized as he glanced over at the other cop, a short woman holstering her drawn pistol. "You all call me back if you need me for any reason."

"Search the room," Pudge instructed his female partner.

"Hold on, sir," Hans shrieked as he shook off the remaining cobwebs. "You need a warrant to do that."

"I got one, scumbag," Pudge said as he showed what appeared to be a typewritten document at Hans. Hans couldn't read the fine print. It was an old receipt for the monthly payment of the cop's leased sports car. The female partner had put gloves on and went to work while Hans was struggling with the towel slipping from his waist.

"Look what I found, Pudge," she said with a sly grin as she held out the skinning knife. "This dopehead has cut somebody up. I don't see evidence of any blood-stains on his thin body." She inspected the dimly handwritten words on the pillboxes found on the bedside table. "Furthermore, the loser has enough dope here to make us all happy-go-lucky and slightly crazy."

Pudge looked sternly at Hans Schmidt and said, "Yes, I get it. You drugged some young teenager, sliced up his face and stole his blue and red headband over there lying on the table. I think we got the makings of a new gang marching into our quiet little town."

The female cop read the Miranda dictum to Schmidt advising him of his right to silence. He ignored her and began to cry. She retrieved a washcloth from the bathroom and threw it at his face. Blood had begun to trickle from his swollen and broken nose.

"I'm calling my lawyer," Hans sniffled, and then picked up the telephone on the small desk.

"Not to happen, sonny," Pudge laughed as he slammed it back down. "No more stalling. You're going for a ride downtown with us. You can make all the calls you want after they book you. Grab your socks and jocks and let's hit the road."

The old innkeeper stumbled out the front office door and flipped "the bird" at the patrol car as it swung away from the motel.

Schmidt was booked, fingerprinted and interrogated for two hours at the police station. He was agitated, still confused and then became belligerent when he was escorted to a holding room. Lieutenant Baldy was informed about the new detainee and decided to join the interrogating detective. He listened intently to the detective's brief summary of events. He didn't feel right about the story and needed more clarification. Something was odd, way out-of-whack about the interview with Hans Schmidt.

Baldy turned to the interrogating detective and said, "He told you he was a nutcase and not sure why he was brought to the station. Is that right?"

"Yes, sir."

"Did you have one of our clinical people check him out?" Baldy showed concern.

"No, sir. He's no different than half the junkies we bring in here."

"How about his fingerprints? Any matches?" The police lieutenant wasn't happy with the detective's flippant responses.

"The results are on the way here as we speak," the detective beamed in triumph as though he'd just completed a four-minute mile."

The lieutenant told him to hustle over to the booking desk, get the print results and return to the holding room. He'd wait for the report at that location.

I think I've seen or heard of this Hans Schmidt character before—not sure when or where. I could be confusing him with some other gang members we've put behind bars. Oh, my Dear Jesus, yes, this thug is a murderer. ME Evelyn Augustin's last inquest revealed Schmidt's prints had been lifted from the index card tied to the deceased Drake's shoe.

The lieutenant had Hans Schmidt escorted to one of the cells, then went upstairs to his office. He called Howard Hill. He got a busy signal and called him three minutes later. Same results—busy signal—left an urgent message to return his call. He decided to ring Boyd Bounder at the hospital. Boyd's secretary answered and reported Bounder was at a tax meeting downtown with the county tax assessor. TCCV had filed a petition to make minor changes to the hospital's legal structure supporting their non-taxable status.

Baldy spun up from his desk chair, exasperated and baffled. Then he plunked down on the couch across from his big desk. He needed to think—try to put the pieces of this developing complex puzzle together in some meaningful format. TCCV-taxation-hospital-psychotic patient-assassin-Hill's non-availability. *What next? A jail riot?*

His telephone rang and he jumped off the couch. "Hello, Howard, I've been—"

"Huh, um, excuse me, hello," a Spanish-sounding dialect broke off Baldy's thought process. "Hello, Mr. San Antonio Police Lieutenant. This is Javier from the Federal Ministerial Police in Monterrey, Mexico."

Baldy strolled back over to his office chair and sat down. His state of confusion heightened. *Am I dreaming here, for Christ's sake? What's going on?*

"Excuse me, sir," the lieutenant said. "Who did you say you were?"

"Javier. We are the Mexican FBI. I have been directed by my superior to report a situation involving one of your people."

"What situation and who is one of my people?" Baldy relaxed, now conducting business in a police-like mode, excited with the new twist working away at his brain cells.

Javier hesitated, then continued. "Our mortuary has the remains of a big Indian hombre from your city. He was crushed over by a garbage truck near our Universidad de Monterrey. His poor body was dragged two blocks by the truck before the driver became aware he'd run over somebody. Sad and Unfortunate. Our policia are treating it as a homicide based on the facts and unusual circumstances."

"Interesting," Baldy said. "How do you know he is from San Antonio?"

"Our men searched his remains. Oh, sorry, sir. Our men searched his clothing and found a motel key in the back pocket. It was hard to read because it was scratched up. We could make out the words 'San' and 'Antonio' though. Has anyone filed a missing person report to your office?"

Baldy had no clue what this was all about. Nor did he care at this point. The Federales are making one big assumption, and he wasn't about to get involved in a witch hunt developing on somebody else's doorstep. He had all he could do to keep his sinking ship afloat.

"Sorry, Javier, we have nothing on this end for you." Baldy was ready to sign off but hesitated. "Wait a minute. Let me ask you one more question. Did your policia fingerprint the corpse? I think you have access to the worldwide bank of notorious villains."

"Yes, we do have that capability. And yes, we did fingerprint him."

"Tremendous," the lieutenant said. "What did you find out?"

Javier moaned. "Nothing registered, sir. His fingers were so scarred up from some incident or accident in his past life. His hands looked like big scorched stove mitts."

Baldy sighed. "In that case, I suggest you contact the US Consulate General's Office in Monterrey and let them investigate this affair. Thank you for calling, Javier. Goodbye."

John C. Payne

Chapter 32
Meanwhile in Houston

Jase Lozen sat by himself in a large hotel room on the outskirts of Houston reflecting on the activities of the recent past. After picking up Chemist at the San Antonio airport, they had motored east on IH 10 to establish a temporary command post in Houston. Chemist insisted on flying into the Alamo City, but Jase didn't want to remain in the San Antonio area for security reasons. Chemist had shared the hotel suite in Houston before being dispatched to San Antonio on his contracted mission.

The hired assassin had devised an acceptable plan to link up with his target. The next day the big Indian bid goodbye to Jase and ripped-off a pickup truck parked in a nearby mall. He drove back toward San Antonio to complete his assignment.

Houston provided Jase with a brief stopover to complete several matters on his to-do list. He visited his local bank and reviewed the status of the tribe's finances. Jase transferred some additional funds deposited in an off-shore Cyprus bank account. He was tempted to visit two older professional mentors but nixed the idea. Social meandering wasn't important enough to sidetrack him from dealing with his mission to glorify the ancient history of his tribe.

He would spend the remainder of his allocated days in Houston going over his manuscript of the upcoming campaign plan. Some minor modifications were necessary.

Two weeks later he received a text from Chieftain. He had mixed feelings when he read the attachment. It contained an article from the San Antonio newspaper covering Drake's murder. Chemist never sent him the mandatory after-action report outlining the step-by-step process undertaken to kill Drake. Though he did learn Chemist briefly visited Chieftain in South Texas before journeying across the border to Mexico. Chemist planned to link up with a professor friend who taught chemistry at Universidad de Monterrey.

The failure of Chieftain to detain Chemist at the encampment until he could get down there infuriated him. Chieftain didn't order the contract—he did. Chieftain wasn't the leader of the clan—he was. *It's time to relieve Chieftain of his responsibilities. I'll re-insert myself as the leader of the movement next week when I return to my full-time duties.*

Jase reflected further on the assassination. He was happy with the way it went down but perplexed with the results.

Drake was no longer a threat to our plans. That fact was irrefutable. Chemist was worth every dollar he was paid for eliminating the cancerous organism threatening the noble cause. According to the newspaper article, he did attach my warning note to the traitor's body. That should alert the hospital leadership they're all going down for how they've vandalized and desecrated our land.

However, I'm extremely frustrated with Chemist. His marching orders were to kill Drake away from the hospital environment by injecting the same chemical solutions used to eliminate Percy Radcliff. There was no need for the savage and spiteful bloodletting that took place.

Jase had been concerned there might be incriminating aftereffects from the vicious slaughter scene. More evidence in terms of blood samples, physical evidence identifying the location of the assault and potential witnesses could result in possible ties to Mission Oaks Treatment Center.

He didn't want his sister implicated in any way. However, he suspected his father was supporting the mission in some hyper-secretive manner. To make affairs worse, he learned in a follow-up text from Chieftain that Drake's tongue was removed and forced down his throat. *Why was that necessary? Was there an underlying animosity toward the victim? Chemist had to be terminated. That could easily be arranged. I'll contact World Funds, LTD again. Enough money in one's bank account can buy any-thing. I learned that simple axiom long ago when falsifying a report on an excavation disproving the existence of a time-honored culture in Columbia.*

Jase was still incensed with Chemist's failure to follow protocol. Before he checked out of his hotel in Houston, he sent a message to his contact at World Funds, LTD. It took two hours before he heard back. The contact scolded him and told him to follow the same security procedures he was forced to follow in his initial appeal to World Funds.

He hated the encryption sequences. He should've initiated the request by using the same "dark" internet channels he'd communicated through before. It was less cumbersome and just as effective on his part—maybe not on their end. The use of a short-wave radio interface was cumbersome. When he finally made contact, he was advised there wasn't enough information on Chemist's whereabouts to negotiate a new contract. Frustrated again by "the system" was annoying. He considered doing the job himself with the aid of a Mexican mafia group known for their extermination of unwanted political adversaries.

Jase spent two days attempting to establish contact with several of the cartels operating across the border. He finally connected with one willing to stage Chemist's assassination. However, the proposed arrangements became too complicated for his liking. He backed out. Jase swallowed his enormous pride and contacted World Funds one last time. He figured he had enough information on Chemist's planned visit with his friend in Monterrey to satisfy the phony financial organization's intake agent. *I'm draining our reserve funds to make this happen, but we can't live with a controversial, loose-cannon Indian threatening our survival with his disdain for following exact orders.*

World Funds relented after receiving more definitive information for the death warrant. The agent told Jase they would take the contract after he wired a million dollars to one of their offshore bank accounts. It took Jase time, but he did as directed. Within hours he received notification the funds had arrived, and a "burial consultant" had already been dispatched to Monterrey Mexico.

Jase checked out of the Houston hotel and drove a hundred miles to their haven in South Texas. The security guards in the outposts manning the outer perimeter defenses were thrilled to see him again. They shared in confidence how the entire movement was being jeopardized by Chieftain's failure to lead the warriors during his absence. They disclosed the fact he had remained on the sidelines allowing less experienced subordinates to design and execute the training protocols.

Meticulousness had been replaced by sloppiness. The young braves didn't mince words, hoping Jase wouldn't share their discussions with Chieftain.

It was past midnight when the security guards waved him through the series of huts and into the center of the encampment. The base camp was quiet. The only sounds heard were from a pack of coyotes yelping and interrupting the noiseless night.

In contrast, he missed the lowing of the livestock around the property caressing his ears in the solitude of the late evenings. As an aside, he laughed out loud. *I wonder if they've been immunized yet with the Micotil supply in storage. Life on the vast frontier had been peaceful—not in these trying times.*

Chieftain was rudely awakened by his young bodyguard. He was shocked to see Jase Lozen standing erect next to his straw cot but recovered quickly. He rose up, placed his arms around his leader and then led him to the hut serving as the council headquarters.

"I'm happy you're finally here with us to take control of our mission," the Chieftain said without conviction. "You've been away for a long time. The clan has missed you more than I can put into words. I often question whether your extended absence was worth it."

Jase stared him down. "Did you think I took the assignment from the Bureau of Indian Affairs for selfish reasons—for personal gratification, or what? The monies I earned was a necessity. We had to augment our treasuries. The excessive costs to relocate our people from Louisiana far exceeded the budget. You kept the books. Of all people, you should be thankful for my efforts to keep us solvent."

"Believe me, we're all beholden by your extreme sacrifice. But, the training to mold our young scouts has suffered through their lack of interest and motivation . . . which I don't understand. The brief presence of that butcher Chemist in our camp caused problems."

"In what way?" Jase asked.

"He was drunk most of the time. Even our medicine woman couldn't stop him from drinking our cactus tree fermentations. His stay here was a nightmare."

[225]

"Go on," Jase said.

"Our men thought he came here as your replacement. There wasn't an advance notification of his arrival. They hated the way the big Indian flaunted himself among the young maidens. They were in constant fear that he was going to rape them."

"And you allowed that type of behavior here in our sacred setting?" Jase was livid.

Chieftain didn't answer. He changed the subject. "I admit the thought of him replacing you had also occurred to me because you were negligent in keeping me informed. Chemist led me to believe he would be our new leader. He implied there were plans in motion to take you out."

"Really? It's difficult for me to believe things were that bad," Jase said, knowing he didn't handle Chemist properly. *I should've arranged Chemist's assassin the day after Drake's murder. Two eradications for the price of one!*

"Oh, yes," Chieftain continued. "One night he informed me he had a greater calling in Mexico explaining how an old associate needed him in Monterrey. The big thug left that beat-up pickup truck he arrived in and stole one of our vehicles from the garage. I should have killed him."

Jase said nothing, his anger rising like hot lava in a volcano.

"We need you back, my faithful leader. New challenges are pending. We need to move up the timetable for our final assault."

"Why," Jase sneered. Nothing made sense to him.

Chieftain hesitated, then answered. "Concurrently, we have to step up training and revitalize the entire compound."

"Specifically, what do you have in mind that you haven't already accomplished during my absence? Never mind."

Jase pulled out his Glock and shot him between the eyes.

Chapter 33
October 2017

Howard Hill was frustrated and in a terrible mood. His kingdom was collapsing in his lap. He feared he was a Humpty Dumpty falling off the wall. There were no "king's horses and king's men" to put him back together again. Tam Lozen was scary and confused every time he called—almost hourly. He was certain the TCCV spokesperson was going to fire him. Boyd Bounder wasn't any better off. Lozen had already threatened him. Molly wasn't around to run interference.

He decided to relieve the mounting pressures at Teddy's Tavern. The saloon was not busy at noon. A small Alamo tour group walked in, didn't see any activity they liked and walked out. Teddy Bear was behind the long bar inventorying his liquor cabinet. Hill slipped in through the front door and grabbed a barstool seat behind his friend, then clapped his hands.

"Jesus on high, Howard, you scared the hell out of me. Shouldn't you be working now? Word on the street hasn't spoken kindly about your serfdom over there on weirdo hill. Haven't Baldy and his boys found that killer yet?"

"I didn't come here to be harassed, Teddy. Give me a shot and a beer."

"No, I won't do that, Howard. I'm your friend. Colleagues don't listen to ridiculous demands."

"If you want to remain my comrade, you'll do what I say." Howard pounded the bar. His face rushed to a crimson blush, the veins on the side of his temples puffed-up.

Teddy lurched back, never having witnessed Howard in such a foul mood. "Things that bad, huh? I can tell it's eating your heart out. Coming off the wagon ain't going to solve the situation at Mission Oaks, my friend."

"I'm going to report you to the Inhumane Society, you mad dog," Howard shouted. "Now get me that drink or I'll jump over the fucking barrier and serve myself."

Teddy knew he wouldn't win this battle with his long-time friend. *I would need several allies to gain leverage over this maddened warrior. It's happened before, but Hill always found a way to regain sobriety again.*

"At your service, sir." Teddy pulled down a bottle of Jack Daniels and retrieved a cold can of Budweiser. "Help yourself, Howard. I got to finish this inventory. Don't have time for your juvenile outburst." He resumed his work at the liquor cabinet but kept glancing back at Howard through the big mirror next to the elongated wooden cupboard.

"Teddy Bear, things are fucked up over there. Baldy and his team of rookies can't get past first base. I think it's time for the whole department to be relieved by the mayor. My old troupe of Eagle Scouts would've tracked the killers down by now." Hill's cellphone jumped into action and startled both of them.

"Answer that damn phone of yours, HH. Are you deaf, or dumb? Probably both conditions as I see it." Teddy was disgusted.

Howard grabbed his phone off the bar. It was Evelyn Augustin from the medical examiner's office.

"Where are you now, Howard? We need to talk. Something big has come up and I think you need to hear what I have to say."

"Well say it, Evelyn. I'm all ears."

"No, I need a face-to-face with you."

"Agreed. Teddy's Tavern, across from the Alamo. I'm getting drunk." Howard had no clue to what the big news she was harping about . . . something good he hoped. *The woman gave no hint. Evelyn was always under control, damn it.*

"I know where it is, Howard, you're babbling. Slow down on the booze. I'll be there in fifteen minutes. Don't leave." *Under normal circumstances, I wouldn't be going to any bar during the day. Howard's situation alarms me. He needs help.*

"I can't wait," Howard said and hung up.

Teddy finished his bottle count and descended the small ladder. "So, what was all that about? You look slightly happier but still ugly as hell. Is the girlfriend not pregnant? The rich uncle dies, and you are about to inherit a million bucks?"

Howard explained that the medical examiner was on her way over. She had some new information to share about the murders involving Mission Oaks.

Twenty minutes later Evelyn popped through the tavern door. She looked around and was glad there were no other customers in the bar—wasn't sure about Howard's fragile mood. He finished his second shot and beer, then introduced her to Teddy. She acknowledged him as Howard led her to a table in the back of the saloon.

"Want something to drink?" Howard asked her.

"Not now. Probably tonight when I get home from work."

"Hey, we're sort of partners now, thanks to the crazy murders at my place of employment," Howard said with a forced chuckle. "How about drinks at my place? I don't know if you've had the opportunity to experience the activity around the Pearl Brewery. I live there."

"I visited once," she said. "Nice place, neat bookstore, great coffee shops. Yes, I'd like that Howard but one quick drink when I come over."

"I need something good to happen in my life," Howard said coyly.

Evelyn changed the subject and told him she'd received a text from an old medical school friend. They had been hip-to-hip in their earlier days living in Montreal. The friend was working as a professional associate to the county morgue director in Monterrey, Mexico. She told Evelyn that a recent corpse run over by a city garbage truck near the University stirred a deep interest in the staff. They weren't able to get fingerprints as requested by the policia because of his deformed fingers, apparently from old burn injuries of both hands.

"So, what caused the big hubbub?" Hill asked patiently.

"Not the dead man's hands, but what they found in his mouth and throat," she said. "Half of his tongue was cut off and shoved down the throat opening. My US-trained physician friend remembered reading about the death of your own Mr. Drake who was found in the hospital Dumpster. She subscribes to the Express-News because her parents live in San Antonio. Plus, she keeps up with all mortuary news and affairs in our various publications. That's her so-called life in the trenches of death."

"Interesting . . . but what's the correlation here?"

"Think hard about it, Howard. A piece of Drake's tongue was cut off and pushed down his lacerated neck."

"Oh, shit!" Howard shrieked. "Do you think he was the dirty thug who killed Drake? Has our beloved police lieutenant been wired-in on this?"

"Yes, I talked to him yesterday. He told me the Mexican FBI had contacted him because a San Antonio motel key was found in the dead man's pocket. Nothing was mentioned by their law enforcement about the tongue situation. That, my dear Howard, came from my trusted crony. You got to keep us morgue-types happy and entertained. We always scope for the 'big story' in our little domain."

"I'm going to call Boyd Bounder and tell him to get over here," Howard said. "He needs a slice of good news to ratchet-up his depleted mojo. The guy's taking this whole death scenario personally. I've noticed he hasn't been eating much lately, either. It's a rarity for the man who claims he could have been a famous chef rather than a hospital paper-pusher. I'm going to call Molly also. She's almost been as derelict as Boyd in the food chain department."

"Please don't," Evelyn said. "I'm against holding an informal inquest in a beer joint. Not deemed professional."

"I hope Teddy didn't hear that bit of slang," Howard mused. "He's sensitive about his place of business, a popular watering hole in the middle of town, frequented by thirsty tourists and local autocrats alike."

"Dead-on," she said. "I changed my opinion about this fantastic location near the Alamo. I'm going to call our police lieutenant and ask him to join us. I have to know what the department is doing since we last spoke yesterday."

"Baldy for Molly, but I also want Boyd here." Howard was assertive, the alcohol having a noticeable effect on his speech. She detected the change.

"As you wish." But no more booze for you today, Howard. That's an order."

He nodded timidly and then carried the bottle of Jack back to Teddy.

Howard laughed and told Teddy she was stopping by his place tonight for a quick drink. His rotten day just turned into an afternoon of glee and anticipation.

"Good move on your part, Howard. The little lady carries a big stick."

Howard and Evelyn both lugged out their cellphones and called their respective parties. Baldy showed up first. Five minutes later Boyd walked in, not knowing for sure why Howard called him. He would soon find out. Evelyn was first up.

"I appreciate you men coming over on short notice. Howard and I have been discussing the latest progress with the murders at Mission Oaks." Evelyn summarized what she and Howard had been discussing. Boyd Bounder was elated. Lieutenant Baldy sat quietly and let her finish the update before speaking.

"Thanks, Evelyn," Baldy said. "I have some more recent information that came in early this morning to add regarding this complicated murder case. My policia contact in Monterrey informed me that a professor of chemistry at the University visited him last night. Bottom line—the prof knew the corpse, an old friend who worked on a research project with him years ago in Spain. They had planned to meet in the science lab the morning he was run over by the garbage truck."

Evelyn jumped in. "Right, I forgot to tell Howard earlier that my mortician friend told me that the professor came in unannounced and made positive identification of the dead body."

"Yes, I was about to tell you folks all about that informative happening," Baldy said. "Please, there's more. Let me continue with my talk to the Mexican police official. It seems our big stiff was a renowned chemist who had published an environmental impact study on a project in Barcelona. You won't believe this, but the undertaking involved chemicals used to inoculate domestic farm animals to protect them against a wide variety of disease organisms. More specifically, those butchered for sale to raw meat vendors in the open market."

"Hold on here," Boyd interrupted. "Are we implying that the two chemists used Micotil in the study? You remember the chemical, or toxin, or poison or whatever. It was discussed in an earlier hearing that just about floored all of us."

Baldy smiled. "Yes, Micotil was one of the agents used in the study I just spoke about."

"Bingo!" Howard yelled out. "This monster was the mysterious beast who also killed our patient Percy Radcliff in the hospital dayroom."

"And let me add, the freaking animal who just followed up his malicious act and then killed Drake," Bounder said.

"Hold on here, boys," Baldy cautioned. "As much that I hate to admit, we can't officially make that correlation. We haven't confirmed the man's name or place of origin. Also, we're unable to validate he was physically present at Mission Oaks to commit the terrible crime—let alone wiping out Drake as an encore. If he were alive and on trial, his defense lawyer would argue the absence of proof connecting his client to both murders."

"So, where do we go from here, lieutenant?" Evelyn asked. "I'm satisfied."

"This is entirely above my pay grade," Baldy said. "I'll defer to higher law enforcement experts in Austin to tie these things together and develop their suppositions."

"Makes sense to me," Howard said. "They have more resources to delve deeper. Thank you from all of us. You did what you could at your operating level, Lieutenant Baldy."

The lieutenant acknowledged the compliment, then got up to leave. He hesitated a few long seconds.

Should I drop the bomb on them now? I shudder what they'll do when we all go back to our workplaces. He turned and faced them. "I have one other bit of news to drop on in your collective laps."

Boyd said with a bit of sarcasm, "Bring it on, Baldy. We're all ears."

The three sat down again, anxious to hear what the lieutenant had on his mind that he hadn't shared with them earlier.

"Alright. On my way over here, I received a disturbing radio message from my lead detective. I hesitated to tell you before because I had difficulty assimilating the impact of his message."

Evelyn wondered what other variables in the investigation could be thrown into the complicated mix. She'd seen it all in her young professional life.

The lieutenant took a deep breath and proceeded to inform them. "Your psychiatric patient Hans Schmidt just made a startling proclamation from his jail cell. His exact words were . . . "I killed Drake!"

Chapter 34
Reflecting back to the night of Drake's murder

Sallie Sake remembered the final scene at Cantina Classica with Drake and Chemist that led to her nightmarish experience and near death.

The men were going at each other so frantically, I feared they'd rip the Cantina Classica apart. I had tried to quiet them down, but it didn't work. I raced out the front door, screaming at the top of my lungs. I hailed a cab and told the driver to take me over to the same motel Hans Schmidt had rented. Schmidt had told me earlier I could stay with him while Drake was entertaining his friend in San Antonio. I told the old innkeeper I was Hans Schmidt's girlfriend and he let me in. I became hysterical, concerned beyond belief that something crazy was going down tonight.

Sallie shook off her frightful thoughts and downed what she'd labeled her miracle pills and chased them with a glass of water. She climbed into one of the twin beds, fully clothed and was sound asleep in a few minutes.

Schmidt and the goon Chemist barged into the room, shouting, clapping their hands and then clunking down on the bed next to Sallie. Hans turned on the bedside lamp. They were out of their minds—higher than a kite on something an excess of alcohol could never achieve. At first, they didn't notice Sallie, and then it happened.

Chemist came over to her bed and slapped her awake. He unhooked his belt and dropped his trousers. "I'm going to give you something that Drake can't do anymore, sweetheart Sallie." His tongue was thick, and his eyes appeared to be bulging out of their sockets. He was shaking in anticipation.

Hans came over and shoved him aside. "No, you fucker, she's mine. I invited her here tonight. Go and find your own woman if you have the guts to venture out after what you've done."

Chemist threw a hard left at his head. Hans toppled down to the floor. The big Indian, with his pants still hanging around his ankles, tripped over him. Hans reached over and grabbed a broken wooden slat from under the bed, got up and slammed it over the big man's head—then fell down again. They ended up sprawled out on the floor in some kind of comical daze, mouths opened wide. Hans tried to tell Sallie something but began choking and then began sobbing. He rolled over, upchucking bloody bile on Chemist's trousers. Chemist wasn't able to deflect the gushy, sour discharge.

Overcome by panic, Sallie high-jumped over both of them, grabbed her backpack still hanging on the inside doorknob and raced out the door. Drake's red Lincoln SUV was parked outside. She climbed in, hoping the keys were still in the ignition. They were. It smelled like shit inside the car, but she ignored the stench. She reached under the driver's seat and pulled out Drake's holstered .38 caliber, snub-nosed police special, stared at it and then tossed it on the passenger's seat next to her backpack.

Her fright turned into rage. She cranked up the motor and caught her breath. It was a horrendous night. *Where the hell was Drake? I wonder if something bad happened to him. I'm going back in there and kill them both. No, not a good idea.*

Sallie put the vehicle in gear and swung it around, heading for the front of the motel. Lights were still on. She saw the old innkeeper come out for a smoke and light up. She quickly shoved Drake's pistol in her backpack and veered off, not knowing where she was headed. *I don't care where I'm going to end up for the night, though I feel great relief to get away from this hellish place.*

The early morning sun was reaching out to announce daylight on the hard pavement underneath the IH-37 freeway near the downtown Houston Street exit. Sallie Sake was rudely awakened by a toothless, obese homeless man that had been sleeping next to her. "It's time for you to get the hell out of here, sister. A pretty mademoiselle like yourself is going to get tumbled real hard by one of these other creeps who makes his home here."

"Leave me alone, Bozo," she shrieked. "I felt your dirty hands fondling me hours ago. I can take care of myself."

"Hey, I'm no clown, for crying out loud. Please call me Charles, my baptized name. And no, darling, you don't have what it takes to defend yourself down here in the streets. It doesn't work that way. Look over there at those losers spread out on crummy blankets. I sheltered you from them when you crashed here a couple hours ago. Anyway, what the hell is wrong with you?"

Sallie didn't respond. She was searching for the answer herself. Her hair was disheveled, clothing was partially torn, and one of her shoes was missing.

"Why do you need to know?" she said curtly. "I didn't probe and ask about you. I don't care about you or your other has-beens sleeping down here. Everyone has their own story, so leave mine alone."

"Well, I'll be," Charles uttered. "I should' a let them have at you, a beautiful body like yours. I could' a charged admission—made me some easy money." He rolled over and tossed the missing shoe at her. "Square yourself away and boogie outta here, babe. Some lucky stud is probably out of his fucking mind roaming the city looking for your sweet ass. Go!"

"Alright—alright, give me five minutes and you won't see me again."

A metro police cruiser passed by, reversed gears and backed up several yards. The driver shot a glance over at Sallie and the homeless character.

"Everything okay over there?" he shouted at Sallie.

"Yes, sir. We're fine here. I was just arguing with my grandfather. He finally agreed to let me take him back home. We'll be out of here after he gathers up his belongings. Thanks for stopping and checking on me."

"Yes, certainly ma'am. Can I give you both a lift and drive him home?"

"No, sir, my car is parked around the corner. You have a great day."

The cop waved and then continued on his surveillance routine.

"Grandfather, you say?" Charles questioned her. "I'm offended by the age implication. I could be your husband, brother. Maybe even your father, but—"

Sallie cut him off and put on her other shoe. "I was about to tell the kind officer you just raped me."

"Huh? What the hell!"

She laughed. "No, I couldn't do that. Not after you protect-ed me and saved me from committing suicide."

"Suicide, huh? Why were you going to kill yourself?" Charles expressed a renewed sense of concern.

"Yes, I intended to take my life. Last night when I ran away from my motel room I was so stressed out. I don't even know how I got down here. Couldn't find my medications—must have left them at the motel."

"You were going to overdose on a prescription drug?"

"Yes." She stared away from him.

"Which one?" he asked, straightened up and frowned. "At one time during my illustrious life, I was a well-known and suc-cessful pharmacist. That is until I found a sweetheart drug that made me float to heaven and talk to my Creator whenever I took it. I was hooked."

She didn't know why she was sharing this sensitive per-sonal information with some street bum. Perhaps, she surmised, he showed genuine concern about her situation.

"They've been giving me Ketamine at the hospital," she said harshly—not proud, but matter-of-fact.

"No way," Charles asserted. "That's an anesthesia drug they use to put you to sleep. I read way back when I was in business they were experimenting on its use for suicidal folks. Is that what this is all about?"

She nodded, now embarrassed. *This guy appears fully legit. He seems to walk-the-talk.*

He puffed out his chest and lectured her, "Lithium or Clozapine might have been better for you. I felt a responsibility to tell those young doctors out of medical school what I know about mind-altering medications. I kept up on the latest and greatest. Are you hooked on that awful pain killer?"

"Well, yes, sort of, but—" She spun around, picked up her backpack and ran as fast as her legs would take her down Houston Street. She passed a small school, turned the corner a block away, and then disappeared out of sight from the freeway.

Sallie found a bench and sat down, out of breath but with a clear mind. *Things need to start getting better real soon. I got to put my life back together again. But where did I leave Drake's car last night? Oh, shit, I can't recall! Let me think.*

Chapter 35

Still, in a state of bewilderment, Sallie didn't notice a fat, meticulously dressed woman plunk down on the bench next to her. The woman thumped Sallie's right shoulder enough to bring her back to reality. She quickly put things in focus, sat up straight and rearranged her disheveled clothing. Sallie patted down her untamed head of long hair and looked over at the woman.

"You in trouble, gal?" the lady asked with a disturbed look.

"No, just taking a short break from my walk." *Where the hell did I leave Drake's car when I bailed out under the bridge last night?*

"Looks to me like you had an all-nighter," the mysterious lady went on. "Oops, sorry, I tend to blurt out the first thing that comes to this old schoolteacher's mind." She pointed back to a building near the freeway. "I was on my way over there. I teach classes in that school."

"I appreciate your concern, ma'am, I got to be on my way."

The schoolteacher looked at Sallie, then slapped her hands to her hips speaking in a soft voice, "You need help, woman."

"Thanks for the personal observation," Sallie said. "But, you need to tend to your little school kids. Teach them about minding their own business and not to talk to strangers."

"Oh, my," the teacher shot off the bench. "Look who's handing out advice, bitch. Another cute cunt walking our beautiful streets and dirtying the sidewalks at the same time."

Sallie ignored the slur and started to walk back toward the freeway. All of a sudden she recalled where she had left Drake's car. Spinning around, she headed to a parking lot next to a downtown hotel. The gleaming, red Lincoln SUV was parked next to several other vehicles. A note was attached to the wiper blade. Sallie tore it off, read it, ripped it into tiny pieces and let the wind carry it away. It was a citation for unauthorized parking.

She called to mind the friendly cop who was on patrol earlier this morning. Smiling, and with a huge sigh of relief, she dug the car keys out of her backpack and climbed in. Sallie punched the ignition button and let the car engine idle again, then reached into her backpack for a particular official document she had stuffed in a zippered pocket some time ago. She was going to take a minute to read it but flipped it on the passenger seat, anxious to hit the road.

Sallie was distracted when a man dressed in a grey suit walked to the car next to her. She thought she recognized him as one of the Mission Oaks clinicians but was mistaken. They acknowledged each other, then he jumped in his Range Rover and drove off.

Sallie hoped Drake would be recovering from his bombastic episode at the restaurant last night. He had to be home at his apartment near the medical center. She drove there. Leaving her backpack in the locked car, she climbed the stairs to the second floor, opened his door and walked in. She was bothered because he never locked his apartment. Drake trusted his fellow mankind, even though dismissed from his leadership role with the tribe. *Hey, the tribe of all places. Maybe that's where he scampered off to after leaving his crazy old army buddy. Yes, the bastard Indian who tried to molest me at the motel.*

She inspected his apartment. His bed was neatly made. There were no dirty dishes stacked in the sink, but his place smelled musty. It appeared he hadn't been home for several days, though mold and other fungi are common challenges in older apartments. Walking into the kitchen, she saw a note pinned to the refrigerator door. It read—"If ever you can't find me, go to South Texas. You know where." The handwritten note confirmed her earlier thought.

Drake had recently shared with her in one of his more serious moments a message he had received from one of his sons at the encampment. He wasn't sure how they knew where he was living. He hadn't left a forwarding address. There was no US Postal Service in the camp. Neither son had ever contacted him before, nor did he ever feel the need to reach out to them. He figured he'd abandoned the boys and didn't seek their recrimination.

The note was brief but urgent. The son told him Chieftain was relieved, and the tribe needed him to return to his old leadership position because things were deteriorating at a rapid rate. It ended with an urgent plea. "Please, father, we won't survive much longer here without you."

Drake had confided with her regarding his mixed feelings on what course of action he should follow. He told Sallie the boys were hard workers, eager to learn and were fervent about the camp's mission. Drake assured her he never walked out of the tribe's requisite to carry out its campaign demand. Yes, he had reminded her the onus was to take back what was legitimately theirs.

She hurried back to the stairwell and got in her car. Retrieving the official document from the passenger seat, she unfolded the crumpled paper and scanned it. Bexar County Courthouse, San Antonio, Texas was printed in large, bold font at the top. It was a dated marriage certificate with her name and printed next to it—Elan R. Drake. She flipped to the backside and was thrilled the handwritten, detailed map to the tribe's encampment in South Texas was still legible.

Sallie was amazed that Drake had thought of everything in the event they were separated for any reason. She knew she'd find him there.

She maneuvered out of the parking lot, drove over to IH-35 and sped south. An hour later she flipped on the car radio and listened to a local news alert.

> **"Another vicious killing took place at Mission Oaks Treatment Center. The victim was discovered in a garbage bin behind the hospital. The deceased male hasn't been identified yet, but the police department is filtering through some important leads. And now back to the weather. Today—"**

She punched the radio off and began to speculate who was the unfortunate soul found dead in the big container.

I would put money on the stiff being Marco Simone. Eduardo Munoz often confided in me that he could no longer tolerate the overbearing little Italian dictator. One day shortly before I left for good, they almost came to blows in the hallway. Marco was chewing Eduardo out so brazenly for constantly speeding in his motorized cart in the courtyard. Marco bullied him and tormented him. He said he'd take the cart away from Munoz and toss it in the nearby famous river.

I heard Eduardo threaten him in response. I think the words were "keep harassing all of us sick patients and you won't be around here for long." He shared with me the fact that ten other residents had joined him in a secretive group to plan Simone's unscheduled departure from the facility. Without question, I would join them in the action. Hans Schmidt would be in line next to me.

Wait. Holy shit. I wonder if he's still back in the motel with that animal. Don't have time to sort it all out—got my own troubles to attend to.

Chapter 36

After fleeing from San Antonio in Drake's car, Sallie Sake stopped several times to reset her GPS. The device worked for about five minutes and then went blank. The encampment's isolation couldn't be tracked accurately, thus the software failed. She had to pull out Drake's handwritten map from the backpack to adjust her route. She made several wrong turns and had to retrace her route. The approximate five hours from the inner city turned into a nightmarish eight-hour foray.

Driving slowly down the barren road that seemed to be leading nowhere, she saw a blinking light up ahead. *At last, I finally arrived—must proceed with caution.*

Moving closer, she noticed the light was on top of a makeshift tower, an interlaced log structure probably no more than ten feet high. It was manned by two men carrying rifles. One stayed behind and shone a bright spotlight on her car. The other started to climb down the rope ladder as she stopped the car at the wooden barrier blocking the roadway. He caught up with her.

She opened the car window to inquire about driving into the compound.

He pointed the rifle at her and shouted, "Turn the engine off and get out of the car, lady. You're about to trespass and get shot."

Sallie killed the motor but stayed in the car. Concern and mounting fear gripped her. She wasn't prepared for a confrontation.

He shot a warning signal over the car and repeated his demand.

She quickly jumped out and walked over to face him. He appeared to be a young Indian brave wearing blue and red smidges broadly across his checks.

He leveled a flashlight in her face and then down across her body. "You are on private property, lady. What are you doing here on our road so late at night? Are you lost?"

"Take that light off me and I'll tell you." She relaxed as his tone seemed more friendlier than his facial expression.

Sallie identified herself and told him she came here to join her husband and two stepsons. She reached in her backpack and pulled out the marriage license. Sallie showed him the document and then put it back in one of her pant pockets.

"There is no such man here on our ranch. You must leave." He became sterner and more demanding, flexing his authority over her.

She refused, demanding to speak to her husband. The young brave waved down the other guard from the tower. He cut the bright tower light and switched it to a lesser intensity. This security guard was older, taller and vicious-looking. She noticed he left the rifle behind—could probably kill another man with his bare hands.

The three talked for a short period, then the older brave pulled out his cellphone and made a call. He nodded several times, then asked several questions to his phone contact. He terminated the call and looked over at her.

"Will you let me in now?" she asked, sensing a breakthrough in hostilities was imminent.

"Yes, lady, but I'm driving."

The other brave came and frisked her—taking too much time patting her down. He was satisfied she wasn't carrying. He pulled an eyeless black mask over her head and shoved her in the passenger seat. The young brave then walked over and re-positioned the heavy wooden barrier enough for the car to slip through.

"Take this damn mask off," she pleaded to the driver as they were moving through the camp. "I can hardly breathe."

"Be quiet, lady. Not my problem."

"Where are you taking me?"

"I was directed to bring you to our Security Mid. He'll decide whether to keep you here, or kill you and spread your innards to the hungry hogs."

"Stop this car right this minute," She demanded. "Don't talk trash with me. My husband Drake is one of the leaders here. Now take me to him."

"Save you breath, lady, we're almost there, and you can plead your trespassing case to our Security Mid. He'll know what to do with you."

He slowed the car to a crawl as they entered the interior of the camp.

Sallie never anticipated her arrival at the encampment would be troublesome. After all, she was the wife of Drake, an esteemed leader of the crusaders. Her homecoming was met with confrontation and hostility usually directed at a rival tribe seeking more living space.

After arriving, the brave removed the mask and walked her to a little hut in the center of the compound. Sallie met with the Security Mid, one of the five mid-management supervisors in the chain of command under Chieftain. The Mid told her that Drake wasn't present at the encampment and no longer involved with their mission. When the question of Drake's two boys came up, she was told information regarding family matters was not his responsibility. She would have to meet with the Training Mid who was performing duties off-site.

Sallie was taken to the command shack where she'd remain until she was interviewed. The Security Mid threw her on the straw-matted floor, removed her shoes and chained one arm to a thick wooden pole in the middle of the bleak space. Then he headed for the door and told her he might be back in the early morning to check on her.

It was difficult for her to reposition herself on the floor. Sallie was physically worn out and mentally depressed. It was around midnight and she was exhausted. She no longer had access to her personal belongings and worried about the pistol still underneath the front seat of Drake's Lincoln. She figured it might be her only ticket out of the prison camp. Finally, she fell into a restless sleep.

Somebody opened the shed door during the early morning and placed a tray on the floor. It was barely within reach. After the person left, Sallie was able to slide the tray closer with her bare left foot.

Ambient light in the shack was minimal, but she was able to check out the contents on the tray. Very simple—two small pieces of bread and what looked like water in a glass pint jar. She devoured the bread, drained the warm contents in the jar, and then fell back asleep. It wasn't until the light of day that all hell broke loose.

The Security Mid she'd met last night showed up with the Training Mid, then quickly left the two alone. The new warrior facing her looked like a creature from pre-historic times. One eye was missing, and an eight-inch scar ran from his forehead across his nose and down the side of his face. He was muscular, taller and reportedly more brutish than the other Mids in camp. He unchained her from the pole.

Standing tall and erect, she pulled the marriage certificate from her pant pocket and thrust it in his face. He glanced at the contents and then disavowed any knowledge of Drake or his alleged two sons. He ripped the marriage certificate into little pieces, opened the door and threw the fragments out into the prevailing winds.

"Stop, please," she shouted. "You're not listening to me. I deserve some respect."

The man ignored her. She began to weep.

"Shut the fuck up, you insulant bitch." He slapped her hard across the face. "Want to see what my young brave outside the hut found in your car."

He pulled out Drake's .38 caliber police special from his jeans, waved it in her face, and then poked it into her belly. "Who did you come here to kill?"

"Stop, stop, I don't own a gun. Somebody in your camp must've hidden that gun under the seat of my car to frame me." She didn't have time to concoct a different story.

"Ha, don't believe you, woman. All outsiders are enemies of the tribe. I should put a bullet in your head and be done with it."

"No, no, I came to find my husband Drake and his sons." She became hysterical, pleading for her life.

"You must be hard of hearing, Miss America. I already told you there are no such persons here." He smirked coarsely at her while reassessing her gorgeous body. "I am a merciful soul but given to lust. Therefore, I will keep you to myself. You will be my slave and belong to me until our esteemed camp leader returns from his mission in San Antonio. Only he can rule on your legitimacy."

"Please . . . for God's sake, will you believe me? I—"

He ripped her clothes off and threw her down on the straw-matted floor.

"I beg you, please let me go. I'll do anything you want and then—"

"Shut your filthy mouth, you slut." He punched her in the face and snap-twisted her left arm, putting her down to her shaking knees. Then he raped her.

Chapter 37
November 2017

Jase Lozen pulled into the San Antonio International Airport parking lot in his silver Lexus thirty minutes before his father's scheduled arrival. An earlier plan to meet in Houston was derailed. He wasn't surprised his father texted him to have a wheelchair ready for him. It was two days after World Funds, LTD confirmed the completion of the Chemist murder contract in Mexico, and he had mixed feelings.

It was worth our rapidly shrinking financial resources to have traitor Drake and the volatile Chemist removed from interfering with our operations from this point forward. And now I'm not sure father is in a position physically and mentally to help complete our mission. I'll make that call when I pick him up, and we get settled in the hotel.

He was shocked when he saw the airline representative wheeling Tam Lozen out of the Homeland Security gate passageway. His hair was white, his right cheek was droopy, slightly sunken. He couldn't raise his right arm to shake Jase's outstretched hand. Jase was convinced his father had suffered a major stroke.

"I'll take him from here young man. Thanks for helping him." Jase steadied his father on to the walker he'd rented instead of a wheelchair.

"Ugh, ahh, thanks, son. Good to finally see you. It's been way too long. How many years? Five, six?" His voice was still firm, maybe terser than Jase had remembered.

"Ten, father."

"Well, get me out of here, Jase. We have much work to do and the clock is ticking away. Why are you staring at me like that? I told you on the phone I had a minor setback—slipped in the shower, hit my old noggin on the side of the tub. Thought I shattered the ceramic beast." He tried to laugh, but empty sound only filtered out one side of his mouth.

"Yes, you told me the bathtub story on the phone," Jase lied.

"Enough about me," Tam said. "You're looking pretty good for your age and the excessive mileage you put on that well-trimmed body. Molly will be happy to see you. You've always kept yourself in good shape, exercising and eating like a vegetarian. I did notice a few specks of grey hair trying to stand at attention," Tam laughed again.

They reached the airport exit. Jase helped him maneuver the four-legged device though a tunnel over to the parking garage. The drive downtown was slowed by a stalled vehicle in the hammer lane near the Grayson Street exit. They valet-parked the Lexus at the downtown Haxton Hotel.

Jase was perspiring and anxious to register. The tall blond receptionist was friendly and polite, putting him at ease. She offered Jase and his father bottles of cold water.

"No thanks, young lady. What's your name?"

"Lacie, sir, and thanks for asking. I know you're in a hurry. Let's get finished."

Jase paid cash for the executive suite she'd recommended. He gave Lacie a phony name, address, and telephone number. She smiled and asked him for his car license number. No problem. It was registered in the name of a deceased corporate executive in Houston. Lacie insisted a uniformed male associate escort them to their suite.

"Enjoy your stay, Mr. Borgstrem." Jase was impressed with her efficiency.

"Call your sister and have her come over," Tam ordered after they checked into their suite.

"Molly is at a conference in Dallas," Jase said. "She'll be back in two days."

"Huh? I just talked to her yesterday. She didn't mention anything about going out of town. Must have been some kind of emergency meeting. You know those hospital-types—too damn many meetings and not enough action. At least that's what I used to hear from my former TCCV comrades. Is my close friend Marco Simone running the place in her absence?"

"Yes, he's in charge now, dad. Did I understand correctly what you just inferred? Are you no longer on the TCCV board?"

"Well, sort of. I'm on a forced medical leave of absence. As far as I'm concerned—it's permanent. Those folks are running off in all screwy directions which have nothing to do with our initial charter. They want to build glitzy hotels and fancy movie theaters for R&R purposes. Hell, we're not even in any wars right now. Our former brave combat soldiers don't need entertainment. They need physical and mental support for their honorable and faithful service. You know what I mean here . . . securing our country from all enemies, foreign and domestic. Do you understand my position, son?"

"I do, father. I certainly do indeed." He was convinced the old man's brain was impaired as the result of damage from the debilitating stroke.

"Anyway, Jase Lozen, I have been dedicating all my remaining efforts to crush those concrete monsters suffocating our celebrated ancestors."

[254]

Jase thought he was referring to the brick and mortar structure of Mission Oaks, but didn't ask for clarification. "I'm calling room service for some tea and pastries. Are you game, dad?"

"Sure, but get me dark, black coffee instead. I need to inject a boost of caffeinated energy."

Jase noticed that his father was limping, even when supported by the walker. He assumed his old army combat injury was thrown out of kilter with his stroke.

Before long, the uniformed young lady from the hotel kitchen wheeled in a cart with a food tray and white and silver carafes containing their hot drinks. She placed the items on a circular coffee table, nodded at Jase and left the room.

They munched and sipped their drinks in silence. Jase knew his father was trying to formulate some meaningful conversation. The man mumbled a few words, then took several long breaths to clarify his utterings. "You ever been to the Alamo?" Tam asked.

"No, dad, and I'm not here to tour this historic city. We've got some heavy-duty decisions to make this afternoon. Let's center our conversation on those topics."

"I understand, Jase. Did you talk to Drake about the explosives he had lined up for us? I'm scheduled to meet with him in the morning to tie down the remaining details for our final charge."

"Drake is no longer working with us," Jase informed him. "I guess you're not aware he left the tribe and is working somewhere in North Dakota—oil fields I heard."

"That's too bad, Jase. He was always loyal to me and dedicated to our cause. Though I have to admit, he was more arduous than most of the other wannabes. Drake should've told me he wasn't fit for the job anymore. I would've relieved him."

"He was a deserter in my mind," Jase said firmly. "That's all I'm going to say about Drake."

His father registered a quizzical gaze at Jase and motioned for him to come closer. "Didn't you call me last week and tell me the young trooper Hans Schmidt took over Drake's assignment building our new weapon of mass destruction, Jase? Don't you remember what we envisioned earlier when we found out about the young hero who would be a worthwhile asset? Why do you think I had him transferred to San Antonio? To visit the famed Alamo?"

Jase didn't answer. He got up and walked over to the window. He could see the red Torch of Friendship abstract structure from their fourth-floor hotel room. It was given to the city by the Mexican government. He'd read about it on an earlier visit to the city. Jase snickered, pondering to himself if that gesture was a belated way of reconciliation for the Alamo massacre almost 175 years ago.

Late afternoon was settling in. He turned to face his bewildered father. "You'll be happy to know I arranged a deal with a demolitions company operating out of a Fort Worth suburb. They'll deliver the necessary commodities to our encampment and then help us assemble the bombs."

"You are so smart, Jase. All that digging and all that sifting through buried skulls and bones didn't change your aggressive ways. I'm proud of you for locating the assets to finish our job."

Tam blinked several times. His left eye bulged.

"On second thought," Tam went on. "I think Drake was losing the significance of our pursuits and more interested in his well-being. Maybe Molly told me that. Is she coming over here to have dinner with us tonight?" Jase was getting impatient with his father's abstract thinking.

"No, I told you she's in Dallas," Jase screamed at him.

"That's amazing. I go there once a year and wade into the crystal-clear waters."

"Let's get serious, father, we have to move on. Did you made any appointments for tomorrow other than with Schmidt that I should be aware of?"

He had to switch the subject, not wanting to confuse the old man about the complicated arrangements being made through the black internet for their munitions. He now had direct access to the top dog in World Funds, LTD. A man with the unusual name of Simian vowed to help him. That is if enough monies were involved to satisfy the greedy monster.

His father finished the last chocolate chip cookie and then downed the rest of his cold black coffee. He got up to secure his walker and then slipped back into the soft chair. "Hmm, I don't remember any people waiting to see me tomorrow, Jase. My main thrust was to get here and let you take over. I would like to see Molly, but you said she's up in Dallas. Too bad she's not available. There are three men of importance at Mission Oaks that I always liked to visit."

"Who are they, father?"

"Let me see now. Er, I forget their names but surely remember their faces."

"I repeat, father, did you make any appointments for tomorrow?"

He looked directly into Jase's eyes and shrugged. "Yes, I'm going to visit Drake."

"I think you're overtired, dad. Why don't you take a nap before dinner? It'd do you good. These short airline hauls can be exasperating at times. Tomorrow is a big day, much to get done on both our ends. I'm going down to the lobby to make some phone calls. When I return, I might even join you for a short nap."

Tam Lozen agreed, and with his son's assistance, he fell into bed. He was asleep in less than five minutes. Jase stared down at his father and shook his head. The man was breathing heavily, completely worn out from the short flight. He took the old man's shoes and socks off before going downstairs.

The Haxton Hotel lobby had become busy with several jovial visitors standing in a queue at the front desk. They appeared to be part of an athletic team—tall, lanky and trash-talking each other. Lacie had no trouble jelling with the youngsters to get them registered.

Jase found a quiet corner near the lounge where he could sit and make two telephone calls. The first call was made to the explosive expert who had already checked in at another downtown hotel. They chatted informally, no names or specifics, as he was certain they were on an unsecured line. Within a short time, they had agreed to meet later tonight at eight o'clock in Travis Park, a location several short blocks from the Alamo. The contact would be wearing a white University of Wisconsin letter-sweater with a red badger affixed to the only pocket.

He hesitated for several minutes before placing the next call. It was a difficult decision but had to be done. Jase was convinced. It was a harsh, unforgiving verdict, but crucial in light of their pledge to right a serious injustice. His sister would surely disagree, but she wasn't in the driver's seat on this important leg of the mission. Jase got up and went to the men's room. He found a stall in the far corner and then initiated the encryption process.

It took fifteen minutes to connect with Simian in the Quebec home office of World Funds. "It's me again, Simian. I'm meeting your contact person tonight. Thanks for the quick turnaround time. I have one last request, and I hope it won't break my bank. I've half-filled your deep money bins already."

"What do you want to be done?" Simian liked to be brief and to the point but veered from preciseness when he got on a roll.

"I need a cleaner, one of your best. I need him tonight. If it can't be arranged in this short time, I'll back off and find a local willing to do the job for a ton less money than you'll demand. Can you do it?"

"Yes, of course. Wire me 100k by tomorrow morning."

"Simian, you didn't hear me. I need it done by midnight tonight, or the deal is off."

"Look, friend, I may be short, stocky with long arms and unattractive to most people, but I'm not stupid. I can arrange a quick cleaning job for a gigantic discount to a new colleague. I'm assured it will bring me repeated business. I'm also taking a chance by agreeing to complete the deal before I get paid. Not the way business is conducted in my chosen profession."

"Does that mean we have a deal?" Jase knew an alternative wasn't within reach.

"Yes, of course. You already have on file the address to wire the funds. Give me the name and short description of the person and the address where you want the cleansing done."

Jase relayed the specifics.

"Are you sure of that young man? Your fucking father?" Simian couldn't believe what he'd just heard.

"Yes, he's already dying a slow death—terminal cancer."

Simian recited a few verses of Elisabeth Kübler-Ross's five stages of dying.

"One last question, if I may ask you?" Jase said, bored with the long-winded Canadian and his homage to the famed author.

"Hurry the hell up," Simian said. "My encryption device is alerting me I have three minutes before this conversation crashes."

"How are you able to get the resources here in San Antonio so quickly after we terminate the call?" Jase was awe-struck but still concerned

"That my friend is what makes me number one in the entire world perfecting this line of work. I'm aware you are going to meet her tonight at eight o'clock."

"A her? How the hell can I—"

"Hold on there, cowboy," Simian said. He spoke in loud short breaths. "Our encryption software doesn't enable voice recognition. She or he is an 'it' person."

"I'm relieved to learn that. I wasn't aware of being routed through to a more complex encryption mode," Jase laughed. "Strange things happen when I'm dealing with the renowned one."

Simian picked up again. "The 'she' person we're talking about is my detonation-explosives expert. The 'he' person I'm referring to is her husband. He elected to accompany her to San Antone on what was going to be a pleasure trip for him. Now, I'm putting him to work for you. He is one of my regional cleaners—the best. He's with her. I don't have to send somebody else down there on an emergency."

"I appreciate that," Jase said.

"Oh, and I just decided not to charge you the 100k for his work to clean up your mess. Gratis, they say in French up here in Q City. It's a Latin word. Who cares—it's free because you have become a good customer. I've already banked your other monies.

"Well, thank you Mr. Simian. I hope—"

The encryption device terminated the lengthy conversation.

[260]

Chapter 38

Jase returned to the hotel room from the Haxton lounge and found his father almost lifeless and spread-eagled on the silk sheet with the top bedding strewn on the floor. The room reeked with a foul odor. He was lying in a smudge of feces. Jase looked down at the skinny body of the decorated war veteran and former Houston city mayor. He glanced at Tam's right thigh. The seven-inch scar from his combat wound was still evident on his bony leg. His father never discussed the useless fighting in Southeast Asia with any of the family members.

Jase never stopped revisiting the senseless hostilities his father had experienced. He also recalled his former close friend Percy Radcliff had served a tour of duty in Afghanistan—another ridiculous notion to convert illiterate tribesmen to our version of democracy.

And what did Percy bring home? A terrible mental disability they call "post-traumatic stress syndrome" in the psych business. Unfortunately for Percy, his disability threatened our little conflict in this country. At first, he was gung-ho, totally on board leading the charge. But then he began to send me bizarre cell-phone texts. I'll never forget the mental struggles he was coping with his expressions of doubt. "Should we be doing this? Innocent people are going to get hurt, even killed. I've experienced more than my fair share of the ruinations of war. Maybe I should abandon hope and take up a different, but worthwhile cause."

Percy was helpless in his struggle for normalcy. He had begged me, "Jase, let me know immediately where and what I need to do before I attempt to take my life, even somebody else's life. I can't hold on much longer."

No question Percy had to be exterminated. Chemist took care of that foaming abscess for us, together with the turncoat Drake. Now, it's goodbye, Chemist . . . ha, ha, ha.

Jase had to move quickly to remove the last remaining obstacle in his plan. He grabbed a loose pillow, folded it in half, and then forced it vigorously over his father's opened mouth. He pushed hard—folding portions of the firm pillow around each side of Tam's head.

A muffled moan burst forth, only making Jase press harder and harder. Tam's thin legs began to kick out, then jerk back and forth. The whiff of putrid excrement seized Jase's nostrils. He started to gulp down the bile surfacing in his throat. Keeping the pillow firmly in place, he felt Tam's chest—no movements suggesting he was still breathing.

He checked the father's wrist for any sign of a pulse—there was none. He decided to keep the pillow firmly rooted to the head for several more minutes. Then pulling the pillow off, he stared aimlessly at the dead man. The lifeless head with the self-righteous picture of death was starting to turn purple. Jase froze at the image of violent death and began to retch, then puked on the already soiled sheet. And then it was over. Tam Lozen, a chiseled warrior, skillful politician and supportive father was dead.

Jase's cell phone startled him. He ignored the interruption and started to question what he'd done.

I hope the Great Spirit taught to me by the Medicine Man won't condemn me for carrying out his wishes. After all, my behavior was sanctioned by the Almighty One. It was through the nocturnal aspirations in the past few nights that I was called to take this action. May the dominant Father Sky God and Mother Earth forgive me.

He jumped off the blemished bed, daring not to take one last look back at his father. Past history—non-factor. Jase elected not to answer the telephone call. They'd leave a message. He checked his watch. The liaison with Simian's team of two was ten minutes away. Jase secured his few belongings, affixed a "Do Not Disturb" card on the hotel door and sped to the elevator. The young girl who brought them the drinks and pastry was exiting the elevator in front of him. "Oh, hi there, Mr. Borgstrem," she gleamed. "I was coming to your room to pick up the tray."

"Oh, no need or that. Someone else came by earlier and took care of it. Hurry, the door is closing. I'll ride down together with you."

"That's fine," she said. "I'm a little late, had to leave work for an hour to take my mother to the doctor. I sure wish she hadn't had that accident. Broke her ankle—can't drive. I guess living at home alone has more responsibilities than I anticipated. Where you from?" She nudged closer to him.

Jase didn't answer, only leered at her, thinking . . . *most women are disguised as vaginal versions of flaming devils pursuing the consumption of flesh.* He exited the elevator ahead of her, crossed the front lobby and headed out the front door. He would be a few minutes late for his rendezvous, but they weren't going anywhere. A big payment would soon be deposited in their bank.

It took fifteen minutes to walk over to Travis Park. Some cops had pulled over five teenagers riding Bird scooters on the sidewalk down Navarre Street disrupting the crowded foot traffic. Several cars ahead of him slowed to watch the animated discussion. The kids dismounted and walked their scooters back to Houston Street. They shouted obscenities at the cops.

Jase located his contacts in the center of Travis Park. The statue of General Robert E. Lee was no longer anchoring the center of the grounds.

They stared at each other. She nodded at him to come closer. The man next to her checked back to ensure nobody else was within earshot range. There were a few homeless characters but near the Navarro Street bus stop. They could care less about some other minor activity being generated across the street by the old hotel.

"Hello, pretty lady," Jase said. "Are you going to meet anybody important tonight?"

She looked him over but didn't say anything. The man next to her moved closer to Jase and eyeballed him intensely. The lady with him was Hollywood-starlet cute. The short man looked like a gorilla—barrelchested, flat nose, long-hanging arms, fifty-shades uglier than grey. They appeared to Jase as a pair of circus-like street performers.

"I'm here to meet an important friend of Simian's," she said stiffly.

"I'm Jase Lozen, the important man. Happy to make your acquaintance."

"You didn't answer my phone call," she admonished him. "We thought maybe we had an aborted mission on our hands."

"Sorry about that. I was, ah, preoccupied."

She loosened up. "Anyway, we normally don't share our names with people we just met. This is an exception for business partners. My name is Blitz. You can call my husband Cleaner. You can refer to us as BC or CB, or use the names I gave you. Let's get down to business before we're joined by some uninvited poor scoundrels looking for a handout."

They discussed several important details. The first order of business was cleaning up Jase's hotel room. He gave Cleaner one of the room keys. The set-up would entail Cleaner dressed in a plumber's uniform on a mission to fix a stopped-up toilet in the hotel room where the corpse was located.

The disguise and inference to a major plumbing problem in a busy hotel worked every time without incident. Management was never happy to deal with a non-revenue producing hotel room. That is, the total cleansing had to take less than fifteen minutes before suspicion arose on several fronts.

Cleaner had a magnetic sign he had slapped on the truck door which read, "AJ Plumbing, Triple-A Rated." He was already attired in the plumber's denim uniform with the logo identifying his phony company affixed to his shirt pocket.

Blitz discussed the next step. Jase was directed to retrieve his car from the hotel garage and park next to Cleanser's big Ford 150, King Ranch Edition sitting across the busy street. Orange and white-circled barrier cones were temporarily placed around the big truck.

Fifteen minutes later, Jase backed up to Cleaner's truck. Blitz hustled over, unlocked the truck bedcover and began to transfer the munitions and a large, locked toolbox into Jase's trunk next to his suitcase.

"Hurry up, please," Jase pled. "I expect the cops check on this popular park, often during the day and for sure, many times during the night. We can't afford a search and destroy operation on their part."

Blitz said nothing and finished loading her gear, and then slammed the trunk door down. "All done, Mr. Worrywart," she said in a mocked tone of voice.

"Fantastic." What all is in there?" Jase looked worried, questioning if this entire setup would prove problematic. It all seemed too choreographed.

"Thought you were in a big hurry," she shot back at him.

"I was before, now we're fine. Shouldn't arouse any suspicion. Do you have the dynamite in the large box? Will it explode if we get into a wreck?"

She looked hard at him. "As a rule, we don't employ dynamite. I prefer to use Composition four. You may have heard it called C-4 when you were in the military."

"Of course," Jase said. "We used it in Iraq when I was in no man's land killing the overzealous radicals," he fibbed with a conceited smile.

She continued. "It's the military's favorite explosive. Fifty-pounds of my favorite 'boom-boom' are safely packaged in the wooden crate. The other gear includes all the supplemental items to arm and detonate the bomb. Hey, there's a black and white cruising this way. Let's go . . . now!"

Jase quickly hopped in the driver's seat, Blitz in the passenger's seat. The car maneuvered away from the curb and on to the street. Blitz opened the window and blew a kiss to Cleaner. He was leaning on his big chariot puffing on a fat stogie.

As Jase and Blitz drove past the oncoming police car, Cleaner removed the yellow safety cones, flipped them into his truck bed and drove off. He headed over to the Haxton Hotel and scrutinized the area in front of and on each side of the street adjoining the hotel. Then he drove around the block several times until he found the most suitable place to park his truck. Darkness was settling in.

Egress was more critical than ingress whenever he did his job. He would cleanse the crime scene, an unappealing routine

[266]

he'd performed many times each year. The specialist was in high demand for his extraordinary, but atypical talent. After "purifying" the contents of the room, he would collect, and then dispose of the remains on his return trip to Fort Worth.

Cleaner had already identified the entombment site north of Waco. He owned the five acres of barren land on a seldom-traveled back road, miles west of IH-35. There were a few non-descript outbuildings scattered around the acreage. A small log home with a huge garden plot sat far behind the sheds. His frequent assignments arranged by Simian more than satisfied the bank mortgage.

Chapter 39
Later that same evening

Howard Hill met Evelyn Augustin at her hotel. It was after seven. He hadn't had a formal dinner date since his "one-and-out" with the slippery Clarisa Rios. She had made at least two amorous overtures in his direction after she was awarded the Mission Oaks dining room contract. He'd had enough of her self-righteous attitude.

He'd enjoyed the brief time he had with Evelyn at his Pearl Brewery apartment for the promised "one quick drink." They had gone to his place after the session at Teddy's Tavern when Baldy shared the news about Hans Schmidt's confession. He'd found Evelyn to be an interesting challenge—well-educated, quick with a joke and extremely talented in her field.

She was temporarily housed at the Haxton Hotel, awaiting the remodeling of the small home she had purchased in the King Wilhelm district south of downtown. Boyd Bounder lived in the neighborhood and had recommended the area to her. "Old, but quaint." She had remembered his description of the wrought-ironed fenced colonials dotting the old streets.

"Good evening, madam," he said as she ushered him into the fifth-story hotel room. Evelyn was dressed in a light blue dress with a short hemline. Her hair was arranged in a tight bun, offset to the right on her head. Howard wasn't sure if left or right positioning mattered. He was only hoping for good things to come his way.

"Nice digs," Howard commented. "Going to be here much longer?"

"Depends. The contractor told me he expected to complete the renovations by the end of the month. Thank goodness. This place is nice, but it's not home. Sit down and relax, Howard. Care for a drink before we go?" She was testing him to learn if he was still on the wagon.

"Of course. Make it water without ice. Squeeze two ounces of fresh lemon juice in and serve the drink in a tall glass."

"Sounds like a winner," she said with a welcomed sigh. "I'll have the same, but no lemons are waiting for you in my fridge." She then disappeared around the corner. He sat on the leather, overstuffed chair by the television set wondering how best to gain her undivided attention squarely on him—in contrast to the goners she eviscerates daily.

They chatted about the interesting people they work with and the wonderful diversity of the San Antonio citizenry. Howard looked at his watch and suggested they leave for the steak restaurant on Houston Street he'd recommended earlier to her as "best in town." She had told him eating out was no longer a big treat for her. She longed to get into her new kitchen and prepare some of her favorite meals.

Howard had learned much more about her past schooling, current interests, and future goals. She was young enough and energetic enough to accomplish those ambitions. McGill School of Medicine in Montreal had already reached out to her for a teaching position. Her good friend and medical school classmate in Monterrey had the same lofty target but never got the call.

They had finished the main course, waiting for the waiter.

Both ordered coffee and a healthy fruit dish for dessert. Howard had done most of the talking, joking and reporting his entire background to a set of interested ears. She was a great listener, having learned long ago on her first big date not to dominate the conversation.

"How is your associate Boyd Bounder doing lately, Howard? I would guess he's encumbered with a ton of stress running that mental health unit."

He pondered why the interest in Boyd. "Not so much for the day-to-day operations, Evelyn, but his resolve has been drained by the abysmal murders. We both have been drawn into the terrible consequences caused by that vicious killer."

Evelyn looked intently at him. "I have the feeling based on the perceived sensitivity of Boyd's body and eye movements at Teddy's today he might have a hard time coping with the Hans Schmidt confession. What're your thoughts?"

"Why are you asking, Evelyn?" He had the outlandish thought she might have an interest in Boyd. It bothered him. *Was this the old Clarisa Rios three ring circus happening again?*

"I'd be interested in learning more about the Hans Schmidt-Boyd Bounder relationship," she said. "Do you think there's a 'gay blade' attraction between the two?"

"Huh? No way my friend Boyd Bounder is gay. I don't know enough about the Schmidt guy to comment. Why are you asking?"

"Just a lady's intuition, not based on facts. Forget I asked."

"Boyd's taking Hans Schmidt's incarceration in jail as a personal failure from strictly a clinical standpoint," Howard assured her. "They seemed to have bonded while Hans was being treated in the long-term unit. Bounder brought in Patrick McDarnel, a local forensic psychiatrist to provide another clinical specialist to assist the in-house psychologist. McD, as he likes to be called had played Longhorn football with Boyd at UT—became super successful."

"I never dated a jock," she smiled.

"Good, I never played sports. I had to work to support my widowed mother until I enlisted in Uncle Sam's' fighting forces. By the way, McD's clinical interpretation of the dreams and hallucinations described by the prisoner was interesting. He believes the reveries were drug-induced rather than outlandish imaginings fueled by his paranoia. An ongoing series of assessments were recommended because the psychiatrist thinks Schmidt might be innocent of the terrible murder charge."

"How do you know this psychiatrist?" She hadn't heard anything mentioned about him in previous conversations.

"I met the popular doctor last July at a police department charity golf event organized by Lieutenant Baldy. He'd ask me to invite Boyd Bounder to join the outing and bring another good golfer with him. McD joined us and proved to be a decent golfer. One problem bothered me, though. He demanded too many mulligans—wouldn't pay for the two extras we offered him."

Evelyn laughed, then said, "I haven't talked lately with your buddy at the police department. Last time we chatted, the lieutenant held forth that we have an open and shut case on Schmidt. The blood samples on the skinning knife were that of Drake's. The fingerprints on the same skinning knife were those of Schmidt's. It didn't help that the innkeeper worm testified he overheard Schmidt one afternoon threatening to kill another man also staying in the motel. Looks pretty obvious to me."

"Not to me," Howard snapped back. "I've lived a long and contentious life in the trenches and experienced more trauma, deaths, and notoriety than a man my age should have been exposed to. Baldy is still staying in constant touch with the higher Dick Tracy super-cops in Austin. They're now committed to investigating every conceivable lead—even non-leads prompted by over-zealous media hypocrites."

"Settle down, Mr. Hill. Do you mean Dick Tracy from comic land? And super-cops? Maybe I shouldn't have expressed my opinion here."

Howard didn't react. *I should've known. Women tend to jump to conclusions.* Then he changed the subject. "You probably don't remember us talking about Eduardo Munoz, one of our long-term patients."

"Boyd has told me some interesting things about the screwball. Must be a three-ring circus over there."

"Well," Howard said. "Eduardo's alleged girlfriend at the radio station is stirring the pot. She's telling anybody who will listen to her that there's a menacing and unpleasant incident about to slam down on our heads. She maintains the hospital is haunted. A ghost, spy or secret agent is going to surface and horrendous chaos is imminent."

"Seems to me she ought to occupy one of the beds in Boyd's hospital," Evelyn smiled. "Anybody working as a radio talk show host is an expert when it comes to generating listener interest in their bombastic oratories."

Howard laughed, then turned serious. "Don't want her type anywhere around my operation."

"Why not, Howard? She may generate some great PR."

"Can't take that chance," he said. "She's convinced Munoz to conduct a daily and nightly surveillance of his long-term compound. He now believes he's the reincarnation of Sherlock Holmes. One afternoon I saw him jetting around the plaza in his motor cart. He was smoking a pipe, fittingly donned in an Inverness Cape and deerstalker cap atop his head. I turned around and walked the other way."

She smiled and said nothing, though she'd like to meet the eccentric—put some humor in her daily work. Stiff dead bodies lack personality.

Howard reiterated. "We're running out of rooms over there. Boyd is doing a bang-up job combined with the constant stream of referrals from the TCCV in Houston. The hospital is running at ninety-percent full. Molly has some capacity available in the long-term unit but not for patients with acute psychiatric disorders. Schmidt is no longer there. Sallie Sake was officially released, and Lefty had a major stroke and is in acute care over at the VA hospital. I'll add in Marco Simone. He's back in Ohio at a VA prosthesis clinic getting refitted for the latest and greatest artificial foot money can buy. I'm sure you knew he had one blown off in Iraq."

"Yes, he shared that with me. Seems to get along well. Hey, we've spent more than our allocated time in this establishment. Let's stop talking shop, finish our fruit du jour and walk back to the hotel."

Howard summoned the waiter, paid the bill, and they sashayed out the restaurant, hand-in-hand. Evelyn wanted to take a slight detour in their walk by strolling past the Alamo. She wanted to see the hallowed Shrine of Texas Liberty lit-up at night in multi-colored streams of light.

He agreed to the slight change of pace on the return back to the Haxton. An extra five blocks would do no further harm to his aching hips. He'd already scheduled a medical consultation with an orthopedic surgeon for a possible hip replacement.

They passed the Alamo, sans brightly-color accent lights. Evelyn wanted to continue their stroll around the back of her hotel.

He was curious. "Hmm, why don't you want to go to the lobby through the front door? Are you looking for another exit in case of fire?"

She said nothing, just continued to walk.

"Perhaps you don't want to be seen there with me," Howard said.

"Stop that mush, Howard. Don't be foolish. I'm a curious person by nature."

"Huh? Why waste time?" *I think it's a tactical delay. We have better things to do upstairs.*

"Do I have to explain everything to you?" She took on a defensive posture. "What I'd like to do tonight with a handsome and fearless escort is to witness what that fellow is up to on the sixth floor in the adjoining hotel. Last night he left the drapes open and performed some kind of bizarre ritual in his birthday suit. I watched in delight, but couldn't figure out the character's routine. Maybe a witch doctor pleading for more rain on the droughted counties adjoining us. I couldn't see if the amateur gymnast had a female admirer poised for action."

"You should've told me," Howard said. "I have a set of expensive binoculars and attached mini-cam which would record the show. Maybe worth a big laugh or two."

"Let's just forget it," she said. "Would you please escort me to the front of this building."

"Of course, Evelyn."

They turned and took three steps when the rear door of the hotel flew open, almost hitting them in the back. A repulsive-looking Neanderthal dressed in a grey denim uniform rushed out quickly, looking in both directions. A tightly rolled-up rug was slung over his right shoulder.

Surprised, he said, "Oh, my apologies, folks. They called in an emergency because of a plumbing problem and our triple-A-rated company responded. A toilet had overflowed on the fourth floor and was seeping down to the unit below. Not a good situation—smelly to say the least. They just don't install the more efficient Kohler toilets in these modern hotels. Be careful back here in the dark. Have a great night."

They didn't question the man, nor see a parked plumbing truck in the vicinity. It seemed a little unusual, but plausible—could have been double-parked on the side of the building. Howard took Evelyn's hand and softly squeezed harder as they walked around to the front lobby. They took an elevator to her fifth-floor apartment and went in. Evelyn enjoyed the night with Howard and asked him to stay for a cup of Earl Grey, the special tea she loved. Howard obliged.

"Please don't take this the wrong way, Evelyn, but I was wondering if you have a love interest back in Canada. A pretty professional lady like you doesn't go around unnoticed."

"I take that as a nice comment, Howard. "Why do you ask?"

Howard lacked suaveness when dealing with the opposite sex. Clarisa Rios had mentioned this to him on their first date. It stung him enough not to continue to pursue her, but pediment that didn't last long. This woman was different.

He plunged ahead. "I'm not too savvy at telling a woman that she is special. I'd like to know more about her before marching forward."

Evelyn took a long sip of her tea. She ignored his question about having a love interest elsewhere. She didn't. He didn't need to know that. Evelyn was aware that the man sitting next to her was direct and truthful. *Yes, more than most of the younger physicians I've dated over the years.*

"What might be your plans for moving ahead, Howard?"

Howard smiled. "It should be obvious that I'm attracted to you, Evelyn. I've never met a woman of your prominence before that would dare spend much time with me. I've been called hard-core, stubborn, intolerable and self-centered. What is . . . is. I hope I don't come across that way to you."

"Absolutely not, Howard. But let's not rush into something that might be interpreted as serious. I would want to continue our relationship on a so-called 'friendship' level for now. Is that agreeable?"

"Sure thing," he said with a frown.

"I'm not sure you're convinced, Howard."

"Huh? You don't intimidate me. I love a challenge. Let's be friends for the time being. I'm comfortable with that status quo. It is what it is."

Evelyn got up and led him to the door without saying another word. She figured he needed some time to fully digest, and accept what went down.

He opened the door and walked out.

"Howard, come back here," she demanded.

He took two steps backward and she hugged him, kissed him on the cheek and whispered, "Thank you for a lovely evening. Let's do it again . . . soon."

Chapter 40
Earlier, that late afternoon

Jase Lozen and Blitz jumped on IH-35 and hightailed it out of San Antonio. They talked little as they began the ride south. He felt relaxed with her professionalism. She didn't waste time getting to know him better or probe into his life. She was under contract, not inclined to meet and enjoy the company of new friends.

"You will refer to me in public as Chieftain from this point forward. I don't care what names you call me when we're alone—matters not. We don't use any given names in camp. Shall I continue to call you Blitz?"

"Yes, I have no reason to be secretive. I'll never see you or anybody else from your tribe again. I'm here to do a job, then leave the wreckage behind in your capable hands."

"Got it," he said. "I want to explain in more detail about our mission, and how you will be an integral part of it. There will be no questions asked on your part—just outstanding performance. That's what I'm paying you for."

"Why all the talk about your mission?" Blitz asked. "Correct me if I wrong, but you're bringing me down there to arm two vehicles with enough explosives to blow up two buildings back in San Antonio. At least that's what my contract reads. Am I missing something here, Jase Lozen?"

"That's your job. I feel compelled to tell you a little bit more about who we are, and what we're trying to achieve."

"If you insist. I'm a good listener and won't interrupt you."

Jase spent an hour detailing every facet of the program from the beginning formation of the special tribal group to their end-stage complete breakup. He'll end his allegiance to the tribe when the mission is accomplished. The clan will relocate to another state after the two buildings come down. He did offer to whisk Blitz back to Fort Worth after the mission in San Antonio is completed.

Blitz listened intently but didn't respond. She was working on her plan of extraction. She hated to be exposed to so much detail. *Was he trying to justify the slaughter of multiple human beings? He has to live with it, certainly not me. Isn't there a more humane way to express themselves and their plight?*

They were finally nearing the encampment entrance after the long drive. Dusk had set in. A threatening squall was approaching from the south. The area drought was due for major relief. The same two sentries that were on guard duty when Sallie Sake arrived a few days earlier were posted in the tower. The younger brave carrying a rifle stepped down from his perch and approached the vehicle. He recognized Jase but not the passenger. The older brave watched the verbal exchange. He already knew the person in the driver's seat.

"Welcome back, Chieftain. Who is that lady riding with you? Does she have papers?"

"Not to worry, son. I have brought her here to help us get ready for the final push."

"Sorry, Chieftain, I don't understand. Why is another female outsider joining us? Should I be concerned?"

Jase ignored the reference to "another outsider." *Did somebody else come to my camp sometime earlier without my knowledge?* "No need to worry, son. You'll be briefed soon enough. I've already cleared her for work on our compound.

[278]

You'll get to know more about her when the last of phased training begins. Open the barrier gate and let us through."

Jase motored in and brought Blitz to the visitor's hutch. A downpour hastened them inside. He told her to get comfortable and not leave the hutch for security purposes. "Believe me, Blitz, wandering around the area in the dark could get you killed. Our young scouts hunt at night for any vermin trying to sneak into the camp looking for scraps of food. A meal will be brought to you a little later. We'll meet at the break of dawn in the morning."

He drove across the compound in the heavy rain to the motor pool shed and unloaded the contents from the Lexus. The motor pool supervisor secured the articles in an old, rusted-out CONEX container of Korean War origin.

"Aha, so this is what we've been waiting a long time for, right Chieftain?"

"Yes, and keep it under your belt until we begin the execution phase."

"I will do so, Chieftain. Welcome back. We missed you."

Jase then went to the command hutch to meet the Training Mid—the designated acting commander of the tribe during his temporary absence. He couldn't believe what he witnessed when he opened the unlocked door, unannounced.

The partially clothed Training Mid was rolling around on top of a naked white lady chained to the wooden pole in the middle of the hutch. The Mid turned to see who interrupted his private party, his face smeared with blood. A deep gash on the side of his face was seeping blood.

"Stand at attention, you fucking pervert," Jase commanded.

Mid . . . shocked, jumped to his feet and saluted Jase. "Chieftain, sir, I can explain—"

"Shut up and wipe that blood off your chin," Jase ordered Mid, at the same time tossing his wet jacket over Sallie Sake's bloody and bruised body. "Unchain that woman! Get down on the floor and shackle both legs to the pole. See what it feels like to be a caged animal. Don't say another word, or I'll kick your face in."

Sallie shook off the after-effects of the powerful sedative that had he been adding to her drinking water during her short stay in confinement. She was convinced the potion functioned similar to the more well-known, date-rape drugs.

She collected the remnants of her clothes, then walked slowly to the corner and dressed as best she could. She even found her shoes. She looked over at Jase when she finished dressing, thankful for saving her from the wretched beast. He observed her rubbing her thighs and lower legs. She grimaced in pain when lifting her left arm.

"That fucking beast has been violating me since I arrived," Sallie screamed out. She marched defiantly over to Training Mid and stomped on his face with tremendous speed and high impact. He couldn't deflect the hard jolts and screamed in pain. He grabbed at his shattered nose. Mid's face started to swell. He screamed out obscenities in his native language.

Jase walked back to him, slammed his foot down hard on Mid's throat and then shouted, "I'll be back. Meanwhile, think long and hard about what I'm going to do to you."

"Wait, Chieftain, please listen to me. You got it all wrong. The whore is a spy. She confessed to me one of our young braves smuggled her into the compound with a loaded weapon. She deserves to die."

Jase didn't say anything. He gently took Sallie's hand and led her out the command hut. The rain had subsided. He secured

[280]

the door with the same lock used by the Mid to sequester her to satisfy his carnal desires.

Sallie sat cross-legged on the wet ground after they had taken several steps. She needed to catch her breath and allow her eyes to adjust to the outside light poles.

Jase allowed the brief interlude, then said, "It's late, we have to move on. The area lighting will soon be dimmed."

Chapter 41

Sallie stood up and they walked on. She turned to Jase and looked intently at him. "Thank you so much for rescuing me from that maniac. Who are you? Where is my husband?"

Jase said nothing as he placed his index finger to his lips. He brought her to his private hooch next door. He offered to have the team medic tend to her cuts and bruises. She agreed because her left arm still hurt. Jase then summoned him.

After her arm was bandaged by the medic, Jase brought her to a soft chair in the corner and sat her down. She acquiesced to his offer of a cup of hot tea. Then he began to question her.

Sallie dove into the entire litany of sequences that brought her to his compound. She included her relationship with Drake and her recruitment to the cause. Jase remembered his father sending him one of his rare notes that included his excitement in converting two new members to their crusade. Tam Lozen had said they were both "head cases" but offered no specifics. He had assured Jase that Sallie Sake and Hans Schmidt would serve them well.

"I am called Chieftain, the tribe's leader that will spearhead this small nation to redemption. You are willing to honor our Coahuiltecan ancestors even though you are Asian. We respect that commitment. For the time being, you will remain in guest quarters with a woman I just brought to our camp. I envision you will be working with her for the next several days."

"Excuse me, Chieftain. Don't refer to me as an Asian. For your information, I am a proud Japanese-American. I have served my country well. What can you tell me about my two stepsons, and where is my husband?"

Jase hesitated, then said, "Yes, I'm told they are young warriors training to fulfill their destinies. I prefer you not to meet or talk with them until we depart this encampment. They are fine young men, and I don't want them exposed to any distractions until they complete their assignments. You'll then have the luxury of time and my consideration to unite with them. Let's go."

"No. I'm not leaving yet. You ignored the question about my husband. Where is he?"

"Nobody knows for sure," Jase lied. "I'm told he left the camp weeks ago for some unknown reason. Sorry about that. We have to move on now. It's late."

"I'll find him sooner or later," she countered. "He's important to me and the boys."

Jase said nothing and then walked Sallie to another hut where Blitz was housed. He introduced her to Blitz and then excused himself.

Blitz and Sallie chatted together and shared their reasons for being in the encampment. Sallie began by relating a short history about Drake and the two sons. Blitz was touched by the emotional narrative. Blitz was brief in discussing her bottom-line mission and wanted to hear more about this interesting woman.

"What the hell!" Blitz screeched when Sallie told her about the rapes. "Did that animal break the arm that's all bandaged up?"

"No, not a break but a severe strain," Sallie frowned. "It could have been much worse the first time he beat me up, though. It'll be okay, the bruises will heal—doesn't seem to limit my activities."

"Are you comfortable in whatever role you're going to play in the grand scheme of things?" Blitz asked.

Sallie had the feeling Blitz was probing too much. "Role? What do you mean by that? I told you earlier I came to this barren desert to find my husband. He's not here. Nobody seems to know where the man went. You might not be aware his two sons are young braves training to become warriors. Do you have any children?"

Blitz smiled. "Don't have time for that . . . er, blessing most women look forward to in a blessed marriage. I understand the quest to reunite with your step-sons is a priority. But, maybe they have other thoughts about their immediate expectations. You should be thinking about your future if you can't find your husband."

Sallie hadn't thought that far ahead and changed the subject. "I told you earlier about my past service in the Coast Guard. Maybe I'll check and see if there's a chance I can get back in if my husband doesn't surface. My sons might like that. I think I'll rest now. Mind if I stretch out here?"

"Of course not, Sallie, be my guest. It's past midnight and you need your rest."

The next morning Jase returned to the command hutch with a muscular security guard in tow to deal with the Training Mid. Before unlocking the door to enter the hutch, he reminded the brave that "a leader of our sacred tribe must maintain dignity and control of his emotions at all times." The brave didn't speak but nodded in agreement.

They entered the hutch and walked directly to the Mid without saying anything. Jase was dressed in his tribal attire. The Mid was still chained to the pole. His legs were quivering in anticipation of what degradation was lurking ahead for him. Jase released Mid from the chains, stood him up and punched him in the throat.

[284]

The punishment was going to be swift and unmerciful in light of the Mid's decision to abandon the strict set of laws established for all male members of the tribe.

He didn't try to defend himself when Jase shoved the sharp butcher knife in his face. The accompanying guard circled behind Mid, stood him taller and bound his hands together. Then re-chained Mid to the wooden pole.

Jase marched over to Mid and punched him in the face, then pulled the sobbing Indian's pants down to his ankles. In a matter of seconds, the defenseless man was castrated and left behind to bleed out the evil bodily juices of moral indiscretion.

Jase and the security guard left the hutch. The tribe medic was told not to render any level of assistance to the battered Mid. A humiliating exile from the tribe would soon follow . . . if the emasculated reprobate survived the gelding.

Chapter 42
Late February 2018

Mission Oaks Treatment Center had a slight dip in admissions after the local news media finished a series of op-eds on the facility. At the same time, the community appeared to overlook the stale negative news realizing the dichotomy that both weird and fantastic happenings are the norms in psych hospitals. Referrals from local psychiatrists remained steady. This narrative was not the case with TCCV.

The leadership had reviewed the written synopsis from the long-haired, bulldog legal consultant who'd visited their San Antonio entity. They were searching for alternatives to gradually phase out the operation—rid themselves of the liability elephant on their collective backs. They hadn't been sued yet, but the future cannot guarantee relief.

The non-profit, military veteran-benefits organization decided to purchase a physician-owned hospital in Louisiana. Half of their mental health patient transfers from Houston-area hospitals were sent to the newly acquired hospital across the border, rather than to San Antonio.

TCCV executives were perplexed with the news their number one advocate for veteran affairs was no longer active in the decision-making processes. Tam Lozen never officially notified the organization he was retiring. He had been sick and on medical leave but kept in touch with two of his counterparts. Then he disappeared off the grid. His closest peer assumed Tam retired to a remote island in the Pacific. Tam frequently joshed about doing a ghost exploit.

It became a dead issue. Nobody in the organization cared to follow it up. Senior officials closed out all banking and financial accounts where Tam was a signatory. His company car was assigned to his replacement.

Marco Simone had proven himself as a reliable and progressive manager. Howard Hill had positioned him to replace Molly Pritchard if she opted to resign as the manager of the long-term facility. He'd developed a strong rapport with all the military residents in the facility. The female who assumed Sallie Sake's role as the patient coordinator had the "hots" for the handsome Italian, but it didn't go any further.

Molly Pritchard was devastated that she'd lost total contact with her father. TCCV disavowed any knowledge of his whereabouts. Furthermore, her brother Jase also fell off the radar screen. She became moody and uncooperative with her peer group. Marco ran the business until her emotional constraints lessened. Boyd Bounder was able to convince her to sit in on several of the open counseling sessions by the staff psychologist.

"Thanks for all your support during my downtime, Marco," Molly said. "You've been a bastion of strength for me."

"Hey, nothing more important for me than maintaining the tight relationship we've had for so many years."

"Marco, I have come to a crossroads in my life. I've decided a career change was necessary for me. I'm not getting any younger. The mental health business is no longer appealing. It was more frustrating and nerve-wracking than I'd ever envisioned."

"It's a strange and challenging world we're tied-to here," Marco said. "But, we've helped those who've opted out of our umbrella of support to get back on track and live a more fulfilling life." He was proud to be a part of their success.

"I've tried to find a better time and place to tell you, Marco, but I'm leaving."

"Huh? What did you say?" He was stunned.

"I accepted a coaching position at a small college in Massachusetts. Volleyball had always remained foremost in my mind, not being trumped by the other more worldly challenges I've been exposed to over the years."

"Yuk! This is a big surprise, but that's all I have to say about it. I wish you the best of luck if this will make you happy."

Boyd Bounder was also contemplating a change in career direction. He'd been heavily recruited by larger, nationally known psychiatric organizations who followed the "crazy" things that happened at Mission Oaks. They shared with him their appreciation for how he had successfully maneuvered through one calamity after another.

Howard Hill had consistently been his biggest ally and always his lead blocker when controversy arose in the trenches. Their friendship was "shaken" at times but never "stirred" during management's attempt to keep the hospital afloat. Their personalities functioned on different cerebral planes, yet they managed to maintain a true balance of contrasting egos to get the job done.

Hill tried to convince him to stay at least one more year and then re-evaluate the other opportunities. He couldn't afford to lose both Molly Pritchard and Boyd Bounder at the same time. It worked in Hill's favor, but only after Bounder demanded two weeks of paid vacation. This allowance was a no-no in Hill's limited inventory of employee benefits. He turned his cheek and approved the request. Or was it a mandate?

John C. Payne

The only long-standing patient at Mission Oaks requiring constant management intervention was Eduardo Munoz. His off-the-wall insistence that the facility is under siege had fallen on deaf ears. The fact that his girlfriend, who nobody had ever seen nor met, continues to embellish him with this fretfulness narrative. Lady Gal, as she's called on her late-night talk radio show has a commanding audience—overwhelmingly male, including Howard Hill.

Lady Gal promotes herself as an esteemed mystic and seer. She received specialized training from an old enchantress in New Orleans. Drunks, homeless, tourists—it mattered not. In less than two years they grew a small business stocked by captivated clients roaming the streets of the French Quarter. Lady Gal broke off the relationship and left town when her pot-smoking mentor proposed to pimp for her.

Boyd Bounder declared Lady Gal off-limits to the Mission Oaks property after she visited Munoz late one night. Her presence and interactions with male patients created a boisterous uproar resulting in property damage in the dayroom and adjoining hallway. Eduardo certainly knew how to "evoke" them—Lady Gal knew how to "stroke" them.

Not one to disengage from organized chaos, Lady Gal found a friend to function as a willing intermediary to carry messages back and forth to Eduardo. The popular radio host frequented the Cantina Classica and casually gained rapport with Clarisa Rios.

Many weeks before the calamity of all calamities was planned to rain down on Mission Oaks, Marco saw Eduardo patrolling the perimeter in his go-go motorized—get out of my way contraption. It was dusk, the sun rapidly performing a disappearing act in the West.

He encountered the motorist circling the Dumpster in the far back corner of the property. Eduardo was outfitted like General Erwin Rommel, the Desert Fox of German military might. Munoz was equipped with a pair of expensive binoculars dangling from his fat neck—his "Panzer tank" wheeling around the complex at breakneck speed.

"Stop, stop," Marco shouted at the ersatz combatant. Eduardo pulled up beside him and rendered a sharp hand-salute.

"Yes, sir, commander, perimeter secure."

"Eduardo, what in the hell are you looking for? Get back to the main building, it's chow time."

"I don't take food when the enemy is swarming our gates. It's time to call out the reserves and deploy them to our front."

Marco was amazed at the patient he'd learned to enjoy, rather than admonish. He had no clue where Eduardo was storing all his gear. Molly had avoided the demented man at all costs. Eduardo was proud to be recognized by all who cared that he was the oldest remaining patient from when the hospital and long-term care facility began operations in 2016.

"Who is the enemy confronting us?" Marco asked, tongue-in-cheek.

"Need I ask you if you ever tune in to my favorite radio show? No, of course not. Lady Gal would be of no interest to a career soldier, limping from a combat wound and never seeking assistance from anyone."

"Enough of your long harangue, Eduardo. Answer my question."

"Of course, commander, you should be so advised. The Indian Nation is going to bomb our buildings and lay siege to the compound."

"Oh, why are they going to do that, Eduardo?"

"Commander, where is your intelligence officer? Colonel Bill Donovan, head of Strategic Services during WWII would've admonished you for lack of foresight in carrying out your official duties. You're being laid bare with a complete lack of tactical information. Our Supreme Commander General Dwight D. Eisenhower would certainly have relieved you on the spot." He then began to motor off.

"Hold on, Eduardo, maybe you can provide the intelligence I seem to be denied for some unknown reason. Please fill me in on what you know. Tell me your source of this critical information."

"Fair enough, sir," he said with a broad grin, rubbing the Prussian Iron Cross Medal hanging under the binoculars. "I'm not sure you met my girlfriend who has a popular radio talk show here in this great city. She—"

Marco interrupted. "You mean Lady Gal, the eccentric who had been blackballed by the compound commander?"

"I don't like the term you used to describe her, sir. She's been asked not to meet me here at the fort with this critical information. We have a pigeon courier who transports our messages." He refrained from mentioning Clarisa Rios as their primary communication conveyance.

"Where does this astonishing young lady get her material?" Marco asked.

"Promise this will go no further than the two of us loyal servants. I am sworn to secrecy."

"Yes, I give you my word—it's just between us," Marco assured him.

Eduardo reached into his grey tunic and pulled out a 3X5 laminated card. He quickly checked the brief narrative, and then shoved it back in his pocket.

"My Lady was born into an Indian family in the deep swamplands of Louisiana," Eduardo said. "Lipan Apache. According to her, but I fully disagree—she was slightly disfigured and so unattractive her parents disowned her. I think they just didn't want another girl."

"Interesting," said Marco.

"Yes it is," Eduardo said. "She had spent many hours boarding with their medicine woman until she ran away to live in the wilderness on her own. Time spent with the spiritual leader was not wasted. My lady learned how to communicate with the stars—a spiritual correlation with the ability to see into the future. Call it a sort of prophecy generator. When Lady Gal moved to New Orleans at an older age, she enhanced her spiritual mystery."

"Stop, Eduardo, enough of your bloviating. Tell me more about the revelation she received from the stars concerning the destruction of our hospital complex."

Eduardo looked up to the heavens. "I can't enlighten you because she never explained to me how the prophecies are imparted to her. I don't care. I am a soldier and nothing more, just following orders. And now I'm tooling over to the mess hall to pick up my cold meal. I've changed my mind about eating with the other troopers."

"Gotcha," Marco said. "One last question, and then I'll dismiss you. When is this massive bombardment going to happen?"

Eduardo gave a concerned look of fright and panic. "Not sure, but I think soon, sir. If I were in command, I'd begin to stock the bomb shelter with food, water, and medicines."

Marco shook his head in skepticism as he returned to his office. He Keuriged a cup of dark roast Columbian coffee and sat deep in thought.

The fool is getting irrational and more fanatical than ever. But, maybe there's some validity in his ranting and raving. We can't afford to overlook anything that could cause major disruption to our smooth-running business.

I'll discuss the situation with Boyd when he gets back to the hospital from dinner at the Cantina Classica. Clarisa wanted to see him about something important. Perhaps there's some correlation here with Eduardo's story. After all, she was his courier. Boyd may have some much-needed answers to this rapidly developing puzzle.

Chapter 43
March 2018

Howard Hill was replaying Lady Gal's last night's program when he got a call from Baldy. He quickly turned off the radio. The police lieutenant informed him there was a big meeting in progress at the police station. He asked Howard to come to the station immediately. He didn't want to discuss the matter over the telephone. Baldy needed to see his friend face-to-face. Howard was insisting on the reason for the call when the lieutenant hung up on him.

When he arrived downtown, Boyd Bounder was sitting in the lieutenant's office with a grim frown and worried look. Evelyn Augustin was perched on the corner of Baldy's desk. Another uniform was sitting next to Bounder.

"What the living hell is going on here, Baldy? Does it have something to do with Boyd? Why does he look half- dead?"

"No, let me explain, Howard. Take a seat, and I'll get to the point."

Howard hesitated, then sat down.

"Hans Schmidt had been found hanging from the jailhouse window," Baldy said. "A children's jump rope, or something comparable was secured to the middle steel bar of the window. The other end was tied around Schmidt's thin neck. Someone had smuggled it in—visitor, custodial person or lawman. Evelyn determined the cause of death was suffocation, no visible evidence of trauma. The drug screen is still being analyzed."

"Well, just our luck," Bounder sighed. "Now we'll never know who killed Drake. Right, Baldy?"

"We never give up on a homicide, Boyd. We didn't turn the motor off on the continuing investigation simply because Schmidt signed a confession document that he had in fact, killed Drake. You should know better than that, Mr. Hospital Administrator of mentally deranged individuals. Maybe he would've beckoned us to his jail cell tomorrow to claim he didn't kill Drake—only that he had experienced a frightening dream of killing Drake."

"Did that noted psychiatrist Patrick . . . whose last name I forgot, share any insight with you about Hans Schmidt?" Boyd asked. "Shouldn't he have developed a working hypothesis of some degree that might hint of innocence or guilt?"

"Patient-physician confidentiality," Evelyn said. "I don't believe the doctor called McD had enough sessions with Schmidt to reach any definitive conclusions."

Boyd ignored her comment and pointed to Baldy. "But, you said it was his fingerprints on the skinning knife that had Drake's blood spattered on it."

"Stop, stop please," the police lieutenant raised his voice in anger. "Let me do what I'm paid to do. I suggest you do the same, Bounder."

Everyone started talking at once—confusion, sniping, arguing.

Evelyn Augustin had heard enough of the squabbling. She shot off Baldy's big desk, startling everyone in the room. "Gentlemen, no more bickering! Start acting like grownups. We're all in this together. I'm sure our professionals working the case will find the assassin."

"What's your take on this, Baldy," Howard came to life. "You work here, have access to all the inmates and visitors."

[295]

Evelyn jumped in and cut him off. "Let's face it. The killer could be Schmidt, Chemist or a new player in the game. It's after duty hours, let's go see Teddy Bear and 'libate' our way back to being amiable cohorts."

Howard broke into a huge grin. "Evelyn hit the nail on the head. I applaud her sensitivity. Naturally, she'll buy the first round of drinks, or I'm not called the Howard I. M. Hill, imperial master of the universe and all living humanoids, foreign or domestic."

Bounder walked outside the room and called Marco. He suggested Marco join them at Teddy's for some interesting updates on the investigation.

"I'll be there," Marco said. He was thrilled they might even consider bringing him back in the loop. He had a reputation.

When Boyd returned to the meeting room, he noticed everybody's mood had changed for the better. They took off for Teddy's place. Evelyn rode with Howard.

"I haven't seen you so animated since our dinner date, Howard."

"What can I say? You're getting to know more of the real me."

"I like the 'real me' guy. You're fun away from the job. I sense you folks over at Mission Oaks continue to be stressed out. Is that the reason Molly left? It amazes me how the care and treatment of our mentally challenged population can drain one's resolve faster than a meteor blazing across the endless Texas skies."

"Does all talk mean you like me, Evelyn? Do we connect?"

Evelyn grasped his hand that wasn't on the steering wheel. "Yes, Howard. We're making headway."

Marco Simone was sitting on a barstool between Baldy and Bounder when they checked into Teddy's Tavern.

"Hey, Marco my man," Howard yelled out when he saw him. "I was about to call you, but I see someone preempted me. Glad you could join us. Too bad Molly's gone. She would've enjoyed this impromptu staff meeting to let off a little steam from the collective overheated engines."

"Maybe," Marco laughed. "I think she prefers to leap up and down near the volleyball net shouting encouragement to her young charges. It's her welcomed new custom to blow off stress."

After two rounds of drinks, the jovial conversations headed in another direction. Marco reported his chance meeting with Eduardo Munoz the other night. He went into great detail about Eduardo's girlfriend and her damaging prognostications.

"I haven't heard of any rumblings from the American Indian population in Texas," Baldy reported. "Other groups are scurrying around the state challenging law enforcement."

Howard cupped his big hands and slid his chin in them. He didn't recall any Lady Gal programs that hinted of such an uprising but wasn't about to admit he was a fan of the radio host. Howard shared an incident with the group that he'd encountered during his active duty military days. His army unit was deployed to augment a law enforcement team to quell an Indian uprising in Utah. It got nasty and several tribesmen spent time in jail.

Marco couldn't let go of poking his nose into police affairs. He walked over and tapped the police lieutenant on the shoulder. "Based on a worst-case scenario instigated by some disenchanted evil tribe, shouldn't you be ordering some surveillance vehicles to Mission Oaks on a rotating schedule?"

"No solid evidence for doing that, Marco," the lieutenant explained. "I can't justify the resources based on a mystic having a bad dream. We're already overcommitted on man-hours, and the city doesn't like to pay for excessive overtime."

"Well, well, let's wait until our buildings get blown away," Marco barked loudly. "Then we'd justify fetching the boys in blue to gallop to our defense."

Howard glanced over at Baldy waiting for a response. There was none. There amiable relationship had taken a brief vacation.

Marco limped toward the door, then turned to face the group. "Thanks for inviting me to the interesting skull session. Molly would've supported me. You folks think I'm a fucking idiot!"

Chapter 44
April 2018

Jase Lozen was thrilled with the completion of training for the culmination of the long campaign to take back what was their rightful real estate—ancient ancestral burial grounds. The new Training Mid surprised him with his extensive knowledge of tutoring the younger warriors.

The offensive was planned to coincide with the grandest party of all in San Antonio . . . Fiesta San Antonio. The Battle of Flowers Parade on Fiesta Friday afternoon traditionally attracted over one-third of the city population. It was an ideal time to strike during the colorful cavalcade honoring the heroism displayed by the patriots of the Alamo. Lozen's tribesmen were generational patriots also. They helped found the city and later were unceremoniously pushed aside by the white supremacist zealots.

Blitz had completed her contracted mission, but Jase convinced her to remain with the tribe to oversee and be a part of the final thrust. She was comfortable with the industrious people and impressed with the seriousness of their plight, though not consumed by it. She enjoyed the newly-formed fellowship with Sallie Sake, the only other woman involved in the dangerous mission. Blitz's passion was making and exploding bombs of all types for any living human willing to pay an extreme price for the weapons. She notified her husband Cleaner that she would be delayed at least another week.

Sallie Sake had fully recovered from her vicious sexual attack by the previous Training Mid. She was thankful there were no early indications of being pregnant from the rapes. The team medic was called in for a final follow-up of her injured arm. The damage had been more severe than he'd initially diagnosed. However, he advised Chieftain she had improved enough to participate in a limited capacity during the upcoming strike against their adversaries.

The fact that her husband Drake was nowhere to be found still was a thorn in her side. It bothered her. Chieftain, the supreme leader of the clan had to know something but refused to discuss the matter with her. Sallie wanted to push him harder. She knew he was under heaps of stress but backed off, hoping he'd relent.

He'd ordered Drake's murder. Explaining all the reasons and ramifications to her would be unwise and not contribute to their successful undertaking. There would be a better time and place for a detailed accounting. Nothing would curtail the established blueprint for the attack.

Sallie was happy that he'd introduced her to Drake's two sons, something he swore he wasn't going to do until the mission was completed. He'd reneged from his earlier position, sensing she'd assimilated enough in their plight to prevent any distractions or disruptions. After all, she volunteered to drive one of the Humvees in the raid next Friday.

Jase was in awe of the woman and became attracted to her over the short period of her stay. Sallie's beauty wasn't blemished by the viciousness of the now-deceased sexual perpetrator. She sensed his continued interest and felt she needed to reward his timely delivery from the hellish sexual pounding she'd endured. They spent many nights together in his command hutch talking and getting to know more about each other.

[300]

John C. Payne

Jase interpreted the vibes radiating from her were now more sensual than much earlier. He assumed she was more interested now, assuming Drake's situation was no longer a compelling drive for her to continue the hunt. *Is this pretty woman offering herself to me? Has she recovered enough from her demoralizing and physical trauma? I need to find out. I can't wait much longer.*

Jase hadn't bedded a woman since his days fulfilling the Bureau of Indian Affairs contract in Mexico. Local prostitutes were abundant and willing to service any man for a reasonable price. He was ready to end the short-lived celibacy. Two hours before the morning sun shone in the corner of his hut, he moved his hands softly up her uninjured arm touching the side of her breast. She smiled but wasn't ready to give herself to him at this time.

A two-day soft rain had let up allowing the camp workers to continue preparing for the armed convoy to San Antonio. The grounds were muddy and slippery, but the labor force had to remain on schedule. The weather for all next week was forecasted to be cloudy until the Thursday before the big Friday parade in downtown San Antonio.

"How do you like them?" the motor pool brave asked Jase when he entered the big shed housing the Humvees.

"Great paint job. Do you remember what those colors mean to us?"

"How could I ever forget, Chieftain. It's inscribed deep in my heart."

"Tell me then," Jase insisted. "Some of the inhabitants on this compound tend to let the colors fade away. I can't live with that."

The supervisor walked up closer to Jase, placed his right hand over his own heart and recited with deep pride, "Blue means we, as a tribe are saddened by the abuse and neglect society has heaped upon us. We're being treated like third or fourth-class citizens in this country. That's beyond sad, sir."

"And the red color?" Jase asked.

The man smiled, took his hand off his heart and shot it in the air with a tight fist. "War, sir. War to take back what is rightfully ours. That's why we're getting these Humvees armed, and alarmed."

"Thank you," Jase patted him on his chest. "You are a good man. Tomorrow I want you to circulate throughout the camp and talk to as many people as you can to impart on them your strong feelings about our colors."

"Chieftain, it is my honor. Consider it done."

Jase changed the subject. "I trust the engines have been serviced to the nth degree to ensure no breakdowns on the excursion north."

"Yes, sir. We did make the modifications inside the units you'd asked for. Plenty of room to house the munitions. Are you certain that lady you brought in for the demolition knows what she's doing?"

Jase smiled. "Well, maybe I should conduct a test to prove her competency. I'll ask her to wire your hut tomorrow with some of her 'toys' and see what happens when you and your wife are sleeping."

"No, no, I trust your judgment, Chieftain. She's great."

"Good," Jase said. "I'll be driving the blue Humvee. You will motor on with the red Humvee. Does that please you?"

"Yes, sir." He stood erect and saluted. "My role in the mission will be paramount. One small mistake and we're doomed. I hope none of the older braves get upset because you selected me."

"Let me worry about that. That's why I'm the leader of this clan. What about the .50 calibers for the Humvee's backing up the one's Drake's young braves are scheduled to drive? Have they been mounted and checked out?"

"Yes, Chieftain, the young braves ran two simulations out in the far perimeter of our land. All went well. You should've heard the blasts of the .50s in the quiet desert. Wow. God forbid anyone who gets punched by one of those massive rounds. They'll be missing several major body parts."

"Keep up the good work," Jase said, then walked away. They would lead the celebrated raid. He in the blue Humvee—the young motor pool brave in the red one. He would suppress any dissension among the ranks . . . for he is the chosen one.

Blitz received a text from Cleaner. He was upset she was remaining behind. Her contract was specific—design the explosives, train the participants and disappear. World Funds, LTD top dog Simian didn't want any of his top operatives enmeshed with political causes or movements. Such commitments would expose his international group of exterminators to possible sanctions. She decided to meet with Jase and have the leader clarify her specific role in the raid.

"Thanks for running me down before we kick off the offensive, Blitz. Your note read you had some reservations. Would you please clarify them for me."

"Yes. Cleaner contacted me and insisted I return to Fort Worth immediately. I told him you'd already assured me you were going to personally deliver me back home when we've achieved the objective. He wasn't happy with my decision to stay—said I could get killed."

"Look, Blitz, you bought into our strategy. We intend to blow up the two buildings sitting atop our sacred burial grounds and then take control of the property. In any war, there are unintended consequences. Some like to refer to this phenomenon as 'collateral damage.' I don't. Simply put, they're the enemies—we're the friendlies. Yes, I will admit that one or two overzealous employees or bystanders might take up arms against us. But, I don't feel that will happen." He didn't specify why.

Blitz continued to question him. "Why have you armed four Humvees with .50 caliber machine guns if you didn't plan on killing anyone or group who dare oppose your glorious conquest? Couldn't you simply arm a few braves with pistols to act in self-defense."

Jase exploded. "We're not setting out to kill poor, mentally deranged veterans of foreign wars, woman! We have the right to protect ourselves if law enforcement agents put up barriers and fire at us. I must keep my warriors safe from any harm directed against us."

"Sorry if my questioning upsets you, Jase Lozen, supreme Chieftain of this clan. Remember, I volunteered to ride in another Humvee on your mission of conquest. I could lose my life. So, bear with me. I have one last question. Where do you intend to put me in the convoy? Upfront with you, or with the second tier of young braves yielding the heavy firepower—certainly not bringing up the rear?"

Jase hesitated. He hadn't decided yet where he would position her. It bothered him she was starting to ask too many questions so late in the planning stages. He'd concluded earlier that

Blitz needed to be with or near the explosive packages in the event of malfunction or misfiring.

"My planning staff is working on every detail as we speak, Blitz. We're indebted to you for agreeing to ride with us. We have no intention of exposing you to danger. You'll be well insulated from harm. You have to believe me. I'm telling you now that Sallie Sake will be riding with you in the attack column."

"That relieves me and makes sense," she said. "We make a good team."

"I have to run now," he said. "There are some details I have to discuss with Sallie. Goodnight and sleep tight."

Blitz couldn't sleep that night. *Cleaner said his concern for me was based on us killing hundreds of vulnerable and unarmed mental patients who'd served our country with the utmost dignity in several past wars.*

She had a difficult time grasping the idea that soon, she may be dead or alive—maybe even severely wounded. Innocent people could be killed because they had no way to alert authorities in advance to vacate the hospital facilities before the attack.

This is inhumane and I'm going to be an accessory to the crime of the century. No way am I going to sacrifice my life for a bunch of Indian malcontents striving for social justice.

I have to concoct something quick to cover my ass. Wait a minute, here's an idea. Tomorrow I'll swipe the key to the locked CONEX container where my explosive packages have already been wired and packaged but not yet armed. I'll make some minor munitions adjustments in the Humvees that should facilitate my freedom from this quagmire of all quagmires.

If anybody catches me, I'm doomed, maybe executed as a traitor to the grand cause. Now I can enlist Sallie Sake to keep an eye out for me. She's going to ride with me in the big assault. We've become friends out here in this isolated compound. If I read her correctly, she had ambivalent feelings about her role in the attack and Jase's sexual interest in her. Why in the hell did I ever take this contract? Somebody reach out to me. I need my head examined.

Chapter 45
Several days earlier

Marco Simone had received a welcomed text from Molly Pritchard. It was the first time she'd reached back to him. Molly told him she was returning to San Antonio to enjoy the many fun events scheduled during Fiesta San Antonio. She'd heard Mission Oaks Treatment Center was planning to have a decorated, flat-bedded vehicle in the Battle of Flowers Parade. She was curious about the float's theme.

He texted back. "We're hailing our courageous warriors. We want to show the public how our charges are combating psychological barriers to relive healthiness and well-being."

She texted back. "That's a mouthful?"

He answered. "Want to ride on the float?"

She returned. "I'll just be a supportive bystander in the crowd trying to catch whatever goodies you're tossing us. See you soon."

He had been responsible for recommending the hospital openly participate in the revelry enjoyed by all of San Antonio and scores of outsiders. It would suggest healing, a refocus of the hospital's main mission. The publicity should achieve untold positive results.

Howard Hill had agreed with Marco's suggestion. "Great idea Marco," Hill said. "You head it up, and I'll get everybody in line to help support your work. Out of curiosity, do you plan on having Eduardo Munoz on the float?"

Marco said nothing, thought the question lacked merit. No way Munoz was going to be an attraction on the float.

Howard felt Marco had finally cooled off from their last meeting with Baldy and the other folks. His close friend Baldy never brought up the subject when speaking or texting Howard. Marco's aggressive questioning of Baldy's refusal to accept his report of impending disaster didn't resonate well with most of the uniforms. They never react to a hoax. More concrete information had to be established before they'd commit valuable time and resources. Hill respected Marco's position, but not as a flame-throwing malcontent.

After several minutes of hesitation, Marco replied to Hill. "Why do you ask, Howard?"

"Because you think he's the second coming of Christ."

Marco didn't know how to take Hill's comment. He wasn't going to resurface Eduardo's passionate expression of disaster heading their way. Nor was he going to talk about Lady Gal. He declined to discuss Munoz.

"Thanks for backing me on the float," Marco said with relief. "I'll move forward and let you know if I need your help putting it in play."

Marco had lunch the following afternoon with Boyd Bounder at a new downtown Mexican restaurant. They hadn't visited Cantina Classica since the recent tragedies. Clarisa Rios had become socially isolated from Mission Oaks personnel. She opined that the mental health hospital operation had been the reason for a decline in her business. She designated one of her trusted supervisors to handle the food service contract with Mission Oaks, further sequestering herself from the hospital clients who normally frequented her restaurant.

"Molly's coming to San Antonio for Fiesta," Marco shared with him. "I'm not sure if she's lonesome for us. My guess is she needs a break from recruiting young volleyball prospects."

He finished-off two green enchiladas in record time, dripping some droplets of green chili sauce on his white shirt.

"How's she doing in the world of collegiate sports?" Boyd asked.

"I have no clue. We haven't kept in touch until recently. We are or were best friends from the battlefields of combat to the shores of Mission Oaks. Maybe she needed more space from me. I can be an asshole at times."

Boyd laughed. "You said it, not me, brother Simone. But, I'm more interested in what's going on with Eduardo Munoz. I haven't noticed him motoring around the compound lately."

"He's spending more time over at Lady Gal's apartment. We've allowed him more off-facility time. One of our clinicians feels his disposition has improved several degrees since his relationship developed with that woman."

"Have you met her yet, Marco?"

"No, but Eduardo is bringing her in tomorrow afternoon for what he called a 'tactical interface with reality.' Maybe I should have a disinterested psychologist present to interpret the conversation."

"Have you listened to her talk show?" Boyd asked. "Howard clues me in periodically when she goes ballistic on any topic he holds dear to his heart."

"Like what?" Marco asked. "I don't have any idea what makes Howard Hill tick. Maybe you do. Hells . . . bells, if you two duked it out in any meaningful manner, something should have rung your bell—and I don't mean his right fist."

Ignoring the question, Boyd took a long swig of iced tea. "I don't have the time, nor the inclination to share with you everything I know about the one and only Howard I. M. Hill. Let's order dessert. I need to get back to the hospital pretty soon."

Marco was at his office early the following morning. His foot had completely healed from the minor surgical revision at the VA Ohio clinic. The new prosthesis had improved his ability to ambulate without a noticeable limp.

It was mid-morning when his office assistant came into his office. Marco was draining his third cup of black coffee. She told him he had a visitor waiting in the lounge.

"Who is it?" he asked. Lady Gal wasn't scheduled until this afternoon.

"I don't know. She wouldn't give me her name—said you were expecting her."

"Fine, please bring her in." He paperclipped several documents he was working on and placed them on the coffee table in the corner.

"I hope you'll forgive me for coming early and without Eddie," the tall, good-looking, dark-skinned lady said with a slight grin. She firmly shook his hand and announced proudly, "I'm known to most of my fans as Lady Gal. You can call me LG if you'd like."

Marco was impressed. Eduardo had described her differently, as though she were a geek, sheltered from the realities of life. Either this lady evolved drastically into a beautiful specimen, or Eduardo had described another old girlfriend to him. She stood as tall as Molly Pritchard, and her athletic-looking body was as supple as Molly's.

He'd never been intimidated by a woman taller than himself, but this could be the one exception. LG wore her hair long and over one shoulder. She displayed a gold ring on every long finger, her thumbs left unattended. Her fingernails were painted a vivid purple. The fake fingernails protruded at least two inches over the fingertips.

"Eddie couldn't make it," she smiled. "He's in my apartment drafting a tactical op-order for the Fiesta San Antonio 'day of reckoning' as he calls it."

She gazed over at the coffee table and commented, "Looks like a diagram of a parade float. Is that for the Battle of Flowers Parade? Eddie told me you intend to have one in the big carnival procession. It's going to rain big time thunder on your parade. May I sit down?"

"Oh, sure, sorry," Marco stuttered, trying to recover from the onslaught of information tossed at him. "You said, Eddie. I trust you meant Eduardo. Care for a cup of coffee?"

"Yes, Eduardo my boyfriend. And certainly, no to coffee. I don't touch the wicked brew—makes me super hyper. I don't need any more stimulation."

Marco agreed in thought.

"Do you like the way I look?" she hoped he'd express approval. "Eddie told me I should campaign for a time slot on our TV programming. Management adores me over there. Then my many fans can appreciate my perception that beauty begets happiness and fulfillment."

Marco declined to comment on her looks. "Tell me about the strategic plan Eduardo is drafting. Scuttlebutt has it that you are predicting an assault on our complex by a group of political activists on parade day next Friday. Care to be more specific?"

"How can one be more explicit than when a passing bad dream streaks across your overly active brain during the REM stage of deep sleep?"

"Your what? Would you care to share this dream with me? And, it'd help if you'd also explain REM."

[311]

"Sure, Mr. Marco. I'll be brief. We all have non-REM stages of sleep that can change over several minutes to the REM stages where dreams take place. Oh, let me clarify. REM is a quotient for rapid eye movement. Just accept my short explanation and I'll proceed."

"Thanks," he said. "I'll file that in my cramped mind. Please go on." *Hopefully it won't keep me awake at night determining what REM stage I'm in when I get up and head to the john.*

"Eddie probably told you I'm a clairvoyant, a person that can look into the future and predict outcomes. Please don't call me a psychic—hate that moniker. I was born with this marvelous capability, but my proficiency was further honed by a famous medicine woman."

Marco nodded repeatedly. He didn't grasp a complete understanding of her enlightenment but let her continue. Nothing gained by trying to slow her down.

"Next Friday during the Battle of Flowers Parade, an armed convoy will travel unabated to your hospital buildings and blow them up. I'm unable to tell you who they are specifically, or where they are coming from. I'm convinced that's all you need to know to mount some kind of counter-offensive to blunt their attack. Many lives will be lost if you, Mr. Marco, allow this calamitous affair to happen on your watch."

"That's a pretty heavy business you're espousing, LG. Can you expand on that so I can put my arms around the tangled mess we are all facing here?"

She jumped up to leave. "Sir, I couldn't be more specific about what's going to happen. Take some time to think more clearly about what I just told you, and you'll be alright."

[312]

"Got it," he said. "Thank you for coming, LG. I'll get together with Eduardo tomorrow and see what strategic plans he's drawn up, and we'll take it from there."

She shook Marco's right hand forcibly and left without saying another word.

His secretary popped in after his guest left the building. "Do you like that fine specimen of a woman, Marco?"

He hesitated to comment. "Don't you have an important memo to get out for me—like ASAP?

Chapter 46
The Following Thursday

Jase Lozen assembled the entire clan in the large open field adjacent to the command hut. It was two o'clock in the hot afternoon. Fifty-five enthusiastic members were standing and cheered him on after he concluded his opening remarks. Some mothers were holding young babies. A few fathers gathered their adolescent sons at their side. Even the medicine woman and team medic were in attendance.

"Today is the day we've been working and praying hard to make happen," Jase announced over a portable loudspeaker. "Tonight, our convoy starts for San Antonio and we will TAKE IT BACK," he screamed to the eager crowd.

It is ours," they responded enthusiastically. "It is ours." The adults were wearing blue and red feathers in their hair. The bald warriors wore them around their necks. "Go blue. Go red."

Jase acknowledged their responses with his right arm raised high. "Yes, yes. Twenty brave warriors will ride with me tonight. The rest of you will start packing for a new home over in New Mexico. We've already purchased the property. You'll enjoy twice as many acres to build permanent homes for your families."

He saw hopeful expressions from all who were near him. "Take only one change of clothes and the few valuables you have in your possession. Destroy everything you leave behind. Our trusted Security Mid will arrange for a ceremonial burning. He will be in charge of your relocation. He already has all the details you'll need to know for your journey. He will brief you tonight after our convoy leaves this encampment for the last time. Our raiding party will join you in our new territorial home next week."

"TAKE IT BACK," the assemblage continued to shout, but much louder.

At dusk, the raiding party met at the large motor pool housing the armed vehicles. Jase gathered the motor pool brave, Blitz, Sallie Sake and the twenty warriors to his side. "I and our motor pool brave will lead the column and drive the blue and red Humvees."

He then pointed to Drake's sons. "You young warriors will follow in the two explosive-laden Humvees to strike the targeted buildings. I know you want to 'suicide-attack' the objectives. That's not how we planned it . . . okay?"

The two youngsters nodded without showing emotion. "The third row will have only one Humvee. Sallie Sake will drive the vehicle. Our explosives expert Blitz will ride with her and wait for my command to initiate the destruction. She will remotely detonate the charges as the Humvees with the bombs smash into the buildings."

"Now, hear me loud and clear," he said as he pointed to Drake's sons. "You will not die martyrs! I order you to jump from your vehicles ten yards before they collide with the structures."

Drake's taller son stopped Jase and begged," Chieftain, sir, I want to die like my father who lived in vain for our just cause. I know you were not aware the medicine woman pulled us aside and told us father had been murdered in the San Antonio slums by three homeless acidheads. Our mother Sallie was with us at the time. The medicine woman gave us a drink of a strong green potion to control our emotions. My brother here feels the same way."

Blitz turned to Sallie with a serious smile. "You hadn't shared that information with me. You seemed relieved accepting some closure now that you know he's gone. I've been thinking about many things since we've met. I learned more about you and respect your predicament. We'll talk later. The Chieftain was watching us—maybe trying to gauge your reaction to the boy's dilemma."

Jase countered the taller son with a loud voice and moved closer to them. "Yes, I know you and your brother are solid. I have plans for both of you when we get to New Mexico. You will be elevated to a new rank of Mids. I will not discuss the details now, but you will not die. I order you to survive."

There was no response from the two. Sallie Sake faced the brothers and spoke up. "Be clear, young men. Remember what the medicine woman told us. There is only one way we can honor your fallen father. Martyrdom is for losers with nothing more to contribute to their nation. You two have been anointed. Listen to Chieftain. He knows what's best for you and the future of the clan."

Jase turned to Blitz. "You and Sallie have prepared your parts of the mission well. I know from our motor pool brave you had rehearsed the actual use of the detonators out on the firing ranges. Summarize for us how the process works."

"Yes, Blitz said without emotion. "I've already programmed the newest version of the GPS-driven signaling device to the electronic receptor inserted into the blocks of C-4 explosives. For the dummy run, I used a remote-controlled apparatus to detonate a bomb-laden, old pickup truck. It had been parked on the perimeter of the range next to an old cement-block structure. It was our ground zero."

"I'm familiar with the location," Jase said. "Please continue."

"Sure," Blitz smiled. "On my electronic signal, the truck exploded, and the blast shattered the small building. I had Drake's older son rehearse his escape from the old truck before impact. Sallie clocked every sequence with her stopwatch."

Jase nodded his head, satisfied with the thoroughness of her preparations.

Blitz picked up again. "Here's what's going to happen for our raid on the hospital. I have a separate GPS signaling device already loaded with receptors in the blocks of C-4s for each Humvee the two sons drive. They're set at the prescribed ten yards from building one and then building two."

"Very well," Jase said. "As we discussed earlier, you both will be in the third tier driving your own Humvee. The fourth tier will have two Humvees armed with members of the raiding team with AK-47s following behind your vehicle. Bringing up the rear is the last segment of the raiding party. Two Humvees loaded with our brave scouts will be manning the .50 caliber weapons."

"Go blue, go red," several braves shouted out. "We will take it back. It is ours alone. We will take it back!"

"Yes, that's exactly what's going to go down. Now, hear me out on this important consideration. If the situation dictates, weaponry will be discharged only on my radio command and not before. This rule of engagement is critical regardless of your pent-up emotions that might call for premature action."

Drake's taller brave son raised his hand. "Sir, Chieftain. You said you and our motor pool brave will lead the convoy in the blue and red Humvees to the targeted area. Right?"

"That is correct," Jase affirmed. "But, I didn't tell you that fifty-yards out from the hospital complex, we will peel off and let you two proceed through our opening and drive your loaded Humvees directly to the target area. This is a crucial point. Am I clear on that?"

"Yes, sir." Both of Drake's sons looked at each other and grinned.

"That is the key component of our plan. Any questions?" Jase wanted to be sure of not omitting important specifics in the planning directive. Nobody asked for clarification.

"We leave tonight at midnight. It's about a three-hour drive to the outskirts of San Antonio. Several days ago, Security Mid told me about his uncle who owned a small ranchette ten miles south of San Antonio. Uncle Tio Bobwhite had raised the young Mid after his parents were killed in a car crash."

Security Mid shot his arm in the air defiantly.

Jase smiled and resumed his briefing. "As you've been informed, Tio Bobwhite will allow us to use his isolated ranchette as the staging area for our mission. He agreed, fully cognizant of our plight with white supremacy. We depart here in groups of two, taking different roadways to San Antonio. We'll rendezvous at the ranchette before the light of day. The exact coordinates of the ranchette are posted in your Humvees—also a county map with the property circled in red."

"WE WILL TAKE IT BACK!" Drake's two sons shrieked out in harmony. The other warriors clapped their hands and hugged each other.

"I suggest your teams pair up and rehearse the plan one last time," Jase suggested. "We'll meet at the motor pool tonight at eleven o'clock. Get some rest. You'll need it."

"Please hold on, everybody," Security Mid ordered the raiding party before they broke up. He'd been silent throughout Chieftain's detailed presentation. "I have one word of caution to you Humvee drivers based on a text I received from my uncle. He is an old man with a passionate heart to let us rendezvous at his small ranchette. Uncle Tio alerted me that major streets and some access roads will be blocked off for the parade route through the middle of San Antonio."

"Listen up, everybody," Jase interrupted. "This is important. Mid informed me late last night about what we might, or might not expect tomorrow."

The Mid acknowledged the interruption and continued his comments. "Last year there was only one street blocked-off south of the city. He felt the same situation might transpire this year, but had no guarantee. He gave me the exact address of that street closure. Anything more you want to add, Chieftain?"

"Yes. I checked our planned routes in and out. We should be good to go. If there is an adjustment, I'll inform everybody in the morning at the courageous uncle's ranchette. And lastly, I'll wait until morning with another specific set of instructions on how we'll proceed out of the battle zone after bringing down those buildings. You are all excused."

Blitz stayed behind to talk to Jase. "I need to know your proposed instructions as soon as possible, not tomorrow morning. You know I need Sallie's help and hope her physical condition won't be a problem. I want to get her squared away as soon as possible."

"Sallie will be okay—she's motivated," Jase assured her. "Why are you in a rush? Your roles are well-defined."

This woman is getting on my nerves. She knows what's going on. Is she going to back out on me at the last minute? Probably not. I'm getting mixed vibes. It doesn't matter now—I have a notion to kill both women after the bombs are detonated—write them off as collateral damage.

"We'll talk about it soon enough tomorrow. Go rest."

"I'll do that, Jase, but you need to answer another question. During the planning stages, I had asked you if you were going to alert the hospital staff to vacate the buildings before we blow them. Your answer was vague."

He gave her a threatening stare before answering. "No, I'm not going to forewarn anybody. We're combatants—people die."

Jase took Sallie's hand and led her to the command hutch. He had begrudged postponing the "honeymoon" phase of their relationship until their last night together. He expected her to be more accommodating on the eve of their grand triumph.

Blitz stayed behind for several minutes after they left. She shook her head in disgust, then went to the guest hut and called Cleaner. She discussed with her husband the final attack plan and her exact role in carrying it out.

After a five-minute discussion, they terminated the encrypted call. She had agreed with Cleaner's suggestion on reverting to a "fail-safe" extraction. Blitz knew what that would involve. She hoped the aberration would happen without incident.

Chapter 47
Friday Morning

Marco Simone and Eduardo Munoz remained at the hospital complex while other staff personnel were fine-tuning the hospital float. The group was off-site at the parade staging area near the Pearl Brewery. Molly had flown in the night before and had dinner with both Boyd Bounder and Howard Hill. She noticed a more delicate rapport had developed between the two men she had come to admire.

She had an early breakfast with her close friend, Marco Simone in the hospital dining room. Only four other people were in the large room. She shared a personal, touching story with him—didn't know why.

"You did what?" he said, staring closely at her.

"Yes, I had to find out my biological lineage which my adopted father Tam Lozen never shared with me. He said one day he'd take me to his Houston bank vault and go over all the documents."

"Please elaborate," Marco asked.

"I learned from TCCV that they presumed my father Tam Lozen was dead. Because of my persistence, they obtained a confidential report about my father from one of their local hospital administrators. He had suffered a severe stroke and signed out against medical advice shortly after initial evaluation and stabilization. The neurologist said he could be dead in a month if left medically unattended. Those involved held to his edict not to notify family members of his condition."

"We'd heard through our network channels he was on medical leave," Marco said. "You talked about a brother. Does he know anything about the current status of your father?"

She made a sad face. "Nobody has heard from Jase Lozen since his last telephone call to me—told me to be careful around here. Someone might be out to harm us all. I just left it at that. He used to smoke loads of pot—could have been stoned when we talked."

"Tell me. Did you go to the bank and get in the vault?"

"Yes. I had been listed as the only other person authorized to access the safety deposit box. Here's the bottom line. My biological father was Swedish, an oral surgeon. Mother was Irish, played basketball in college. I was the only child and physically and mentally abused by both parents. It got so bad the state took me away from them at an early age. I was placed in foster care. Tam wanted a girl as a part of his family. The rest is history."

"Wow, Molly, let's move on to the present. I'm glad you declined to sit on the hospital float during the parade, insisting the honor be given the military patients and not current or former staff. Hill had concurred. Bounder had no preference. Each military service will be represented with one staff exception. The recreational therapist Donna Rae Phelps will act as the 'figurehead' for the float."

"Thanks for asking me for breakfast, Marco. It was great seeing you again. Let's keep in touch. I have to get going now, don't want to be late for the big parade. I'm told parking is a chore. I like to walk, so won't drive anywhere near the parade route."

"Wise choice, Molly. I suggest you hunt for a location near the Alamo. One of my senior staff members told me he always rents a chair on the sidewalk in front of Teddy's Tavern. The crowd is boisterous."

"Are the troops assembled, Eddie?" Marco asked Eduardo, slowly smiling when he mouthed the man's nickname. They were drinking coffee and eating glazed donuts brought in by his associate.

"Yes, sir," Eduardo said. "All present and accounted for. We ran through the drills last night."

"I suppose my ass will-be-grass when this whole shindig is over," Marco sneered. He didn't care. Baldy and his cronies in law enforcement weren't going to do anything. Marco had always displayed an active role under stress—highly averse to those nitwits who wait patiently for guidance to stroke them. Regardless, he'd act on Eddie's scheme.

"Not as I see it," Eduardo said staunchly. "I have never been defeated in combat," he bragged. "I've fought many battles as an underdog, never outwitted or outflanked by the enemy. We were highly outnumbered by the Krauts in The Battle of the Bulge. I was with Brigadier General McAuliffe of the 101st Airborne Division when he responded to the German written surrender demand with his 'NUTS' response. We gutted it out, fought like demons and repelled their all-out attack. The tides of WWII changed dramatically. When I—"

"Shut the fuck up for one minute and tell me your plan for this afternoon."

"Of course, Sir Marco, I'll be brief."

"Please. I'm supposed to be at a complaint session in an hour. Two of our newer residents petitioned us to subscribe to more movie channels for in-room TVs. How do you feel about it, Eduardo? You live here."

[323]

"Ha, ha, ha. I'd tell them if they want to live in a 5-star hotel—go downtown. I don't watch any TV because I thrive on being pre-emptive, not a lazy bum having to be entertained every swinging minute of the day and night. They ought to—"

"Enough, Eduardo. I get your point. Hold your tongue for a few moments, then give me the facts."

Marco downed the last donut in two big chomps. He ate little with Molly at breakfast. It didn't matter, Clarisa Rios arranged to have a Cantina Classica float in the parade and declared a minimal staff holiday for kitchen services. Toast and jelly, hard-boiled eggs, and orange juice were available.

Munoz began to describe his plan of action to defend the complex. "I've recruited three SEALs and one marine sniper from their 'fun and sun' games in the hospital pool. After I briefed them on Lady Gal's prognostication, we got together in the lounge and devised a tactical plot to brunt the attack. I think the flow charts are still up there."

"That's fine," Marco said. "Go on, I can't hold out much longer."

"Right, commander. We mapped out every conceivable approach to the hospital grounds that an armed convoy would take to strike us. My four troopers are armed with shovels and pick-axes we swiped from maintenance. No weapons. For shame, we didn't find any down there."

Simone shook his head in wonderment. "How do you plan on repelling their attack?" he asked. "There may be as many as twenty or forty heavily armed insurgents."

"No, my LG never envisioned a large horde to breach our defenses."

Marco thought for a few seconds. "Must've been dreaming. I guess REM Stage 3 kicked in."

"That happens with my LG, sir. Let me continue. After our skull session, two SEALs left the hospital grounds to go talk with one of the policemen they knew from the murder investigations. The cop agreed to deliver several spools of those spiked, barrier strips designed to puncture the tires of wheeled vehicles. At the SEALs urging, he also threw in several boxes of orange parking cones and ten rolls of black and yellow barricade tape. Everything is packed in sealed boxes behind the hospital Dumpster waiting for deployment."

"What's all this going to cost me?" Marco asked.

Eduardo grinned. "Only a five-hundred-dollar donation to the police union widow's fund."

"I should've known. I'll live with that bestowment if we all survive." *Bastard must've been in bed with the cops knowing about my tiffs with the police lieutenant.*

"Marco, my man, I've told you before . . . I've never been defeated. Trust me."

"My life and those of the rest of the contingent here are in your capable hands, General Eddie. Do you have the exact time tied-down when our adversaries are scheduled to deploy?"

"Sweetheart LG predicted the enemy will enter our gates at three o'clock this afternoon. The marine sniper will climb that big oak tree at the far end of the employee parking lot. He will signal the enemy's approach in time for us to lay the spiked barrier strips. We've already coned-off and yellow-taped adjacent avenues of approach into our complex. This action will force the striking force into a narrow lane where our barrier will deflate their tires and stop them cold. We'll then attack them with our primitive weapons until the police SWAT team arrives."

"Had your collective brainpower ruled out the fact that your adversaries will be armed to their teeth? Wait, hold on. SWAT team? What's that all about?"

Eduardo grinned. "You have underestimated the ingenuity of our beloved SEALs. Their supplier of goodies at the police department is a decorated, former Army Green Beret. He also serves as the leader of their SWAT team. Based on the SEALs' overwhelming enlightenment of impending doom, the blue uniform agreed to have six members of his team on hold for positioning this afternoon. They'll be in place by two o'clock, two blocks east of Mission Oaks. Our marine camouflaged in the tree has the private cellphone number to call and initiate the action."

"And what is your role in this campaign, Eddie?"

"Stop calling me Eddie, for Christ's sake, Simone. Only one living person in this universe has the right to use that terrible aberration of a sacred name."

"Sorry about that," Marco smiled. "And you're going to do—"

"Sir, please allow me to remind you again. I am the general in charge of this operation. I will oversee the command and control function from the rooftop pool of the hospital. I'll be equipped with my binoculars and cellphone. The rest is up to the experts in the hallowed field of juggling war and peace in their collective struggle against the evil forces of humanity. Now, if you'll excuse me, I have to attend to business."

"Wait one minute, Eduardo. I have—"

Eduardo Munoz wheeled his motorized wagon around and raced out of the office.

Marco Simone shook his head in amazement and watched the outlandish man disappear.

Chapter 48
Friday Noon

Jase Lozen's band of armed warriors had arrived at the rendezvous site without incident. Four different routes were taken on the trek north. One Humvee driver reported he'd been followed by a state trooper for at least five miles but not pulled over. Jase couldn't believe the level of excitement and anticipation exuded by his task force. This was going to be a day of joy for the Indian nations.

However, the last night in bed with Sallie Sake was a disappointment. He almost strangled her to death. There was no honeymoon. She feigned illness, even wretched many times in the open bathroom. She begged for him to wait one more night before they physically consummated their relationship. When she did fall off to sleep, she kept softly moaning Drake's name. There wasn't going to be one more night in her life. He had already decided to kill her after their successful attack on the hospital.

A last-minute decision was made to move the striking hour up to noon, rather than three, as initially programmed. Jase couldn't contain the animated warriors any longer. The younger braves had begun to sing ancient battle hymns passed down by their ancestors. Several began dancing and whopping-it-up around their assigned Humvees. One brave blasted off several rounds of his AK-47 in the air. He was severely reprimanded, kicked in the groin by an older leader and threatened dismemberment by another brave. They mounted their vehicles at eleven o'clock and then moved out rapidly.

The motorcade reached a secondary, almost isolated highway parallel to IH-35 into the city. The lead blue and red Humvees were side-by-side, both roaring down the roadway—their diesel engines squealing higher acceleration. The remaining contingent followed in a tight formation. They only encountered two vehicles on the route to the hospital. Both vehicles raced for a shoulder unscathed. The motorcade was ten-minutes out.

Jase radioed the motor pool brave rumbling closely alongside his racing vehicle. "When we pass through the rear parking lot, peel hard to the right and let the bomb-laden vehicles pass through. I'll veer off to the left."

"Roger that," he replied.

He radioed Drake's two braves and advised them to accelerate at their highest speed when they see the blue and red Humvees spin out of their tight formation.

His last radio message was to Blitz. "We're a few seconds from your detonations. Do what you've been paid for and the success of our mission will be realized."

"Aye, aye, commander," she said, then readied her GPS screen and punched in the signal to ignite the first Humvee with the C-4 explosives . . . just twenty yards short of the target. Drake's older son was blown high in the air, bloody strips of body parts draping the big Dumpster where his father had been temporarily entombed. His Humvee was shattered in fiery pieces of metal. What remained of the vehicle's mainframe came to a sudden halt—a foot from the hospital building.

The red Humvee driven by the young motor pool brave had already swerved severely to the right, overturned, and pinned him under the huge motor vehicle with a broken neck.

Jase had curled off to the left and momentarily stopped to witness the appalling misfortune that took place to the far right of

[328]

his position. A chunk of a rubber tire from the backblast slapped his right shoulder. He howled in pain.

Blitz then sent a signal to the detonator on the younger son's Humvee headed for the secondary target. Thirty yards from the second building the Humvee exploded. Drake's son flew skyward in the Humvee shattered seat, headless and still bound securely by his seatbelt.

Jase recovered quickly, not believing what was transpiring before his eyes. Both bomb-loaded strike vehicles were obliterated. He grabbed his radio and called Blitz. "What the fuck are you doing to us, you crazy bitch of a devil. I—"

His blue Humvee exploded in the same precise manner as the previous two but with more blast-shattering effects. Shards of hot steel, scorched clothing, and Jase Lozen's body parts were flung in every direction. The hospital plaza area resembled an active combat zone.

Unbeknownst to everybody in the camp, she had snuck out early in the morning at the rendezvous site to arm his blue vehicle with three blocks of C-4. She wanted to be doubly sure he'd never survive, so added an extra block of C-4 rather than two blocks secured in the other two Humvees.

The remaining Humvees in the strike force spun around and raced away from the devastation as rapidly as their souped-up trucks would take them. Out of desperation, three crazed warriors discharged their AK-47s into the passing treelined escape route.

Eduardo's collection of seasoned combat soldiers hadn't arrived yet for deployment. They weren't needed.

Sallie watched in awe the fireworks detonated by Blitz in their Humvee, safely distanced away from the onslaught. She was in a minor state of shock. Her two sons became the martyrs they were ordered not to become by the supreme Chieftain. She had mixed feelings about Jase being blown apart. Blitz had forewarned Sallie of her scheme two miles from the attack site.

"Sallie Sake, we need to get out of this mess as fast as possible. The local cops will be swarming this battlefield before you know it. Hurry, step on it!"

Sallie saluted Blitz with a smile. "Hang on, sister." She spun the Humvee around and raced off in a westerly direction from the hospital. Within minutes they were swallowed-up by remnants of the heavy parade traffic, blasting horns and shooting off firecrackers in every direction.

High above the hospital complex, near the outdoor pool, a fascinated Eduardo Munoz trained his binoculars down on the annihilation of the brazen enemy. Lady Gal stood beside him gazing upward at the sky. Three dark clouds slowly encircled a bright white cumulus and began bouncing back and forth. The bright cloud expanded like a spitball in a jar of water, then engulfed the dark clouds. Within minutes, it began to spray droplets of light rain down on the ill-fated vestiges of mortal battle.

Epilogue

The new TCCV leadership in Houston made a strategic decision to cease operations at their San Antonio Mission Oaks Treatment Center. The short-lived undertaking to operate an intricate and problematic mental health business was wrought with bizarre consequences. They were able to relocate the remaining four inpatients and three long-term care residents to treatment facilities throughout Texas.

After the transfer was completed, the buildings were locked-up and secured by roving police patrols. Pending legal disputes were resolved and TCCV contracted a local demolition company to level all the buildings on the compound.

Crowds of people gathered to witness the structural annihilation. TCCV elected not to send a representative. They were still breathing a cautious sigh of relief that another rambunctious law firm wouldn't pursue additional costly litigation.

The dynamite pyrotechnics exhibition took place three months shy of the second-anniversary date of the hospital's grand opening. A giant excavator finished-off the task and cleared the debris from the vacant property. Local media covered the event with a variety of controversial op-eds about the downfall.

Marco Simone was absolved of his past articulated sins against law enforcement. He joined his old nemesis Lieutenant Edgar J. Wactenshutt at the local police department in a PR capacity. He was forced to take up golf in his infrequent spare hours.

Howard Hill had left San Antonio before the razing of his ill-fated empire. He retired to the family homestead in the Blue Ridge Mountains and raised a flock of award-winning show goats. His old comrade in arms, Grizzly went AWOL from his Alabama long-term facility to join him. Grizzly soon became a well-respected goatherder.

Boyd Bounder became the head football coach at a private high school in Austin. He married the head coach of the Texas Longhorns varsity cheer-team. Twin Bounder females arrived a year later.

Eduardo Munoz secretly eloped with Lady Gal. The couple joined an offshoot organization of the Ringling Brother's traveling circus which performed primarily in South America. They called New Orleans their permanent home of record.

Blitz secreted Sallie Sake out of San Antonio and returned to Fort Worth. Blitz, Cleaner, and Sallie formed a compatible alliance, scaling down from emotional highs to a more casual existence. Sallie was invited to work a few high-profile cases with Cleaner. Before too many moons, she was then recruited by Simian of World Funds, LTD. Sallie Sake became a notorious contracted assassin.

Blitz and Cleaner retired to their farm acreage west of Waco. They built a two-story mansion overlooking a small, walled-off and gate-locked cemetery of nameless gravestones.

The TCCV donated the property to the Bureau of Indian Affairs. The Bureau repurposed the site as a sacred Indian burial grounds commemorating the plight of the ancient Coahuiltecan Tribes of Texas. A small adobe brick building was constructed on the southern tip of the property. Former ranchette owner Tio Bobwhite moved to San Antonio and became the full-time custodian of the sacred grounds.